PRAISE FOR *LATE AIR*

"*Late Air* is a story of the world of elite female athletic performance like no other novel I can think of. In her debut, Gilbert is alternately a miner, a sculptor, a guiding ghost, but always a virtuoso—showing us the athlete's body as a perfectible object, a vessel for obsessions, a target, and a site for the recuperation of the athlete's humanity."
—Alexander Chee, author of *Edinburgh, The Queen of the Night*, and *How to Write an Autobiographical Novel*

"Gilbert's shatteringly gorgeous debut is part Megan Abbott in its can't-take-your-eyes-off-the-page depiction of the competitive world of girls' running and part Elizabeth Strout in the way she so deftly explores and understands her characters, all of them desperate to love even in the face of ruin. A deeply original look at how tragedy shape-shifts a marriage, and so rich and alive, it's impossible to believe this is a first novel."
—Caroline Leavitt, author of *Cruel Beautiful World* and the *New York Times* bestsellers *Pictures of You* and *Is This Tomorrow*

"In this mesmerizing debut, Jaclyn Gilbert has given us a deep and nuanced study of the ways that loss can ravage a marriage, how passion becomes obsession, and the body as a site of devastation and healing. Gilbert's prose is luminous and hypnotic, so finely wrought it cuts. This book riveted me, broke my heart, and revived me."
—Melissa Febos, author of *Whip Smart* and *Abandon Me*

"To read *Late Air* is to be deeply immersed in the inner worlds of beautifully complex characters torn apart by time, memory, and trauma. Gilbert gracefully resurrects wisdom from the smallest details, each moment as finely wrought as the last, showing us who we are and how we love. A truly impressive debut from this gifted writer."
—Marian Thurm, author of *Today Is Not Your Day* and *The Good Life*

"*Late Air* breathes some welcome oxygen into the modern novel. The characters, both major and minor, are created with great care, and the story is moving and extremely readable. Jaclyn Gilbert is up and running!"

—Richard Cohen, author of *By the Sword, Chasing the Sun*, and *How to Write Like Tolstoy*

"Jaclyn Gilbert's *Late Air* is an exquisite meditation on marriage, loss, and the redemptive power of distance running. Gilbert's gloriously complex characters circle each other at arm's length, swallowing words when they should speak up, turning away instead of reaching out, even as they crumple beneath the weight of their desire for connection. In exploring the many faces of grief—and of resilience—Gilbert has delivered a wise, nuanced, and utterly unforgettable story."

—Kirstin Chen, author of *Bury What We Cannot Take* and *Soy Sauce for Beginners*

LATE
AIR

LATE AIR

Jaclyn Gilbert

A Novel

Grateful acknowledgement is made to the following for permission to reprint previously published material: Camille T. Dungy: Excerpt from the poem "Notes on What Is Always with Us," Trophic Cascade by Camille T. Dungy. Wesleyan University Press: 2017. Reprinted by permission of Camille T. Dungy.

Published by Little A, New York

www.apub.com

Amazon, the Amazon logo, and Little A are trademarks of Amazon.com, Inc., or its affiliates.

ISBN-13: 9781503903586 (hardcover)
ISBN-10: 1503903583 (hardcover)
ISBN-13: 9781503903579 (paperback)
ISBN-10: 1503903575 (paperback)

Cover design by Emily Mahon

Printed in the United States of America

First edition

For Jared

There are things I do not want to say . . .
Except the not saying won't return anything you love.

—Camille T. Dungy,
"Notes on What Is Always with Us"

PART I

ONE

Late August, Monday
5:33:05 a.m.

"Remember our goals," Coach Murray said. He and his number one runner, Becky Sanders, were in his car headed to the campus golf course. Through the darkness, the empty streets, Murray relied on his headlights. He tuned the radio to a clear station: the Doors.

"We're aiming for 5:10 pace," he said.

"Okay." Becky was peeling a small blood orange, one long sheath unfurling on her lap. At 5'2" and ninety-five pounds, she reminded him of his two-time cross-country All-American Sarah Lloyd. As a senior, Sarah had set a course record of 16:23.14 in the 5K. Becky was only a sophomore, but Murray believed she had even greater potential than Sarah; he saw Becky winning Nationals this year, maybe even competing in the Olympics one day.

Murray hadn't showered or shaved in three days. It was humid in the car, and the gray stubble around his long mustache felt damp.

He hadn't always had a mustache. In his youth, Murray was clean shaven, but he'd worn his blond hair a little long through his own college running days. He'd run on full scholarship for the University of Scranton. Growing up in Luzerne County, he'd gone by his first name, Samuel, but on Scranton's track, the chant *Mur-ray* had sounded best—especially at the age of twenty-seven, when he'd qualified for the '84 Summer Olympics in the 10,000-meter run.

Now, almost four decades later, Murray was sixty-two and no longer ran. His two knee replacements made walking so difficult that at the golf course, he'd have to use a cart to get around. He couldn't miss a split.

At a red light, Murray noticed as Becky carefully removed two strings of pulp from the orange, then divided out the first quarter section. She raised a sliver to her lips and bit in slowly.

Murray's breakfast sandwich still lay warm on his lap. No cheese, just ketchup and egg. He smelled oil and toasted bread, and then the juice misting the air as Becky's thumbs pressed down.

He'd grown accustomed to their prolonged silences. In fact, he'd come to welcome them. Becky never challenged his insistence on their two-a-day practices, the first of which always happened in the morning, and the second later in the afternoon, when he held practice for the whole team. Murray had started this precedent in '01, when he'd been named head coach—the year after Sarah Lloyd had joined his ranks— and he had groomed at least a dozen other phenoms since then, each as hungry as the last to qualify for Regionals, then Nationals, to earn the elite status Murray had tasted in college too. Every record Murray had set depended on running before daylight, the darkness an ideal time for finding focus, this protected space where he could demand only the best from his girls.

Becky warmed up at the fairway of the first hole. She did some form drills: high-knees, butt kicks, some rabbit hops. The sun had partially risen, mist clouding the first hill a soft, dusty green. Becky's father, Doug, was an ardent golfer, and he had met Murray for eighteen holes the summer he'd started recruiting Becky. It was then that Murray had told Doug about his recruiting plan to help earn Becky's admission to Yale, given her slightly subpar grades and test scores. In the end, she'd chosen him over all the other coaches vying, even those offering full scholarships. The pressure for her to keep up academically remained high, but he felt assured by her 3.6 average last year, when she was still a freshman.

He marked a tall elm as the start line and read her target splits from there. He told her to focus on her foot strike, keeping her weight centered. She'd have two minutes of rest between sets. "Four of them," he said.

Becky rolled her neck around. She jounced her knees. When she readied her stance, he began his three-second countdown, stopwatch tight by his thumb. He clicked hard, and she bounded forward, her stride chiseling the mist. Her tan calves parted as they pushed into the fairway grass. Her thin, muscular arms sliced the breeze.

To Murray, Becky would always be like a Belgian warmblood, this magnificent breed he'd once bet on as a child, with his father, at the Erdenheim Steeplechase. The horse had a pinwheel brand on its left thigh. Becky had a scar, too, but on her right shoulder.

Last year, Becky had placed third at Regionals. Murray had taken her to a diner for a pancake breakfast to celebrate. It was there, her fork circling tiny slivers of pancake, that she told him how she'd been burned by someone's still-lit cigarette. She'd been walking with Doug on Atlantic City's crowded boardwalk when someone brushed her hard. She hadn't really eaten any breakfast that morning, so Murray had finished the pancakes for her, a heaviness in his stomach he'd disliked; it was the hunger he longed for, the exertion that earned it.

Murray watched Becky in the distance as she hooked around the first bend, the quarter-mile mark.

Her forward lean looked good, legs kicking back nicely. Gravity was taking her, he thought. She *let* gravity take her.

He lumbered over to his golf cart but had a difficult time lifting his right leg and stepping in; even more cumbersome was crouching down into the seat.

Just two minutes to get to the finish at the base of the fairway on the second hole. He turned the key and floored it. He kept one hand steady on the wheel, the other over his notepad. A breeze cooled his face and the sweat that had gathered along the back of his neck. He focused on the bluish grass unspooling beneath him.

At the finish point, he pushed hard on the brake. He checked his watch: 4:55.16. He squinted his eyes, waited for a sign. Checked again: 5:10.39. *Where is she?*

5:25.16. He slammed hard on the pedal and careened up a side path. He called her name several times, but nothing came back.

It wasn't until several minutes later, in the distance, that he saw the white of her T-shirt, shapeless and crumpled. The closer he approached, the more he could discern of her body: fetal, motionless. He checked his stopwatch—10:23.57—and clicked stop. Frantically, he thrust his body forward, shoulders jerking unevenly to make up for his wobbly stride. He bent over where she lay in the grass. A dark purple bruise marred her right temple. He squeezed two fingers together and touched the side of her neck. A pulse. He lowered to his belly, met her at eye level. With a middle finger and thumb, he peeled the right lid open. It was dilated. He leaned in toward her mouth, careful not to move her head. A difficult angle, so he had to drag his cheek over the grass. Her warm breath emanated, but it was ragged and shallow: one deep inhale followed by two seconds of apnea.

"Becky." He spoke close to her ear. "Blink if you can hear me." When there was no movement, he shouted, "Please, Becky! Blink!" He waited three more seconds, close to her mouth, monitoring the warmth, and then he was fumbling for his cell phone, fingers pressing for 911; he was shaking. He heard himself on the phone, specifying Becky's head trauma as severe, maybe a level 6 if he went by his years of sports medicine training. A first responder asked him to keep close watch of the time, to note any changes in her vital signs. He reminded Murray to stay calm and—above all—not to touch her neck. Estimated wait was seven minutes.

Murray dropped his phone into his pocket.

Last night he'd called ahead to the clubhouse; no golfers had been scheduled. They were on a slope by the woods. Could the ball have rolled? He thought he saw a shadow moving from behind a tree. He called out, asking if anyone was there. But no one answered: there was just his own voice resounding, and then the deadening silence after that.

Becky's hands were curled tight and close to her chest. Like an infant—silent, spine tucked into her mother's womb. He thought he sensed a blue light passing overhead, lucid and wavering, then this slow ascension of her body.

Murray refocused his eyes, took several breaths. He felt again for her pulse. Still there, but the skin on her neck was growing paler. She was chilled, goose pimpled and clammy.

He waited five minutes, seconds like droplets, before ambulance lights flashed in the distance. He'd specified the second hole, but he worried it was too difficult to locate. He didn't want to leave her side for a moment, so he flailed his arms as high and wildly as he could. When the truck saw him, it tore off the main path. Two technicians ran out. One heavyset, a white duffel slung across his chest, the other a slim woman with *Paramedic* printed on her badge.

She shouted, "Closed trauma," and then "Upper-right contusion." The EMT was still catching his breath. Murray was sure his lack of fitness would delay the process. Murray scrutinized the man's thick fingers, how awkwardly they grasped a thin ballpoint pen for recording essential information. He was relieved by how swiftly the paramedic worked in comparison.

"Is she in a coma?" Murray stayed close as the paramedic flashed light into Becky's pupils, noting a sustained dilation of the right one, yellowing around the sclera. The left pupil hadn't dilated, but from what he could tell, it was equally unresponsive to light.

"Open the airway!" the paramedic shouted. Immediately, the EMT performed a jaw-thrust maneuver, one Murray remembered learning about in his training class. The only method that would protect Becky's cervical spine from further harm.

He watched a mask grip Becky's face, and then he began praying for a miracle as a steady supply of oxygen flowed into her mouth through a clear plastic tube that looped a small pressurized tank.

He tried not to think about the color of her forehead, which was turning a grayish blue. Livid. A blackish raccoon ring was already forming around her right eye. The EMT might have noted both as signs that the skull was fractured, capillaries ruptured, Becky's brain swelling more with each second.

"Blood pressure skyrocketing. Pulse low at forty." The paramedic was testing a radial artery, while the EMT fastened a pulse oximeter to Becky's finger. Splinting material crowded her neck.

As they worked, Murray estimated fifteen minutes since the time of injury. "Maybe twenty—shit, I don't know!"

The paramedic wanted his help in holding Becky's head while they eased her out of the fetal position and lowered her, safely, onto a long-board. After they shuttled her into the ambulance, Murray tried to leverage himself into the truck, but his hips wouldn't let him lift his legs. He asked for help, but the paramedic just shook her head. "Not without clearance."

Murray collapsed off the bumper, then recovered himself and reached the driver's side before the paramedic could close the door. He thrust his hand out, gripping the hinge. "Please!" he said.

"You're holding us up!" she cried. He relaxed his hand, and the door closed. Lights flashed on, bleating, as the truck sped away.

His hands shook as Murray dialed campus administration. He left a message for the athletic director, Rick Warner, even though Rick wouldn't be in until after 8:30.

The grass stank of bitter chemicals, making it harder for Murray to breathe. Sirens still rang in his ears.

~

The main lobby of the hospital was fluorescently lit, with high white ceilings and shiny linoleum floors. Murray sat facing the reception desk, watching the minute hand of the clock. 8:03 a.m. Almost two hours he'd been waiting. Becky's parents had driven from their home in Danbury and were with her in the neuro ICU. They wouldn't answer his latest calls. He'd already tried them seven times and asked the receptionist repeatedly for help, but she wouldn't let him use the hospital line.

Murray kept seeing Becky's ponytail bob. Even in the morning haze, it had been this clear, lustrous ebony. Her face vivid. *Cyanotic* had been written on the report. Murray shivered, picturing the same gray-blue of her skin.

There were at least a dozen other people waiting there. A few seats to his left sat an Indian couple, wife dressed in a traditional sari, husband in a white T-shirt and jeans. They weren't holding hands.

To his right, a man waited alone. He wore a red cap and loose-fitted jeans. He slumped low in his seat while he checked his phone.

Directly across from him—Murray couldn't help but stare—was a mother with her son. The mother's hair had been dyed platinum. She had gray slivers for eyes. He couldn't tell if they were real, or colored contacts.

"What are you looking at?" she asked, her accent thick, maybe Brooklyn or Yonkers.

"Sorry," he said. "Long morning."

She nodded. She had small wrinkles around her mouth that broke through heavy pinkish-white compact powder. The woman kissed her child's head. Bangles clinked. Her boy uncurled his thumb.

To test for responsiveness, the paramedic had had to rub forcefully over Becky's sternum. Her clavicle had protruded through translucent skin.

"I want a donut," the boy whined. "I'm hungry."

"Danny," the woman said, "this isn't the time." The boy burrowed close to her chest. Then she looked back at Murray. "Why are you here?"

"An accident," he said, glancing at his stopwatch. Somehow the numbers had started running again. The time read 2:15:27. His fingers trembled. He wanted to, but didn't click it off.

"What kind of accident?" she asked.

"I'm a coach," he said. "One of my runners was hit."

"Oh my God," she said. "How?"

"By a golf ball," he said. "We train on a course."

He'd lost sight of Becky just after the first 800 meters, at 2:30–2:31. He was sure he'd stopped his watch at 10:23.57. Exactly 7:53.57 that he'd been away. *Wasn't it?*

"Freaky," the mother said.

Danny's head nuzzled deeper, closer to his mother's breast. He wanted to ask her why she was here and not in the ICU.

Had this woman done something that barred her proximity? Or was it simpler than that? Hospital rules were strict. She, like him, wasn't immediate family.

"She gonna make it?"

When Murray didn't answer, she said, "I'll pray for her." And then, "What's her name?"

"Jean," he said, figuring that it had definitely been no longer than seventeen minutes by the time the medics arrived to give her oxygen.

"Jean," the woman said. "She's in my prayers."

Murray's fist tightened over his watch, numbers slipping like sand.

TWO

The night they conceived, Nancy would call her husband a liar. It was September, twenty years ago, Nancy and Murray's second anniversary. Nancy had gone to the trouble of baking fresh halibut with potatoes au gratin and—hoping he'd indulge her that night—a strawberry short-cake for dessert. But he hadn't shown. She was about to dump his portion in the trash, when she decided she might like to bring it to work with her tomorrow. She unpeeled a sticky note from a block on the kitchen counter by the telephone, wrote *DO NOT TOUCH* in thick red marker, and set the container in the refrigerator. Then she squirted soap into the pans in the sink, holding the spray nozzle like a gun as foam began to rise.

Nancy had pinned up her rust-colored hair—in certain light it looked more gray—and had ironed her blouse, a clean blue paisley, before putting it on, leaving a few extra buttons open to expose some lace in her bra. She'd worn the pearl-drop necklace Murray had given her for their first anniversary to accentuate the freckles he liked along her breastbone. She unclasped the necklace before their bathroom mirror but didn't bother putting it away. She splashed water over her face, working in cleanser gradually, head over the sink, then reached for a towel to pat her skin dry; she held the towel over her cheek as she looked back up into the mirror, scrutinizing a stubborn black streak below her left eye, part residue from crying, part new, from the futility of cleaning.

She went to her dresser drawer for an oversized Michigan T-shirt. She'd grown up in Bloomfield Hills, to parents who'd wanted her to marry a doctor or lawyer, *at the very least* a professor, who'd have shared her fine taste in literature, art, music, her passion for travel. Murray barely read outside of the sports section of the newspaper (at least it was the *Times*), obsessively memorizing every stat. His coaching brain had no room to remember their anniversary. Nancy sat cross-legged in bed, circling this thought and craving a cigarette, even though she'd given up the habit, this other aspect of herself, for him. He had refused to marry her unless she quit.

She heard his keys jingling at their apartment door, then his footsteps in the kitchen, not trepid, but audacious and confident, as he opened and closed the refrigerator and poured something—milk, she assumed—into a glass. She imagined him gulping as she slid under the covers and turned her back to the slightly cracked door. A few minutes later, he entered the room and called to her: "Nancy." He walked around to her side of the bed. She looked up at him, wide-eyed and still, like a deer before a man discovers it.

"How could you forget?" she said, knowing full well that if she hadn't broken the silence, he would have pretended all was fine and just gone on with his routine of showering before bed. He answered, "I didn't forget." But he would not look at her carefully, guiltily, like she wanted him to do—to at least acknowledge her this. He just turned and headed straight for the bathroom and turned the hot water on.

"Don't walk away!" she yelled. She listened to the snapping shut of their wicker hamper. Either he hadn't heard her or he was pretending not to. "You forgot. Just admit it!"

He let the water run and returned to the bedroom naked. Even in the dim light, Nancy could detect every ridge of his abdomen: long, clean lines that separated oblique muscles and framed his narrow pelvis. At forty-two, he maintained the body of a twenty-eight-year-old.

"I didn't know about dinner. You didn't say anything."

"You're such a liar." *There*, she'd said it, crying this time.

Murray remained in the crinkle of light, shower water raining heavily from behind. She turned her focus to the single lamp still burning, the one for reading; it was green shaded with a yellow porcelain base.

He went on about his need to work late, to clock an extra training run, the pressure he was under. But she didn't want to hear it; she stuffed her face into a pillow, felt the heat in her tired cheeks, the tears that wanted to come down harder.

"I'm so close. Remember?" he said. "The promotion?"

He had gotten into bed next to her. "I love you," he said. He held her hands and kissed her mouth. Tears mixed with the salt on his skin. "I didn't forget," he said, his hand brushing her collarbone. He kissed her breast.

She said, "I don't believe you," but her voice wasn't forceful anymore. His lips moved around her belly button, between her thighs and over the side of her hips, where goose bumps formed.

He removed her shirt and guided her to the bathroom. They paused and kissed by the sink. The steam made her heavy. Droplets had condensed over their metal toothbrush holder. When they moved to the shower, he turned her body, which she knew, at forty, had begun to droop. She gripped the metal safety bar as he entered her from behind, his palm pressed into the space between her shoulder blades. Her hands were plastered against the blue tile when they finished. She smelled the minty bar of soap as he ran it gently along the nape of her neck, then down her back. She'd been born with a minor case of scoliosis, a left-leaning curve of ten degrees that caused unevenness in her shoulders and hips. That he forgave such deficiency was one of the things she loved most about him.

She took the soap from him, afraid it might slip in her hands, but managed to run it carefully over every rippling crevice, every bony edge. They shampooed and conditioned separately, taking turns rinsing, and then afterward Nancy shut off the faucet, while Murray reached for a single towel to wrap them in. They made it into bed, where Murray's blue eyes seemed softer, and then a clean click of the lamp sent them into darkness.

~

Three weeks later, they went to Mystic Seaport for the weekend and passed a cart selling hot dogs. Never had the scent of oiled meat smelled so vile. Nancy ran to a ledge rail off the boardwalk to vomit. She told Murray she was sure she'd caught some sort of stomach bug, but the next day it happened again, when they sat down for lunch at the marina. Grilled cheese sandwich, french fries, plus most of the chips that'd come with Murray's: Nancy ate all of it. But when a woman nearby lit a cigarette, Nancy felt the food begin to rise.

She said nothing at first, but then her curiosity bloomed, and *bloomed*. A few nights later, Nancy found herself light and dizzy in their bathroom, gripping the edges of the sink, studying her face in the mirror for balance. The pregnancy test showed a plus sign through its gray oval. In the mirror, Nancy had more miniature wrinkles around her eyes and mouth than she could count, and her hair seemed to turn grayer by the minute. She and Murray had married late in life, both so focused on their careers a child hadn't seemed part of the picture. Even if they'd wanted one, or had agreed they wanted to try, she'd assumed it would have been a planned effort. How would he handle the surprise?

They were seated on their bed when she told him. She had her hand pressed to her belly. Murray just stared at his feet and nervously twisted the end of his mustache.

"What are you thinking?"

When he didn't answer, she reached for his hand. "Are you happy?" His face went rigid. He waited several more seconds and worked his mouth into a smile.

"Yes," he said. "Of course I am." Two years before, just after they'd married, she'd been so quick to anger any time he didn't express the right emotion, but she was learning to accept Murray's reticence. He implied his love, didn't he?

The morning after their anniversary, he'd proved he hadn't forgotten it by surprising her with a first-edition copy of *Giovanni's Room* from Argosy Book Store in the city; he had rushed to the Metro-North after practice, but then had missed the 6:47 p.m. train coming back.

It was true, she could be too hard on him sometimes, defensive, like her mother had been with her father, accusing him unfairly, ruminating over the slightest mistakes. Nancy was trying to be different. More patient.

They sat together in silence for several long minutes, until Murray said, "We should move things around this weekend. To gauge space for the baby." Nancy sighed, then nodded, surveying their queen-sized bed, their two old dressers from the Salvation Army, their single bookcase tilting from the weight of her literary anthologies and reference texts competing for space with Murray's training manuals. The room's only window was steel blue in the early evening light. It had rained for most of that day, and for the first time, they felt the lingering dampness, the quiet of time stopping. They turned to one another confounded. Nancy laughed, then Murray did too. Was there something forced in *his?* she wondered, but then thought she was once again being too hard on him. She shouldn't overanalyze; it wasn't worth that now. They leaned back on the bed together, fingers locked.

Over a week later, a Monday, they both took off from work and went to see an obstetrician. Because Nancy was technically a high-risk case—any woman over thirty-five was—she had pushed hard to see Dr. Edmund Weiss, a world-renowned expert on fetal therapy. While they waited in the exam room, Nancy was possessed by another violent bout of morning sickness and thought about leaving the appointment. But in strode Dr. Weiss as she was pacing the room. He was tall and thin, with crow-black hair, and held a miniature Dixie cup with a tiny pocket of water.

"Take a seat," he said, and she calmed. He smiled. "The test didn't lie. We're looking at a four-week-old embryo." He went through the results of Nancy's physical exam and blood tests. Everything was looking good: her weight, blood pressure, reproductive health. "Since you want to be conservative, we should run a few screenings. An amnio at seventeen weeks can tell us a lot more."

"Like what?" Nancy asked. Her body ached. She sipped from her cup, fingers clammy and tremulous.

"Down syndrome is the big one," he said. "There is a one in one hundred chance."

"That high?" said Murray. His shoulders scrunched to his ears.

"None of this is meant to scare you. It's simply important to be aware. Especially since many abnormalities can be prevented. I'd advise you to read these."

He handed Nancy a stack of pamphlets listing terms like *gestational diabetes*, *preeclampsia*, and *vascular disease*, and a folder with information on the risks of miscarriage and preterm birth.

"The most important thing," he said, washing his hands, "is that you're both in good health, with strong genetic histories." He turned the faucet off and reached for a paper towel. "I recommend checkups every other week. If we find anything along the way, we can always up the visits."

Nancy bit her lip and shook her head slightly. She had slipped on her reading glasses and was perusing a sheet on metabolic disorders.

"Lots of fluids and simple foods," Dr. Weiss reminded her. "See you in two weeks."

In the car on the way home, Nancy burst into tears. She was suffo-
cating and asked Murray to roll down the window. Murray pulled over
and unbuckled his seat belt. As she went on about how she couldn't quit
her job at Beinecke Library, that she didn't know if she could make it
through all these tests, he told her to take deep breaths. "It's alright,"
he said. "Doctors always give worst-case scenarios." He reminded her
they needed to take things one day at a time, that certain factors *were*
in their control. For instance, she could try to cut back her hours. He
would apply for a raise and start running private training classes. He
could help prepare meals and regiment her exercise. They would figure
out finances. Nancy was rubbing her reddened knuckles. She nodded
but words wouldn't come. They drove the rest of the way in silence.
Murray steered with one hand. The other he rested over Nancy's, her
fist bound tight with a clump of tissues.

The next day, Nancy checked out every book she could find on
pregnancy planning and fetal development. She went into the stacks,
where it was quiet, and read about the first trimester. Already their baby
was the size of a green pea, with a primitive backbone curled like a tail.
A U-shaped tube formed the heart, rapidly pumping.

She confirmed all signs of early pregnancy, penciling tiny check
marks on sticky notes inside the pages. She'd need to consume a delicate
balance of vitamins, protein, and fat, she learned, but the things she
craved most were full of empty calories: fresh bread, mashed potatoes,
and butter-drenched noodles with parmesan. Ice cream.

A little boy in the elementary school Nancy had attended as a girl
had walked around with an oxygen tank. He had a congenital heart
condition that made his lips blue. Years later when Nancy was selling
magazine subscriptions for a fund-raiser, she'd rung his doorbell. His
mother had answered, her skin bone colored, eyelids swollen. Behind
her there'd been an empty wheelchair and discarded tank, its discon-
nected tubing visible.

~

Some form of exercise every day was ideal, Nancy knew. She'd never liked running, even after Murray had tried to help her build up to a mile around their neighborhood last summer—but cardiovascular health was important, especially with her lungs at a disadvantage already, after all the time she'd spent smoking during her PhD, when the pressure of producing pages for her dissertation, all those hours spent alone in the archives, had weighed on her.

Nancy started a daily habit of fifty jumping jacks and thirty toe touches. Murray showed her how to lift his free weights, the ten-pound dumbbells he used to practice his arm swing before the mirror, and she learned to focus on the different core muscle groups Murray said she'd need to keep strong these nine months.

Although several books made an allowance for the occasional slice of cake, block of chocolate, or celebratory sip of champagne, she tried not to indulge. To prevent dietary slips, she posted a note with *Every bite counts* over the refrigerator door, next to a magazine clipping of a perfect baby.

One morning over breakfast, Murray commented on the photo. Usually Nancy didn't rise this early with him, but she'd been unable to sleep. He asked her if she really believed their baby would match the image.

"Why does that matter?" She was sipping orange juice, aware of the bitterness in her tone but more concerned about the pH level of the juice. She'd left her diet books upstairs by their bed, by her glasses and the reading light.

"Just curious." He sighed and tore his slice of toast in half. He scribbled notes on his pad.

"Don't you ever get bored?" she asked, the irritation still there, exacerbated by this pressing need for her nutrition checklist.

"How do you mean?"

"Tweaking the same plan?"

"It's not the same," he said, gulping the last of his juice.

"More or less."

Well into his second year as assistant coach, Murray was obsessed with proving himself, physically and professionally. She wondered if he'd always be this way. Would he be a good father, a healthy model for their child? Did he even want to be a parent, or was he ambivalent?

Murray hadn't yet affirmed, at least not fully, Nancy's growing desire, her curiosity, about what it might be like to guide a young mind through life. She could admit she'd felt, since her late twenties, some envy for mothers with children at bus stops, or in restaurants and shops. How wonderful it seemed to explain simple words and arithmetic for the first time, and to be confronted with much larger conundrums, such as why up was *up* . . . or a sound, *a sound* . . . or the question of forgetting; she had once heard a child ask, *Mommy, why do you forget?*

Nancy's own mother had *forgotten* nothing, the way she'd been quick to remind her of every possible threat, every potential germ or disease. Most days, her mother had been too afraid to leave the house, and Nancy would run countless errands for her, mostly to the drugstore for all the special creams and vitamins her mother claimed she depended on.

Murray mumbled something when he stood up from the table. She wanted him to speak louder, but he shrugged her off. She pressed him again by the door on his way out, where he stood with his coffee mug and newspaper. "I'm doing the best I can," he said. "For us."

She pinched away tears, said she was sorry. Then she trudged upstairs to try and sleep off the last hour before she had to get ready for work. But when she couldn't relax in bed, too distracted by her books, which she'd thrown onto the floor, she slipped on a pair of sweatpants and took a walk around the neighborhood. The sun had just begun its ascent, illuminating a distant bridge of girder steel.

Nancy was thankful for the fresh air. Walking helped her clear her mind before the day grew too busy or weighted down by other concerns. She resolved to make this her habit: a long walk every morning, well before sunrise. She could exercise and let her shape disappear into shadow. She could think. And when she finished, even though Murray wasn't there to see her, she began a habit of stretching her hamstrings and calves in the yard. Sometimes she added a set of lunges, like she'd watched him complete many times after a run.

~

When she and Murray first met, Nancy had wanted to understand marathons, what it felt like to complete one.

They had taken ham sandwiches to a bench in the Luxembourg Gardens, in Paris, where Murray used to train every morning, and she still liked to picture the stone-faced guards during each one of his laps: twelve times around the perimeter.

When she'd asked him about marathon training, Murray had looked at her concernedly, rubbing a little bristle on his chin. He'd started at square one: the essence of establishing a base of thirty miles per week. It was all about weekly long runs, about working one's way to eight miles, adding a mile every week after that, until twenty miles was reached. After several twenty-milers, *a runner knows she's ready,* he'd said with a smile. Nancy had been too distracted by the scent of tuberose, and the small muscles in his arms while he ate, to ask: How do you know you're ready for the *full* twenty-six? Wasn't the difference of six miles significant, especially at the end of a race? She supposed she'd been afraid, was still afraid, of appearing foolish, in knowing so little about his world.

Yet it was Murray who had walked into hers that first afternoon, into the café where she'd been reading for her dissertation. He'd shown up sweaty in his running clothes like only an American would, and this had made her smile—though at the time, she'd acted like she hadn't noticed him. She was good at that, she thought, pretending to be oblivious to a change in a room. Oblivion had always seemed easier than risking the tiniest of failures, or worse, admitting them to herself out loud.

~

In high school her mother used to scold her: If her nose was always in a book, and she never went to social events, how was she to meet anyone? But then Nancy *had* met someone, the final year of her PhD, for that matter; she had written her mother of the news, and her mother had written back congratulating her, insisting that she and her father visit as soon as possible. Her mother was terrified of overseas travel, so Nancy had been deeply moved by this gesture. But both parents were beyond disapproving of Murray's background: his father had worked in a coal mine; and Murray had majored in anatomy and was a college running coach. What of the doctor, the lawyer, the possibility of a desk, of real colleagues? Murray had insisted on wearing his track jacket over a T-shirt with jeans, despite Nancy's repeated suggestion that a blazer—at the very least, a button-down—would be best. This had frustrated him, his irksome tone suggesting the importance of *being himself,* and so she'd yielded, because wasn't that what one did for love?

She shuddered to think of the way her mother had been at the dinner table that night, not smiling once under the dim lighting of the restaurant, La Petite Chaise, a space so small and warm it seemed carved into the side of some great topography. And Murray had gone to such great lengths to secure a reservation. Both her parents had ordered steak au poivre, and Nancy had found herself forgetting to eat as she studied the slow and careful rhythm of her mother's knife, comparing it with Murray's hasty pace. At one point, she'd watched, stomach clenching, as he'd used the edge of his pinky to push some risotto onto his fork.

Murray competed in the Olympics, she'd said, reaching for Murray's knee under the table. Her own father had played golf for Brown, after all. Nancy's mother, who always wore her white hair pinned with two black clips, had merely pursed her lips, and her father had nodded faintly, the same nod she'd often witnessed as a child; once, he'd given it to a plumber, after the plumber had asked for a glass of water before the job was over, and then, as her father had put it, *gone so far as to detail the troubles of his personal life.*

~

Neither Mother nor Father would ever accept him, Nancy knew. But it didn't matter. Shouldn't matter. Murray was her life now, her family.

She recalled with fondness those first months together in Paris—how slow and full the days had felt, yet how quickly the weeks had amassed. Murray had abandoned his hotel to stay with her in the apartment she'd rented from a widow, Madame Arnaud, on Boulevard Raspail. Nancy guessed the Madame fed a stray black cat that liked to lurk about the building; on a few occasions, she'd caught it perched on the ledge of her bedroom window, watching her and Murray through filmy panes.

She liked to reminisce over the many mornings they'd spent waking up next to one another, gazing around at the strange array of paintings lining the walls. She used to speculate over different stylistic techniques and the historical influences behind them, and Murray would listen patiently, same as when she'd gone on about Monet's *Water Lilies* in the Orangerie, or Rodin's bronze bust of Balzac in his sculpture garden. She could still see Murray's eyes, how fixed they were on the smallest details she'd needed to account for: the size of the boat Monet had painted his masterpieces from, the proportion of green to turquoise Rodin used for his patinas, the dates on the newspapers Picasso cut up for his collages. Until she met Murray, Nancy had always assumed herself alone in her passion for precision, for noting each and every choice that went into producing a perfect object.

Her mother had answered the phone when she'd called with the news they were expecting. Afterward, she didn't tell Murray about the call—the management of her weight, the consumption of the right calories, her exercise were so much easier to discuss. She hadn't spoken to her parents since they had refused to acknowledge her marriage. She hoped their child might level things, bring them to their senses.

Nancy, her mother had nearly whispered, *did you leave him yet? There'd* been a long pause. *Or are you just now planning to?*

Nancy almost hung up the phone, but she'd found the courage. *We're pregnant,* she'd said. *I thought you should know.* And then she'd pressed the power button on the cordless and listened to the dial tone. She'd held the earpiece and receiver to her chest, then lower by her belly, as if Baby might affirm they were both still living, that the pain would pass. The first weeks had been the worst; she'd had no way of fully anticipating the degree of her disappointment, her guilt. Her anger. Why was it so hard for them to acknowledge her marriage? Even after Murray was offered his coaching position, and she—after less than three weeks of searching—had secured a job at Yale, too, as Beinecke Library's American literature curator. Surely the stars would continue to work in their favor. Couldn't her parents see that too?

There was nothing more to say to them, but why did she still feel like she needed to justify her choices? As if it were possible to point to a single moment that could explain everything. Was there even one?

~

She supposed that there had been that one hot afternoon in early July, when it had been over ninety degrees; somehow she and Murray had resolved it wasn't bad enough to stay inside, and they'd taken the metro to Montmartre, since Nancy had insisted on showing Murray the Sacré-Coeur.

Even as beads of sweat dripped from his chin, Murray coached her up the hill, at least three hundred steps. She'd had to pause at every landing, hoping he wouldn't notice her smoker's hack, the kerchief she'd had to untie from her hair to cough into. When he'd asked if she was alright, she'd claimed the start of a cold—and then she'd cringed when she'd had to use that soiled kerchief to cover her shoulders before stepping into the basilica. At least she'd found some solace in the dusty pews, sunlight splintering through the open doors.

Silently they'd admired the stained glass together and the magnificent apse mural with the Holy Trinity above, and they'd donated a few francs to light a votive on the way out. Afterward, they'd gone for gelato. Murray only ever had ice cream once or twice a year, he'd explained, but then he'd smiled, and she knew that this was *his* idea, that he wanted to impress her.

As they waited in line, she'd clutched the strap of her satchel, but then after they'd gotten their cones and began weaving through tourists—she wasn't sure when—she'd felt the strap loosen over her shoulder. The buckle had come undone, and her wallet was gone.

Murray reacted frantically, sprinting through more throngs of people in the narrow streets. She'd teetered after him in sandals, legs aching, down more steps, fingers sticky with her discarded gelato cone. She followed him to the police station, a tiny office buzzing with fans, Murray leaning in close over the front counter, shouting fruitless English. She'd had to take over as translator, and he'd nearly been kicked out for seizing the office telephone so she could cancel her credit card; he'd helped her jog her memory, to account for the exact amount that had been stolen, a little over two hundred in US dollars. It could have been worse, but Murray's concern, his utter devotion until the end, had proved he was more than a lover; he was a partner, a friend.

It was 6:00 p.m. by the time they'd left the station, both of them starving. They'd eaten dinner at a little crêperie, sharing a bottle of wine. It seemed crazy that they'd stayed, but Murray had wanted to treat her, and after the wine, they were both too tired to travel all the way back. They decided to spend the night in a small hotel. Bastille Day was at least a week away, but there'd been a fireworks display over the Tuileries. They'd hurried after the distant cracks, the throb of sound—to a stone wall at the edge of the hill, promising a clear view of the city. As they watched tiny blossoms of light against the black sky, she'd felt her faith in Murray burgeon. Something about him made her body feel light and grounded all at once. Two weeks later: a proposal, an acceptance.

Nancy could not discuss her anguish over her parents with Murray. Not only was it a sore subject after their visit, but both of Murray's parents had passed: his father when he was a child, and his mother just last year. He no longer kept in touch with his younger brother, Patrick, after he'd moved out west to work at a casino, leaving Murray to care for their mother after she fell ill. Nancy never wanted to remind Murray of his many losses.

Nancy had visited his hometown in Luzerne County, Pennsylvania, only twice: first, in October after they married and moved to New Haven, just a few months after the July proposal. Murray's mother had recently had a stroke. The second visit was just four months later, in February, after she'd died. Nancy held just a few images of the place: hills arched in autumn red and gold, hills ridged with snow; afternoon skies, a cold, crisp blue. She remembered feeling oddly compelled by the spectral feel of forgotten industry, of a past waiting to be reclaimed. This was the place that had produced her husband, the determined set of his lips, his need for the clock and its calculations. Though Murray never spoke of returning there, she hoped one day he'd show their child the land he knew.

THREE

After Murray had waited four hours in the hospital, with still no word from Becky's parents, he headed to the exhibition pool on campus, this dark, cavernous hole below the first level of the gym. A series of tunnels ran behind the stadium seating, and Murray entered from high up, at the fifteenth-level row. Every Monday, when the diving team was in the middle of practice, he came here. The intermittent spring of the board calmed him, as did the stillness of the water afterward, when he could be left alone with its deep, electric blue.

But now he crouched into a seat, the scent of chlorine burning his nose. Humidity made it difficult to relax. He rolled up his jacket sleeves and noticed a hint of blood, dried, along the inner part of his forearm. The wound was bleeding? He saw the bruise, the red rim before he searched for her pulse. Had he touched her head?

He looked up to where a male diver stood on the board, at least twenty-five feet above the water. The diver had strong pectoral muscles, rounded ever so slightly at the edges. His abdominals were the same, clear cut and striated.

Murray wasn't close friends with the diving coach, Theo Fischer, but they respected one another. They'd spoken a few times at administrative meetings, mostly about their common approach. Success, they both believed, depended on a careful mixture of repetition and focus, in honing the athlete's attention to the most minor details: keeping the shoulders perfectly square and relaxed, engaging both big toes to activate inner thighs and arches—squeezing the gluteal muscles during push off—or, in the case of this diver, during the jounce. Murray watched him now, three measured pulses before the creak, the fated zing, as the diver sprung up and twisted, suspended midair before he fell, clean and melodious against the water's skin.

Theo had assured Murray he didn't mind his presence. He'd told him to come anytime. Usually he waved when Murray found his seat in the third or fourth row, or else Murray would raise his pad in acknowledgment, but today he'd snuck in just high enough not to be noticed, covered in shadows.

A young woman approached the board. She didn't bother testing the spring, just stared fixedly ahead. The water filter lapped. Overhead lights buzzed. A glare rippled over the water, disfiguring it.

Before the jump, she squeezed in her body, then arced perfectly through the air. She slid in palms first, minimal splash.

When she popped up, her teammates clapped. "Good, Lydia!" Theo yelled from behind. But she never smiled, only absently parted the water with her strong arms until she'd reached the stepladder and slowly climbed up.

Murray looked down at his pad, still turned to the page with Becky's name and all her splits. He noticed some coffee spilled over the paper, and some grease from the breakfast sandwich he'd never opened in the car. He'd been planning to give her the other half of it after practice as a reward.

～

Could Murray be accused of negligence? After all the time he'd invested—thoughtfully, meticulously? Becky's parents, like everyone else, knew Division I running required morning practices for top athletes, countless hours of solo time.

Take Nationals last year, in Terre Haute. Becky had qualified at Heptagonals, the biggest meet of the season against all the other Ivy Leagues. She'd run an exceptional time of 16:35.42, even after they'd only had three weeks to prepare. He'd had to keep her over Thanksgiving break, since the race was always held two days before, and though Doug had questioned him about that at first, he'd understood when Becky placed second, overall, in a time of 15:22.08.

He and Becky had left early for the race one Tuesday morning, and he thought of how she'd refused to place her backpack in the overhead stow. She'd held it on her lap instead, hugging it like a stuffed animal, while he'd spread out a copy of the newspaper to review seed times. At one point, she unzipped her backpack for a water bottle filled with a pale pink liquid, most likely Pedialyte, and then she'd pulled out a copy of Spenser's *Faerie Queene*.

Becky's deciding on the English major still surprised him. He'd assumed she'd pursue science or math, something more concrete and useful. But Becky had seemed passionately focused on her reading through the whole flight, turning each page carefully, almost exactly a page per minute. She'd kept her pen poised, ready to underline, and when the flight attendant came, she'd foregone the complimentary beverage and peanuts. He'd asked for seltzer water, somewhat self-conscious about shaking salty peanuts onto his cocktail napkin, studying their seams and considering his blood pressure.

Becky hadn't spoken until the ground came into view, these gray and brown specks of trees and neighborhoods she'd pointed to. She'd said though her mother was from Ohio, she'd never been to the Midwest, mostly because her grandparents didn't live there anymore. He'd asked where they lived now, and she'd said *Florida*, nearly whispering.

The first time Murray had met Becky, with her mother, Lisa, in his office, she'd been exuberant. Becky must have weighed ten, maybe fifteen, pounds more then. She'd been small, but she had flesh around her smile, a bright color to her lips. She'd asked him all kinds of questions about the program and where she could expect to compete. Her eyes had been bright, too, as he'd listed all the opportunities that would open up to her, especially since she hadn't peaked yet. As a high school junior, she'd already run 17:23—under mediocre coaching and a low mileage plan, at that—so Murray had told her, if she was willing to commit herself to *his* program, honed since his own Olympic days, they could expect to see great things.

Why couldn't they still? Why jump to any conclusions? Murray didn't know that she wouldn't run this season, or next.

~

Nancy used to comment about how careful he was about every detail when it came to coaching, but was blind to the *bigger picture*, especially when it involved their marriage. It was her tone, always, that had carried her judgment of him. His ex-wife was chronically jealous of the time he spent coaching. It had been so easy for her to assume he was responsible for all that had gone wrong in their lives.

Mary Hannan's torn hamstring in '97, or Kim Degrise's bulging disk in '98—Nancy had been quick to link those first injuries to her own dissatisfactions with him, when he came home *too late*, or spent *too much* time on the field. Nancy wasn't an athlete—any true athlete knew injuries came with the package. More often than not, he'd had to remind her, it was the culture of the team, not the coach, that spread bad habits. Coaches didn't have control over other girls setting a poor precedent around diet and sleep—from too much studying or partying— or trying to slim down by cutting calories. All coaches faced the same predicament, Murray thought. Even Theo here. Murray was sure Theo had the same problems if one of his divers started eating less because one of her teammates was.

~

Murray was sweating. He hadn't felt it, not at first, but along his wrists were small beads. He breathed deeply.

The only thing a coach could do, he'd remind himself again, and again, was *focus on the present*. The present was the only thing that mattered in sports: schedules, itineraries, workouts.

Murray turned his pad to a fresh page, hands quavering. He wrote *Anna Bradley* at the top. Technically, Anna was next in line on his roster—nowhere near Becky's talent—but at least she was disciplined enough, a fierce competitor.

Anna had been running 5:55 pace up to this point. He needed her closer to 5:30. There were only two weeks until the first meet of the season.

By the time the medics came, a string of pink saliva had hung from Becky's mouth. Blood had bubbled from her nostril—that was where the blood on his forearm had come from? But she had been breathing, he reminded himself. There had not been a lapse in Becky's breath, no hidden symptoms, no sudden pause.

Murray's hands felt clammier as he watched a female diver venture onto the board. She had broad shoulders, well-articulated collarbones.

Once Anna got the feeling of number one, thought Murray, her speed would adapt to the mind-set. Dropping twenty seconds per mile was significant. It would call for drastic training modifications. He'd have to increase her mileage from fifty to sixty. Add an extra set of everything the team was doing, like Becky did. Murray's eyes twitched. He touched his lips.

The first male diver was up again. His back faced the water, skin glistening. A hard spring to tuck and then a flip forward. Though the splash was loud, rough, the team clapped.

Murray glanced back down at Anna's chart: sixty miles per week equaled a little over eight miles per day, but as he went to write the numbers in, he stopped, more sweat on his hands.

The paramedic had noted some vomit obstructing Becky's airway. Murray had caught sight of it, too, bloody mucus mixed with fibrous strips of orange.

~

On his way to the men's locker room, he nearly slammed into the athletic director. Rick Warner had been around longer than Murray. Formerly the lightweight men's rowing coach, Rick had seen his rowers through five National Championship wins.

"Murray." Rick sounded breathless. "I couldn't find you. Why didn't you come to see me in person? The message you left—I can't believe it about Becky."

Murray felt Rick's eyes on his soiled sneakers, then on his lips, as if he could sense the taste in his mouth, its rancid tingling.

"Have you heard anything more about the injury? The severity?" Rick kept in good shape, biceps bulging beneath a crisp navy sports polo.

"No."

"She could die." Rick had his arms crossed. "Aren't you worried about that?"

Murray turned away. Rick—even he would suggest *negligence*?

"Look, it's horrific." Rick's voice lowered. "A nightmare. I'll understand if you need to cancel practice after you break it to the team."

"Thanks, Rick." Murray barely heard himself speak.

"Let's keep each other posted, okay?" He patted Murray's shoulder as he brushed past, eyes and mouth pinched in false condolence. Certainly, Rick wanted Becky to pull through, but did he wish the best for Murray as a coach? Murray thought, *No.* Rick had always looked down on him for coaching girls in the first place. He'd once asked why he hadn't waited around for the men's cross-country coach to retire, but when Murray explained his belief that girls responded better to a male figure, Rick had laughed.

Then Murray thought that it shouldn't have been news to Rick that there were still plenty of male coaches for women's distance running teams around.

The tradition had started with Ken Foreman and his Olympian Doris Brown in the sixties. Foreman had endured the worst discrimination too. Murray had read the coach's autobiography in one siting, all about how Foreman used to have to hide in closets to stretch Doris's hamstrings, how he'd been bullied off tracks, suffered countless sideline threats and intolerable rants because he'd been a male coach with young women under his charge. People liked to make assumptions, project their own insecurities onto what they hadn't experienced firsthand . . . "Rick," Murray muttered as he rinsed his face in the locker room . . . *Rick* didn't understand Murray's particular way with his team, *how hard* all of his girls worked for his approval, *how much* his quiet authority urged them to achieve.

~

It had been the same for Murray and his father, who'd rarely affirmed Murray as a child. The first time Murray could remember was after he'd won the mile in seventh grade. His father had told his friends, the men he worked with at Blaschak Coal—Frank Stoltz and Lee Murphy—his father had told them Murray was going to break the high school record as a middle schooler, but the next year, when Murray didn't, his father hadn't said anything—he'd just looked away, down at his newspaper. He'd been sitting in a plastic patio chair in the yard, and Murray had said, *Dad, I still won*—but there had just been silence outside in their yard, the still trees and the near crinkle of his father's newspaper, Murray's hands in his pockets, digging at lint.

The only time Murray's father ever broke his silence was out of anger. When Murray was a boy, no older than eight or nine, he'd found a robin's nest in the large elm he liked to climb. Murray had kept a jar of worms ready for when the eggs hatched, but one day, when he went by the nest, there'd only been the crushed blue shells. Murray had run inside crying. His father had called him foolish. *Larger animals simply eat smaller animals,* he'd said, but then Murray had cried harder, and his father had braced his shoulders and screamed at him. *Stop it,* he'd said. *Stop it right now.*

Murray's father died before Murray could achieve anything substantial. When he was fifteen, a methane gas buildup caused an explosion in the mine his father worked in. The mine had collapsed and trapped his father and ten others. As the eldest, Murray had had no other choice but to fill his father's place, taking care of Patrick, only eleven then, while his mother went to work. Murray had helped cook dinners and do the laundry, had packed lunches. He'd been in charge of running his way to a college scholarship.

It was there, at the University of Scranton, that Murray found his freedom. He'd been raised a fairly religious boy, Catholic, but he had not kept up his churchgoing over the course of those four years. He'd devoted himself to training, even on Sundays. His body, this hardened casing he'd come to imagine flowing with blood, became his religion. That, and the necessity of pain, its ability to blur boundaries of time and space, only if he surrendered to it utterly.

He believed in the singularity of agony: the searing of his legs and lungs that could carry him into an oblivion more all-knowing than any God he'd ever read about or felt, even in "the holiest of moments" when he'd married Nancy that September day in 1996, or when he'd received the Eucharist every Sunday, certain she'd change her mind those first three months after they divorced, officially, six years later.

~

It was already 2:57 p.m., and all the girls were waiting for him in the gym lobby. Under normal circumstances, they took a shuttle to the field house, and then ran two miles from there to the golf course as warm-up. Murray's knees ached as he descended the stairs from his office to the lobby, and his hands shook over the sheet he'd scribbled his notes on—words like *tragedy*, *act of God*, and *head in the game* to frame their perspective, keep things general enough, so as not to upset them.

Ginny and Emily were pushing off on a wall, stretching their calves. Rodney (who went by her last name), Anna, and Patricia were all doing the butterfly stretch, laughing about something. Liu was readjusting her silky black ponytail, so long it nearly reached her bottom. And then there was Victoria, who always came with her Differential Equation notes tucked into her sports bra. She mouthed the formulas with closed eyes. Tanya, a newer walk-on, sat cross-legged, hugging her shoulders.

"Listen up," Murray said before them. "Becky's injured." A few of the girls looked at one another; others stared straight ahead, eyes large. "She had an accident on the golf course." He paused, took a breath. "She was hit by a ball . . . is in the hospital for head trauma. I don't know anything more." Liu gasped.

How many times would he have to say this out loud? It had been the same for him and Nancy, when people wanted clean answers about what had happened. And he guessed she'd always blamed him—for pretending he hadn't heard certain questions, looking down at his pad and scribbling numbers instead of engaging. Once, she'd cursed at him and shoved his pad from the table before he could reach for it.

Victoria had begun to cry. "The chance of this occurring is one in ten billion," he said, fighting to keep his voice firm. "Less than that." He tried to picture a clean gray road ahead, not one undulation deterring his pace.

"Will she be alright?" Anna's eyes searched him. "Can we go to the hospital?"

"I know very little," he said. "Her parents have been with her since early this morning. As soon as I have news, I'll tell you."

Tanya was looking out toward the door, as if she assumed practice was cancelled, or wanted it to just go on—so she wouldn't have to think any longer?

"I know it might not seem possible to run today—" He sensed the machine in his tone, automatic, unflinching. He tried to embrace it. "But I want to argue for the opposite." He covered his mouth with a sleeve, the acid rising up again, and breathed. "But like with every race," he said, "we must stay in the moment. Becky wouldn't want us to give up. She would want us to train."

Victoria looked at him with disgust. Rodney stared at the linoleum floor. She hadn't been running well since a performance peak during her sophomore year. Murray wondered whether this news would serve as some kind of tipping point for her to quit. She didn't believe in his high-volume method, had come to his office at the end of last season to tell him so. He'd never seen her cry before, so when she looked up, her eyes and face red, he was startled. He took another breath, sent signals to his heart to calm. Let it settle.

"We'll do an easier four-mile tempo run around campus." He told Anna to shoot for a 5:50 or 6:00 pace and reminded the team that he'd be at the two-mile mark and the finish for giving times. A few of the girls went to the bathroom. Rodney led the remaining bunch outside. Through the main doors, he saw her gesticulating furiously to Patricia—she appeared to be venting about something—while Patricia stood with her arms crossed, listening. Patricia, a junior recovering from a hamstring strain, wiped her face with a sleeve.

Just then, Anna came out of the bathroom with Tanya and Victoria. "Anna!" he called and motioned her over, hoping she'd separate herself from the other girls. She did, and he felt a balm of gratitude for her. He pointed to what was written on his pad.

"I was taking a look at your times, Anna, and think you could do something great by November, at Regionals. I think we could have you under 18:00 by the Iona Invitational in two weeks."

Anna's eyes darted nervously, but he went on: "It will require some extra training. Some serious dedication on your part. But if we amp up the intensity now and factor in a taper, it's doable."

"Oh," she said. "If you think so." She had begun chewing a lip. "But I guess I don't understand. Are you assuming Becky won't be back?"

"Of course not. I'm just saying that while she's out, we have to stay focused, think like competitors."

They had a few classes together, he guessed. Introduction to Psychology and another one he couldn't remember. He pointed to his pad and told her to aim for 5:30 pace.

Anna sighed, then forcibly nodded. She had a pale, freckled face and fox-colored hair, such similar features to Nancy's. Her green eyes were locked with his now, this time in desperation.

"I want you to go out there and remind the team of what I said. You're a natural leader. The other girls respect you. We can't afford to let unknowns get in the way of moving forward."

None of the girls ran well. Anna's splits were almost twenty seconds slower than usual. It was a terrible makeshift course, full of traffic lights and interruptions, but even if he subtracted a minute from each runner's total time, numbers were still slow. Anna apologized afterward, sweat dripping from her lips. But he told her today was done; what was important was tomorrow. Eyes on the horizon. Get back on the horse. More tropes he'd come to live by as a coach.

In the car, at a stoplight, he checked his phone again. No missed calls or messages. He considered driving back to the hospital and waiting in the parking lot, but depending on the severity, the schedule for surgeries, there was no guarantee Becky's parents would ever be leaving, the chance of running into them slim to none.

Instead of turning right on Edgewood Avenue like usual, Murray turned left, in the direction of the golf course. He passed Central Avenue, which overlapped with the two-mile course the girls had run today—the exact point where he'd caught Rodney walking. Her Adidas shorts had been grazing her knees, her broad shoulders outstretching her tank top. He'd been parked on the corner taking splits, had yelled at her to get going, but she'd only scowled at him.

Murray had never really admitted it to himself before, but he wondered if Rodney had feelings for Becky, if Becky was the reason why she'd stayed on the team so long, even after last year, when her times and grades had begun to plummet. Rodney liked to make jokes about Becky lapping her at practice, and a few times he'd caught them immersed in conversation. He didn't understand what they had in common, except that they were both majoring in the humanities. Or were these thoughts about Becky and Rodney—were they just him being paranoid?

Murray did not feel his foot pushing harder on the gas pedal or his clenched grip over the wheel, just his mind spewing images uncontrollably, of Rodney trying to cause a stir, pushing her way to see Becky before he did, telling the team a different story about what had happened, just because she was rebellious. Because she could.

At the entrance, he slowed to a stop and searched for a water bottle in the car. He kept dozens of spares rolling around on the floor—as he searched, he noticed some dried orange peel, some seeds. He stuffed the peels into an empty plastic bag and rushed out of the car, looking for a trash can, suppressing an urge to vomit. He focused on the clubhouse, the clear structure of its stone facade. But the heat, this humidity outside, made it impossible to focus—Murray wanted nothing more than for September to arrive. Just three more days until then.

"How are we, Coach?" Jamie, the manager, asked when Murray was inside. The man had small moonbeam eyes that sometimes looked crossed. How did the man hit a straight shot? But when Murray told Jamie about the accident, he looked genuinely stricken.

"We wondered what had caused the turf damage this morning—it must have been the ambulance." Immediately, he got on the phone to call Seth Arthur, the director of the club.

There was a hardened yellow spot over Jamie's desk, and Murray watched as Jamie scraped at it with his index finger while he waited for the phone to ring. He thought of the daisy border in the bedroom he had scraped and scraped, because he'd thought Nancy had wanted it removed—but before he could see the white he'd scraped down to, there was the question of Becky's ear, whether it showed Battle's sign, this discoloration that could appear a day after severe trauma, tiny purplish-red splotches potentially populating her skin.

Murray swallowed, mouth still parched, before walking over to a large bag full of newly minted clubs. He brushed the tops of wedges and irons, gripped the head of a thick titanium driver. This place smelled like paint and fresh tennis balls. He noticed a shelf with speed sensors that measured swings between thirty and two hundred miles per hour.

"No one can believe it," Jamie said, hanging up the phone. "Seth is sending out a club-wide memo."

Then Murray asked to see a copy of this week's schedule, to make sure the morning hadn't been booked.

"Nothing," Jamie said, pointing to a large spiral-bound day calendar on his desk, pencil poised over the blank lines by 5:00 a.m. As far as Murray could see, there were no erasure marks. He quickly registered the names of a few people that had been slotted later in the morning: Simpson, McDonald, Chadha.

"Will you let me know if you see anything suspicious, or anyone who wants to book early morning?"

"God," Jamie said. "Of course. Let us know as soon as you hear anything. I just hope she's okay."

Murray nodded. Baseball players suffered comparable injuries. He'd once read an article about one hit in the back of the head by a foul ball, but the player had not seemed injured; he'd gone on playing the game. It was only later, on the subway, when he'd keeled over. Brain swelling.

Outside, Murray used the golf cart key he'd held on to and drove to the precise place where Becky had fallen. He kept his eyes on the edge of the woodland, a thicket of pines. He stopped when he saw a group of golfers approaching tee-off.

After Murray parked nearby, he watched a bull-necked gentleman sip beer in his cart. Most likely an early retiree, or perhaps he'd grown up with a trust fund and never had to work.

Another man descended from the driver's seat, black visor shadowing his face, but when he gripped his club by the tee, shoulders hugged the shaft to reveal small, taut breasts.

The woman hit a stunning shot. There were some gasps, then laughs, most likely because she was better than everyone else. The woman laughed too.

Becky's nail beds had begun to blue. *Hypoxic,* the paramedic had said, pinching the tips of her fingers to trigger a motor reflex.

Still another player left to hit. An older gentleman of medium height took a few practice swings, then paused to cough his smoker's cough, like Nancy when they'd climbed up the stairs of Montmartre that day in the heat. The man swung hard and cracked the ball on its side, too late for him to help the angle as he followed through over his shoulder. Everyone watched the ball spin left toward a hem of trees, like when he and Nancy had once played tennis on the campus's outdoor courts, and she'd accidentally hit a ball over the green caged fence, out of bounds.

"Shit!" he yelled, slamming his club into the ground. He raised and pounded its head several more times, enough to divot the soft green earth.

No matter how many ways Murray imagined it, if a golfer had been preparing to tee off from the holes nearest to where Becky fell, Becky would have been visible enough. Or maybe it had still been too dark then. No, he was sure of it: the sun had risen enough. The golfers were the ones expected to follow the rules, take every precaution. Everyone knew this was Yale's course, that his girls trained here.

"Sir." The woman had stopped her cart in front of Murray's, one ungloved hand over the parking brake. She smiled. "It's all yours."

"Oh—" He looked around skittishly. "I don't have clubs."

"That's funny," she said. She glanced at his cart.

"You haven't come across any strays?" he asked. "Seen anyone lurking about?"

"No one but you!" said the oldest man, smiling.

"This is serious," said Murray. And then: "A criminal could be among us." His tone surprised him.

"Oh my God," said the woman. She'd removed her visor and was adjusting the band. Why would she make it so tight?

"Did you hear me, sir?" she said. The bull-necked man plucked peanuts from his hand.

Murray heard his own voice: "This is serious."

"Sir?"

Murray couldn't remember if the medics had started an IV for Becky, an infusion of saline solution that would've stabilized her faster.

"Something is wrong with him, Kate," the man said, pulling the woman's arm defensively. "Just get us to the next hole."

"Wait," said Murray. "Do you ever play here early?"

Before the woman pressed on the gas, she shook her head. "Look, I'm not answering any of your strange questions. We will report *you*."

As she sped away, Murray was almost certain no one had done anything about saline solution.

~

Murray went to Widdy's to eat something, just enough to raise his blood sugar. He walked dizzily through the door and looked around at everyone just going about their business, drinking and talking.

At his table, Murray reminded himself to breathe deeply, while a server poured water into his glass and recited some of the specials. Snapper soup, a salad with endives, rib eye steak.

"Just a turkey club," Murray said. "And a gin and tonic."

On the course, his cell phone hadn't been able to secure a clear signal, so when he saw three full bars rise, he became hopeful for a stream of stalled messages. But after five long minutes, not one vibrated—he thought it possible that Lisa Sanders had tried him at home or his office. No, that didn't make sense. Everyone used cells in an emergency.

He tried to relax his back more comfortably into his chair, kept his watch on his knee.

Murray looked around as an unlikely pair—a younger man with his daughter on his shoulders—filled the last stools. She had strawberry-blonde pigtails and was holding a small plastic container in her hands.

This father didn't seem to think twice about placing her on the stool next to him and ordering her a Shirley Temple, plus a glass bowl full of maraschino cherries.

A group of four loud men dominating the bar called him out. "That's the way to prime her for college!" one said.

Another man with snarled brown hair laughed. "Right!"

The father had been wearing a hat, and when he took it off, he waved it dismissively at the group. He nudged his daughter's bowl of cherries close to her. Though he couldn't have been much over thirty, his hair was sprouting patches of gray.

The focus of the loud men shifted to how badly the second nine holes had gone.

No matter how closely Murray listened for evidence, he heard nothing of *girl*, nothing of *mist* or *blue morning light*—of forgetting to call the clubhouse.

When his sandwich arrived, he realized he'd forgotten to ask for no mayonnaise. He reached for his knife and scraped off the fat and asked the waiter for a side of Dijon mustard. Nancy used to despise this about him, his need to special order, until she'd become pregnant and done the same thing. For a moment he felt as though she were here, in this room. He could see the wicker chairs of the little café where they'd met, on Boulevard Saint-Germain in the Latin Quarter.

He'd entered soaking wet—it had started raining in the middle of his long run, a dozen times around the Luxembourg Gardens. It was still raining as he stood at the zinc counter of the café, just a few feet from Nancy's table, where she'd been working. He'd kept an open stance, just close enough to notice the red lipstick stain on her cup. He'd tried to take patient sips of his espresso—was as careful about breaking apart the flaky center of his croissant and spreading blackberry jam over the flesh. Rain had poured steadily over the café's windows, a beating that had seemed to soften his every gesture next to hers, as she'd copied page after page of her notes.

Murray cut one triangle of his club sandwich into a smaller triangle. He considered the amount of salt, then decided he wasn't very hungry after all, that the gin and tonic would be enough to raise his blood sugar. He drank from his glass until ice knocked his lips. The sounds of the bar were growing louder. Murray slid down the back of his chair a few inches more. He closed his eyes. What was the first word he'd read on Nancy's pad? Just something to ground him: the one word in English that had lent him the courage, after several long hours of watching her, to say hello?

"Are you alright?" Murray opened his eyes to the waiter's scrunched features. He nodded vaguely at the suggestion of water. He watched the waiter's hands wavering pink through the pitcher.

He still could not remember the word Nancy had written down, but when he had said hello, asking her about her project, she said she'd been working on her dissertation, on James Baldwin's writings. *He came here and sat in this café. He had nothing.* She'd held her cup by her mouth. *Enough for bread. And coffee,* she'd said with a laugh.

Room, he thought. That had been the word he'd recognized, for *Giovanni's Room,* the book her research had focused on. Nancy wouldn't have wanted him to say *book.* She would have corrected with *novel,* or *manuscript.*

He tried to stop the words, wanting all of them—all of *her*—out of his head, but it wasn't possible not to recall that first day they'd spent together, how he'd described the Paris marathon he'd placed eighth in, how she'd told him about her "life in letters," or her joking that she often spent whole days at the archives of the National Library, taking breaks only for a curbside smoke, he'd find out later. She'd said she admired him for his health, his optimism.

He'd never really considered himself optimistic, just someone who measured days by exertion. Nancy brought him out of that, showing him the different quarters of the city, telling him about the writers and painters implied on different street corners. He had fallen in love with her willingness to forgive his upbringing, his uneducated family, his absent father, the strip mines they'd depended on.

For a moment, Murray saw them, at the dinner table. His father pulling apart one of his mother's soft rolls, black beneath his fingernails, even after washing. Murray saw his father's shoulders hunched over the kitchen sink as he scrubbed along a bar of soap, his crooked fingers moving back and forth.

Murray held a napkin to his lips without wiping. He watched as a large ice cream sundae was placed before the girl and her father. Three chocolate scoops covered in whipped cream. The father stole a cherry from his daughter's bowl and placed it on top. Her stool had been angled toward him, and she was smiling from all the sugar.

The girl held her spoon tight in her little fist, elbow jutting sideways as she worked out bites. She fed several tastes to her father, who leaned in and made enthusiastic faces each time. Murray looked away, back at his watch on his knee, still running numbers. Then he looked back up at the table, at the boldness of the red tablecloth.

Murray supposed he could say it had all come crashing down with Nancy, finally, one scorching day in August 2002, even though who's to know when the foundations of all you'd built together really started to crack? Crooked posts and rotting piers, dirty sand or too much water poured into a concrete perimeter, things you didn't notice until one morning there were puddles in the basement, a bulge in the wall, flakes of white everywhere, signs his father had taught him to look for, those summers he and Patrick spent repairing old houses on River Street. It was easier when it was someone else's life, he thought, when there were diagnosable symptoms.

When his star Sarah Lloyd was a junior, he'd taken her out to some trails in New London for a long run, and afterward he went for an ice cream cone. He hardly ever indulged, but she'd had a particularly good workout, and it was a hot day in mid-August. At first he'd stayed parked in the lot going over splits, looking up here and there to think, factor a specific calculation. Then on a small deck that wrapped around the parlor—how hadn't he noticed sooner?—he saw her: *Nancy*. Sharing a milkshake with a man. He was handsome, with a full head of dark curly hair. A bulkier man.

"I'm sorry, I should have asked." The waiter came back with a menu. "Did you want anything else?" Murray shook his head, taking too long to realize where he was, surrounded by golfers, to slide out his credit card and place it over the bill tray, hands quavering.

That August day sixteen years ago, he'd reminded himself: *Stay in control.* He'd been careful not to overreact. Maybe the curly-haired man was just a coworker from Beinecke? She collaborated on big projects, events, with all kinds of people on campus.

But then that man—*Richard*, he later learned—had leaned in and licked some cream from her lips. They'd kissed.

FOUR

Marjorie was Nancy's closest colleague, and friend, at Beinecke. Making new friends had never come easily, and in their first year of marriage, Nancy had resented Murray a bit, for the suddenness of their transition into the unknowns of New Haven—also this feeling that they'd moved here for *his work*, not hers, when she'd invested just as much in her career as he had. Nancy was grateful for Marjorie's camaraderie; she was a curator, too, in Modern Manuscripts, and they'd bonded over a shared passion for James Baldwin and French surrealist poetry. She'd turned Nancy onto the unpublished works of Desnos, Éluard, and René Char written during the Second World War, and just yesterday Marjorie had suggested going to a Master's Tea at Saybrook College this afternoon, on *La Résistance*, over lunch.

At first Nancy hesitated; such events were reserved for undergraduates—their attendance seemed intrusive. But Marjorie assured her she was good friends with the professor giving the lecture, Richard Nevins, and that he'd be delighted to see them there.

At a quarter till one, Nancy was surprised, irritated really, not to find Marjorie in the front lobby according to plan. Nancy hated when someone was even a minute late—she and Murray both did—for the valuable time *lost* waiting. She distracted herself by looking out through the library's glass doors to Commons dining hall, where a handful of students in hats and mittens juggled books and coffee thermoses.

She slipped on her own leather gloves. Outside, she brushed some snow from the low marble wall that divided the library from the rest of campus. It was cold, but not so terrible for February. Her peacoat was lined, and she hoped to get through the winter without needing a larger one. At eighteen weeks, her bump could still be hidden, and she was glad for that, not to be so noticeable. Coworkers might think less of her, assume she wouldn't accomplish as much before she took leave. Maybe times had changed, but still she felt it: how quick people were to judge by appearances, especially women's, reducing them to their bodies.

"How's it going?" Marjorie laughed, a warmth that always lifted Nancy's mood. Marjorie looked radiant as ever in her fur-hooded parka, her black hair luminous despite winter. She had spent last month in Casablanca, and Nancy hadn't been able to help feeling some envy when Marjorie first described the sunshine, the slow-cooked tagine, the reading she'd done for pleasure.

Luckily Saybrook was just around the corner. They had to hurry and slip through the college's gate before a student exited, iron clanging heavily behind them. Inside, the stone courtyard was crisp with cold light, the benches rimmed with more snow, more students and faculty bundled up and hurrying for the Master's House. A floating lotus plant on an ivory stand marked the entryway; oriental rugs and a stunning array of mahogany furniture filled the living room.

Nancy was glad to recognize the Master, Annette Woodson, an art history professor who'd written on Beinecke's rare indigenous map of Mexico City, though Annette didn't offer the same recognition— because maybe Nancy hadn't worked here long enough? Was her face too bloated?

"Your house is beautiful." Nancy filled the silence.

"Home," Annette said. "This is my *home*."

"Well, it's beautiful," Nancy snapped, which surprised her. Luckily Annette was too distracted by other students coming in to respond. Nancy drifted over to the table for tea. She sifted through flavors, comparing mint and chamomile, as if they were more complicated than their names. Marjorie was already busy socializing with other faculty, so Nancy joined them, taking a few timid sips of hot water and biting her lip.

"Nancy"—Marjorie reached for her arm—"this is Fareed, our expert on Proust, and here," she said, "our famous Richard. Richard helped me with that symposium last fall, the one on Gide, and he loves Colette." Marjorie smiled, as if waiting for Nancy to affirm the magic of *Chéri*, but Nancy couldn't distill her thoughts in so little time—she felt this fog; she only nodded, took another sip of tea. Richard just looked at her, as if perplexed by her own sense of fraudulence.

Then the lights dimmed, and Nancy and Marjorie found their seats while the Master began an introduction. Nancy felt a pin drop. She made a tenuous hash mark on her pad, the one she'd brought exclusively for the talk. She took another sip of tea.

Richard was at the podium now, a projector flashing its empty white light on the wall behind him. Eventually the image of a novelist—Jean Giono—appeared sidewise; the lens adjusted, zoomed in.

Richard had thick curly hair and a bit of a paunch, but it was soft, inviting in its own way—and the minute he'd launched into his first slide about Giono's origins, he was waving his hand freely. When he arrived at an important point, he slowed, just enough to make his idea clear, emphasizing certain words, first in French, then in English. He took long pauses between slides to reflect, and when he became particularly eager, he raised his hand higher, like he might seize something to write with.

In the end, he'd use a whiteboard to make a diagram, squeaking boxes around each major event in Giono's life, starring the most tumultuous period in the 1930s—when Giono had started a pacifist commune on the Contadour Plateau in Haute Provence, a group that had been misconstrued by the Resistance Movement as evidence of Giono's collaboration with the Vichy regime—but Richard fervently refuted these allegations. He explained how Giono had suffered post-traumatic stress disorder from the Great War, how the French country-side had always been sacred to his writing; Giono had spent most of his life in the tiny mountain town of Manosque, had drafted all of his novels from a small library whose largest window had overlooked the quiet of the Alps—*total war*, Richard said, had threatened to destroy the safety of that perspective—*sa sécurité*—he repeated several times. Eventually he stopped and looked around, as if he had one more bit to add, but instead he only blinked into the quiet, lips turning in a little smile toward his audience. There were a few claps, then more, until everyone finally joined.

Richard's face was glazed with sweat. Nancy did not know so much perspiration was possible without more physical labor. He was differ-ent from other academics, she thought, and continued to think as he pointed enthusiastically at each student with a question.

Nancy could not remember when she and Murray had last had sex; well, she could, but she didn't like to think about how long it had been. Murray had been the first to object, before they'd made it through the amnio last week. He'd said he was worried the fetus was *too fragile*. She'd felt like such a fool for unhooking her bra before their bed, waiting for him like that, so exposed, expectant.

~

Richard was flooded by students afterward, and though she'd hoped to have just one word, to ask her question about historical narrative, she and Marjorie couldn't stay any longer. Marjorie just waved—then on their walk back, she'd turned to Nancy. "Wasn't that great?"

"It was," she said, realizing her shortness of breath, her expanding ribs, the air colder, harsher to her lungs.

Murray often asked how she was feeling physically, but never about her work, the disruption, how suddenly her focus would have to shift, and in the middle of her first major exhibition at Beinecke. As she pushed through the building's heavy doors—Marjorie insisted on going in first, on holding the door for her—she was surprised by the suddenness of tears brimming, though Marjorie didn't seem to notice. In her office, Nancy continued to ruminate over the feeling that she gave more emotionally than Murray did, letting him go on about his practices day and night, attending as many meets as she could, never complaining when he used his only free day—Sunday—for his own training instead of spending time together. Was it so much to ask for the same support, the same level of understanding?

She'd confided in Marjorie before, about her fears and doubts, how they'd worsened these past weeks, but Marjorie had assured her it was all hormones, that they *heightened everything.* She said she'd felt the same when she was pregnant with her twins; she'd been as enraged by Bill's neglect, the hours he'd put in at the office when she'd needed him most. Later she said Bill confessed how worried he'd been about making ends meet, and though Marjorie was like Nancy in that she didn't believe in strict role divisions, Marjorie said she could understand now where Bill had been coming from. She felt that Bill—Murray, too—needed to cope with uncertainty in his own way.

∼

So the following week, when Murray called her at work and suggested they go to the hardware store for a can of low-VOC paint, Nancy jotted a note in her planner: *Murray channels his worries through action.* She felt as assured when he didn't want her on a stepladder or breathing in toxins—so she would alternate between watching him from the doorway and resting in the living room. She tried to make herself comfortable in Murray's recliner, using the back pages of an old wall calendar to sketch out the dimensions of Baby's sleigh crib and the antique dresser they'd found at a yard sale.

"What do you think about the black and white of Boulevard du Montparnasse in the rain above the changing table?" she called.

"It's a little formal, isn't it?" he called louder. She didn't want to have a full conversation like this, so she went to watch him from the doorway again. He was standing tiptoed on the ladder. His ankles quivered.

"I could paint a picture," she said. "Maybe something neutral like a mouse or a lion. Are those neutral?" She imagined his nose scrunched, lips raised in a snarl, how he always looked when he worked.

"What?" he asked.

"You won't listen. A mouse or lion? Which is better?"

"Neither. Look, Nancy, I can't pay attention to what I'm doing. How about a cheetah? Neutral enough, and fast."

"Perfect!" she said, laughing at the lemon-shaded streaks of paint over his gray T-shirt. His biceps squirmed as he stiffly held the paintbrush—his blue jeans were also stained, and when he turned to face the wall again, she wondered if their child would inherit his pancake bottom. There were only a few things she felt sure of: that Baby would have long, lean legs—something she and Murray shared in common—and narrow shoulders, light eyebrows, and dimples, though she only had one on her left side. She was 5'4", Murray 5'9". She often worried their child would inherit her lack of athletic ability, her crooked spine.

"Let's keep track of measurements on that part of the wall." She pointed with her pencil. "I want to start as soon as our baby can stand. One year and up."

Sometimes she wondered if they were silly for wanting the gender to be a surprise, but she remained resolute she didn't want skewed expectations—not just in the first moments, but as their child continued to grow.

Murray nodded. "After we finish laying out everything." He gestured toward the separate list Nancy had been keeping for the other things they still needed: a bassinet, crib mobile, baby monitor, high chair, bibs, bath towels and toys, extra blankets and pillows. Marjorie had wanted to throw her a shower, but Nancy had resisted because it was embarrassing having so few outside friends and family to invite. She had one close friend from college, Caroline, who'd just had her first child, too, and was full of all kinds of advice when Nancy had called with her own news. It would be too much to ask Caroline to travel to the city for a shower, and she figured it would be easier to buy the basic things they needed anyway, even if Murray was worried about the accruing costs, the receipts he insisted on saving in a jar.

"We'll have plenty of space," she said, too quietly for him to hear, now that she'd returned to the living room. They used to keep an ongoing Scrabble game on the coffee table. A few weeks ago, Murray had gotten lucky with *syzygy*, at twenty-one points, and at first she'd assumed he'd used a reference text, but when she'd looked up the word and realized it was a term used to describe celestial bodies, she'd been impressed by his secret knowledge of astronomy.

They'd moved the game to Murray's desk, then to the bedroom to make space for Baby, and sometimes she couldn't help but think of all the time he spent there, most often watching "form videos" of his girls. He claimed he was analyzing their gait and turnover speed, measures he felt *in constant need of improvement*. Nancy had been tempted to open the door, to pretend to ask him what he wanted for dinner, or double-check their Sunday plans—but the next weekend he was away, couldn't she just watch the videos alone, without worrying he might catch her, accuse her of spying?

She heard Murray's footsteps in the room.

"I'm glad you're resting." Some sweat had seeped through his T-shirt, more yellow paint on his cheek. "I'm going to take a shower," he said.

She closed her eyes, waiting for her stomach to settle.

Before he reached their bedroom, she breathed deeply. "Thank you for painting the room." She wanted to say something else, something about her gratitude for him, but what—what could she say?

"Tomorrow I'll add another coat." He smiled, his way again: always focused on the next task.

As the shower water ran, she felt the extent of her guilt, how easily her mind latched on to things to worry about: images of him with his girls. She'd never told anyone she was paranoid, not even Marjorie. She was ashamed of her insecurity, her need to assume the worst because it was easier than embracing the reality of their situation—this unknown thread she sometimes felt them teetering along, for no apparent reason.

FIVE

Murray drove ever so slowly with the window down. He listened for any sound: a car door opening or closing, the rumbling of a garage, footsteps creaking over a wooden deck, the jangling collar of a dog, any noise from a backyard. The crack of a golf ball would be impossible to miss in such silence.

Minutes slipped in and out, approaching the time yesterday when he'd been at the course with Becky, then moving beyond, leveling at 5:40, then 5:46. By now, he would have sent her out. Eventually he completed eight laps, jotted a few notes down about early-morning walkers, a couple of slow joggers, a house where a woman stood before her kitchen window washing dishes, gazing out absently. He passed a house with a broken gate, listened as its iron latch banged against its hook, the weight of heavy wood driving forward and back. One woman entered her car carrying an infant in a car seat.

He remembered: people woke at all hours of the morning, or night, to drive their infants to sleep. Babies were calmed by the thrum of an engine.

Unconsciously Murray rubbed the tender indent of his temple with a calloused index finger. Around 6:00 a.m., he unbuckled his seat belt and limped toward Maltby Lakes Trail, where the winding dirt paths made for better backyard views.

He stepped over tree roots and half-submerged stones. Amid some brambles, he found a long, knobby stick for steadying his balance as he glimpsed more lives. Brick or stone patios, some with picnic tables and benches, others with glass tables and wrung-up umbrella tops, black nylon hoods cloaking grills. Bill and Marjorie, that Labor Day barbecue they'd had . . . but he still couldn't place it, the exact moment things had started to slip.

He peered into a few other yards with swimming pools. The most luxurious was eight feet deep with gold leaves skimming its top.

The morning wind had stilled itself to a breeze. He and Nancy had never succeeded in buying a house together. She had loved to swim, and he imagined the space she inhabited now came with certain comforts, the calm of a pool.

~

There were no drivers lying about lawns, no suspicious golf bags, no unclaimed piles of balls.

Titanium drivers covered the farthest distance at the lowest trajectory; titanium struck the hardest.

Assuming he'd done all of the math correctly, Becky would have been unconscious for no more than thirty-five minutes before she reached the emergency room, well within the "golden hour" doctors used to predict survival.

~

The news wouldn't come until much later that night when Lisa called him, hysterical. She said Becky's trauma was severe, that she'd undergone emergency surgery to remove several blood clots and was officially in a coma, had been for the past forty hours. No telling whether she'd wake up, or if she did, the extent of the damage.

Why did you single out Becky for these practices? Lisa had cried through the phone. *My baby,* she'd wailed.

He told himself to stay calm, stay in control. He would not let this woman crack his optimism—would assure her of his tradition, how carefully he plotted each and every workout, the steps he'd taken to communicate with the club beforehand, and now all the research he was doing to locate the source of the accident. There would be some justice here, he promised. She'd been quiet through the phone. She'd listened to him. He needed to see Becky, he said, and he wanted to help her and Doug, if there was anything he could do. Eventually she'd yielded. She and Doug were taking turns driving home to shower, to check on the house, and it was Doug's turn now. He could come now, if he hurried, she'd said—she would be standing outside Becky's room. He was on his way, but even so, he'd have no more than five minutes with her.

～

Inside, the cervical collar still clasped Becky's frail neck. A monitor tracked her heart rate, oxygen saturation, blood pressure; another, her brain's electrical activity. He knelt down beside her.

A ventilator worked her lungs, her chest rising and falling to the rhythm of the machine's hiss of oxygen into her windpipe. Intertwining tubes covered her chest. One, thin and yellow, fed nutrients in through her nose.

"Becky," he said, barely able to produce more than a whisper, the constriction in his throat, this sense of having been here before, though he wouldn't let the thoughts seep in, not fully. He focused on Becky, here, in this bed.

The right side of her head had been shaved, a half-moon of sutures. Both eyelids were bulbous and charcoal hued, the right one deeply raised, still rimmed.

"Please," he whispered, crouching close. A small part of her bloated thigh showed between her hospital gown and compression boots, her tan skin ashen.

He dropped his face to his hands and repeated her name. He wanted sound from her, coherent or not, to affirm that she heard him, that she was alive. He reached out toward her curled palms. To elicit something instinctive in her, like the desire to grasp.

One of her monitors started to beep. He looked around, unclear which monitor was signaling. A voice rushed in, a nurse. "It's her temperature!" she said.

Lisa entered next, weeping, screaming questions at him, while the nurse prepared for cold water to be pumped through a blanket.

"Get out!" Lisa yelled.

"You need to put ice bags under her arms," he said. "She shouldn't have a blanket—"

He wasn't clear on the difference between minutes and seconds, just this blur of Lisa shouting again for him to leave. *Out!* echoed through his ears. What had he done but try to help, ensure her safety? Becky's temperature could rise again if they didn't change the protocol, didn't adapt to Becky's particular needs right *now*, the only moment they ever had—he almost rushed back inside the room, but a nurse brushed past him first, nearly pushed him away, bringing more ice for Becky. Murray closed his eyes. Anything but the image of Becky's swollen arms, shivering and cyan blue.

Just before Nancy's due date, Murray had gone with her for a tour of the hospital. And as he passed through a series of halls to the elevator now, he thought of the neonatal care unit where there had been miniature drip meters and ventilators, a dialysis machine and a cart carrying forceps, scissors, bandages. He shuddered over the image of tiny spectral lungs, air sacs thin enough to explode.

~

The Yale Art Gallery was on Chapel Street, just across from Atticus, where Murray and Nancy used to meet for lunch every Wednesday. His legs were weak as he ascended the gallery's center staircase. It had been *designed to create the sense of an abyss*, a tour guide had described the first time he and Nancy visited together. Murray never looked down from the top; he always stopped at the second level, winding his way through a maze of periwinkle until he found the painting. There was no one here yet.

Murray hadn't dated much in high school or college, and the fact that he'd asked Nancy to go to a museum when they first met always felt like it was from a dream. Also the way she'd smiled at him, eyes like sunlit glass. *Right now?* she'd asked.

He'd been ashamed by his wet clothes, his missing umbrella, but she must have sensed his discomfort, because she'd reached for one poking from her handbag. *We'll share*, she'd said. And he'd felt this uncertain tug that made him forget his plans for the day. She'd guided him the few short blocks under her own umbrella to the metro, and then they'd transferred at Châtelet before getting off at Concorde.

Orangerie. He didn't understand naming a museum after oranges, but he'd been too afraid to ask Nancy to explain. She'd taken him to see the *Water Lilies*, and in the room enshrouded by water lilies, willow branches, and cloud reflections, she'd explained the water as a mirror for the sky. She'd said the light from the sun filled everything, this *illusion of an endless whole*. They'd sat there for a long time, drenched in silence, in grays and greens and blues, afternoon seeping into evening. Nancy told him how Monet woke every morning before dawn to paint the sun's first glimmers from his canoe, how he spent a whole day tracing its shifting energies and undulations. Murray wanted to squeeze her hand then, but it had been too early for that, so he'd focused on remembering instead, on imprinting every fact and detail to his mind. He was good at this.

~

Camille on the Beach in Trouville, a Monet in the Yale gallery—he and Nancy had first gone to see it together the weekend they found their New Haven apartment. Ed Swanson, the women's head coach at the time, had connected him with a broker in the area. Murray saw their apartment, the one he still lived in, just as it had been that first day: the fresh yellow clapboard, the way they'd walked around to the private entrance, the broker going on about the size of the kitchen, the abundance of natural light, the in-unit washer and dryer.

Murray pictured the dusty, empty look of it all after they'd stepped inside, speckles of light dancing over hardwood floors, the oily electric burners and rusting oven in the adjoining kitchen. He'd opened the oven, wiping his finger along the top rack, and then afterward he'd hoped Nancy hadn't noticed the grime he'd had to wash off. He'd worried reality was setting in. They'd only been married six weeks, and these amenities should have been inexcusable, considering Nancy's roots. But she hadn't brought it up and he hadn't apologized, because apologizing admitted a weakness. The worst kind.

Murray thought of that dinner when he was thirteen, just two years before his father died, when his mother had gone on about their day at the library. His mother had loved the library, and if he and Patrick finished their chores quickly after school, she'd take them to pick out one new book each. The library was an old brick building with a copper bell in front, and he and his brother used to hurry up to the second floor, where all the science books were. Murray usually picked one on astronomy.

That dinner, Murray's mother had wanted to share all the details about a travel guidebook she'd found on South America, her hopes of flying there. His father had asked her to be quiet. Murray had watched his mother's lips straighten, had watched her slowly rise from her chair and set her plate in the sink. Then she'd turned. She'd pointed her finger at his father and said, voice raised, something else about speaking her mind, about having her own dreams. Then his father stood up, grabbing her wrist. There had been a glass jug of milk on the kitchen counter from when Patrick had poured himself a cup, and he must have forgotten to put the jug back in the refrigerator—their mother didn't notice him forgetting—because their father had reached for the jug and thrown it at the wall. The glass had shattered, and milk had beaded along the edge of the counter and started trickling down, and Murray had clambered to pick up the shards while his mother blotted the counter with a towel. Sobbing, she'd crouched down next to Murray to help. It wasn't long before she cut her finger, sucking the blood and crying, and his father walked outside into the cold. It had been February, and sometimes his father drove to the nearest bar where everyone from Blaschak went.

～

Murray was glad Nancy never met his father, but he wished his mother might have been more recognizable, like the one he'd grown up with, when they'd first visited her in Luzerne. At the home, they'd talked about books, since his mother's long-term memory was still intact. She loved *The Secret Garden*, and Nancy knew it well, as she did most books, and they'd exchanged thoughts about characters. He'd been proud to marry Nancy, someone so well versed in literature, as his mother would have been if she'd gone to college. It had made him happy to show off his new bride before his mother passed, because just before he'd left for Paris for the marathon, when her health had started its decline, she'd told him that was her greatest wish for him—that he might find his match one day in a wife. Even if they had come back to the States to marry, she would have been too weak to attend, but they'd shown her photographs, and he'd watched his mother trace her finger over the light and shadow around Nancy's short veil, smiling crookedly at him. Then she'd said *beautiful* and reached for Nancy's hand.

~

Nancy's parents' reaction couldn't have been more opposing. Nancy's mother had arrived to meet them in Paris in pearls and shiny heels, her father a suit of pressed linen. They had been quick to total the sum of Murray's parts, his jeans and T-shirt, his sideburns. He still wished she'd properly warned him. That had been their first real argument. He'd wanted a clearer sense of the kind of people they were, the wealth she'd come from, but he often wondered if her parents' disapproval of him was more than a matter of class. If it was the idea of an athlete— of making a career out of unknowns—that they couldn't stand. Most people were too afraid to test themselves that way, he thought. You risked failure every time you stepped on the line. Risked injury the minute your laces were tied.

They'd eloped in September. The wedding took place in a small public garden in Cernay-la-Ville, just outside of the city. A local priest Nancy had befriended during her arts fellowship officiated because they'd wanted to avoid their disparate religious backgrounds: he Catholic, she Protestant. He remembered the smell of rhododendron, Nancy's simple ivory blazer and skirt, her shoes studded with tiny beads. He'd given her a plain gold band, using up what had been left of his race earnings.

Then, as if by fate, Ed Swanson's offer had come to Murray two weeks later by mail. Murray had given his Olympic coach, Phil Friedman, his hotel address in Paris, in case of an emergency, since his mother had been in poor health, and by the time Phil forwarded Ed's query to him, Murray had feared it was already too late. He'd hurried to the nearest newsstand and bought a phone card. He'd connected with Ed in a phone booth, and Ed had offered to fly Murray back for an interview. Somehow, in just a matter of weeks, it had all worked out for Nancy to return officially with him.

Whenever he thought back to that moment, of stepping off the train in New Haven, just one suitcase each, the memory felt as unreal as that first day had. Nancy had had all of her papers and books shipped separately, so she'd narrowed her bag down to the essentials. He remembered that, on the plane, he'd had this strange sense of riding a hot-air balloon without a compass, fire blowing beneath them, this burning lightness to their departure; they were starting over, free to become the best versions of themselves in a new city.

That first afternoon downtown they'd gotten lunch at Claire's, since Ed had recommended their homemade bread and salads. Nancy had started eating healthier after they married, and he'd watched her poke her fork at threads of carrot, laughing about how the States never had a shortage of fresh vegetables. Unlike in France, where she used to scout out all the best Niçoise options for him. He had always been religious about a light, healthy lunch, especially during the peak of his training. He thought of how Nancy had quit smoking for him, how she'd gotten rid of most of her clothes because of the nicotine. He'd been struck by her discipline, the way she, like him, could achieve any goal she set her mind to.

They'd just had those two suitcases, and it had been easy enough to check them at the gallery—Nancy had needed to see the gallery before they met the broker to see apartments—as if Yale's own French collection would let her pretend she'd never left Paris. She'd looked up the sole Monet in advance, and the room it was in, European Painting—had circled it on the map she'd procured from an informational office on campus, and couldn't wait to examine the painting up close, then at a distance. Her thumb pressed to her lip as she thought. She'd said, *It's wonderful, isn't it?*

He'd nodded, said, *Yes*, and then that he liked that it was a beach scene. He'd always struggled to say something more profound, but it'd been all he could think of then.

It's about a transitory moment, I think—at least that's what he thought she'd said—*You see how there's the finest suggestion of movement in the veil from her hat? While the lines of her parasol and chair are fixed . . . He's able to capture air, I think. Motion.*

Right, he'd said. He'd pulled out a pen from his jacket as though he had something to write, some calculation to make. *Always something to do,* she used to say—and later—that it *stopped him from being in the moment.* As though she were any better at that than he was.

He heard sound entering the room, and when he turned, he saw a petite woman and her son. She was holding a video camera, slowly scanning each painting, walking in this perfect square around the room. When she reached where he was sitting, she called loudly for her son to meet her, and he hurried dutifully to her side. At one point, the little boy looked at Murray, his brown eyes intent, as if he wanted something, but Murray wouldn't indulge him—he looked away toward the security guard, wondering why she just stood there and let strangers take video. Shouldn't it be illegal, like burning movies off the Internet? *This was a sacred place,* he wanted to tell her, but she just stood there, with her buckled gold belt.

The year Nancy left him, he'd started coming here once a month. He hadn't yet given up. He'd thought if he came and thought of something new to say about the Monet, something measured, insightful, she might change her mind about him eventually. He thought he'd say something about the child in the painting, the one at the water's edge. The angle of the boy's foot relative to the ripple of foam on a wave. He might even have suggested they go on a trip, just the two of them, to the beach, not just to the marina, but to a nice beach in Long Island. He could have taken more weekends off to spend time with her, especially those first years, when he hadn't had his promotion. Although *hindsight,* she used to always say, *was twenty-twenty.* He'd put in all that time so they might have more to work with, a better life as a family. There'd been much to prepare for.

～

A whole group entered, a French class. The professor, this tall, lithe man with thick brown hair, made a sweeping motion toward the artwork.

Murray couldn't make out more than the most common pronouns, such as *je* and *nous*, a few words like *ne . . . pas* and *jamais* and *rien*, for negation, but he'd forgotten their specific usage.

The professor had his students line up, and a young woman ambled toward the small bench where Murray was sitting. He stood up, and the professor said, "No, no, sir. It's fine." He had his hands clasped together under his chin, as if in apology, but Murray shrugged. He couldn't stand French professors. They seemed the worst combination of pretentious and cowardly.

"I'm leaving anyway," he muttered.

"Oh, alright then," the other man said.

But before Murray reached the door, he paused and turned to where the young student stood, hair black as Becky's—the room was silent as the girl pointed to bits of the painting, her voice trepid, but her pronunciation smooth, and he watched the professor's overly emphatic nod, his loathsome *oui, oui* when she finished, in 3:02, almost exactly— if he subtracted elapsed time from the remaining time on his watch. The professor tapped his watch: *Fini*, and then the girl smiled faintly, shoulders collapsing in relief.

~

When Murray first called Becky to say he'd put her at the top of his recruiting list, her voice had grown breathless through the phone, energetic and light. *Oh my God*, she'd said. *I can't believe it!*

He heard the sound of her voice then, in its absence now. He couldn't pinpoint when it had grown dimmer, her words less frequent. Maybe sometime during her freshman year. Those early weeks of practice, she'd spoken assuredly about where she was from, used to ask questions about workouts and meets. Yet with each major accomplishment she'd only grown quieter, more cautious. The little bits of food she ate—he didn't know when that had started either—but it was like she'd been trying to disappear rather than fill a room, as she should have wanted to, to *seize* the space that was required of a champion.

～

Nancy always said he set impossible standards for his girls. That he needed a female assistant, someone comfortable talking about eating issues—not because of anything he'd told her—but based on her own observations at meets. She'd once called Sarah Lloyd *skeletal,* said it disturbed her. Even worse, she'd said, was his apathy. *Your indifference scares me,* and he'd felt the words, her eyes glassy with a fear that seemed to run deep within her, beneath both of them. She'd begged him to book a few sessions with a nutritionist, but he'd dismissed her, pretended he hadn't heard. After all, coaching had always been his field.

Nancy has no business crossing that line, he'd thought, but then he remembered it had been one of those times when she'd grown quiet afterward. In her eyes, he knew she'd had more to say, but he had not wanted to hear it. He saw Nancy in all the things he hadn't done, the referrals to counseling he could have put in for Sarah, and Becky, too, and the countless others who had shrunk in size, some slowly, others quickly, in the four years he had with them.

It wasn't all coincidence, maybe. But who knew if things would have been any different if they'd stayed together? If they'd kept trying to be a family, if Nancy had actually changed her mind. Would he have listened then? The only thing he knew was that he could still hear her everywhere, in this empty room that was his life.

SIX

Her contractions began on a Sunday morning. On a whim, Nancy had offered to join Murray at the track, had hoisted herself up the cold metal bleachers for a seat near the top. It was only when the liquid spilled over the seat and made a light tapping noise on a rail beneath her that she looked down and screamed. Murray was crossing the 200-meter mark on the other side—she was yelling as loud as she could—but she had to wait until he rounded the corner and noticed her waving her arms. He sprinted, elegant even in alarm.

In the car on the way over, he handed her a stopwatch to hold while he drove. The next contraction lasted for fifty-eight seconds, exactly six minutes after the first. Nancy was wearing a cornflower-blue sundress, and as a nurse helped her into a wheelchair, she saw how the damp of her fluids had turned the fabric a splotched navy. Murray jogged alongside the wheelchair as they headed to the laboring room. He helped her into the bed and propped pillows behind her neck, and she had another contraction, this time forty-five seconds. He said he was getting her some ice chips.

"Dr. Weiss will be here any minute," said the nurse, a middle-aged woman just over 5′ tall with dark brown hair pinned into a bun. "My name is Lena." She spoke behind a jade mask. "I'm just going to get you set up." Nancy closed her eyes and waited for a cold needle to enter her forearm. "You have good veins. Lots of exercise?" Nancy nodded, imagining with closed eyes the drip of IV fluids.

Another contraction made her jolt. Her feet cramped, and when she reached for the nurse's hand, she felt the chill in her own. "Forty-seven seconds," Lena said. Through watery eyes, Nancy watched her set up the heart rate monitor.

"How are we?" Dr. Weiss had rushed in. He pressed his stethoscope to her belly as Lena began reviewing her chart out loud. "All good," he said. "Baby's heart rate is coming in around 130."

The monitor had already printed two sheets of connected paper folded like an accordion.

"Can I see it?" Nancy reached her arm out.

Dr. Weiss ripped off the first sheet and traced a jagged black line on the bottom with his finger. "That's the fetus," he said. "Above, that's you." She was five centimeters dilated. "Halfway there," he said, confirming her baby was still in perfect position. "We are looking at another six, maybe ten, hours."

Nancy started another contraction before she could answer. She began the patterned breathing they'd learned in Lamaze, short soft inhales, followed by a long blow of air.

"Breathe, Nancy," Dr. Weiss said. "Look at me. Where is your focal point?"

Murray came a few minutes later, one arm looped through a thick duffel bag, the other with a large cup of ice.

"You are doing great," he said. He reached for her clammy hand.

When she could rest again, Murray sat down next to her. A half-drawn curtain exposed the next bed over. She noticed a basket on the floor, spilling out a white T-shirt and asthma inhaler. Minutes later a woman entered, dragging her IV pole. She appeared distraught, her eyes and skin shadowed greenish gray. When Lena returned, she quietly explained that the woman had been in labor for the past thirty-six hours.

"That's horrible," said Nancy, squeezing her eyes shut for another contraction.

~

Two hours later and one and a half more centimeters dilated, Nancy would hear that that woman had been rushed out for an emergency caesarean, her baby's head turned the other way in the uterus. She would recall reading about the effects of such trauma on a newborn's psychological health, that a mother was likely to harbor more long-term resentment, and C-section babies were often more colicky. No, she didn't want this. And so, though Dr. Weiss would eventually suggest an episiotomy, an option he'd urged her to consider several times already, she would say no. He would try to persuade her that delivery would be much less painful, that her *stretching* would be less traumatic. But Nancy would just shake her head repeatedly. If women in ancient times could do it standing up or kneeling over birthing bricks—gravity coaxing out a head, then arms and legs—she could too.

Soon, her patterned breaths regressed into loud grunts, the sweat between her legs indistinguishable from amniotic fluid, urine, the scent of crushed flowers. Just as Lena positioned Nancy into the birthing stirrups, she felt Murray by her side coaching just as she'd hoped, telling her how close she was, over and over—until she got to a certain point, where the pain brought her so high, to a place of such impossibility, that she had no other choice but to let go.

Murray had once called it an *out-of-body experience*, the moment when physical agony transcends suffering—he'd compared it to a final lap, the cattle bell ringing, when his number one had to kick, give everything she had to the finish. Nancy couldn't quite say whether this analogy felt true to her, but she found warmth in his investment, his belief that their experiences as parents were shared, equalized somehow. True, she'd felt her body merely gliding, sifting through space, no longer conscious of minutes passing. And some part of her had heard a bell, imagined it acutely in the blur of her numb and throbbing body. There was definitely a sound that echoed, reverberated through the cavities of her skull, when she felt Baby's head crown, fully, and the wind of the bluish-purple cord, the excesses of her discarded placenta, lay like gold beneath her.

She cried. Tears of joy, or sadness, something in her felt she'd experienced an important departure, but from what, she couldn't be certain.

Murray cut the umbilical cord. Their child screamed, and Murray smiled at her, his eyes soft, the blue in them hazy.

"It's a little girl," he said.

"Congratulations," Dr. Weiss said. "She's perfect."

"Beautiful." Murray spoke so low and softly, Nancy could feel him holding back his own tears. As Nancy cradled their child, she sensed Murray's hand reaching to wipe some cold sweat from her face, then to brush a clump of hair away from her eyes. She held their baby tight by her chest, absorbing the sound of her quieting, this soundless rush of air.

"Let's call her Jean," Nancy said.

They had mentioned this name only once or twice, after Jeanne Moreau, the French actress they loved, but only one *n*, no *e*, fit her best.

"Fine," Murray said. His eyes glowing brighter than the light. He was still smiling.

Jean's skin looked very red, no more than a sheer curtain over her circulatory system. Nancy used her pinky to stroke the little dents for temples, the button nose. She admired her shapely ribbon of purplish lips. Her delicate eyelids.

An Apgar score of eight, her heartbeat over 100 beats per minute, her cry full and vigorous, her muscle tone solid, skin color even. "You should try feeding her," Lena said.

Nancy was terrified, another test of her body. She nodded weakly, cradling Jean nearer her breast, and unbuttoned the top of her gown enough to guide a nipple closer. It took a few attempts for Jean to take, but when she did, Nancy absorbed these new rhythms, this raw energy. She traced a finger over her fuzzy forehead. Lena reminded her that Jean would need to eat often, every one to two hours, that it was normal to experience some discomfort, especially in the first weeks.

"So far, so good." Nancy laughed nervously. When Jean finished, Nancy wiped some creamy yellow milk from her teeny lips, some more that had dribbled onto Nancy's gown. She stroked sleeping lids hatched with lines, like rivulets on a map. *We did it,* she thought to herself.

Then Murray knelt beside her, and he kissed Jean's head. She wished he'd say he was proud of her, her strength these months, but it was his quiet way, wasn't it, never able to affirm with words?

~

The 2:00 a.m. shrieks didn't help. Just a week in, and Nancy's resentment seemed to double by the day. They weren't using formula, she wasn't pumping, at least not yet, but couldn't Murray still rise with her? The feedings were painful. Her nipples had become dry and cracked, little trickles of blood she had to blot. She longed for breaks, for Murray to ask about her pain, but he rarely asked or offered to help. Once, in the middle of the night, she'd muttered, *Get up, will you?* but he'd only grumbled back, *You're talking in your sleep.* She'd raised her voice: *I was talking to you!* But it didn't faze him; he'd asked her, his eyes closed, *What's the point of sitting there?*

She began to believe marriage, parenthood, was full of these little hurts, these little incisions that started one day, only to deepen. It should have been easy to tell him this, what she needed from him, but it wasn't. She wanted him to recognize his lack, the void he left, even when they were in the same room; she wanted him to acknowledge that and to offer to fill it with his time, his attention—was that so much to ask? Even if it wasn't expected of him to drop everything like she'd had to—because she could breastfeed, because she'd carried Jean, because a woman was supposed to absorb these duties instinctually, sacrifice her wants and needs. As though every accomplishment in Nancy's life had been pointing to this one simple truth: she would be a wife and mother for the world. She'd never disrupt the silence; she'd never complain.

She remembered how her parents used to talk to each other, all the nights they'd spent arguing about where to travel to, which boarding school she was to apply for, which activities would round out her schedule. She thought of all the smaller conversations her mother had wanted to have with her father over dinner, how she'd kept notebooks with talking points, budgets, though money had never been an issue. Maybe her mother had needed something objective to cling to. Her father would eat his food, only half his gaze on her, the other on the newspaper, or his work, nodding as distractedly as Murray did.

Once Nancy, no more than six, had asked her mother why her father wouldn't listen, and her mother had said, *That's what men do. They can't do two things at the same time.* When Nancy still hadn't understood, she'd said, *Men can't read and talk, listen and work. They compartmentalize,* like it was a new vocabulary word Nancy should memorize for an exam in school. She'd felt that detached disdain in her mother's voice, indestructible, until eventually her mother had erupted; it had happened one evening, when her parents assumed she was sleeping. Nancy felt she understood it now, her mother's unquenchable rage.

Nancy wept many nights over the loneliness, but in time she learned to bear her burdens in silence. During the day, when Murray was at work, she bit her lip, drank as much water as she could, even though it nauseated her. Worse was the numbness she felt around her child, to see Jean as no more than this screeching bird she hardly knew at all. Most mothers, good mothers, she was sure, fell in love with their newborns instantly. Happy mothers were delighted to nurse, relished the animal bond—this extension of that symbiotic miracle that had begun in the womb. It was all skin to skin, outside scents mixing, and

Nancy wanted to experience joy; she longed for some sign that this was her calling.

Who knew she'd be so clumsy with a diaper? That she'd have a hard time tempering Jean's thrashing kicks while securing one sticky tab over the front, or how often she'd mistakenly position it backward? There were more physical pains, but these, too, were invisible to Murray, and if they weren't going to talk about how she felt, then her mind flipped to how Murray hadn't suggested sex, not once—even though she consoled herself with what Dr. Weiss had said—that it was best to wait at least four weeks after birth. But she wanted to know her husband still wanted her. Sometimes she wondered about others who might caress her, someone who'd desire her in any shape.

When fantasies arose, she learned to fight them. She put all of her energy into Jean, into feeling love for her baby. How much she wanted to look at her intently, to stare fixedly into her eyes, their clearest of blues, and not think, *This is it?* All the agony, the preparation, *And now?* What she felt but could never say was that the pleasure she'd once relished, the excitement over meeting Murray in the middle of the day for lunch, or to sit in the art museum, had dissipated. She felt these feelings had vanished.

On the worst days, when she was home alone with the baby, she found calm in music. James Taylor, Bob Dylan, the Beatles, the Stones. Her taste in music changed as rapidly as her moods. At least Jean didn't seem to mind the variety, though when Édith Piaf came on, this one held her attention especially.

"I love you, Baby," Nancy forced herself to say every day. She hoped the more she practiced, the more the feeling would become real.

Even on those mornings when she struggled to rise out of bed, the silence of the bedroom punctured by wails from the nursery, she asked herself: *Are you loving?* Or those afternoons when she wanted nothing more than to take a walk in the fresh July sun but knew the heat would be too much for Jean: *Are you true?* And then, the answer: *It doesn't matter about you, Nancy.*

After six weeks, she and Murray took Jean for her first standard checkup. Dr. Sharp was a tall, slender woman with gray hair and eyes. She praised Nancy and Murray for Jean's health. The baby's heart was beating normally, and her ears and mouth showed no signs of infection. More numbers: Jean was now ten pounds six ounces—in the eighty-fifth percentile for her age, sixtieth percentile in length, twentieth percentile in head size. Nancy watched as Dr. Sharp poked and prodded her baby, placing her hand over Jean's skull to feel the shape and make sure her brain wasn't pushing out disproportionately. "Great." She nodded, then pressed softly on the top, confirming the necessary flat spot. No organs felt enlarged when the doctor squished her tummy. The joints in Jean's hips and legs moved fluidly.

"How are *you* feeling?" Dr. Sharp said, after she'd asked for some time alone to talk with Nancy. Murray had already left with Jean to sit in the waiting room. Dr. Sharp's eyes squinted a bit. "I know it's not my place to ask, but have you spoken with your GP?"

"About what?" Nancy asked, feeling her fists tighten.

"I have to say I'm a bit concerned," the doctor continued. "You look like you've lost any baby weight very quickly. Are you eating enough?"

Nancy said she hadn't really noticed, not that she wasn't eating—she was—though she knew she could have been better about it, the way she'd begun to subsist on a slice of toast here or there, maybe a piece of fruit or a yogurt when she felt light-headed. But she supposed she hadn't been weighing herself regularly, or looking in the mirror, afraid of what she might see—her fatigued eyes, her washed-out cheeks.

"I am eating," she said finally, defensively, but Dr. Sharp just stared at her, perplexed. Fatigue, soreness, some irregular bleeding, she said, were all normal, but the gauntness of her face, it wasn't right.

"I don't have time," Nancy said, tears rising. The doctor excused herself for a few minutes and returned with Murray. He had Jean's head nestled over his shoulder.

"Hold her closer by your chest," Nancy told him. "I only ever hold her like that after a feeding." Her hand was on her forehead. "Where is her car seat? He doesn't even have it. Did you leave it in the waiting room?"

"Wait," Dr. Sharp said. She looked at Nancy, then Murray. "Your wife is depleted," she said. "Will you make sure she eats?"

Murray made a face, one Nancy knew too well, his brow furrowed, eyes narrowing. Then he looked away, as if distracted by some ambient noise coming through the wall. He was cradling Jean. *Jean Bean,* he'd started calling her when he took her into his willowy arms. As she watched him, she felt more tears collect. Suddenly he asked her to hold Jean while he got the car seat. Her arms trembled as she brought Jean close to her chest. She wondered if Dr. Sharp noticed. Could anyone actually see how she felt? Could anyone see her?

Jean squirmed in her arms and began to cry, and Nancy scrambled to search for her diaper bag, to make sure she had enough extras if this was the problem, but it was likely Jean was hungry, so she asked Dr. Sharp if they were through, if she could go home and see her again next month. The doctor said that was fine, but offered one final word of advice. "I know you and Murray want to be as attentive as possible, but sometimes Jean will have to self-soothe. If she's been recently fed and still goes on, it's okay to let her cry a little bit. It will ease your stress too." She smiled in a way meant to comfort, but the look of concern in her eyes, clear even behind the thick lenses of her glasses, set some kind of dread in Nancy's stomach.

As she positioned Jean into the car seat later that day, she considered what Dr. Sharp had said to her right before they'd left. She'd asked what her plans were for returning to work, and Nancy said she hoped to return next month. "We need the money" was Nancy's explanation. Murray had stood silently beside Nancy, his arms full of Jean. Nancy could feel him next to her, his watchful presence, possibly calibrating how Nancy would handle the question.

Dr. Sharp had looked at them and smiled. "You do whatever you need to do," she had said. "You're good parents."

A few days later, Murray would go to the toy store and surprise Jean with an enormous teddy bear made of a powder-blue terry cloth that matched some of her bath towels. When he brought it home, he'd wave the squishy gargantuan thing at her and then pretend to claw her little belly with it. He'd growl, too, but Jean would only stare at him blankly, a slate sheen over her eyes, which were still learning how to focus. Nancy would feel herself laughing then, perhaps out of pure nerves, perhaps out of the absurdity of Murray's whim, this simple act of love. She wasn't sure. She wasn't sure of many things anymore. But, yes, it still felt good to laugh.

SEVEN

Murray was waiting for the girls to arrive for pool practice. Once a week they jogged in the water to flush their muscles of the lactic acid accrued from workouts.

Anna arrived early. She wore a one-piece that accentuated her strong arms and thighs. Fuller than Becky's, but no less lean. She didn't smile at him, or wave; he kept his gaze half on his pad, pretending he might not have noticed her. He drew little lines under the interval sets he'd plotted out. When he finished, Anna was leaning over by the edge of the pool, struggling to touch her toes. He appreciated her effort to make use of every little pocket of time, to prepare, stretch.

A few more girls entered. Liu and Victoria. Rodney, Tanya, and Ginny arrived next, laughing. There was always someone laughing, he thought, like they were children, and he wasn't here to babysit. He told them to get in the water and stay in the first two lanes. Twenty minutes of warm-up. But not too easy. They had to focus on keeping their torsos straight, abs tight as they drew their hamstrings back. He yelled out reminders, especially for Victoria, who liked to lean forward and get ahead. In high school, she'd once broken eighteen minutes in the 5K, but he'd yet to see her do it again. He used to have patience with burnouts, but some days, like today, he wanted to tell Victoria her time was better spent studying in the library.

"Two minutes on!" he shouted. He followed the large round clock to the left of the pool. A long red needle marked seconds for tracking each interval.

Becky would have worked double their pace. Even in the water, she moved as fluidly as air. Like at Nationals, in Terre Haute, how light she'd looked in her midriff tunic and briefs. It had been twenty degrees that day in late November, and when she'd passed him at mile one, there'd been a sheen on her face and arms, Vaseline to prevent chapping, her eyes frozen with determination.

By the end of her freshman season, Becky's swimsuit had begun to hang from her at pool practice, bagging around her chest and bottom. She'd rubber banded the back straps together. Anna and Victoria had expressed their worries to him at that time, and he assured them it was being taken care of, said he'd have a talk with her, but then the season had gotten busy. She'd cleared the BMI minimum at her first mandatory weigh-in for the season, but now there were rumors she'd tied little weights to the inseams of her shorts. He'd heard Rodney tell Anna this on the course, at their second practice back after summer break, when the team had been in the middle of doing their form drills. If Rodney was gifted at anything, he thought, it was spreading rumors.

After the last interval, he clapped his hands twice. "Everyone out of the water!" Told them to find a spot for core work. Had them hold a plank position for one minute on their elbows, then it was time for push-ups.

"On your knuckles!" he said. After twenty, everyone but Anna could stop. He crouched down and started counting twenty more. The other girls were cheering her on, but after fifteen, she cried out she had to stop; her knuckles were raw.

"For Becky!" he shouted.

The girls fell silent. Anna collapsed onto her chest and whimpered. Rodney grabbed her towel from the bench and jogged for the locker room, slamming her body through the swinging door.

"Hey!" he said. Liu, already wrapped in a towel, used the end to wipe her eyes. He excused them all. Anna's knees wobbled as she stood up, but she just waited there in front of him, clutching her shoulders for warmth.

"How could you say that?" she said. She was looking right at him, her eyes quivering.

"Where's your towel?" he asked.

"I don't know," she said, looking around. "But I asked you—" Her voice had softened.

"I heard you," he said. "Don't you think she'd want you to work hard?" When she began to speak, he stopped her. "You know, you're right," he said. "I was out of line." *It wasn't a big deal*—his eyes twitched—*wasn't his fault* if the words came off wrong. But he couldn't let her leave like this, risk it damaging her times. Complaining to Rick.

"Did you hear from her parents?" Her shoulders had relaxed a little.

"No," he said, a twitch in his cheek.

"Can we visit her?" she asked. "I could help organize something," she said, her voice still soft.

"Not yet," he said. "Her parents aren't ready."

When she shivered, he told her she had to find her towel, but she wouldn't go.

"I can't sleep," she said. "It could have happened to any of us." Her voice cracked.

"You heard me," he said. "Dry off before you catch a cold."

~

Three days later, at the Iona Invitational, Murray thought he heard Rodney say something about holding a vigil in Battell Chapel. The girls were loading their duffels out of the bus's luggage carrier. Tanya and Victoria had nodded. "It's not right," Liu nearly whispered.

He may have been getting older, but his hearing was immaculate. Something he wished he'd reminded Nancy of more often. She used to accuse him of not listening, not truly *hearing* what she was trying to say, but she had no way of being inside his head to judge what he had taken in.

Battell Chapel stood opposite the campus green, which was wide enough for thousands of students to gather. It didn't make any sense to Murray, except that Yale was a dramatic place in which students and administration continually sought various pedestals for voicing their fixations. Wasn't quiet meditation better? Silent prayer?

Anna was drinking from her water bottle under the team tent. He called her over, gripping his clipboard with both hands. "Nestle in with Lisa Gates and Bernadette Morgan. Lisa is U Conn. Blue. Bernadette, Iona. Red. They're five seconds faster per mile than your best."

When he went over her mile targets, he alternated between pointing his stopwatch over the numbers and locking eyes with hers, which looked more hazel in the sunlight.

"If you hold on to those two," he said, "I know you can outkick them." She didn't nod like usual, and he wondered if she knew more about Becky than he did.

"Choose a focal point, color, clothing tag, anything. Just don't lose sight. Hear me?"

For a moment, he felt Nancy's eyes, sweat on her brow, looking up at him in pain.

He knew she—*Anna*—wanted him to confirm a hospital visit, but he couldn't just yet. Even if he could, there was no telling how it would affect her season. Of all Division I courses, Van Cortlandt's was the toughest, back-loaded with hills, the last half mile always much longer than it looked. Wednesday he'd had Anna do mile repeats on the road, up Prospect Avenue. She'd looked stronger than ever; there would be no disrupting her streak.

A half hour before the start, Anna rounded up the girls for a twenty-minute warm-up through the woods. Tanya would be closest after Anna, though her last two workouts had been mediocre.

He blamed Rodney. She was a bad influence all around, especially given her grades. She struggled to maintain a B-minus average, and he was sure that the combination of two required courses, one in ecology and another in neurology, alongside those required for her major in women's studies, would keep her on the same downward spiral this semester. Rodney brought down the team GPA, lessened morale. He had all the notes, lists of Rodney's infractions to date, between coming late to practices, putting in zero effort, and talking out of turn. Her grades were just the icing on the cake. Murray still had to get the final approval from Rick to let her go.

He migrated closer to some of the other coaches gathered by the start. Casually he knew Coach David Marcus from Fordham, and Allan Mosley from Iona, but the U Conn coach, Dena Winters, was new. None of the other Ivies were present, but it was important to establish a precedent here, show Harvard and Princeton what to expect at the Heptagonal meet in a few weeks.

His girls were warmed up. They went to the tent to shed layers and apply more Vaseline between their thighs. He heard Ginny ask Anna for the bag with extra spikes, then for the wrench, but Murray hollered at them. It was too late. They should have taken care of these things sooner. Ginny threw her jacket in the corner and made a sullen face before her run to the start, where a few other girls had already started doing form drills or practicing striders. He yelled at Tanya to keep her back straight, for Victoria and Liu to shift their weight forward, plant their feet midstrike.

He felt a tap on his shoulder. It was Allan Mosley.

"Coach," he said. "I wanted to tell you how sorry I am. I was devastated to hear about Becky." He swept his arm to where his own girls huddled in a nearby mass. "We're so moved you're all out here in her spirit. Actually we did a group meditation for her this morning."

Murray nodded without making eye contact. "Thanks," he said. "I appreciate it. We're hopeful she'll be back soon."

"My God, really?" Allan's eyes went wide.

Years ago, Murray had run into Allan at the supermarket, and Allan had given him the same spiel about how *sorry* he was to hear about Murray's divorce. His heartfelt consolation had felt just as disingenuous then. Allan had invited Murray to join his family for church once. He and his wife, Mary, and their two kids, a little boy and girl. This must have been some time before Murray's knees gave out, because he'd jogged with his cart to an aisle on the other end of the store, claiming he needed Dixie cups, then had secured an express checkout lane and paid with a credit card.

"Well, she's making progress," Murray said. His curtness seemed to rattle Allan—and he was glad—the guy needed to back off a little. Iona was a religious school, Catholic, and Murray guessed Allan was praying for him "to find a way back."

Murray had stopped shaving and doing his laundry on a regular basis, and he assumed most of the other coaches considered him a hermit, a recluse. Sometimes he felt they looked at him like he was a homeless person, like the man he sometimes saw on a park bench by the city green: the man with his long gray beard and high cheekbones, his blue eyes. Once he'd watched the man peel a piece of beef jerky from its wrapper, and Murray had wondered how he—with his dirty face and toenails poking from taped-up shoes, his garbage bags stuffed with blankets—had gotten the jerky. How did he manage at all?

There'd been a time when Murray had looked after himself—in the first years after Nancy left, even—when he'd spent seventy dollars a week at the health food store on vitamins to improve his energy levels.

Chaga tea and liquid iron, and other supplements like cordyceps, cardiovascular boosts, brain boosts—"highs" that would only augment his running. Coaching was the same, like a drug: as long as he had his mind on his athletes and their races, he could forget himself.

"I've got to set my clock," Murray said suddenly, unsure if it had been to himself or to Allan, who he was surprised to find still standing there, looking at him, confused. How long had it been, the silence?

"Of course," Allan said, as if maybe seconds, not minutes, had passed. "Good luck," he said.

~

On Thursday, Nancy had reached out to Murray. After sixteen years of silence, it somehow seemed *perfect* that his number one runner was the reason Nancy wanted to see him. She heard about what happened, she'd said, wondered if he wanted to have coffee next week.

In the last minute before the gun, Anna did three high jumps. Her feet kicked backward toward her gluteal muscles. Murray had secured her a set of longer metal spikes for the race, and as the starter went over instructions—the importance of staying inside the neon cones, elbows in—Murray silently extolled the power of shoes: how Anna would have a real advantage cleaving the mud.

"I'll be at one!" he shouted to her.

She didn't turn. No backward nod either. When the gun went off, she broke out of the pack immediately and maintained a lead of about four feet in front of Iona's number one. Anna's blue tunic gleamed in the sunlight. It was just several short-lived seconds before the Iona runner passed her, but she was already fighting her way back up. Sometimes he thought her stride bore an even closer resemblance to Sarah Lloyd's than Becky's did.

Some jostling happened amid the riffraff—then Murray heard the scream.

Jaclyn Gilbert

It took a few seconds to see the trampled girl. There was at least one in every meet. This time it was a U Conn girl, her calves lacerated by passing spikes. Her coach helped her stand up and limp back to their tent.

Becky's line of sutures had been U-shaped, licorice tinged, around her right ear. Hydrocephalus, fluid buildup in the brain. Babies were born with it sometimes. *Neural tube defects could be detected in early ultrasounds,* he thought, almost automatically.

~

Murray drove to mile one in a cart he'd rented from the park. More often than not, at least in his experience, the runners who got trampled had female coaches. Female coaches didn't inculcate body shoving as a necessary part of the game. He'd always thought girls should be trained from an early age to run aggressively. He practiced what he preached.

From where he was waiting at mile one, he picked out Anna approaching in the distance. Only three away from the lead. She looked strong, in control of her breathing and stride, on pace for a 17:45 finish. He could expect her next mile, the middle one, to be at least ten seconds slower, but she might drop another ten during the last.

Drop foot happened often inside hospital compression boots, he thought, pushing out the image of lifeless toes bent, pointing downward. Gravity. The way the tendons of the ankle could shorten.

Tanya was on pace for a twenty-second personal record, and Murray gave the rest of the girls his routine encouragement. "Hold on now," he'd say.

He had about ten minutes before the finish and opted for a shortcut. As he blazed over winding dirt trails, he focused on the brown earth, its silken darkness. The sound of his cart masked the trail of cheers behind him; he focused on stones, tree roots, anything threatening his path.

One minute from the finish, he heard the roar of the crowds again, clapping and finger whistling that rallied the top finishers through the final stretch. Murray had a difficult time differentiating between the first three girls, torsos thrashing for the win. Eventually he pinpointed the body of Jenny Reese from Iona. Still leagues behind where Becky would have been, but Jenny had performed well at the Eastern Athletic Conference last year. She was 5'3" tall, with a longer stride than U Conn's Mary Winterson. Mary was 5'9" and struggling to match Jenny's fury. Then, turning out of the woods, he caught Anna approaching. She might hit *17:30*; Murray could barely contain his excitement—he steadied himself out of the cart and shouted after her, waving his watch.

"Use the stretch. That's it! Foot speed, turnover. That's it! You're setting your record!"

She made eye contact with him, her head and neck still evenly aligned, a clear sign she wasn't exhausted, that there would be plenty left for Monday's practice.

Two days ago, he'd heard from Rick—somehow Lisa had agreed to speak to him—that Becky had opened and closed a fist sporadically. He hadn't lied to Allan, Murray assured himself, Becky *was* showing progress. Another day soon she might flutter an eyelid or try to pull out a tube. When he'd visited, next to her blood pressure cuffs, he'd noticed the soft cloth ties around her arms. Suddenly he imagined her strength rising, her desire to outstrip those temporary bounds.

Maybe he would take Anna with him to the hospital next week. Lisa and Doug would be more open to a teammate. The two of them could stop by the toy store beforehand and pick out a teddy bear. One with terry cloth would be best. Some even came with stimulating rattles. Bells.

Two days before movers had come to their apartment, Nancy had placed a bouquet of hydrangeas in fresh water on the kitchen counter. Said she clipped them from the communal garden outside their apartment, that she'd wanted something nice for him to come home to. She had cried, claimed how sorry she was. She had started toward him, as if she might reach out and hold him, but he had felt that same stiffness of his body. He'd felt numb to her then, but he'd known he wouldn't always—that he would one day long again for the heat of her against him.

Murray looked up at the sky. For the first time this morning, he noticed its vibrancy. Sunlight piercing the atmosphere and scattering blue.

EIGHT

Three months had passed, and then Nancy finally found something in Jean's eyes to hold on to. It happened one day during a diaper change, when her baby squirmed more than usual, and Nancy found herself saying, "Steady there." She grabbed a knee and tickled the tiny crease behind it, this soft line separating rolls of skin. That did it: Jean's eyes locked with hers. Little lips began to separate and stretch into a smile. They worked hard to match Nancy's.

"Oh!" Nancy laughed. "Beautiful girl you are." She smiled wider for her baby and scooped her up.

When Jean smiled, her eyes squinted like Murray's in the sunlight. Nancy was already seeing so much of him in her. Not a speck of red in her baby-blonde hair. "It's too early to tell at three months. Give her at least a year," Murray said, when she told him about Jean's smile. But the first time Jean smiled *for him*, one night when they were all on the sofa watching television, he turned to her and laughed. "I believe this is me. I'll have to dig up a baby photo."

He stroked Jean's soft arm and looked into Nancy's eyes, his as blue and warm as she'd known them when they were first falling in love, just a few years ago, as hard as it was for her to believe—she felt she was falling in love again, in this found wholeness of their family.

Jean brought her and Murray closer, she thought, each time they took a walk together on the weekends or shared more changings and giving Jean her baths. Murray seemed to enjoy the baths as much as Nancy did, in the plastic tub they nestled into the kitchen sink. Once she'd caught him singing "Row, Row, Row Your Boat" while he squeezed a puffy sponge over Jean's arms and legs. He was as careful as Nancy, too, softly coaxing the water over her head and rinsing her belly button.

She and Murray began reading to Jean together in the evenings too. She'd gotten an illustrated version of Aesop's *The Tortoise and the Hare*. The fact that it was Murray's favorite came as no surprise, but when he explained why, when he said *he felt sorry* for the hare, she'd had to resist laughing. And she'd been glad for her restraint; he'd been so serious explaining his disappointment, his frustration, over how the hare's risk-taking had gone unrewarded. Nancy was learning to appreciate every little moment Murray opened himself up, made himself vulnerable.

∿

Nancy knew that Murray's father, for those years he'd been alive for Murray, had put great pressure on him to succeed. *It was important to achieve something*, Murray had once said of his father, this phrase that had been sown into him over time—this idea that things were black and white: you won or you lost; you took risks or you didn't; you pushed your body to the utmost or else you had regrets.

She tried to accept this about him, the extreme conditions upon which he'd founded his life, but she did worry about Jean, that he might apply his philosophy to her one day—teach her to equate pain and physical exhaustion with achievement and self-worth.

They were all in bed together: Jean on Murray's chest as Nancy turned pages in her sleepiest voice. Murray rubbed Jean's back, soft with thin cotton. Jean's eyes were soundly closed, breath steady with sleep, so that Nancy could quietly close the book and reach, even more quietly, to place it on the nightstand. As they waited for Jean's sleep to deepen between them, she felt them embrace a stillness, a peace, and then she thought, How could she let her fear overburden the moment, as they made room for themselves to become different parents, better ones, than their own had been?

$\sim$

The next sunny day, not too hot or humid for late August, Murray suggested they drive up to East Rock Park for a picnic. Nancy packed a hat for Jean, and on the drive over, she said, "How about a picnic, Jean Bean?" She'd made her voice high. "Won't you like that?"

Murray parked the car just outside the entrance. Nancy had brought water, which she used to rinse the grapes, some of it splattering over the pavement as she shook the bag. In the shadiest spot they could find, Nancy spread out a blanket. She unpacked the rest of their food as Murray held Jean by his chest, her floppy white hat brushing his chin.

"She's like a little flower," she said.

"A tulip." He rolled his eyes.

Nancy couldn't believe that in just two weeks she'd be back at work already. She wished they could afford a nanny—even though Yale promised many of the best options for day care—but still she couldn't imagine leaving her child with a stranger.

Jean started to fuss. Nancy had just fed her before they left, so she told Murray it was her diaper. He reached for a fresh one from their bag, filling his eyes with that look, since he'd started a game of having her time his speed with her watch. There was something exciting in his every move, as he folded up the sides especially, securing tape in two even strokes. His record was 1:20, but today fell just short of that at 1:22. Jean seemed to enjoy the fury, Nancy thought.

"You're getting red." Murray looked at her, touching his chest.

And when she looked down at her own, she could confirm the splotches. They came on so quickly.

"I'll get sunscreen from the car," he said.

Suddenly she heard "Look!" She realized an older couple was standing behind them, the wife somewhere in her seventies, sporting long shorts and a safari hat, the husband with a baseball cap and binoculars. "Isn't it wonderful?" the woman said just as loudly.

"Different times," the husband said.

"How old is she?" the woman asked Nancy.

"Three months." Nancy tried not to sound curt, but it was better than Murray, his typical pretending no one else was there; he hated *making conversation* this way. He tied Jean's floppy hat a bit tighter.

"Well, keep that one," the woman told her.

"I will," Nancy said, but inside she cringed. No one ever extolled her for the dozens of diapers she changed a week. It was merely expected, and sometimes she thought a man could do half as much and reap double the gain.

But after the couple left, she had to remind herself not to fall into such generalizations, since her particular situation *was different*. These past weeks, Murray had grown into a great help. He'd started getting up with her now that she was pumping, so she felt less alone in her exhaustion. They both fantasized about naps, any pocket of time they might seize for just fifteen extra minutes of rest. And he had yet to complain about the break in his training routine like she'd expected. He seemed to be riding on pure adrenaline, channeling it into his work more than ever, so she wasn't surprised when he returned from the car with her SPF 50 and one of his pads.

"I thought it was your day off," she said.

"It is," he said. "I needed to check something."

"Couldn't you have done it in the car?" She felt gratitude slip.

"Nance—"

"What could be so important?" She had been planning to bring up what their schedule would be once she returned to the office, how she wanted to take turns leaving early to pick up Jean. Beinecke had already been so generous; there had to be a limit to their flexibility.

He had his finger on a newspaper clipping, switching between it and his notes.

"Murray," she said again—starting to spin, one reaction yielding to another. Wasn't her work just as important? He hadn't asked, not once, about how scary her transition might be. This tightness in her stomach was digging a pit.

"Do you really want to know?" he muttered.

Do you really want to know me? was what she should have said. Murray's self-absorption only seemed to double as time passed, and before she could take a step back, let her feelings settle, she said: "*I actually do* want to know." It had been impossible for her to hide the bitterness in her tone, her frustration over how clueless he was to her needs—or maybe it was something about the realness of Jean in her arms that made her wonder if he'd ever understand her silent struggle: Could she balance her desire to stay home with Jean a few months longer— she'd never get this time back—with her hope to be able to lose herself in her work again, to know she could live and breathe it as she used to, as easily as Murray still seemed to?

Her anger stewed, waiting for his answer. Finally, when he'd had the luxury of finishing his thoughts—she heard her mother again: *men can't do two things at the same time*—he said, "There's this new phenom from Maine that Ed and I are talking to, and she might race at Franklin Park next weekend."

"Oh," she said. That did seem *really* urgent, she thought sarcastically. She pushed a pacifier into Jean's squirming mouth.

"Last year she won Foot Locker." And when that meant nothing to Nancy, he added, "You know, for high schoolers. The national cross-country championships."

No, she didn't know. Was she supposed to have memorized this detail he might have told her once in passing? What had her last symposium been on? Could he tell her that?

"Ed and I are going to try to meet with her next Sunday to see about her grades and test scores, see if we can get her down for a recruiting weekend to stay with one of the upperclassmen, meet the team." He scribbled something else down. He passed Nancy the clipping. "That's her," he said.

At first she was appalled: He was carrying this around with him? On his day off? This close-up of a teenager who couldn't have weighed more than ninety pounds, wearing nothing but a tunic and briefs, chiseled arms and thighs.

"That's healthy?" she said.

"What?"

"She's skeletal." Nancy was surprised, not only that she'd said it out loud, but that she'd had to explain herself.

"She's young," he said. "Most runners her age are smaller to begin with—"

"Oh. That makes it okay then." She looked back down at Jean, whose eyes were blinking slowly, struggling to stay awake. "If Jean ran, you wouldn't mind?"

"What?"

"You wouldn't have a second thought about her health?" Did she really have to spell everything out for him?

"This has nothing to do with *Jean*."

Maybe it didn't; maybe she'd forced this analogy—but wasn't it implied, what he'd expect of their little girl one day? But she didn't say this. She focused on the concrete, the objective, the only language that ever seemed to resonate with him.

"What were we going to do next Sunday?" She said it bitterly, scolding, like her mother would have, and she hated that, her wont to embrace the pure, insatiable heat of her mother's anger suddenly, without warning.

He just looked at her. "I don't know," he said, rubbing his chin, and then reaching for Jean's foot to tug it, as if that made everything better, these little shows of affection.

"We were going to try that church," she said. "I made an appointment with the pastor." Tears brimmed, but she held them back; this was not a moment to appear delicate, shaky. She must hold her ground: last week they couldn't go because he was driving the team to the trails—he wouldn't be able to go once the season officially started—and the one before that, he'd needed to run. If he kept this up, it would only get later and later. Jean would be two by the time she was baptized.

"Right," he said, seeming genuinely surprised he'd forgotten. "I bet I can reschedule it." He put his pad away. "I'm sorry I keep forgetting," he said.

Jean had fallen asleep in the shade, in Nancy's arms. He moved closer to her; he kissed her head.

That night, he insisted on making dinner, and she knew she'd been wrong. As angry as he made her sometimes, especially in his obsession over his athletes, she could not ignore the love she felt from him. She knew she had to find an appreciation, a love in herself, she could really cling to, to *accept* and savor all the good things. Like the other night, when he'd confessed that something in his body felt different. He'd said he couldn't describe it exactly, but Jean made him feel part of the *continuance of life*. Those were the very words he'd used, and she'd been stunned, proof that his perspective, around time especially, was shifting.

Later that night, as she drew a hot bath, she thought again that she shouldn't take her insecurities out on him. She breathed in the scent of garlic and cooking oil from the chicken Murray was sautéing, Jean fast asleep in her bassinet. Murray had fed her, too, so Nancy could rest.

But now *work*, going back to it in a few weeks and all the thoughts she'd been pushing down, crept up: images of mail stockpiled on her desk, all the prints, the spreadsheets with which she'd have to refamiliarize herself.

The other day, over the phone, Marjorie had assured her it was like riding a bike. Even if the wheels were rusty, she'd find a way to get by.

~

And she did. Nancy found a way to balance her hours at the library with those she spent at home. The first time she left Jean in day care, she cried the whole bus ride to work, but had consoled herself that Jean hadn't seemed so upset. Her eyes had been wide, just staring at all the new faces and the toys Nancy and the day care worker had waved before her, and Nancy had kissed her many times, assuring her she was safe, that she was going to like day care, even though Nancy knew she'd only been assuring herself, assuaging her own guilt.

It took some time getting used to seeing Jean so exhausted from all the new stimulation; after work, she only had to feed her and then Jean was asleep. Nancy hated wondering about all the new things her child might have perceived without her or Murray being there to witness every moment. But eventually they both adjusted, got into a rhythm of trading days leaving work early; Ed was understanding about Murray's needs, and Marjorie promised to call Nancy at home if anything at the office was so urgent she needed to come back. Actually it was a joke between both of them—her and Marjorie—that rare manuscripts could be so life-and-death as they sometimes seemed, all the threads of a project raveling or unraveling on any given week. *Nothing is as urgent as Jean, watching her grow,* Marjorie had said. *You don't want to miss it.*

Nancy was overjoyed when she could be there, with Murray, too, one Thursday night, to celebrate the first time Jean grasped a toy, firmly, in her tiny hand at four months—and a few weeks later, when she'd started babbling. They'd been deciding what to make for dinner, Jean at Nancy's hip. "Ba-baba," Jean said, waving her fist. Nancy and Murray had looked at one another, eyes matching in brightness. "Yes!" Nancy had said. "That's a good girl. Can you say *Da da? Da daa?* . . . or *Ma maa?*" She and Murray repeated both a few times, but Jean just smiled back at them. "Soon," Nancy had joked, kissing Murray's cheek. "I promise I won't be too offended if she says your name first." She'd laughed again.

At five months, Jean was right on target during tummy time, lifting her head and balancing its weight against her little neck, trying to sit without Nancy or Murray's support. "That's it!" Murray coached, his hand just grazing the back of her neck. She was surprised he didn't have a timer or his notepad to log the time. But Nancy was keeping track; she kept a board in the nursery, charting each of Jean's milestones: the first time she rolled over from her belly to her back and then back to belly; the first time Jean recognized herself in the mirror by the foyer one morning; the first time she started solid foods—just a piece of banana Nancy had smooshed into the tiniest taste for her to try. Jean's eyes had gone wide as Nancy lifted the banana to her mouth and nudged it in, and she and Murray watched her little lips work around the food, deciding its texture, before swallowing; they cheered her on. "Another one?" Nancy asked. Jean had smiled back at her and Murray both, slapping her high chair tray.

Next weekend, they had plans to take her to a fall party Marjorie was hosting at her home, and Nancy couldn't wait to show Jean off there. Maybe they could give her a nibble of pumpkin puree, if Marjorie was making pie.

Nancy laughed silently to herself. Marjorie hated baking—so she thought, *I'll bring my own.*

NINE

Inside Mary's Toy Shop on High Street, there were plastic kitchen setups and miniature strollers, rows of dolls and stuffed animals on display.

"I used to have one just like this," Anna said. She held up a baby doll, its head naked, eyes two beads.

Murray fingered the edge of his jacket sleeve. "Did we come here to look at that stuff?"

Last night Lisa had called him. She hadn't sounded as angry on the phone as she told him about Becky. About how her eyes had fluttered six times since the first flutter two days ago. On Friday.

"How about this one?" Anna reached amid a row of stuffed animals for a teddy bear. She squeezed its soft brown fur.

"I said terry cloth," said Murray, thinking of the bear he'd brought home and the way Nancy had laughed at its largeness, but she had kissed him. She had called him thoughtful.

"I don't think they sell them," Anna said, her eyes confused, her cheeks still red. Just before they'd met, Anna had done her thirteen-mile-long run, clocking in at 1:34:06, or 7:23 minutes per mile. They'd gone over her splits in the gym lobby, and he hadn't given her time to shower before walking to the toy store.

"Did you hear me?" she asked again. "I don't think they have them."

"They do," Murray said. He was moving toward a doorway that led to a smaller room brightly lit by a series of overhead fixtures. It was the same as he remembered, from when Nancy had wanted to pick up more things, more bath toys and linking rings.

"Here's something." Anna held up a gray octopus. "It's not terry cloth, but the arms might be good?"

When she passed him the creature, he felt for tiny rubber suction cups.

"A little one at home?" The clerk had come up behind them. She smiled, eyes dark, unlike the room.

"We're shopping for someone else," Anna said. Her ponytail had loosened, rust-colored strands grazing her neck.

"I said terry cloth. Like this bear." Murray went immediately to the register and paid for it with two crumpled twenties. He didn't wait for change.

"I'll carry it," Anna said. Did she think him incapable?

Tissue crinkled as the clerk began to pack the bear in a box. Murray watched as her hands readied pink ribbon from a long spindle. They reached for thick-bladed scissors.

"No!" he said. "We don't need it wrapped."

"Oh," the woman said. "I should have asked." She handed Anna the bear to hold.

Outside, Murray told Anna where his car was parked, but she wanted to walk. "It's only a mile," she said, squeezing the bear to her chest. "It's so nice out."

Murray nodded, not because he agreed, but because this way she would avoid cramping. She could stretch out her legs.

"When did Becky's mother tell you about her eyelids?" Anna asked.

"Last week. Again this morning. Will you stop and fix that?"

"That's great." Anna stopped and handed him the bear. "Isn't it?" She knelt over her shoe, laces unfurling, dirty. Then she looked up at him, hoping, he guessed, for approval.

"Sure," he said. He liked that the girls wanted this from him, but sometimes he thought it made them weak. Men didn't operate this way. They just said what they thought. Did what they had to do.

At the next crosswalk, a woman was also waiting for the light to change. She wore a purple blazer, her hair in a french twist, like Sarah used to wear it, for special occasions—banquets, award ceremonies.

"We can cross," Anna said.

"You know Sarah Lloyd?" asked Murray. He was searching for a better sign, such as the birthmark on her right cheek, but it was impossible from this distance.

"Who?"

"Sarah Lloyd. Her picture is on the recruiting brochures. Her name's on the record board for the 5K. In the gym." He was speaking quickly, hopeful she might pass them so he'd know. But if it was her, wouldn't she recognize him? She would, wouldn't she?

"Right," Anna said. "I think—I've heard of her."

His first prodigy's induction into the hall of fame. Already eight years ago. Becky's accident was in the news, but as far as he knew, there'd been no picture of him. Rick was managing it, not for personal reasons, only because the school's reputation was on the line. It would take some other means, such as a reporter contacting Sarah, to ask her about her experience running under him.

Murray refused to take any of their calls—all of the reporters'. One had been so brash as to try and stop him on his way out of the gym, to see if he would answer any questions, but Murray had said he was late for a meeting.

"Watch it!" screamed Anna. "The car!" Murray stumbled back and fell. His palm pressed into the ground and scraped against the asphalt. When he looked up, the car's grille was there, gleaming silver, and it waited while Anna helped him up. She guided him, one hand on his arm in a firefighter's grip, the other still clutching the bear.

"How did you not see it?" she asked.

"But it was our turn," he said, shaking her arm off.

"No, it wasn't," she said. They'd stopped, and she was looking at him like he was crazy. An embarrassment. "Are you going to be okay to walk?"

"I'm fine." He looked around, but the woman—Sarah—she was also gone. And he had badly scraped his hand. Red splotched, bleeding just a little, burning. He brushed off some debris.

"I'm worried about you," she said. "Let's find a restaurant or something so you can wash your hands."

He didn't see one anywhere, just an industrial lot with dumpsters. The smell of grease and spoiled milk. He might vomit.

"No," he said. "Let's just get there." He swallowed, pressed his hand along his tracksuit and thought it was just a few more minutes, maybe five, until the hospital, but he couldn't show up with blood on his hand.

"I'm sorry," she said. But when he didn't say anything, she went on. "We are all really worried about you."

She had her head turned toward him. He kept looking straight ahead.

"We want to talk about it with you. I don't know what to tell the team either. They don't understand why I'm visiting alone."

"Why would you tell them?" He'd raised his voice. "I thought you'd use your common sense and not tell them."

"But it's not fair," she said, and then, "I'm sorry." She said it more softly this time. "But I don't think it's fair."

"Do me a favor," he said. "Stop apologizing. And speak louder if you have something to say."

"Coach—" She was whining, like a child. He wanted to cover his ears.

"What!" said Murray. "What is that? Do you hear that?" They were cutting past the parking lot of a strip mall. The blur of a pizza parlor, a nail salon, an Indian restaurant, its gold name glinting. "There's crying," he said.

There was, wasn't there?

"Just traffic," Anna said, her words muddled, like the liaison Nancy had once tried to teach him in French; he did not know where the letters of one word ended and the next began. But still he'd heard it. The crying.

"Why don't you go into that pizza parlor? To wash off. Please, will you?" Her eyes searched him again, pitifully, it seemed, but he refused to let her guide him inside.

He limped inside alone, where a man behind the counter was ladling marinara sauce over freshly rolled dough. The bathroom was dark and cold, its mirror fogged with film. He let the cold water sting him, cleanse him. He thought of how he needed to act: calm and assured. His tone even, like he had acted when Nancy had required that of him, to wake up and get dressed and walk out the door—he saw her then, *Nancy*, behind him in the mirror, her mouth about to open, to tell him something—or was it Anna? Anna had come in?

He was in a pizza parlor, he thought. In the bathroom. He breathed, stared hard at the mirror, until the image of his wife faded, until there was quiet again. He continued to breathe as he dried his hands, as he walked back outside.

"Are you okay?" Anna asked.

He nodded, and they made it another hundred yards, to another light, when she turned to him.

"Can we still talk about it?" she asked.

"About what?"

Murray's hands were cold and tremulous, this tingling sensation, over his watch, in his pocket.

"What?"

"I don't know what to tell them. The other girls, about the visit." She was looking at the sidewalk now, hugging the bear tighter to her chest. He wanted to tell her to grow up and realize their conversation was over. He was an adult, an authority, and she'd better learn to listen, but before he could translate that, this thought, others unfurled.

"Organize whatever you need to prepare for her delivery."

"You're not making sense," Anna said. "You mean recovery?"

"That's what I said."

"No, you said *delivery*," she said and paused. Into that silence: "But we don't know about her recovery, at least not really. Right?"

York Street, the street the hospital was on. They were close, where sirens rang day and night. Becky's dorm, Branford College, faced York, and once, the day of a race, she'd complained about the alarms keeping her up. *Recovery. Delivery? Which had he said?*

"Don't worry about it, Anna. I will," he muttered. "I'll talk to the team about visiting."

There was a sever, a crack in the sidewalk, one slab tilted far above the other. "Watch!" he'd nearly shouted. But Anna gracefully side-stepped the slab. She extended her hand to help him. Pain pierced his lower back.

"Do you have water or anything?" she said. "I'm worried." Anna's hair had spidered like red veins along her neck. She looked distracted. She looked away from him, then back.

"Don't you think we should have brought something else too?" Anna said. "Like flowers or a card or something? From the team?"

Sweat. More sweat had soaked Murray's back by the time they stepped through the automatic doors. In the elevator it was cool, though it smelled like latex, like cleaning products, smells he couldn't bear.

Lisa was waiting for them outside Becky's room. She wore a white T-shirt under loose overalls. She hugged Anna, not him.

"Thank you for coming," she said, still looking only at Anna. "They took out her trach today. We're happy. It's a big step." She blotted her eyes. "Doug's not here. He's in the cafeteria."

"It's okay," Anna said. She held out the bear. "It was Coach's idea."

"How thoughtful." Lisa looked at him this time, smiling faintly, but she didn't take the bear. He could still feel Lisa's rigidity, her distance. How could she, even after nearly two weeks, not see it was an accident of the most impossible kind?

Anna placed her hand over Lisa's, reassuring her that the team was doing okay. As Lisa explained Becky's state carefully to Anna, Murray began to wonder how old Lisa was. She was a young mother. She couldn't have been more than forty, which would have made her twenty, at most, when Becky was born.

Murray studied Lisa's tan face, her wavy blonde hair. So unlike Becky's black. Doug's was gray from what he remembered, not as gray as Murray's—but *gray*.

"We're going together, right, Coach?" Anna hugged the bear even closer to her chest, as if she'd never registered that Lisa hadn't taken it. Hadn't accepted their gift.

$\sim$

Then, inside the room, he felt Anna's jolt, her gasp. She turned to him, as if to verify it was Becky's violet face and body they saw. Her arms were bound to the bed by restraints, her stomach, rising and falling beneath thin blue bedsheets. Her life they were watching.

No more tracheal tube: the stable rhythms of her heart rate monitor, the ventilator's steady surge and hush.

Anna reached for him, pressing her firm body into his, the way Nancy had as they'd waited for news. The doctor's quiet footsteps over linoleum, approaching.

Where was Anna going now? So close, too close, to the bed.

"Don't!" he said.

"What?" Anna wept.

"Don't touch her," he said.

"I wasn't," she said. "I didn't." She turned and laid the bear by Becky's side. She crouched over her teammate, weeping. When she looked up, he saw Nancy's green eyes, her mouth white and covered in tears outside the emergency room.

~

"*Sleeping* isn't the right word," Anna said later. How much later, he didn't know.

"What, no—I—"

"You said, *Let her sleep*."

"I did?"

Anna looked straight at him. She walked to the sink in the room and leaned over it. Murray could have comforted her, placed his hand over hers. He saw only Nancy's back, her loose nightgown those mornings she'd been unable to rise. She'd resented him for it, how he'd sought to resume his work those first months.

"Coach," Lisa said.

He'd walked out and left Anna alone in the room.

"How did it go?" Lisa's hands clutched a tattered tissue.

"Okay," he said, but his eyes avoided hers too. In his periphery, a woman on the other side of the room. She was in a wheelchair, reading a magazine.

When Anna emerged, she reached for Lisa. More red hair, wet along her neck. Her back quavered.

"Doug is coming," Lisa said. She wiped her eyes. "I'm sorry. But you both have to leave."

~

Hours later, at 5:00 p.m., Murray went to the empty natatorium to regain himself. He wore his swimming trunks and brought his own towel. At first he considered water running, but it had been so long since he'd last tried. He sat along the edge of the water, looking down at his shrunken, sun-spotted thighs. A regimen of fifty squats a day, at least one hundred jumping jacks, that was what he needed. He swirled his feet, toenails gnarled and yellow, in the water.

Once, not long after they'd married and moved to New Haven, he and Nancy had gone to a small swimming hole in Old Lyme. Murray had brazenly peeled his clothes off and watched Nancy do the same. They usually made love in the dark, but by the swimming hole, where the sun slit the river and had cast shadows around their feet, he'd seen her shape clearly, the perfect line of her hip bone, her long neck.

Murray closed his eyes and slipped into the deep water. He began to push, frog-style. Without gravity, his hips relaxed and opened, a little more with each stroke. His eyes burned from the bitterness of the chlorine. He closed them tighter. He tried to take long, full breaths, but the capacity wasn't there, in his lungs. He felt his heart, the thrum of overhead lights, saw in his mind a mosaic of Nancy's soft back and legs. Then he saw her on her back, faceup at the sky, in the swimming hole, the sunlight warm and scintillating, before she turned over on her belly. She pushed toward him, several long strokes, before she reached him, pressing her lips gently into his.

She said the blue hour was her favorite time of the day, after the sun had sunk beneath the clouds and turned its glittering face to a dimmer, more diffuse pulse. He saw this same blue she liked in everything, when life was both lonely and full.

His legs felt heavy with fatigue, his breath growing shorter. He'd switched to freestyle, set on five more strong laps, from end to end, as if to erase the thought that it hadn't been her beauty that took him, not even her intelligence. Not entirely. Something else. Something about the way she balanced him: how the earth stopped spinning on its tilt when he was with her.

The police station in Montmartre. How calm she'd been with the fans blowing in that squalid office, tucked into a crooked street, the view of the gridded city below them impossibly far away. When Nancy got pickpocketed, she hadn't panicked like he had. She'd found him there, in the office, screaming, and she'd taken over, pleading with those indifferent officers, not in tears, but through an overwhelming grace, an ease. She'd resisted his desperation. Had brought him back to land. He needed that sometimes, he thought. To be brought back, *to breathe.* He imagined air moving through his chest, down his back, the cramped space between his shoulder blades.

He thought of her shoulders, their unevenness. How he'd once believed they made her more human.

He stared up at the dark ceiling, over at rows upon rows of wooden seats, their emptiness, as if in reminder, and he couldn't forget: Nancy had betrayed him.

TEN

Marjorie and Bill lived in a beautiful neighborhood by the campus golf course, and Nancy could admit more jealousy: any time Marjorie mentioned eating at the clubhouse with Bill and the twins. Growing up, Nancy had belonged to a club, so maybe that was part of it, that this option had once been available and was no longer; Murray would never work in finance like Bill, and even if she and Murray both got promotions, she could hardly imagine affording a house even half the size of theirs. Marjorie had a nanny, too—Bridget, her name was—this elusive Indian woman Nancy had met once before, her long black hair loose at her shoulders, a mole in the center of her right cheek. It was Bridget who'd answered the door and welcomed them in for the party. Marjorie was in the kitchen refilling a water pitcher.

"Hi!" she nearly squealed. Marjorie couldn't be more enthusiastic about Jean. When Jean was only two weeks old, Marjorie had visited with a gift, a stack of cotton onesies, but Nancy hadn't felt comfortable letting her hold Jean then, not until her immune system was stronger. Now, Nancy passed her five-month-old over to her friend freely—*she was practically family,* she thought as Marjorie tugged at one of Jean's sock feet. Just last week she'd dropped off several boxes of hand-me-downs, all the onesies Nancy was surprised she'd saved from her twins. Nancy had been grateful—there'd been no shower, no grandma to help her—and maybe Marjorie pitied her, which Nancy never liked to think, but she couldn't help but wonder.

"Everyone's out back." Marjorie smiled.

"This is for you." Nancy handed over the pumpkin pie she'd baked from scratch, and an expensive bottle of wine she'd researched. She couldn't partake yet, not for another few months, but when Jean started fussing in the kitchen, and Murray offered to feed her the bottle she'd pumped earlier that morning, it lessened her frustration somehow.

"Bill never helped like that," Marjorie told Nancy after she'd set Murray up in an armchair in the living room. Nancy smiled, but she wondered if Marjorie's tone was slightly accusing. As if she didn't believe Nancy's earlier concerns about Murray as a father, when Nancy was still pregnant, especially, were real.

As Marjorie passed Murray a towel and asked if he wanted anything to drink, and he shook his head, Nancy knew she was overanalyzing things again. Incapable of seeing the positive: how focused Murray was on every task, remembering to sprinkle a few drops of milk on his wrist, then the way he nestled Jean close, letting her grip his pinky, a slight smile on his lips as she relaxed.

"How's it been going?" Marjorie looked at her, her eyes soft.

"Fine," Nancy said, unsure if Marjorie meant spending less time with Jean now that she was back at work, or her marriage, or both. She felt her stomach tightening again, and when they left Murray for the sunroom, where Marjorie's boys, Brad and Kyle, were filling their cups to the tip-top with cider, she could have asked, *How was it for you, leaving them?* But she didn't; she just watched Brad with Marjorie's dark hair, grown out long to tell him apart from Kyle, watched as the two of them ran out into the lawn, past Bridget, who was carrying the pitcher of ice water Marjorie had been filling when they arrived. Now Marjorie was chasing after them. "Slow down!" she shouted, cider splashing everywhere.

It was an abnormally warm day for early November, and on the lawn, Nancy noted a few young families, many of them in short sleeves. Young husbands huddled around Bill as he told some story, waving his Corona. More husbands by the grill, flipping hamburgers, mothers watching their children, a handful of toddlers by an inflatable pool Marjorie must have had kicking around in the garage, and then there were a few other coworkers from Beinecke. Holly, a conservator who'd once helped Nancy mock up a bookcase for an event, and George, the head of Early Americana, with whom it was dangerous to converse for too long; one question about his work, and he was apt to take his listener through the history of the Spanish Southwest, and early Mormonism, too, before arriving at his point about a particular manuscript.

And there were some college faculty, most of them without children. Or maybe she'd judged the mothers by the kiddie pool prematurely; maybe some of them *were* faculty. Anyone might have thought the same of her, that she was just another mother here, another wealthy suburban neighbor.

~

"Are you hungry?" Marjorie had returned to the sunroom with an empty cup of cider. Nancy was about to say no, she wasn't, and she wasn't, not really. The skin still felt loose around her belly, the back of her arms and inner thighs, and she could not imagine resuming any semblance of an exercise routine anytime soon. Yet she stayed silent as Marjorie heaped her plate with the mashed potatoes that'd been catered, clearly, in their aluminum trays.

"Hope you like burgers." Marjorie smiled. They looked over by the grill, where one of the husbands had already begun serving; Nancy watched as he bent down with his tongs to secure a plain hamburger on the plate Kyle was holding up in earnest. "He loves to be first." Marjorie laughed.

There were a few seats at the picnic table where George was sitting, and while Marjorie headed over to help Kyle open a new bottle of ketchup, Nancy told herself at least she'd have a way to interrupt George without being rude, that she could say she needed to check on her baby.

"Do you mind if I sit here?"

Another man was ready to fill the space across from her. "Of course not." She smiled. It must have been the lack of sleep, because she knew she'd seen him before—she just wasn't sure where.

He was carefully positioning lettuce and tomato into his bun, and when he glanced up at her again awkwardly, and she pushed some mashed potato around on her fork, she placed it: the French professor Marjorie knew. Richard.

"You gave the Master's Tea," she said. "The one last February?"

Richard's brow furrowed, like he had a long list of lectures to file through. "Right," he said. "Good memory. Well, I'm Richard."

"Nancy." She smiled again. "It was an excellent talk," she said, irritated by her need to state the obvious; it had been so long since she'd had a conversation about literature. Even though she was already two months back at the office, she was still playing administrative catch-up, with so little time to read and do research for new projects to the same extent that she had before she left.

Richard asked if she taught, and when she said no, she worked in the library, and he asked the division, and she told him, it came back to her: all of her favorite books she loved to discuss.

"I'm so glad you found each other," Marjorie said. She was holding a picnic basket full of party napkins and plastic cutlery. "What did I miss?"

"Not much," Nancy began. She had gotten some soap under her ring during Jean's last bath, and she'd developed eczema, some blistering she tried not to itch.

"That's not true," Richard said. And then Murray appeared on the patio with Jean, who was dressed in a jumper Nancy considered the perfect shade of burnt orange. She still had to slice the pie, to let her have a taste.

"Murray," he said, before she could introduce her husband properly.

"Richard." Their hands shook.

"How's the food?" Murray smiled. Jean was wide-awake in his arms, waving a fist.

"Delicious," said Richard. He crunched a potato chip.

Jean started fussing again. "Why don't you eat?" Nancy said. "I'll change her."

"Sounds great," Murray said. He passed her over carefully.

Marjorie followed her into the house. "You're welcome to do it in the living room. I can grab a blanket, or—" She paused as she seemed to see some defensiveness in Nancy's face. "Or whatever you prefer."

"Thank you. But the bathroom's fine."

"I can help," Marjorie said, reaching for Jean. "I miss it." She smiled.

"It's okay," Nancy said, pulling back. "Only takes me a minute." She smiled dimly, realizing she was afraid Marjorie might demonstrate an ease, a flow of motion, she still hadn't mastered. Or was it more than that? She needed time alone, to collect herself?

Calm as she could, Nancy wiped Jean's bottom, then dusted a little powder there, rubbing her soft skin. She relaxed into a smile because Jean was smiling, kicking her legs.

Suddenly she felt warm hands on her bare shoulders. She flinched.

"Better?" Murray's voice said. He scooped Jean from the mat and kissed her head.

"I should change her clothes," Nancy said. "I brought a lighter T-shirt, in case she's too warm."

"I think she's okay," he said. "You're okay?" He held Jean before him, her legs dangling down, kicking reflexively.

They passed back through the kitchen, and he reached for a ripening cherry tomato in a small bowl. "I don't think those are for the party."

She shook her head, but Murray didn't seem to hear her. "I'll cool off with her in here," he said. "Go enjoy yourself."

"No, I'll take her," Nancy insisted. "Why don't you have a beer with Bill—you've met Frank, right, their neighbor? Frank wants to try a turkey trot. You should talk to him." She regretted feeling responsible for Murray. He never tried to make friends, not if he didn't have anything in common with them. He was the worst at these kinds of parties, so she was surprised when he just nodded and walked toward the grill, where the two men were, grabbing a beer from a cooler.

"Nancy," Marjorie called. "Over here!"

Marjorie was sitting with Richard on the edge of the patio, facing the lawn. Nancy still doubted she'd enjoy herself with Murray so close, wondering if he was having a good time.

"She's beautiful." Richard pulled up a chair for her; she almost said she needed more shade by a tree in the lawn, because she hadn't thought to bring a hat for a party in November.

"What's her name?" Richard had crouched beside them, brushing Jean's fist with his thumb.

When Nancy told him and explained the namesake, he smiled. "You're film buffs?"

"No. Not actually," she said. "But we saw *Jules et Jim* at the Christine and loved it." Didn't she sound trite? She focused on Jean in her arms, her contented gaze.

Then he asked if she'd spent a lot of time in Paris, and though she didn't want to go into it, Marjorie urged her to talk about her research, the transatlantic exhibition she was planning.

"*Had been* planning," Nancy said.

"Oh, come on," Marjorie said. "You're so dramatic. You'll be able to focus on it again soon."

"How long have you been working on it?" Richard seemed genuinely curious.

"I don't know," she said, realizing more of time's fog. How long had it been: two and a half or three? "Three years," she said, clinging to the whole number.

But he wouldn't stop there. He wanted to know about the period her exhibit would cover, and it turned out he knew as much as she did about post–Second World War expatriate literature; he was fascinated by the newest archive Beinecke had acquired with all of Baldwin's letters, his first manuscript drafts.

Then, as Richard mentioned some correspondence he'd been trying to track down, from the corner of her eye, Nancy noticed a young mother in a cropped top and frayed jean shorts crossing the lawn, approaching the patio with her toddler. They passed by the grill, and she saw a few heads turn, including Murray's.

"Have you read his essay?" Richard asked. She felt herself flinch again but took a moment, hoping maybe he hadn't noticed her distraction.

"Which one?"

Then he laughed and said, "His notes on Beauford Delaney?" and she knew she'd lost the thread.

"Of course." Nancy looked down at Jean to hide. Jean sleeping so peacefully in her arms. When she was awake again, she could taste the pie, and Nancy decided she'd get it from the kitchen, an excuse for going back inside. She stood up.

"What do you need?" Marjorie said softly.

"The pie." She continued to look down, fighting the shakiness in her voice, the fatigue.

"I have to go in anyway," Marjorie said. "I'll get it."

Nancy felt Richard waiting for her; what else could she say about an essay she might have read a decade ago?

"How old is she?" Richard smiled.

"Five months," she said, trying to appear less embarrassed.

He asked when she'd lived in Paris, and they discovered he'd been living in the Marais, finishing up his dissertation around the same time. He said he was looking for a typescript of Baldwin's unpublished notes on Delaney—was that the bit she'd missed earlier?—and he wondered if she could help him. "Yes," she said, relieved by this chance to redeem herself when she returned to work. She brushed Jean's hand, her baby still sleeping so soundly, and she looked out at all the other children on the lawn.

~

Jean wouldn't attempt crawling until a month later. One morning in December, the day after Christmas, when she was already seven months, and they had decorated the tree and hung stockings, opening a few small gifts with her on the floor. Murray decided to crouch low, a few feet away. "Jean," he said, "come over here." She looked up at him. They waited as she reached for a small piece of leftover wrapping paper on the floor, straining arms and neck. Murray patiently waited. "Come on, Jean." Then she reached out her arms farther, just grasping the edge of the paper, and pushed herself forward, slithering another half inch, neck still straining. Nancy turned to Murray, her eyes bright, placing her palms behind Jean's feet to guide her.

"She's advanced!" Murray cried, hurrying to his study for the video camera.

"I bet she'll skip walking," Nancy called out, "and just run!" Her voice was full of playful sarcasm, but Murray didn't seem amused. He already had the camera and was focusing it.

Nancy had to agree—Jean *was advanced*. All of her books said most babies first attempted crawling at eight months, and here Jean was, not far from all fours.

But later that night, all the excitement must have been too much, because Jean became fussy, refusing mashed sweet potato, her new

114

favorite. She had another tooth coming in, Nancy said, "That must be it." Murray wasn't convinced—he thought maybe he should try and change her.

She went to Jean's table first for the Desitin, then their bedroom, since sometimes they changed her there, but she couldn't find it.

"I swear I saw an extra right here," Murray said, shuffling around a stack of diapers on the kitchen table.

Nancy offered to take her, but Murray told her to rest. "I got it," he said. He paced around her room, repeating, *shh, shh* in sets of three.

Nancy remembered she'd set Jean's pacifiers in the fridge to keep yeast from building up—these white patches that might appear in Jean's mouth at any time and lead to thrush.

Maybe they should check Jean's temperature. But Nancy was always on high alert, more than most, she guessed. How could she be sure she wasn't overreacting?

Murray continued to pace between the living room and Jean's room. Selfishly, Nancy couldn't help but wish for the moment they'd find sleep, that it might reset her somehow. It was already 9:00, past when they usually put Jean down, the sky through the window dark—darkening.

"What do you usually do?" Murray said, his voice desperate. "Has she ever done this before?"

She was a bit annoyed, since it wasn't as if she spent much more time with Jean than he did these days. He was holding a bottle he'd heated up in case she was hungry, since she hadn't touched the sweet potatoes. Some milk had dribbled over his T-shirt.

"I don't remember the last time she was like this," Nancy said. She was desperate enough to offer to breastfeed, but if they gave in to the temptation, it would be that much harder to wean her later. She reached to take her from him, and pressed Jean to her chest, kissed the back of her head, rubbed her back.

"Maybe she's sick," Murray said, and Nancy felt better—that she wasn't the only one who worried this far. She told him where the thermometer was, but when he tried it, Jean's temperature came back normal, and it had only made things worse, Jean's cry louder, shriller.

"We could try playing some music," Nancy said, sounding panicked. She'd just gotten a cassette tape, in the box by the bookshelf, for playing the sound of the ocean. Murray found the player and put the tape in. He turned the volume up. Nancy stroked Jean's feet, her red arms and sweaty forehead, but the cries wouldn't subside.

"What if we took her in the car?" Murray's eyes searched hers. "For a drive."

It was brilliant. Nancy hurried to change Jean into her pajamas, struggling over Jean's thrashing legs. Nancy continued Murray's *shh, shh* in sets of three, as if the trick was repetition, consistency.

She stayed with Jean in the back seat, one hand by her knee, the other on *Goodnight Moon*—Jean's favorite—that she'd snatched from their nightstand just in case. There were several red lights until they merged onto 95. Nancy didn't know where they would head to. She hoped Murray had an idea; it was nearing ten o'clock, and she needed to be sure. "What about Meriden?" She pictured the hike they'd taken there once, one spring, where there'd been a beautiful park, a ridge they could drive up to, for the view.

"Okay," Murray said. About ten miles in, they heard the first break in Jean's cries, and gradually they became more intermittent whimpers. Nancy stroked her warm leg; she whispered, "That's it, little girl. My sweet girl."

Jean's chest rose and fell, ever more quietly, her neck relaxing, head drooping with tiredness, and Nancy brushed her cheek as lightly as possible. They were only halfway to Meriden, but Murray took the next exit. He was peering into the rearview mirror, a partial smile on his lips.

They pulled into the lot of a Kmart in Wallingford. Murray let the engine hum. He opened his door and stepped out carefully in the cold, and she opened hers as softly, and they looked at one another, then at Jean, so still, her mouth quivering slightly, the air seeming more frigid against the warmth of the car. Nancy pulled her jacket closer and squeezed Murray's hand, after he'd gotten in the back next to her, gently closing the door, to lock in the warmth.

They were a good team, Nancy thought, as they let Jean sleep.

~

The next night, after Nancy put Jean down, she decided she would do it: she'd surprise him with the lingerie set she'd gotten on sale around Christmas. She'd been planning to wait another month or two, until she'd at least tried to get into better shape, but there was no time like the present. *I have to remember this,* she told herself, slipping on the first piece, a black silk chemise with lace that furled around her bottom. The second was a garter belt, but she had to hurry and fasten the sheer knee-highs that came with it before he finished brushing his teeth in the bathroom.

She had left only the green reading light on when he entered in his boxer shorts. In the warm glow, she wasn't sure how well he could distinguish her shape, and even if it was easy enough for him to, did she look alright? He smiled at her and climbed onto their bed. He waited for her on his knees, arms spread out. She sauntered over, shimmying her hips and laughing. Her breasts were still so much larger than they'd ever been, but at least they no longer hurt. Murray lifted the bottom of her top and began kissing between her thighs. He tugged at the loose strings hanging from her belt. She bent over and nuzzled his neck, smelling the ordinary bar soap he used, his fresh scent. His hair was still wet from the shower, and she rubbed her hands through it, this blond that shone silvery gray in certain light. Murray unhooked her belt and began inching down her thong. When they heard Jean crying, Nancy looked up and paused. She remembered again what Dr. Sharp had said about self-soothing. How Jean would learn to sleep longer overall if she let her go more.

Jaclyn Gilbert

"She'll be fine," Murray said. He pulled her close to him, her back pressed against his chest as he kissed an earlobe, then reached down with one hand to tenderly squeeze a fleshy cheek. The closer she was, the more force she could feel in his erection. Jean had already quieted, which allowed her to close her eyes again and enjoy each sensation.

Usually Nancy had one ear on the monitor without thinking about it—the white noise of Jean's breath and the creaking sound of her moving in her crib. But just after she and Murray finished, about ten minutes later, she noticed the intense quiet. She crawled over Murray, out of the bed. His body slackened, and he stretched his arms and legs out. "Really?" He pressed his temples. Nancy had slipped on her robe and was hurrying to the nursery.

~

She would scream. A wild shrieking through the whole bones of the house. A shrieking that tore through its foundations, lasting the lifetime it took Murray to make it to the crib.

"She's not breathing!" Nancy was still screaming when he rounded the doorway and found her, holding Jean in her arms as gently as she could manage. Murray took Jean from her and laid her on the floor. Nancy fell beside him, sobbing. "Christ," he shouted. "Pick up the phone! Call an ambulance!"

Ambulance, ambulance, yes. Nancy's hands were shaking as she dialed frantically, fingers finding buttons, shouting at the first responder. Murray was on his knees on the floor now, pressing his head over Jean's chest, listening for a heartbeat.

"I don't want to hurt her," he was yelling. "I don't want to hurt her lungs or press too hard." Nancy was begging him to hurry and try. *"CPR!"* she screamed. "Something!" Anything, is what she meant. She felt an assumption rise in her: He should know these things, shouldn't

118

he? Who was supposed to know these things? She was outside of her body again, shaking above him now, hovering, a dark bodilessness.

Murray tried chest compressions with three fingers. He was doing one hundred half-inch presses within the minute, he yelled. "Her chest isn't rising," he yelled louder, crying this time. He bent over her mouth, those tiny petal lips—lips Nancy had made—covering them with his own, and gave one full breath, waiting a second, then another. Mucus had begun to drip down Jean's rigid nose and neck.

Nancy was arching over the table now, convulsing and wheezing for Murray to try again.

"I don't want to hurt her." He began to weep in earnest. "I don't want to hurt her." But he would repeat these compressions fifteen more times. Finally, he pulled back from her still body, heaving, shoulders collapsed.

They waited, sirens crushing the darkness, and Nancy did the only thing she could: recite her name every few seconds. "Jean," she said. "Please, Jeanie," and then she heard herself begging for God to take her too. Murray held her, her arms thrashing in the late December darkness.

PART II

ELEVEN

Murray waited in the gym for the girls to finish a regular training run. He paced rows of treadmills and stationary bikes and step machines: the predictable thrum of varying speeds and pulses, the clank of barbells.

Pop music, had it leaked from headphones? A girl on the StairMaster had large muffs over her ears. Her eyes were closed as if in meditation, her feet forcing rapid, resistanceless steps. Impossible to read the calorie count, how long she'd been going for, but she wasn't building muscle; she wasn't gaining anything.

"What's your problem?" the girl said. She craned her neck to look at him. Her mascara was running, and the biking shorts she had on were way too small. "Creepy," she muttered. She stopped her machine, grabbed her towel, stepped off, still looking at him that way, like she really thought he'd done something wrong.

Then Murray spotted Liu on a stationary bike. How had he missed her? Up close her frail wrists looked blanched from gripping the side handles too hard. She'd suffered two stress fractures last year, and Dr. Owens, the team physician, had recommended twice weekly cross-training to cut down on mileage. But sometimes she went for two hours like this, pedaling slowly, at *real* resistance, between 16 and 20.

Becky had been injured once. Only once, she'd suffered a minor gluteal strain, but Owens had said she could bike, so Murray had custom designed a series of workouts, alternating hill grades and speeds to target Becky's heart rate at 180 beats per minute. Even injured, she'd work out for as long as he wanted, three hours sometimes, and she always came back the next day hungry for more.

"That's enough, Liu." Murray set his hand on the monitor. Liu looked up at him, slowly, even more slowly than her legs were working. Her face as white as her wrists.

"But I've only done forty-five minutes," she said. Liu had lost ten pounds over the summer, cheeks hollowed out, limbs reduced to muscle and bone. Right now her BMI was at 17, a half point less than Becky's, but Becky's situation was different in that Becky's physical exam and blood work had come back healthy. Anything abnormal would have been mentioned in his monthly meeting with Owens, wouldn't it?

~

The female athlete triad—Nancy had brought it up with Murray once, sometime before or after that picnic in East Rock the year Jean died— when he'd been in the middle of recruiting Sarah. Nancy had done her research on the syndrome, had outlined its components for him. *Disordered eating, amenorrhea, osteoporosis.*

That was before the year of the stress fractures—one year after Nancy left—Liesel Kennedy's and Jo Delancey's fractures were the first he'd encountered before Sarah's set in by her senior year, and then anemia had brought all their times down, too, but nothing that a prescription iron supplement hadn't been able to fix. *Lingering bruises, low self-esteem, depression*, these were all symptoms Nancy had pointed out.

Becky had a few bruises along her quads, but that was normal. Almost every athlete had them from working out knotted muscle tissue. Murray had relied on a rolling pin in his racing days, but now there were all kinds of technology his girls used to relieve tightness. Foam rollers and knobbed sticks. A few times he'd caught Becky using her knuckles to knead her quads in the car, and once he'd even said, *Easy there.* He'd tried to make a joke, just some light humor, even though it had never been his strength. Still, Becky hadn't smiled, her brown eyes penetrating, her smile faint.

"Coach?" Anna was standing there, beside him, as if it were still Sunday and they were on York Street, a few blocks from the hospital.

But three days had passed, he thought. It was Wednesday. September. Anna's face healthy and flushed from running outside.

He was still gripping the monitor above Liu's bike—he peeled his hand away, but now Rodney was here; she had come up behind Anna. How long had they both been standing by him?

Liu was still on the bike—as if this silence, his pause—had condoned her reluctance to stop. As if she could hide her slow, sustained calorie burn from him. He told her again, "That's enough."

He himself had skipped dinner last night and hadn't really slept, the red pixilated numbers on his alarm clock blinking out minutes between 2:00 and 4:30 a.m. But it was 4:55 in the evening, and there were matters to take care of.

"Why did you run together?" he asked.

Anna turned to Rodney. She made a face, or was it Rodney? Anna wouldn't disrespect him—it *was* Rodney, of course it was—looking at him this way.

Liu finally stopped her legs and used a towel to wipe her neck, then her wrists and forearms, her machine. She stepped off, still barely moving. She picked up her organic chemistry book on the floor and opened the pages. He could see sweaty fingerprints on the paper, wet rippling along the binding.

"Hydrate yourself," he said.

Anna had her arms crossed now, but Rodney spoke first: "I'm too slow for Anna?"

"I didn't say that," he said, eyes firm on Rodney. The way his own father had shunned him, silently, the first time he took a second banana from the fruit bowl, when it was just one banana each. Unlike Murray, Rodney's eyes were wet, weak with tears in her shame, in resisting his authority.

"We saw her," Rodney said. She wiped her eyes. "Because you wouldn't take us."

"What?" he said, hearing his voice suddenly rise.

"I offered to take them," Anna said. "Since I know how to—I know her parents."

"What do you mean you took them?" he said, louder still.

Liu remained in eye range, paused over the nearest water fountain. It took time for her to lift her head up. The girls claimed she barely ate, only fruit. The orange Becky had peeled in his car, that single wind of skin. He turned back to Anna and Rodney, their faces blurred, the sweat on them. His sweat or theirs, cold at his palms? He looked down at the floor, anything but the thought of his own sweat. The orange.

~

"We'll talk about this later," he managed to say calmly. He looked right at Rodney as he spoke, her eyes piercing his, but eventually she turned and walked away, joining the other girls waiting for him to unlock the varsity training room.

~

Did Lisa Sanders have no problem with a whole crowd in Becky's room? he thought. Threatening her state? He imagined Becky's labored breath, her ventilator more forceful, with all of them there. Why hadn't Lisa called to check with him first? Or at the very least called him after? And Anna, she had gone behind his back?

He sorted out their charts, called each one up to take hers, focusing on names, calling them out, calmly as possible.

Ginny. Victoria. Patricia.

Anna was working the hardest, and so she'd *deserved* to see Becky first.

Emily. Tanya. Rodney.

The others needed results before they earned their privileges. He would never have dared expect his father to give him the ten cents he and Patrick got for weekly chores; they'd had to wait for their father to bequeath his generosity unexpectedly. The point had been *not to expect anything*—it was the same for an athlete—you worked and worked, harder and harder, until fate smiled upon you. That word, *fate*, suddenly in his brain, and the thought made him shudder.

Anna, he wanted to say, as he called her name, handing her chart over last—he wanted to say, *What is wrong with you?*

Don't you ever disrespect my house, Murray's father had said, the second time Murray had stolen more than one banana from the bowl, the peel limp in his hands, as he looked down at his shoes.

Anna had taken her chart, nonchalantly as ever, it seemed, and joined Rodney by the free weights. He watched them find their weights, ready for their lunges.

He'd drive the course again tonight, Murray decided, then he'd leave a message with Lisa, reminding her it wasn't safe for the girls to visit on their own, not without supervision around Howard Avenue, where crime was high. And seeing Becky would lead to more questions about her injury that couldn't be answered yet, would—though he couldn't tell Lisa this—distract them from racing well against Princeton and Harvard on Saturday.

He looked over at Anna and Rodney gripping two dumbbells each by their sides as they lowered into walking lunges. Anna's ponytail had loosened again, splaying the same red, sweat-soaked strands, and she seemed to be whispering something to Rodney.

Murray was sure Rodney had pressured Anna to organize that trip to the hospital. Anna wasn't so calculating or rebellious on her own, he thought as she pumped her arms through the mirror now. Ten-pound weights, same as the ones he'd given Nancy when she'd been just four months in.

~

Before Nancy was angry at him, she was quiet, Murray thought. His wife flashed before him again, this time in their bathroom, wrapped in a towel. He thought of those mornings, when she'd rushed for a towel to cover herself—how she'd stood like that, all covered, before the mirror, combing the knots from her hair slowly, blank eyes not meeting his once through the mirror. He'd thought of coming up from behind and kissing her neck, the soft place she'd once liked, that they'd once shared on her body, but hadn't been able to bring himself to. The touch might have broken them both.

~

Victoria cheered for Patricia through a round of push-ups. Patricia was in a sorority and still had summer weight to shed. But Owens liked to remind him not to be so hard on the girls after the summer. The doctor claimed each season of training demanded at least two months of recovery. Plus, he said, they were college kids like everyone else. Didn't they deserve to have some fun? Once Owens had called Murray's office after a bad season of injuries, warning that if he didn't relax the reins, their physical and mental health would suffer for the long term. Just like Nancy believed, but Owens, like Nancy, didn't understand the rigor that had to be sustained over months for times to drop, and it wasn't his fault if some weren't as well equipped as others for that challenge.

Four years of college running, Murray had reminded Owens, wouldn't be the thing that barred them from living normal lives one day. If any-thing, they should blame the pressures of an Ivy League education. Every program was brutally competitive, across the board. It was what you signed up for, and you got your investment back. No matter how well you fared academically or athletically, Yale was a brand you wore for life. Need he list the countless successes of each one of his alumni over the past twenty-two years? Many of them were on Wall Street, or in the best corporate law firms, medical practices, and hospitals in the nation.

He would have killed for an opportunity like the one his girls had—he and Nancy both, he thought, watching Anna and Rodney at the bench press now. They were still whispering about something, and he saw Anna smile. But maybe that was just her habit, to smile as she spoke.

Nancy had always been full of such small kindnesses. All the times she'd helped out their neighbors, Walt and Lauren Peters, after Lauren had to have surgery for a small tumor in her breast. It had proved benign, but Nancy had brought over mounds of leftovers and offered to watch their two children several evenings.

The Peterses had wanted to return Nancy's support. One weekend when Murray had been away at a meet, Walt had called him to let Murray know Nancy was okay. He hadn't known what he meant until he'd gotten home and found Nancy locked in the bathroom, refusing to let him in. She'd locked herself inside and wasn't eating, and later when Walt called again to check on her, he'd told Murray that Nancy had called him and Lauren, weeping over Jean's empty room, the boxes Murray had packed, and the daisy border, and the crib he had taken down and delivered to the Salvation Army as soon as possible—to make it all more bearable for Nancy. He'd assumed she'd see that, not that he was heartless. Emotionally *dead* was what she had called him from inside their bathroom the day he'd returned.

Anna lowered into a squat. Rodney must have said something new to make her laugh, because she smiled again, reflected in the mirror.

He saw their apartment as it had been before they'd left for the hospital, and then how they'd had to come back to the bags of diapers, the bibs, the towels, and bootees folded by the dryer. The bottles drying by the sink. The rocker and the high chair, the boxes of Marjorie's hand-me-downs. The car seat.

People had tried to help—in delivering food, Murray thought—but Nancy had dumped it all in the trash silently, and then had washed her hands for long intervals at the kitchen sink afterward, or in the bathroom, if she'd needed to close the door and cry beneath the sound of running water.

"Go, go!" Victoria cheered Emily through a series of toe taps and side shuffles for agility and increased lactate threshold.

Anna and Rodney walked toward him. They both refused eye contact, and he heard Rodney make a joke about one of her classes, some double entendre he couldn't follow, and Anna laughed. Nancy again, walking out of the elevator that last day they'd met outside Beinecke, for one of their last lunches, as perfunctory as ever—not a hint of the old excitement in seeing one another in the middle of the day.

Knee-length blue dress, rose-gold hoop earrings he'd given her one Christmas, red lipstick. He felt her staring back at him, scissoring a cigarette, blowing smoke in a thin, wistful stream. And now he was just supposed to reply to her email? As if nearly two decades didn't divide them.

When the girls finished, he had them line up by the door. Rodney blinked dramatically at him, like he'd been staring at her. Had he been staring? That was the wrong word. *No, he was supervising*. This was his job. He collected their charts, reminded them of pool practice tomorrow morning, then their prerace run on Friday before Saturday's meet. The bus was leaving at 6:30 a.m., so they had to eat breakfast early, at least an hour to let things digest. But the girls weren't listening; they were packing their bags and talking about which dining hall to go to.

Murray used to join them for these post-workout dinners—especially during his first years of coaching, when he'd had the energy, the interest, to ask about classes and professors.

Murray always assumed Becky managed well enough in her classes, that if she was earning Bs, she was getting the support she needed, though it might have been on the lower end of the team's 3.7 average. He'd never asked her about the pressure she might have felt, but he saw it in her rush to the library immediately after meals. She spent every long bus ride studying, too, while the other girls chattered on about weekend parties. She usually sat alone, in the front seat opposite his. The last book he'd seen her with was John Donne's poetry, this pale green book stickered with *USED*. Sometimes he caught her looking out the window, staring off.

~

He thought of that March after it happened: how Nancy would stand in the kitchen and look out its only small window, smoking in her bathrobe, the silken green one she'd bought in Paris.

She'd been so quick to regain her shape after pregnancy, he thought. Three months of sleeplessness that kept her in bed until late afternoon most weekends. And then the three after they lost Jean—*after they lost her*—words that never consciously entered Murray's mind. There was only the image of his wife, skeletal—after she'd fallen back to her old cigarette diet, but he'd had no room to criticize then.

Not during those days she couldn't rise from bed, her spine sharp under the bedsheets. He'd smelled smoke in everything. And later, long after she was gone, he relied on Febreze, plugging air fresheners into every room.

~

That first March into April, he guessed she'd been trying to tell him something, in what she hadn't said, the impenetrable quiet that had filled their apartment and his car, as he drove to work, fixing the radio to as many different stations as he could to drown out the lack of noise.

He would make her breakfast. All those months, relentlessly—dry toast, the glass of milk she wouldn't touch. And then one day, she'd looked up from her full plate, about to speak, dents below her eyes, lips chapped. She'd coughed in place of words, and he'd been about to get up and help her, rub her back, ask her what she needed, but there'd been this feeling that if he touched her, she would shatter—and so he'd waited for her cough to settle, for her to find her breath. She had looked up at him, her eyes bright as if in alarm, and then he'd watched that light dim from them, turn milky and faraway. Was it then he'd known she was gone and wasn't coming back?

~

In his car, on his way to the course, the sun began to drain from the sky, slivers of light lowering closer to his eyes, and he had to squint. It was after seven o'clock, but by the time he reached the course, he'd still have enough light left to monitor any activity, see what new clues might surface. Already a little over two weeks since the accident, and so far he'd averaged four trips per week, varying the time of day and nature of his loops. He had yet to spot anyone suspicious along the first or second holes or in the surrounding trails and neighborhoods. Groaning mowers or the ticking arches of sprinklers might be dulling his senses, but weren't these the conditions he needed for determining plausibility?

In his office, the light on his answering machine was always red. At least five calls a day from reporters he didn't return. But there was no use speculating out loud to them, without evidence, without doing the work they weren't willing to do out here on the links.

Murray determined that somewhere near the tee blocks on the second hole was the most likely point someone would have hit from. Assuming a low, wayward drive shot had caused the accident, this golfer was an amateur. Murray set the ball on a white tee, in line with the slope where Becky had fallen.

He looked through a laser range finder he'd purchased from the clubhouse and confirmed no targets obstructed his path. He went to his bag for his best driver, one with a lightweight titanium head and thin speed face for maximum speed and distance. At the tee, he pointed its shaft at twelve o'clock, then three, since he had to know what was straight to know what wasn't. He thought about the rough under Becky's feet, the border of woods to her left.

His stomach constricted. He had to wait, to breathe, to suppress shaking in his forearms, but it was now or never, so he dipped his whole body in, jumping at the whish, the crack. He watched the ball curve toward the fairway, then into the woods.

He'd read about a forty-five-year-old groundskeeper in Sanford, Florida, who'd been hit on his temple by a ball struck one hundred feet away. The hole had been a par five, and the worker had been cleaning debris near a tree. Paramedics had spent ten minutes trying to revive him.

$\sim$

Murray was looking for his own ball in the woods now. His back ached as he crouched down, rummaging beneath leaves, wishing he'd purchased a ball finder online, one he'd researched, with a vibrating camera and blue-lit LCD screen for guiding him to the exact spot. But this advanced technology made it seem more absurd that the simplest precautions hadn't been taken before the ball was struck—binoculars or yelling *fore*, anything that might have offered *foresight*—wasn't that the point of the word?

In 2009, a sixty-five-year-old woman had been killed by her son-in-law's wayward shot on a course in Scotland. The ball had struck the woman in the back of her head; the same thing happened to a seventy-year-old man walking ahead of his group at a course in Chino, California. This ball had been hit from a tee only ten yards away, and the man had spent several days in the hospital before he died. Murray had only pinpointed one case involving a coma, a young spectator who'd been hit, and that young person had woken up, because younger people recovered faster, and Becky was recovering.

He found his ball behind a rock, and he held it for a few minutes, examining its dimples and wondering about the power of a synthetic core.

When he came out of the woods, a group of elderly women sped by, white puffs of hair beneath visors. He heard them laughing, as if they used their cart for assisted living instead of efficacy, and he guessed these women might also giggle off a bad shot, never bothering to look for their balls. Because why, because they wanted to drive around and laugh and drink iced tea? Did they consider what they might have done to an innocent girl, one with such an athletic career ahead of her, such promise? He was still holding his ball, clammy in his hand, and his head felt light, his knees aching.

He drove his cart back to the clubhouse and went inside Widdy's and asked for a glass of ice water. The bar was empty. He would stay for a drink. A straight shot of bourbon. The US Open played from a wide-screen TV behind the counter, these two players he'd never heard of: a twenty-year-old Serbian woman against a nineteen-year-old from Italy, and they were in the middle of the third set. The announcers went on about rankings, and at one point, the Italian's height-to-weight ratio got mentioned, because ever since Monica Seles, grunting was supposed to compensate for a lack of strength and speed—that trend in the nineties, before she was stabbed.

Murmurs of conversations behind him matched the shuffling feet of the players between hits. Becky's rasp through a tube, her threads of breath when he found her.

If conversations around him amplified, maybe he could pick up something, anything about the event, but he didn't want to hear them talking about him, if they were speculating about his back arched over the counter.

"Can you change the channel?" Murray took a large sip from his drink and kept his glass up, the coolness over his hands, then another sip.

"I'm sorry," the bartender said. He was a tall, lean man in black suspenders, drying a wineglass.

"What do you mean?" Murray asked. The cloth looked stained, specked in purple, one of the spots blooming deeper the more the bartender dried.

"Club orders," he said. "We have to play relevant sports—and it's the Open."

"What other sports outside tennis and golf? Polo, rugby?"

"I don't know," the bartender said. "We can't play football or anything, if that's what you want."

"Does it look like I do?" Murray was wearing a tracksuit, had been in the paper, was a legend here, but he was glad for this, should be glad, not to have yet been identified.

Love–fifteen. A British announcer's voice echoed through his ears, the arbitrariness of scoring. *Love* instead of *zero*, fifteen-point increments instead of one, as if such adjustments softened loss.

Nancy might not have cared for many sports, but she related to those that required a singular vision. This was what she'd understood about his running and coaching, and why he supposed she'd said she liked tennis, too, watching and playing it, despite her horrendous hand-eye coordination. She had been afforded lessons as a child, and once, he'd taken her to the courts by the field house. They had snuck in after hours and played under the lights. Most of Murray's serves had been like bullets, low and hard into the net, or else he whiffed, and this had made her laugh. He had taught himself to play at a park one summer during college, and he supposed she'd guessed this—that he'd never had lessons—but she'd barely been able to serve herself, so they had not kept score. They had only counted how many balls they could hit in a row.

He did not know if she had remarried, or if she lived alone, or how much to ask, say, or not ask or say in his reply, if he replied at all. When he couldn't sleep and did research, he kept his email open, her message running in the background. By now, he had read the message twenty-two times.

One of the players grunted too loud, and he wanted the volume turned down.

"I'm sorry," the bartender said. "Club orders." He was using the same dirty cloth to dry the counter behind him. Then he leaned back on its ledge and crossed his arms.

"It's stained," Murray said. "You could be spreading bacteria. *Listeria.*" The deli meat he'd watched Nancy abstain from, the lists she'd made from her books, all the things to avoid—the things she *had* avoided.

"What?" The bartender looked at the cloth. "It's clean," he said, and then laughed. "You need to get your eyes checked."

They were interrupted by a couple taking seats one stool over from Murray. The man looked young enough to be in college; his arm was around the woman, who seemed even younger.

Murray could smell the woman's heavy perfume; also he could detect the diamond on her ring, scintillating in the amber light. When the man opened a menu and ordered cocktails, Murray noticed his ring too. Titanium.

"Charge it to account 9117," the man said.

Murray looked up at the screen to see the Italian was winning this last set, four games to three.

"Good stuff," the husband said, gesturing to the match. He loosened his tie.

"Whaddya get us?" his wife said. "You never tell me!" She sat slouched over a black sequined handbag. Her hair was a vivid blonde that reminded him of Sarah.

"Thanks, Patrick," the husband said after the drinks were ready.

"How's the little one?" the bartender asked. "I haven't seen her in a while."

"She's good, wonderful." The wife unwedged the orange from her drink and sloppily bit into it, discarding the rind on her napkin.

"She's starting school," the husband said. "Can you believe it?" He looked at Murray as if he'd asked to be a part of their conversation.

The woman tipped her head to rest on her husband's shoulder. "Nice to have a night out," she said.

"How long has it been?" The husband looked at her. "January?"

"Nooo," she said. "Liar." She laughed. "For you maybe, but me, it's been foreverrr!" Her hands became two fists on the counter.

"What are you talking about?" he said. "I'm the one up at dawn." He looked hard at Murray and shook his head. Murray was about to say something, but the wife spoke first.

"Yurr life is so hard," she said. "So hard!" Her shoulders collapsed as she laughed. "They call it golfer's widow, right?" she said. "Isn't that what it's called?"

Murray wanted to say something again. He wasn't drunk, but had trouble holding his second bourbon steady, nearly dropping it, when the Serbian double-faulted and screamed. He wanted to cover his ears, wanted to reach across the counter for the television's power button.

But the wife and his own trembling kept distracting him. She was reaching for the burnt orange of a prescription bottle from her purse, but before she could open the lid, her husband grabbed her wrist.

"Stop that!" she giggled.

"Put it away," the husband mouthed, guiding the bottle back to her bag.

"Where do you play?" Murray asked. He looked straight at the man.

"Greenwich, Norfolk, Stanton. We live in Greenwich."

"Why are you here?" Murray asked.

"We went to Yale," the husband said. He slid the cherry off the little sword in his drink.

"Yay," the woman laughed. "Yeah," she corrected herself. She gripped the edges of her purse like it would solve her mind's disarray; if she pinched her purse hard enough, the chaos wouldn't escalate.

"What's it to you?" the husband asked. Murray was still looking at them, imagining the golfer's early habit, the lies he told himself after hearing about a young girl in the news. *It couldn't have been my ball,* that golfer must tell himself every morning he had to wake up and live with himself, look into the bathroom mirror.

"This guy's nuts," the man said to Murray's silence, his sustained stare.

"Yeah, we're alumni, or is it *alumna?*" The woman's mouth stretched.

"Alumni." The man shook his head. Nancy had done the same to Murray, any time he failed to use the term properly about his graduates. *Alumn*ae, she'd said one evening, brushing away pink flecks of pencil eraser from a document.

"Give me that." The husband took his wife's drink from her and finished it. Then he ate the orange slice off his own glass's rim.

"Do you always go early?" Murray persisted, focusing his gaze to better detect the lie, like in a show he'd watched about facial expressions, lies emerging out of the slightest twitch.

"I know you." The woman leaned in, her eyes coming into focus. "Weren't you in the paper?" She was still gripping her purse, and he couldn't understand why her husband didn't just snap it shut for her. Didn't he see all of its contents about to scatter?

"That girl, is she going to live?" Her husband braced her back after she nearly tipped from her stool. "I thought so maybe before." Her voice trailed off. "But now I really see it. The resemblance," she said. "Do you read the paper?" She looked right at him.

The husband had his phone out like he was making a call—to the hospital—because maybe those pills weren't antidepressants but for a neurological condition, a degenerative disease that affected speech.

"I looked you up," the man said. He showed Murray the screen of his smartphone. The article had his photo pinned next to Becky's, a photo of her midstride in Van Cortlandt Park. But Murray's photo was much older, this close-up of him in profile, wind blowing his light hair as he leaned in with his stopwatch, waiting for Sarah Lloyd to cross the finish line in 2000—to cross and place in the top five at cross-country Nationals.

He could not hear other noises in the restaurant, only the screams of the crowd as they'd all waited for Sarah, could not hear Patrick asking him if he needed water or help out of his chair, or if he needed someone to call a car. He was still trembling. He felt the wind on his face, the dry November air, the watch cool in his hand, the numbers locked into the screen that no one could ever take away from him: 15:45.36.

"It's *him*—" He heard the husband say this through the noise. And then, "You look so much younger." Murray thought he heard "What happened?" but then Patrick leaned across the bar and asked him if he wanted his bill.

"What's my time?" Murray asked.

"Your time?"

"I can't remember my time." He noticed the husband helping the wife down from her stool, then mouthing something to Patrick or to him, but he couldn't tell if they were still talking about the news, the pictures on the husband's phone.

The man had his hand pressed into the middle of his wife's tiny back as they exited, and Murray felt for the watch, the number at 383:13:29. He did not know how long it could run for.

TWELVE

July 2002, two years and seven months after Jean's death, Nancy woke to the hum of Richard's air-conditioning unit. He lived in a small apartment, not far from the New Haven train station. Richard had already awoken; she heard him in the bathroom. He suffered from postnasal drip at night, and a good portion of his morning routine was spent clearing his throat. He sounded like some combination of a dog barking and a cat hissing. Worse was that he didn't use a tissue to wipe any leftover phlegm from the sink.

Nancy lit a cigarette. At least running water muffled sound. But it had to compete with the air-conditioning machine, its thirsty thrum. She knew Richard would want her to open a window, even if it wasn't *energy efficient*—his favorite term for being cheap. Nancy let smoke burn her throat and circle her lungs. When she closed her eyes, she felt some tears there. For months, she'd been waking up to the same nightmare: Jean's body slipping through her fingers, face suffocated against her breasts, head caught between crib bars. She realized her right hand, the one not holding the cigarette, rested over nipples that no longer felt tender.

Richard opened the bathroom door.

"You're up," he said. Nancy nodded and blew out more smoke. Black hair covered Richard's head, and his large stomach testified to the Italian wine he drank weekly while editing student papers.

"Are you hungry?" He used the end of his towel to clean an ear. Nancy turned away from him, choosing to stare into the heavy maroon curtains Richard used to cover his windows. Then he said it: "Open the window at least."

"The air conditioner," she said. She felt her left wrist quiver and closed her eyes as Richard stopped the machine's power. She lingered over the long beep, then the way it gurgled and moaned, swallowing its last breaths. When Richard pulled back the curtains, he wiped a film of dust from the sill. She watched empty particles float into filtered sunlight.

"How about some eggs?"

"Coffee's plenty." She would not look at him.

Richard was recently hired as an assistant professor of French, and for the past nine years, he'd been trying to publish a book on poet Francis Ponge's fixation with simple objects, such as a candle or blade of grass. At the age of forty-six, it was clear: Richard had no prospect of tenure.

Nancy stepped out of bed naked. She asked Richard for an old T-shirt, since his were worn thin and soft and smelled freshly of laundry detergent. Richard was compulsive about going to the laundromat every week. He liked to work there sometimes. At the local one in East Rock. But that's not where she'd first seen him after Marjorie's party. She hadn't seen him again until over a year after Jean died, that day he'd appeared in her office in June, still wondering about the notes on Beauford Delaney, the unpublished ones from Baldwin's archive.

"How about a hike?" he asked her in the kitchen. "Or we could splurge. What about Sunday brunch at the Omni? Have you been?" He ran both hands through his hair, these dark clusters around his neck.

"Come on," said Nancy. She was slouched over a copy of the *Times* Richard had left open on the table. "Of course I have. Remember my presentation on Eliot's letters. In their ballroom. Twenty-second floor."

"She must have been desperate," said Richard.

"What?"

"George Eliot. Pretending to write a book as a man. Would you do that?"

"That's not a fair question. I don't desire to write a book."

"What about Jean—that's not a gender-specific name?"

Nancy was gripping a full cup of coffee, eyes fixed on oily black because she no longer added a dash of cream and a half tablespoon of sugar. When she lifted the mug to her lips and slammed it down again, liquid splashed the paper. "What's wrong with you?" Weakness flooded her body as she stood up. In the bedroom, she found the pair of blue jeans she'd shown up in last night. Her brown leather purse.

Richard came up behind her. He grabbed her wrist. "Darling," he said. "I'm so sorry."

"Don't call me that."

"I was just trying to help."

"Help?"

"You said you were trying to talk more openly. I thought that was what Katherine said about moving forward."

"Don't mention my therapist," she said. "Fuck you."

Richard, like a lot of people, Nancy's coworkers especially, was eager for her to get over her loss, *to get back to her old self*, as Holly had put it at the last holiday party, a glass of bourbon in her hands. As if only knowing Jean seven months made her pain less than if she'd lost a child who could walk or speak or understand, but that was the point: Nancy would never have those memories, only the constant shadow of what could have been.

Just last week, Richard had proposed she leave Murray and that they move to West Haven for a change of scenery. He thought it would give them at least *some* privacy, a break from all the rumors about the kind of wife she was, the mother she had been.

Nancy asked for some water. She had her head tucked in her arms. Richard had been boiling eggs, steam now steadily rising from the small saucepan he used for everything. She listened to the eggshells clattering against metal. She smelled toast burning.

Richard's hand was pressed between her sharp shoulder blades, caressing a little square of space. "Forget it!" He waved away the smoke. "Let me grab a shirt." He popped the toast and dropped it on a plate. "The alarm won't go off. Let's get out of here."

Neither of them had ever been to Laurel Beach in Milford, but Richard had heard good things about the clamming. Murray was in New Hampshire with the team for preseason training, so there was no chance of being seen, and Richard owned all of the necessary supplies. Richard always drove because Nancy no longer knew how to stay focused on a task. Images of Jean flooded her brain, or she'd hear the sound of her breathing, the break in breaths through the monitor, sounds she should have heard.

~

Richard drove a 1984 Subaru hatchback. Today he'd cranked the windows down. Even on rainy days, Nancy wore sunglasses to hide her tears, but today, a sunny day when she needed them, she'd forgotten them at home. She tried to use her hand as a visor, but her shoulders felt heavy, her neck strained. On a shadier strip of road, she let her hand fall. She noticed red specks of nail polish. She did not remember painting her nails, or even going to a salon, letting the polish fade away. When Richard told her to stop scratching, she did not realize this either. She clamped her fists and looked out the window. They were approaching water already, sunlit and sparkling, and she worked to see that in the landscape, the realness of it, the beauty and order of nature.

The laws in Connecticut had required an autopsy after they'd received official word at the hospital. Detectives had taken pictures of the setup of Jean's room. Nancy had lain in their bedroom during the investigation. Murray was somewhere in the house answering questions—while she had heaved in the bedroom; she had felt herself bleeding, the phantom sensation of knives kicking her ribs.

"I packed sandwiches," Richard said.

"How many times do I have to say I'm not hungry?"

"Everyone has to eat."

"I'm not hungry," she said again, this same quiet resignation in her voice he'd learned not to disrupt any further.

In the parking area, Richard squeezed between two cars. The process was long, as he backed in and out, sputtering gravel.

They followed a woodsy path to the beach. Nancy paused to roll up her jeans. Lately she was never in sync with the weather, often dressing for autumn in July. She carried the cooler, while Richard balanced empty buckets and clam rakes. She watched him struggle around rocks. He wondered openly about poison ivy and snakes.

But Nancy was more concerned about her spider veins. One on her right side, started during pregnancy, had spread vehemently up her calf and into the adjoining crease of knee.

"What do you think? Should we cool off first?" Richard had already removed his T-shirt. His belly sagged over red swimming trunks.

"It's so calm," Nancy said, after fixing her eyes on the seaweed color of the water.

"Which means yes or no?" His hand brushed her back, then moved to the edge of her earlobe. He kissed there. "I'm very sorry," he said, aware of the anger she had held on to since breakfast.

Unlike Murray, who'd always avoided conflict like the plague, made himself blind to her feelings. And then when she couldn't contain those feelings anymore—by the time they exploded—*she was crazy*, or his favorite term: *overreacting*.

145

A seagull squawked as it lowered toward the water, circling for fish.

Nancy stopped and opened the cooler for an ice cube, then let it rest on her tongue. After Jean, there had been days of subsisting on ice. Now she used ice for the pure chill of it, as proof of her ability to feel—sliding an ice cube along her inner wrist while reading or in front of the television at night. She held the ice by the blue vein of her wrist, the one that beat with her pulse, and closed her eyes.

When she opened them, she saw Richard holding the crusts of his peanut butter sandwich. Like a child, he never ate that part. He dropped the crusts on the beach.

"You'll attract a swarm," she said. Above she saw more of them circling, like they'd been waiting behind the clouds all along.

But Richard didn't care about their screeches. He left the crusts and picked up the buckets and rakes and moved on, as if this was how the world worked. One left one's ugliness behind and never thought about it again.

Murray was that way too; the day after they came home from the hospital, he'd disassembled Jean's crib and changing table. Scraped off with a cake knife the daisy border they'd added to her room and emptied the dishwasher of bottles and pacifiers. Jean's ashen lips whitewashed from his brain, that last moment they'd held her at the hospital, behind the curtain of the grieving room.

She had screamed at him—*FUCK YOU*—screaming to no one when she saw the room emptied before she'd had a chance to say goodbye to Jean's things. She had cried there on the floor alone, while Murray was at work—at a meet somewhere, forgetting her—she had cried over all the boxes he'd packed up without her, one day while she'd been in the bedroom, a day she'd slept through, the days into weeks, only to find Jean's vacant, borderless room. She'd wept on the floor, crying into the phone, until the neighbors came, Walt and Lauren Peters, to help her regain herself, because she had not known if she would—if she hadn't called someone, the only two people near enough—she might have died there in that room.

~

She and Richard were nearing the water's edge now, each wave threatening to spread, in shallow undulations, over their footprints.

Katherine claimed she'd entered the third stage of grief, known as *bargaining: I hear you saying a lot of if-onlys and what-ifs. That's normal . . . The important thing is that you feel less angry.*

Katherine said recovery was not possible. She would not heal; she'd only adapt, learn to live with her loss.

When Nancy did simple things, like open a jar of mustard or type a short note at her desk, lift one foot after the other into the shower, her wrists and ankles ached. When she took showers, she often shut her eyes and wept. Before she went to bed each night, she tried reading into oblivion—romance and fantasy fiction—whatever it took for other images to fill her brain. Sometimes she drank wine with sleeping pills. And then, upon waking, she'd consider how many days she could pass in bed without losing her job or Richard. How many days without food or water. She was staring at Richard, who'd already reached a sandbar, where there was only one other person, a frail elderly man, digging.

"Aren't you going to help me?" Richard called. He held the two buckets, his shorts rolled up and squeezing his meaty thighs.

Nancy sighed. She did not answer him, just kept her hand where it was, shielding her face. She felt a trickle of sweat along her forehead.

Richard made it back to shore with a clam that was far too small, one he'd have to toss back. He rubbed his thumb over its thick gray shell and handed it to her.

"I'm going to get the ingredients for a bake," Richard said.

The day they'd met again, Richard had knocked on her office door boldly. She had stopped wearing makeup, papers everywhere on her desk, but he hadn't said anything. He'd just waited as she wrote down the box number, 7, and then the folder, 280; he'd commented on the neatness of her script over a Post-it.

"We should try again," Richard said, still gripping his bucket.

Katherine said the stages of grief didn't follow a particular order. Some days might seem like she'd reverted to an earlier stage. Katherine claimed grief wasn't linear, that it worked in circles she wanted Nancy to imagine around her, shrouded in a soft blue light.

Richard was wading out again. These long, heroic strides, though he wasn't the least bit athletic. Sometimes she thought she liked this about him best—that he didn't suggest she exercise, like Murray had, like it would have changed the outcome.

~

It took time to reach Richard at the sandbar. Her pants felt heavy, but she felt she should try to sift through the weight, the resistance of the water.

According to Katherine, there was chronological time and "Kairos" time—the years it would take for trauma to integrate itself into her body—so she could stop seeing time in terms of what could have been, but time as it was. In time, Katherine claimed, she'd learn to accept her understanding of the world, her relationships to others, her ability to relate to others, as irrevocably changed.

One hour later, Richard dug his second clam. Nancy observed—she was closer to him now, yet he still felt far away, like she was observing him and herself at the same time. Somewhere, outside them, she watched his excitement, and his disappointment, in discovering another undersized clam, and then she watched herself, too, trying to laugh as Richard cursed the sizing ring. She felt guilty about this forced laughter, but if she made it a habit, she thought maybe she could relearn the feeling, rediscover it as spontaneous and pure.

At least Richard always promised her a physical presence, that comfort, she thought.

She thought of how he'd called her—after he'd stopped by her office that first time in June—he'd called to make sure everything was alright. She'd said she was fine, but he'd continued to check on her, bringing her coffee. In time, she opened up to him; she told him about Jean, and he had held her in a way Murray was unable to. Richard showed her she could still feel in her body the sensations she'd assumed had fallen dead, numb.

When Richard returned, he asked if she thought anyone would inspect them. He handed her another tiny clam.

"How should I know?" she said. "Just leave it."

"Come on," he said.

"It is too hot for me," she said. "I'll meet you back by the car whenever you're ready."

"I see how it is," he said. He used the top of his hand to wipe his forehead. How easily he sweat—and so much of it—even in bed, she always woke to his sweat, the heavy smell of it, as if he were the one having nightmares, but he claimed it was genetic. He said that in fact he slept like a baby, that he never remembered his dreams.

~

Nancy followed a small boarded path after she passed the parking lot. The boards kept her bare feet from burning. It took her about twenty minutes to notice the first beach umbrella, green-and-yellow striped. She took stock of a few obsessive sunbathers, too, brown and oiled up over towels and lounge chairs.

Nancy was never sure how she felt about sex with Richard, whether it was love—but the act of lovemaking filled her somehow. Somehow it shadowed the emptiness and let her detach. When they were first together, he'd let her cry as long as she needed to. Murray was always at work, or on the road, running.

She'd wanted him to come with her to therapy, had wanted to believe they could touch each other again, without the image of Jean— her rigid body, her bluing lips—inside their own bodies; any touch, even the slightest brush of their hands, felt as selfish as taking a full breath or bite of food, or finding easy sleep. The things everyone else seemed to do so easily—so uninterrupted and unfazed—and she loathed the world for that, all the people who took their children for granted, who'd neglected to love their children enough, as she felt her own parents had, because they assumed they'd leave this earth before she did.

~

Nancy kept an extra set of sheets and towels hidden among sweaters at home. She washed Richard's dusty, slept-in scent away as often as possible. She supposed it reminded her of the nightmare she wanted and didn't want to forget. It would always be easier sleeping with a man who'd never fully understand her grief than one who should have been able to.

~

It had been the last day of December, Jean's funeral. Not so cold they'd needed thick gloves, but there'd been a light rain, too, and Nancy had not been able to separate the constant thrum of her body heaving from her own shivering.

Murray had helped the pallbearers lower Jean's tiny casket into the earth. Not once had he looked over at her weeping. The dull-colored grass, the gray sky, collapsing in and out of itself, so that Nancy did not know what was up, what was down, and she'd wanted to hurl herself into the hole with her child, had watched herself screaming for Murray to push her in, into the nightmare of that disembodied silence, that cold.

Marjorie had come, along with a few other coaches, and a few of Murray's girls—a fact that enraged her, too, this visible evidence that he'd been able to resume his training with the team afterward—that he didn't love her or their child enough to suffer the way she did now.

The week after the funeral, Murray had resumed his schedule. He'd wake at 4:00 or 5:00 to run, sometimes earlier, depending on how early he was meeting Sarah; he'd shower while Nancy was still in bed, and then there'd be the steady sounds of him pouring coffee and spooning cereal, the clink of metal against ceramic, hammering at Nancy's eardrums. He went on with his rhythms while she was too weak to rise from bed or steady one foot before the other and reach the bathroom, unable to separate the difference between the hot and cold shower knobs.

At Jean's funeral, she had wanted just one person to look at her and understand, eyes to say: *You're alive, breathing. You're going to live.* It had taken Nancy everything to turn her head toward Marjorie, waiting for her to meet her eyes, but when she did, there'd only been distance, this insurmountable absence. Marjorie wouldn't console her, no one would, and it was then that Nancy knew how utterly alone she was, and would always be, in the depth of her loss, the hollowness of her rib cage, her aching limbs.

~

She was nearing a public area. Sounds like the faint echo of radio music, the squeal of children. Nancy often heard Jean crying, calling to her. Those rare nights she was able to sleep, she often awoke to the sound of it. Jean crying to be fed.

Now, close to the water, she let her feet stick into the wet sand. She watched as a child flopped over on his belly, waiting for a wave's salty rush. She did not see the child's parents anywhere. There was no lifeguard.

"Be careful," Nancy said, nearly reaching for his arm. She felt a sudden rage, not for the child, but for the mother: her neglect. A mother didn't understand how precious time was until it was gone.

"Simon! Simon!"

The mother helped her little boy up, then out of the water. A Mediterranean tan bathed her body: taut calves, thighs, and hips. A sheer cover danced over her one-piece. She had red oval-shaped sunglasses.

Nancy tried smiling casually, pretending she'd never said anything to the boy, who was whining as his mother dragged him toward their umbrella. There were so many children here, and Jean stood there, vividly in each of them. Her blue eyes and happy smile up close, her grasping hands.

All Nancy had was emptiness, this cistern of emptiness pulling her in. She seized her knees, then the sand as it continued to slip through her fingers. Her chest felt crushed in and the heaves wouldn't quiet and she did not know how to make space for her breath—like the ocean before the moon finally lets go.

THIRTEEN

Saturday
7:08:45 a.m.

Every year in early September, Murray took his girls for the infamous tri-team meet against Harvard and Princeton, and this time Harvard was hosting at Franklin Park in Boston. It was one of the rare occasions Yale men and women ran simultaneously, and though Murray and the men's coach, Ross Kennedy, had never really been close friends, Ross had expressed his support these past weeks and his own concerns about training on the golf course.

"How's it going?" Ross was using his team's cooler to refill a dented Poland Spring bottle. He gulped the water, saving just a few sips, never rescrewing the cap.

"Fine," said Murray. "Yourself?"

"Good," he said, taking another gulp. "Hey, did you get my messages? Burger night Sunday?"

Murray had gotten them, was about to say he hadn't had a free moment to answer, but they were interrupted by one of Ross's athletes, Joe Valdez. Joe had rushed into the tent and dropped down for push-ups, blowing out air forcefully each time he lowered his chest. He was a 1500-meter runner whose best was just short of Murray's at his age. He ran cross-country just to stay in shape for spring.

"Joe, you'll tire yourself out," Ross said. *"Joe!"*

When Joe kept going, Ross crouched down next to him and pulled out an earbud. "Joe, get up!"

Murray flinched. His own heart had accelerated, but sometimes that happened when the seasons changed. Made his joints ache more too. He thought of his girls already ten minutes into their warm-up, the crisp breeze, crisper in their lungs.

Franklin Park's course started in an open field before it led into a series of trails. Not nearly as hilly as Van Cortlandt, but there'd be a steep incline around mile two.

"Coach."

Murray looked up from his pad, where he'd been tinkering with Anna's target splits. It was the Harvard coach, Jeff Evans. Jeff wore his same crimson cap, the *H* sallow at its center. The same piece of gum by his lower jaw he talked around. "I've been trying to keep up with the latest, but you know—"

"It's fine." Murray had a sheet with seed times folded in his pocket. He pretended to read it as if he hadn't thirty times already.

"I wanted to tell you, Lily and I—Becky's in our thoughts." Lily Walker was Jeff's assistant. Just a few years out of college, she was still racing professionally. Other coaches speculated Jeff had been cheating with her for years. He had three kids.

Ross came up and slapped Jeff's shoulder with his crushed water bottle.

Murray looked back down at the sheet with Anna's official seed time: 17:45, just a few seconds behind Georgia Manning, Jeff's number two.

When he looked up, Jeff stood poised before him, arms crossed, gum suddenly wedged between his front teeth.

"All I can say is feel lucky for the clear skies. God bless." He brought his fingers to his mouth and kissed them. His gum snapped.

Jeff's number one was Amy Fossie, Becky's closest rival last year. Amy was warming up on the field when Jeff interrupted her to talk, gesturing with his stopwatch. Amy nodded as Jeff leaned in. Jeff gripped her narrow shoulders. It was all about pacing, who to look out for along the way, always saving just enough for the last hundred yards.

Murray looked around for Princeton's Jana Carlsson, but he didn't see her anywhere. She'd only been coaching for two, maybe three, years, but she boasted some insane Danish method. Had three young children too. One of them, her nine-year-old daughter (Murray couldn't remember her name), had already run a 5K in Lawrenceville under twenty minutes.

A gun went off. Murray jerked his head around to look. Someone shouted, "False alarm!"

"Jesus, you would think they've done this before." Ross was in a squat, stretching inner thighs. "One of these days someone is going to get hurt."

Wind shuddered the top of their tent. Murray only had seventeen minutes to collect the girls before the start. Anna was just coming out of the woods, leading the team. She jogged beside Tanya. They seemed to be going a little too quickly for a warm-up, and when they got to him, they didn't disperse like usual for that last drink of water, porta-potty runs, more spikes in need of tightening. Anna and Tanya stood talking. At one point, they looked over at him.

He pretended not to see by glancing at his pad again. Pages fluttered. All the way back to the beginning, where Becky's numbers were. It would be three weeks ago Monday. He flipped the page and started fresh, furiously drawing out rows, filling in names.

When he glanced back, the girls were still talking.

"Drills!" he shouted.

Anna tilted her head up, mouth fixed in a cold smile. Murray had learned this lesson many times throughout his marriage: people pleasers were slow to boil, but when they did, there was no quelling them. The rage.

"Who?" Anna's face was close to him now. When had she run up? "You were talking to yourself but looking at me," she said. Her eyes glistened as she clasped her hands from behind and stretched back. "And you said 'them.'"

"Them?"

"Yes," she laughed. Her teeth, perhaps they weren't as crooked as Nancy's, just mildly overlapped.

The wind had calmed to a breeze, blowing a few stray pieces of hair around her face.

"What are you doing?" he said. "Five minutes until the start."

Last night after the team dinner, he'd told Anna to keep her distance from Rodney. She was a waste of her time, a bad influence, and she wouldn't be on the team much longer anyway; she was on academic probation. They'd been by the vending machines in the athletic lounge. She'd gotten a bag of pretzels, crunching and sucking the salt from each piece. When he'd told her the bit about Rodney's grades, she'd looked up at him sternly. Her eyes had narrowed, and she'd asked to be excused. But he hadn't excused her officially. She'd just gotten up and kicked in her chair.

Maybe she was hormonal, he thought, had broken up with her boyfriend, if she had one? Either way, he reminded himself, anger could be good—the best runners found a little before stepping onto the line. They found it in the middle of a race, too, like Murray had always used suppressed rage, every ounce he could muster, to pass man after man on the track.

Ross offered to drive them in his Jeep to mile one. Murray said he'd forgotten his stopwatch in his car, that he'd have to meet him there.

"You mean the one in your hand?"

"Oh—" In the distance, a gunman was giving instructions. Ross leaned in, his own watch poised.

Murray cleared his time to zero. "It's a monitor so we can hear her at night."

"What?" Ross squinted. "What the hell are you talking about?"

"A watch. I meant."

"Anna looks good." Ross nodded. "She's built some muscle."

"I hadn't noticed," Murray said, but it was hard not to look: her parting calves.

On the way to Ross's Jeep, another gust of wind blew some dirt into Murray's eye. He swore and asked if Ross would hold the door for him; he shuffled all his papers together. Then they got stuck behind a line of cars on the road. More coaches, a few obsessive parents. A black Subaru pulled up next to them and started its blinker.

"Look at this jackass," Ross said. The car nudged closer, threatening an accident if they didn't let him in.

Ross clenched his fist and pounded the steering wheel. "Fucking move!"

He was going to miss Anna at mile one. The car in front inched forward, but rather than close the gap, Ross pulled out and drove off the side of the road.

"What are you doing?"

Ross put the car in park and kicked his door open, balancing the multiple stopwatches on his lap, his own pad and clipboard.

"Run!"

Murray manually unlocked the passenger side to get out. He braced himself, hips too stiff for the slowest jog, but he remembered the short-cut to mile two, deep in the woods. Knees ached for oxygenated blood; birds and squirrels twitched more nimbly among trees. Dry foliage, the start of it hard and thick below his beaten shoes.

Eventually he saw Jana leaning in with her watch. Then someone . . . Jeff calling to Amy, "Get ready!" Where was Ross?

Murray heard the rattle of a large plastic hand. A chorus of finger whistles, the distant chanting of names.

Jana began calling out to her number one, Rita Santiago, leading the pack. Anna less than ten feet behind her.

"Get up there, get up there!" Murray shouted through cupped hands. One quick sprint and she'd close the gap—but then maybe she should wait, save her energy until the last—"Go now!" he said. "Compete!"

Behind him, a spectator yelled "Dig deep!" Words that meant nothing outside a coach.

The course was a loop, the finish line not far from where he stood. Wind pushed more debris around. A man on a bicycle passed him. Some idiot who hadn't read the writing on the wall.

"This is a meet!" Murray shouted. "Get off the path!" No one else seemed to care or notice.

Once, shortly after they married, he'd taken Nancy for a bike ride, but hadn't had the patience to stay with her; he'd been fixated on his ideal cardio zone. One hundred and eighty beats per minute.

Then, through yellow goggles, the man looked at him. A balloon, cream colored and dirty, hung from his baseball cap like a tassel. Slowly he pedaled away. Gravel crunched.

"Who is this guy?" Murray pointed his stopwatch at him. He elbowed Jana.

"What guy?" she asked. Her eyes must have been so fixed on her next runner that she couldn't have noticed, but when he looked around at others, other bystanders even, no one affirmed what he'd seen. He'd have to file a report later. Only another forty seconds until Anna came through. Maybe less than that, if she was beating his projected time.

By the finish, a large clock with red numbers bled forward. Jeff's Amy Fossie crossed in 17:12. Three seconds later: Jana's Rita Santiago.

More coaches and spectators cheered, but Anna was nowhere. He counted four, then eight more seconds, eyes set on the lip of the woods. Only weaker runners emerged, among them Tanya, Victoria, Emily, Ginny; he clocked them all. When he heard his name, he had to squint into the sun.

"Anna's down. Happened sometime after mile two." It was Jeff, cupping the bill of his hat. "I have to stay by the finish. But the trainers know."

"What?"

"Must have tripped over a rock or something. A root. Nothing ice can't take care of, right?" Jeff repositioned his cap loosely.

Fifteen minutes later, a half mile from the finish, he saw the bright red jacket, the white cross of a medical aide.

Anna sat upright, gripping the ground. He said her name, and she cried, head wincing in the opposite direction of her ankle. A knot the size of an egg. The trainer was an older woman, her hair chopped short. "I don't think she broke anything. But I would get an X-ray."

Murray watched white tape crisscross over joints and bones.

"I don't know how it happened." Anna gripped his arm. "I didn't see a rock or anything." Several strips of tape were added along her shin, the last piece cut with the trainer's teeth.

"That should do it," the woman said. "Lots of ice. Fifteen minutes on, fifteen off. Keep that up every couple of hours. Take it easy."

By the finish, the big clock said 40:55.19. There'd been one in the ICU, in waiting rooms as staff updated records. He'd done the math: Becky had been unconscious for 456 hours, ten minutes, and seconds he could not measure.

~

In the car, Murray made Anna keep her leg propped, elevated above her heart to reduce swelling faster. The car stunk of sweat and muscle cream. It was normal for him to drive his athletes when their injuries were minor. It was faster—more efficient—any coach in his shoes would do the same.

"Sure nobody pushed you?" he asked.

"Honestly," she said, "my ankle has been feeling sore for the past few weeks."

"Why didn't you say anything?"

"I don't know. Started bothering me after a long run." Anna's head was turned from him. She was focused on the window. It had started to rain.

In the car, Nancy used to sit with her arms draped limply over her lap, wrists curled. He still had not replied to her email. Tonight, maybe, depending on how things looked.

"You better get an MRI," he said. "You could have fractured it." They'd been driving for seventy-four minutes. In just another hour and fifteen, they could be in New Haven, if he hurried to make up for any unexpected traffic delays: Murray increased his speed by seven miles per hour.

At the peak of her senior year cross-country season, Sarah Lloyd had suffered two hairline fractures. One along each femur. The films had shown calcium deposits, two halos of white.

"You have to keep your hand on the bag. It'll slide."

"It's already leaking."

At a stoplight, Anna removed the sweatshirt she was wearing and wrapped it around the soggy ice. Goose bumps on her forearms.

They were just one mile before the exit, so he accelerated, but after a few minutes, he heard sirens.

"Awesome," Anna said.

He pulled over, then dug around for his wallet. He rolled down a window for the officer.

"Are you aware you were going fifteen over the limit?" The sound of rain on his cap, droplets lining the brim.

"We were on our way to the hospital," Murray said. "She fell." But when he turned to Anna, she was sorting through some papers that had fallen out of the glove compartment: a mixture of maps, legal pad sheets, some photos.

"You're in pain?" The officer squinted.

Anna didn't answer, so Murray did. "She turned her ankle," he said. Anna shrugged her shoulders, still refusing to acknowledge him.

The officer just continued scribbling over his pad. He took Murray's information, told them to wait.

"Keep it propped," he said.

"I didn't know you were married." Anna held up a wrinkled photo he didn't remember saving. "She's really lovely." Anna looked up at him.

"Put that back," he said. "Now."

When the officer returned with the ticket, he reminded Murray to read the fine print about paying the ticket. If he wanted to dispute it, here was the date.

Murray and Anna didn't speak the rest of the drive. Before stopping at the hospital, he parked the car by her dorm, in Silliman, and offered to help her to her room so she could change into dry clothes first.

"No," she said, face contorted, as though he'd offended her. "I'm fine alone." But as he unlocked the car door, his cell phone rang.

Anna was watching him, her hand on the door. When he hung up, he told her the news. "Becky's awake," he said.

"What?" Anna's eyes widened. He felt his own face, light, his toes numb. "Can we see her?" Her bag was really dripping.

"Not now. You need the MRI. X-rays at least." He thought of the pictures Nancy had printed and posted on their refrigerator. Every ultrasound, all of them filed neatly in her desk drawer. Nancy thought she saw her nose and his chin in one of the images, tracing the tiny outlines, and then she had kissed him, had said they were right on track.

Anna turned to face the window again. "We will already be at the hospital. I don't understand why we can't just see her."

"Lisa said she isn't ready yet. In a few days. I'm sure she'll be even better then." He felt his voice trail off.

"Of what?" she asked.

He turned for a moment, looking confused, then back at the parking lot.

"You said this was just the beginning," Anna said. "You were muttering something about her recovery."

He hadn't, he thought. He wasn't one to make those assumptions, not without facts, proof. His lips were quivering. They were hard to feel.

Suddenly Anna moved to open the door, then turned to look right at him and said, "You think because she's Becky, it won't be hard for her?"

"I didn't—"

"You think she's just going to get back to her life?" She'd started crying. "We don't even know how bad it is. What if she can't speak? Write her name?"

"That's enough," Murray said, feeling his father's voice rise in him, his father averting his gaze.

"What if she has to spend the rest of her life in a wheelchair?"

"I said that's enough!"

"I've seen her break," she said.

"What?" He tried to block him out again, his father slamming the door, his father leaving while his mother had cried about the broken glass, the beads of milk he'd helped her clean.

"I've seen her stooped over off the trail before a race, vomiting." Anna had become hysterical. "I always meet her at the end too. Did you know that? She always asks me to meet her. But she told me not to tell anyone. Made me swear."

A fighter risked everything. Murray had not needed his father to tell him that: his own college coach had. Murray had raced with the flu before, shingles. He'd thrown up dozens of times, more than that, had been there when his teammates did too.

Anna turned away, small, clear beads still steady along the window. "You're obsessed with her," she said. "We all know it. We—"

He reached for her arm, but she was already outside in the pouring rain. She sank into a puddle. He heard the water splash, heard her whimper.

"Be careful." He'd restrained himself from shouting.

She wobbled over to the curb and fell. She barely regained herself. Mud had splattered her white-and-blue jacket. He set the car in park, got out; he tried to steady her, but she kept saying she wanted to be left alone. She called him insane, her wet hair plastered scarlet, eyes blinking through the water. Even raised her arm to push him away like Nancy had done when she'd wanted him to feel. She'd been in her bathrobe that day, too, *the anniversary of,* he couldn't finish the thought, only Nancy's words consumed that space: *Feel something!* she'd practically screamed.

Now Murray had fallen and scraped his hands. He called to her, "Anna," urging her back. But it was too late. She'd closed the door to Silliman.

Anna had left her bag in the car, the melted ice an expanding splotch on the seat. There'd been the ice chips Murray brought Nancy in the delivery room—and later, the ice packs she'd pressed to her chest, leaning over the hot bath water, suspending her breasts over it, the absence of his hand on her back, steadying her.

The door to Silliman was locked, he repeated in his mind. *Key card only.*

FOURTEEN

One Friday in October when Nancy was living with Richard—already four years of being together—she'd made plans to surprise him that night with an early birthday dinner for his fiftieth. She was standing in Shaw's Supermarket, examining the shapes of sweet potatoes. She ran her fingers over their divots, the coarse sprouts that marked eyes.

Then she felt a tap on her shoulder. It took time to register the woman dressed in blue jeans and a peach sweater. Her hair was blonder than she remembered, and she had the same sinewy limbs.

"Hi, Sarah," Nancy said, putting the potatoes back. Sarah must have been twenty-three, maybe twenty-four. Her cart held a car seat with a child inside. Sarah was still so young.

"This is Taylor," Sarah said.

A soft sheen covered the baby's head, just as Sarah must have looked as a child. Nancy had kept hoping Jean's hair might show some ginger, or even turn a deeper red, but she'd maintained Murray's blonde until the end. It still devastated Nancy to never know how Jean might have looked or acted at one year.

"You know, I saw you," Sarah said. "And I thought, What are the odds? We actually live in Greenwich now but decided to visit a friend today. Didn't we?" Sarah smiled and stroked the baby's ear. Nancy wasn't sure whether Taylor was a boy or girl, and she didn't ask. She guessed thirteen, maybe fourteen months, old enough to walk—the baby had sneakers on. Nancy's lips trembled. She sucked in her cheeks to make saliva.

"My friend just started her second year at the law school." Sarah was looking at the fresh fruit and vegetables crowding the car seat in the middle of the cart. The baby kicked its legs. "She's been on a peanut butter diet. I'm restocking the essentials."

The cart didn't seem safe. A jar of food, something even heavier, might topple on her child.

"I'm sure your friend appreciates it," Nancy said, cringing at the forced sound of her voice. She tried to distract herself by thinking of what she still needed for Richard's birthday, but there was the silence to fill. "You look great," she managed. "And congratulations."

"Thank you." Sarah's skin was more lustrous than Nancy remembered it. She'd left Murray when Sarah was a junior. Just after that, she'd seen a photograph of Sarah in the paper during the fall cross-country season. In the photo, Sarah's tight ponytail accented her hollow cheeks, her small, tight eyes—the article had been printed before Sarah's cycle of injuries began her senior year, the multiple stress fractures Nancy had heard about from someone in her office who followed sports—Sarah unable to continue running after college like she knew Murray had been planning for.

"What else have you been up to?" Nancy asked, trying to sound curious. "Are you working?" She felt her eyes twitch as she looked down at her cart, finding it empty; she hadn't even chosen the potatoes yet.

"I'm really . . . lucky." Sarah hesitated. "My husband Paul and I agreed that it makes most sense for me to stay at home."

The last time Nancy had seen Sarah in person was at an awards banquet, eleven months after Jean; she thought of how Sarah had sat warming her hands by a glass candle at the center of the table, her shoulders hunched as Murray lauded her times, their successes, before everyone, and Nancy had wanted to run out, make a scene right there, show everyone how incapable her husband was of grieving.

"How are you?" Sarah asked, though she seemed distracted, her eyes focused on something else, someone else maybe, in the store.

"I'm still at the library." Nancy felt herself rub the empty space where her ring had been. "Murray and I—"

"Oh," Sarah said. "I didn't realize." Sarah's voice almost sounded cold, but Nancy wondered if she was reading into things, projecting that onto her.

Nancy changed the topic, because most people waited for that, for the conversation to circle back to the present, to what was positive and life-affirming. "Taylor is *beautiful*," she said, but uttering those words made Nancy's throat tighten. She thought of tummy time, Jean straining to lift up her head, smiling. She and Murray had started at five minutes, when Jean was still a newborn, then worked their way to thirty, forty-five, gradually reaching two hours by Jean's seventh month—she and Murray had been so proud, so elated the first time Jean sat up, held her head up, entirely on her own.

～

Sarah had said something else, something about the park or what else she'd planned to do with her friend over the weekend, but all Nancy could focus on were Taylor's shoes, the mini Converses the baby wore.

Jean would have just started first grade this year, old enough to run down the aisles, picking out her favorite cereal. Nancy tried to breathe, to fill her lungs with air.

"I haven't spoken to Murray. Not for a while," Sarah said suddenly, tugging Taylor's shoe. And Taylor smiled, kicking two little feet. "But I guess send my hello."

"No, I don't—" Nancy felt herself snap. "I don't talk to him."

"Right," Sarah said. She looked at her watch. "I better get back," she said. "My friend will be home soon. It was nice running into you." Nancy nodded. "Yes," she said. "Take care."

She could not risk seeing this woman again at checkout, so she went to the express lane after she'd gathered a bare minimum of items.

Was it Nancy, or had Sarah been acting strangely? As she unloaded her cart, she decided she was reading into things again, always looking for something wrong, something *off*. Because she was uncomfortable making daily conversation, all the inane things she said to make others feel comfortable, safe from the words of what she'd lost; she allowed them that delusion, that forgetting.

Just outside, as she was returning her cart, holding back tears, she noticed a barrel full of pumpkins and gourds. Nancy unconsciously walked toward them. She reached in and ran her fingers over the bumps of a gourd, one lichen green and white speckled. Then she lifted a tiny pumpkin, one she could set on the table in the foyer, or the dining room table, but both were crowded with mail she hadn't answered, bills she hadn't totaled. She put them back and reached for a larger pumpkin and held it to her chest. She felt her heart, first dim, then heavy, throbbing.

After Jean, Nancy's breasts had become too full to sustain. For months, she'd had to pump them to relieve tiny amounts of pressure. Just enough so that gradually they'd stop producing milk. She'd hid leakages with extra-large cardigans, clutching them tight in her cold, overly air-conditioned office. She'd wept nearly every day in the bathroom, over aching muscles and joints, this image of Jean pressed close, her suckling sounds, fist balled around her pinky. She'd suppressed cries each time someone entered the next stall. Lingering over the sound of the latch securing itself, she had waited for the rumble of toilet paper from its roll, the kind one inevitably had to keep tugging at, because the paper, too thin, always tore easily. There was never enough.

Now, moisture clung to the air, and farther down the parking lot, she watched an attendant return an empty cart.

She listened to its wheels roll, its empty clamoring.

~

Later, and already two hours behind schedule, Nancy peeled potatoes, and when Richard walked in from work, she said nothing of the encounter. She let him go on about the essay he'd finished and his plans for submission. Words dampened by the rapid clinking of her peeler. He continued over running water, after she'd turned the knob to full blast to rinse her hands.

"What do you think?" he asked.

"Plan sounds good," she said.

"I almost forgot," he said, looping arms around her belly. "Strawberries for dessert."

"You went to the grocery store too?"

"No, passed a stand on my way home from work."

"They can't be local."

"They were cheap," he said. He was growing a beard again, after she'd finally convinced him to shave it.

"I guess I can't argue with fruit." Nancy smiled dimly at Richard now that he'd squeezed in beside her, kissing her neck. As he rinsed strawberries, she wondered, as she sometimes did, on bad days—like this one—about questionable bacteria, slips during her pregnancy. A picnic on the campus green with Murray one Sunday in May. He'd bought a container of nonorganic grapes. Had hand-fed them to her, unwashed.

Nancy still made lists in her head of all the times they could have been more careful—Murray especially. He was a coach; wasn't he supposed to plan ahead? Prevent injuries?

Painting the nursery. She thought of how she hadn't worn a face mask that afternoon. She'd stayed away from the toxins, but still, Murray could have thought of that—the mask she could have worn for those hours—and keeping the door closed; had it been closed as they waited between coats, or had they kept the door open to ventilate, to speed up the process?

~

Nancy's hands shook as she filled a pot with water to boil the potatoes. The chicken, she reminded herself, had another ten minutes in the oven.

"This weekend I thought we should go to the movies," Richard said. "I'm not working Saturday night." He smiled, waiting for her to acknowledge his birthday tomorrow. But she couldn't, not yet—the dinner, the effort she was putting in—she hoped it was clear.

"Anything you want to see?" he persisted.

Richard was across from her now, gripping the edges of their small kitchen table spread with today's newspaper. Sarah's cart had contained at least ten jars of pureed apricot, she remembered, and several others: peas, applesauce.

Nancy told Richard she wanted to see the sports section. When he didn't hear her, she leaned over him, flipping pages to find it.

"Where is it?"

"Relax," he said, cupping her clenched hand. "It's probably on my desk. I'll get it for you—"

"It's okay," she said, counting silently to ten. Katherine's formula for controlling her reactions, for letting air into the panic room.

She began wiping the sink of potato skins stuck to its edges and reorganized the condiments in the refrigerator, which Richard was always messing up from his addiction to whipped cream, spraying it directly into his mouth in the middle of the night; sometimes the sound woke her up, and her heart quickened, wondering if the dishwasher had started on its own—but *no*, she'd realize, he wasn't beside her in bed or in the bathroom. He was flooding his mouth with sugar.

When they'd first started seeing each other, she'd liked this about Richard best, his readiness to indulge in pleasures Murray wouldn't. Richard used to take her out for ice cream often, and when they'd gone to New London that day, she'd thought they'd driven out far enough not to be seen. Somehow she had forgotten Murray's habit of taking his top runners to the trails around Connecticut College for summer training. And now that would be Murray's last memory of her, this image of her casually eating ice cream with a French professor, as if she'd ceased to grieve. He had no way of knowing it was the oppositeness that Richard had always represented for her that let her compartmentalize, let her escape temporarily.

She couldn't admit that to him—not after he told her what he'd seen when she got home. *You were in the car with Sarah, weren't you?* She'd yelled it through the kitchen, refusing to answer his questions, calm and still as he always was, a fact that had enraged her more. She had run out the front door and walked the whole way to town, waiting for Richard at the diner to pick her up there. She and Murray never spoke of it again, not as she packed up her things the next week and clung to her side of the story—*Murray had started his affair first*—all through the months that led to a settlement.

Sarah would have seen it, too, she thought, her August ice cream cone, and that was why Sarah had acted so strangely in the grocery store. Sarah had seen the end of everything.

The water had begun to boil, so Nancy lowered the temperature and added the potatoes. She breathed steam, her favorite part about cooking, the only part that relaxed her.

"So what movie?" His finger poised over a listing for the one he wanted to see, his asking a mere formality. The kind he liked were always Sundance or Cannes finalists at the Criterion Theater on Temple Street.

They never used to plan weekends in advance. It used to be about surprise, secrets. If Murray asked who was on the phone, she'd say it was a coworker about a project.

"How about this one? A documentary on the Occupation. You never mind subtitles."

"Sounds fine." Nancy chose to speak softly. She slipped on a red oven mitt, half of it scorched from a small kitchen fire in college.

It was Richard's birthday tomorrow. Couldn't she just indulge him that? She could have at least remembered candles at the grocery store, a mix for his favorite chocolate cake.

"Do you want to read the review?"

"I trust your judgment." She removed the chicken breasts from the oven and cut into one, finding it pink, slick with life. "Another ten," she said.

Eight months after they lost Jean, Murray started a habit of watching form videos of Sarah in his home office for hours on end. Sometimes late into the night, rewinding and rewatching. He drew diagrams and ate Ritz crackers. Sarah had just started her freshman cross-country season; Nancy assumed it was porn for him, the kind he could get away with when he wasn't training her, wasn't sleeping with her, as Nancy was sure he had been. A book she'd read about grief said that most men desired sex more after the loss of a child. Said it was their way of healing, but they hadn't been able to touch each other, and Nancy had been left to believe Sarah fulfilled his needs.

Nancy drained, patted dry, and cut the potatoes. She regretted rushing out of the store and not buying another vegetable, like green beans or broccoli. She didn't have time to make or dress a simple spinach salad, because Richard was already lighting candles on the dining table, the one they'd purchased together last year at a garage sale. They only ate over it on rare occasions, in a small nook they'd carved out by the living room.

The kitchen smelled of tender meat and olive oil, the dried rosemary she'd sprinkled over the breasts, which would have been a better way to cook the potatoes. She added sea salt and freshly ground pepper, diced them into quarters, and piled them into a half-moon along each plate.

When they sat down to eat, she thanked Richard for the candles. She heard Katherine remind her: *Gratitude, Nancy. It's the hardest but most important thing to focus on.* Katherine had her logging moments like these in a small journal, but this habit, like so many others, easily slipped.

Soft candlelight flickered over the table as they began to eat. Murray never liked candles, the way you had to blow them out so abruptly—or else worry about a fire if one had been left going, long after you'd left the house, with no easy way of returning after you remembered its burning.

"How is your work coming along?" Richard asked. The orange of a sweet potato clung to his fork, which reminded Nancy of the pumpkins in the bin at the supermarket, and she regretted not buying plain white potatoes instead—a fact that caused her eyes to linger over Richard's fork longer—remembering that Murray had insisted she take all the dinnerware, all the things they'd bought in sets the week they'd moved to New Haven. They'd driven to the mall in Milford, and she hadn't been able to wait to unpack it all once they were home, to find a place for each piece that would be easy enough to recall, reach for in a pinch; she had been glad for such facility with Jean at her hip, especially, stirring noodles or oatmeal. *Potatoes.*

"You make it sound so serious," Nancy said, after Richard had asked her again about her work, and she'd forgotten—all those other projects, this life spent organizing, and planning years in advance, for what?

"It is serious," he said.

"Come over tomorrow then," she said, smiling forcibly. "I'll show you."

"I wish I could. Have that faculty meeting, and then I set a deadline for Friday. For this paper—"

"Maybe some other time."

Richard wiped his mouth with his napkin. A paper one, since she hadn't felt like using good linens. "Tell me," he said. "What's up?"

"Nothing," she said. "I'm fine." But in her mind she saw the image of Sarah walking along the brightly lit corridors of her Greenwich apartment, Taylor's warm head nestled by the young mother's chin.

"Did you hear about the guy in Alabama?" Richard always brought part of the newspaper to the dinner table. How many times had she asked him not to?

"No."

"Apparently this guy went into a community college with an AR-15." He dug his knife into the chicken, impatient for a large chunk. When he finished, he failed to set it down and shift his fork to the right hand.

"Killed one person. Injured three." Richard had grown up in rural Ohio, the son of a plumber and kindergarten teacher. Murray's situation in Pennsylvania had been worse, but even his single, depressed mother had found time to teach him manners.

"Did he work there?"

"No—I don't think so," Richard said, mouth full. "The rest of the story is in my office. I'll get it."

"That's alright. I don't need to see it."

Murray hadn't met Sarah only for early-morning practices those first months after Jean; sometimes he stayed late with her after practices too. One April night, toward the end of Sarah's freshman year—not long before Nancy began her affair with Richard—she decided to stop by his office after she'd left her own. To offer to pick up dinner, feeling hopeful about that, the first time she'd felt this desire before Jean—to think ahead about what they needed. She'd opened Murray's office door just like she used to, ready to ask him the question—and then she'd found them, Murray and Sarah, sitting cross-legged on the floor by his desk, holding hands. Later in their apartment, when she'd broken down, he'd insisted it was nothing, that they'd been practicing simple race-day visualization.

But then a few months later, she'd gone to Murray's car to grab his road map—it had been pouring rain, and Nancy had wanted to look up the fastest route to Amherst for a meeting with a bookseller; she'd found the photo then, the note on the back of it. *Thanks for everything* it had said, a heart around the words. She'd cried, alone in the car, over the racing shoes Sarah held up like a prize, the medal around her neck. She'd felt this rage, this hatred, too, that Murray could smile, could give so much to someone else's eighteen-year-old, while their child—Jean, who would have been six now—lay underground.

~

"Tell me." Richard reached into the silence, across the table, for her hand. She had started sleeping with this man not long after finding the photo in Murray's car. She could be numb with Richard, she could feel her body, the comfort of his touch, and not feel anything at all; she could smoke and stare off.

But Richard was waiting for her reaction: his brow furrowed, lips almost pouting. She'd begun to wonder if Richard was all pretense, as false in his ability to truly empathize as Murray had been—and it had taken her four years to discover this? Katherine, she thought, would disagree. Katherine would say it all went back to Nancy's neglectful, workaholic father, even more so than her compulsive mother—that Nancy still had work to do, to give in to Richard's love, to accept and forgive herself, but Nancy didn't know. Her therapist, she thought, let them—Murray and Richard—off the hook.

~

Katherine had come recommended by a coworker, Sylvia, whose young son was battling depression and social anxiety; Sylvia was a younger conservator Nancy didn't know that well, but her son's therapy had come up in conversation, and Sylvia had shared Katherine's name when Nancy asked. Nancy had been too overwhelmed by her work at the library to commit to seeing a therapist herself, but Sylvia's description—someone more than a name on a Rolodex—had given Nancy the courage to make an appointment.

Katherine's office was bright yellow, shelves stacked with children's books and art supplies, and Nancy had felt foolish for not assuming this, that Katherine's office might be designed for children, too, since Sylvia's son saw her.

For their first session Katherine had agreed to turn the lights off for Nancy, because Nancy said she couldn't come back otherwise, and they always met in the afternoon, when there was just enough light through the windows. Katherine always sat in a wooden chair with her notepad. Sometimes, she held her hand at her stomach when Nancy spoke, as if she suffered the same void.

In the quiet, Nancy took a long sip of water. She didn't look at Richard while he ate quickly—his habit—and she tried not to think about the empty chairs that suddenly seemed egregious, compared with what Sarah's table might have looked like with Taylor at home.

Despair. Katherine often cut her off midthought, the moment she began this loop, because it was the easier narrative, she'd say, over hope—which came through absorbing the moment, through gentle, easy breathing.

"Oh no," Richard said. "The wine—I almost forgot!"

"Really?" she said calmly, evenly. "I don't think we need it." Then she realized she'd forgotten—his birthday—she hadn't said it yet like she'd planned, in serving the food: *Happy birthday, Richard. I made this for you.* All the moments she tried to plan but couldn't execute, the thoughtful things she used to be able to do and say automatically, because there'd been an order, a logic to them.

"How often do we drink together anymore?" Richard smiled.

When she didn't answer, he stole three bites of potato from her plate.

He was still chewing as he walked to the kitchen. She imagined him winding down their cheap corkscrew, and then thrusting his weight into the bottle. The bottle's pop shook her and was only further exacerbated by Richard rummaging for the right glass, and then the liquid's gurgle. He stockpiled the same label from a winery in the Finger Lakes. How hard was it to remember her one request for a cheap chardonnay?

"I poured you a small glass anyway," he said. Then he took a few swigs from his own glass, quickly depleting it by half.

"I hate red," she said. She exaggerated a sip of water and pushed her wineglass toward him. "Take it," she said.

She placed her fork and knife across her plate, then her napkin, covering less than one-third of her meal. She contemplated a cigarette on the fire escape.

"If you're not going to eat, give that to me too." Richard laughed. He said it through his wineglass, his voice echoey, nose and lips concave.

"If you're finished, I'll take your plate," she said. She rinsed it in the kitchen as Richard's fork clinked ravenously over hers. He liked her to be in the mood these nights, but tonight she really wasn't. She thought she'd apply some lubricant next time she had to use the bathroom. She was premenopausal, and the dryness, the frequency of yeast infections, was excruciating.

First there were strawberries, so she went for the carton and rinsed them again. She poured the fruit into a ceramic bowl, listening to their wet, quiet toppling. She picked up a berry and admired its rich red.

Underneath her turtleneck, she wore a supportive navy-blue bra and black panties she'd purchased on summer clearance at the mall. Richard would have to make do with them.

She plucked a few strawberries, holding on to the green tops in her hand.

"Richard," she said, sitting down across from him again.

"Yes?" he said, his own finger poised over the paper, since he sometimes read articles twice for no apparent reason.

"Have you thought more about it?"

"About what?"

"Children," she said. "Adopting."

"Nancy." He sighed and took two large gulps of wine. "We've been through this."

"And you said you'd think about it."

"I did? Well, I don't remember saying that. But anyway," he said, gulping more wine. He had a perfectly clean napkin, but still he used his fist to wipe his mouth. "I suppose I've thought about it, and decided we really aren't in the financial place to raise a child. Not until I have tenure and you—"

"What?"

"Nothing."

"Until I what?"

"Until you get a grip on yourself. Look at yourself."

She peered at her lap, the empty roll of her belly, hands still clenching berry tops.

"It's been years, and you're still on the verge of tears all the time. Do you think raising a child will really make that easier?"

"You know something?" she said. "You can be a real prick." She walked to the kitchen and dropped the leaves into the sink and washed her hands, breathing deeply, thinking about Katherine's pause button, the way she made her hand like a stop sign for a street it wasn't time to cross.

Nancy wasn't certain if she'd ever go through with adopting a child, but in the end, it didn't work with Richard because he could not open his heart to this possibility, not even after he was offered a tenured position at Yale the following year. In the weeks leading up to her decision to leave him, she told herself it was because he never cleaned his phlegm from the bathroom sink, because of the whipped cream at night, because he drank too much. The last time they had sex, both of them lying on their backs afterward, a thick squiggle of bedsheet between them, looking up at the ceiling and talking about literature, as they always did, she'd changed the subject, asking him again if he'd thought more about adopting. He'd said he had—but the truth was that a child would ruin things; he wanted passion without responsibility. *Conditions.*

~

It would take Nancy another year to leave him officially. She left one Friday morning in early February, after six blurry years. Quietly she gathered a few of her possessions, enough to fit in a suitcase. She had her books and a box with Jean's birth certificate, her tiny footprints. Her pink fleece hat from the hospital. She regretted not taking more photographs, but at least she had one of Jean smiling, looking up wide-eyed from her changing table, her legs stretched long. Another from the day she was born, Nancy's back pressed into a blue hospital pillow, Murray decked out in scrubs with his arm around her, smile wide as she'd ever seen it. She had added this one to a baby book with congratulatory cards from friends and coworkers, and now she slid in sympathy cards she'd saved in a box. Last, she packed one of Jean's sleepers, one she'd found in the laundry after Murray packed all the boxes. The sleeper still carried, even if Nancy only imagined it, a tinge of her child's sweet, milky scent. Their bodies together, folded into the cotton, the warmth and oneness she still felt if she held it close and breathed in.

FIFTEEN

Lisa Sanders, Becky's mother, had wanted to meet at a restaurant called the Pantry on Mechanic Street, not far from the hospital. It was always crowded here, even on weekday mornings, and as he waited by the door, he had to keep moving out of the way for people. He and Nancy used to come sometimes; she would get scrambled eggs with mushrooms and avocado.

The walls were painted the same bright orange, covered in posters from various jazz festivals. Light piano played in the background, too, but he didn't recognize the artist. Nancy was good at that. Miles Davis was a favorite. Charlie Haden.

Lisa walked in wearing a jean jacket and sunglasses. She didn't hug him or say anything, just hooked her glasses over her collar when they sat down at a small table by the window. Nearby an older couple shared a Belgian waffle with a side order of home fries.

"Doug doesn't know I'm here," she said.

He nodded, watching as she removed her jacket. She had a tight black T-shirt on—Becky's same tan, bony shoulders. When the waitress brought coffee without even asking them, he thought maybe Lisa had been coming here often. She flicked two packets of sweetener.

"I guess I'll start with the good news." She tipped one full packet, half another. "She's able to make solid eye contact. Not speaking yet, but she can recognize Doug and me."

"That's great," he said, surprised by his lilt.

"And the other day, when the doctor asked her to hold up two fingers, she did."

Murray shifted in his seat. "When can I see her?"

"I don't know. I'm more open to the idea, you know. But Doug's still having a really hard time—"

The waitress asked if they were ready. "Blueberry pancakes," Lisa said. "A short stack."

Murray wanted a spinach-and-tomato omelet with wheat toast. No home fries.

"I'm not even hungry," she said. "But pancakes sound good." She looked out the window. The streets were still wet from rain, leaves slick on the pavement. Murray waited for her to speak again. He partially focused on the brick building across the street: *AGENCY ONE*, it said. For selling insurance.

"She still has a feeding tube, but she'll likely transition soon."

Murray's legs twitched. He placed his hands between his knees to steady them.

"Doug—" she said. "The truth is, he's really angry. I don't know." She reached for her coffee, but she didn't lift it from the table.

"How many hours has it been?"

Lisa's eyes tightened. "Since when?"

"Since she's been more responsive?" He pinched the inside of his thigh.

"A little over two days. Right before I called you on Saturday."

"Oh."

"The right side of her face is less mobile than the left, but it's getting better. The doctors are hopeful, if she's made this much progress already."

"What about her limbs? Her legs?" Murray's knees were twitching more forcefully. It usually happened when he watched his runners run. He could feel his heart thrumming through his stomach.

"She can move them—that's good. And she's been getting massages. But she's still very weak." She lined up her knife with the edge of her place mat.

"Shouldn't she be seeing a physical therapist?"

Lisa sat back in her chair. "Look," she said, but she didn't continue.

The waitress set down maple syrup and a plate with four dabs of butter.

"She's going to have to relearn everything. The doctor said she might suffer from chronic headaches. Dizziness. She could develop epilepsy." Her voice broke. "You understand?" She blotted her eyes with a napkin. Pushed her butter plate away.

"I could come and bring Anna again," he said.

"I don't know," she said. "We should give it at least a few more weeks. Maybe even a month."

"What?"

"She needs time—"

"But I don't know what to tell the girls. When they ask me." He was louder. He wanted to see Becky today, to follow Lisa to the hospital, but the waitress, pupils pinpricked, cat-eye glasses, had already arrived with their food.

"Please just ask for their prayers," Lisa said, wiping more tears.

They ate in silence, Lisa using the side of her fork to cut syrupy pieces. For a moment, it was Becky there—he and Becky, when they'd gone for breakfast after Regionals.

Lisa dropped her napkin on the table.

"It's just really hard," she said. "I'm so tired of fighting with Doug."

The place was small enough to hear dishes clanking from the kitchen. The swinging door screeched too much; louder was their waitress stacking dishes from the older couple who had left. He jolted when he thought he heard her drop something. A plate, or was it the throb of a knife, landing on its point?

Lisa wiped her nose with a napkin. "The worst thing is feeling like you didn't do enough. To protect her." She swallowed. "Do you ever feel like that?"

Murray stared at his hands. He imagined the time on his watch, how it had passed 528 hours. But then she opened her purse, rifling for dollar bills, some loose change to make up the difference. He told her to leave it, that he'd get this one.

"She moans in her sleep," she cried, still rummaging. "The other night I thought I heard her say your name. It might have been *Mom*, or *Mommy*, but it sounded more like *Murray*.

"I want to make it work," she went on. "For you to bring the girls. For the team to come back again. I'll let you know."

He reached across the table for her arm, told her it was alright, but she cried the whole way to the car into a napkin he'd grabbed on the way out. After he'd closed the door, he was about to motion her to roll down the window. To remind her to call him as soon as he could visit, but she was already backing out. She didn't wave goodbye, just stayed hunched, napkin still in her hand over the wheel.

~

On the way home, Murray kept seeing the syrup-drenched pancakes—blueberries bleeding blue. Then that diner he'd taken Becky to in the Bronx right after she'd placed second at Regionals. She'd already qualified for Nationals with her time of 16:12.07, but then she'd dropped another eight seconds at Regionals, and since Doug and Lisa hadn't been able to make it up, he'd wanted to do something special to treat her. He'd been surprised when she ordered pancakes with butter and whipped cream, thought maybe it was part of some ritual he hadn't been aware of.

He remembered how slowly she'd worked a dab of butter around the brown centers, how she'd used her fork to cut off the white rims. She'd made the tiniest nibbles between sips of water. He'd gone on about what she'd done well that race: how she'd attacked the hills early and used the downgrades perfectly—saving just enough for the deceivingly long last half mile. Despite the slight incline, she'd sprinted to catch up with Delaware's number one, but she'd finished just a hair behind—though she blazed by that girl at Nationals a few weeks later, just like he'd known she would.

Then he recalled something she'd said, curtly, almost disrespectfully. She'd said, *I get it.* She'd had her tunic on, her bare shoulders showing, and she'd looked away from him. She'd absently picked at some skin, too, where a wound looked to be, but when he asked how it happened, she told him about the cigarette burn from when she was small, with Doug in Atlantic City. The burn wasn't new, she'd said. It was just that she'd gotten sunburned during practice, and it was peeling.

Practices were never that sunny in November, so that couldn't be true. Murray also didn't understand why a father would take a young child to such a place, when there were plenty of better, safer beaches and boardwalks around New Jersey. And now Doug wanted to blame *him*? One of those tyrants who controlled his wife too. Wasn't that how it worked: the most distrustful were also the most untrustworthy? Out of shame. Guilt.

Anna trusted him, didn't she? Or maybe she only *pretended* to—and that was how she'd orchestrated the team visit? Lisa mentioning when the team could come again, not just when *he* could come again. No one was asking his permission or his opinion about anything. He thought of what his father used to say. *Life isn't fair. I'm your superior. You listen when I tell you to do something.* He and Patrick never argued; they knew this about life, that it *was* unfair, and that you learned to live with the unfairness. You learned not to ask too many questions, learned that it was never your place, as the child, to rebel.

~

Later that afternoon he drove to the track. The girls were doing triangles today: one lap, two laps, one. Three repetitions, between a five-and-a-half- and six-minute pace.

Anna had officially sprained her ankle. She had shown him Dr. Owens's note, and no signs of a stress fracture had shown up on the scans. She would be working with a trainer twice a day to improve her core strength. She had a shot at the race next weekend. But she wasn't answering his messages. Not just phone calls, text messages too.

He'd gotten here at least twenty minutes early because he couldn't stand his office any longer, the chance of running into Rick and other coaches. It was damp in his car. Slightly chilled.

He stared at the empty track through the gate. There was mostly pavement around it, and tunnels for the football stadium, but if he looked past that, he could see part of the intramural fields, where the girls sometimes trained. Only if he wanted a more controlled circumference than the course. What if he'd taken Becky here, if he'd kept her on the fields?

No. Foul play could happen on any field. Any turf. He of all people knew that. Besides, there were plenty of other sports that practiced off campus. Like the equestrian team. They went a full hour away, to Rivendell Farm in Durham. What if a rider was thrown off? Or kicked? The coach wasn't blamed.

Murray had grown up near stables himself and used to know the old riding coach, Mitchell Emory, pretty well. He'd told Mitchell stories about the Erdenheim Steeplechase his father had taken him and Patrick to once—the year before his father died.

His father used to work with this man, Jake Klimer, who left mining to care for horses at a farm just outside of Philadelphia. Jake had offered up a tour of the property one Saturday on his ATV. There were three hundred acres of open land, and Jake told them about the town steeplechase the farm was hosting the next day, where the best horses raced two miles of fence line. He'd managed to get them rooms for the night, and Murray's father had let him and Patrick each put down two dollars on their favorite horses. Murray had chosen this bay-colored mare, named Quinn, for her sloping shoulders and long croup. He'd gotten a good look, too, through his father's binoculars, and he could still feel its small black dial, coarse against his fingers, as he watched Quinn leap through the thick meadowland: the smell of the grass in his nose, the beating of hard hooves in his ears.

Quinn hadn't won, though. A Selle Français with white markings had, but Murray had followed Quinn's stats for months in an equestrian magazine the library kept. She'd once placed third in open fences at a national competition in Devon.

~

It was 3:28:14 p.m. Just two minutes before he'd consider everyone *late*, because fifteen minutes early was on time, and today practice started at 3:45. He rounded them up, had them hurry through form drills. As he was breaking down the workout, the gate creaked. Anna entered, wearing her foot brace.

Silently she walked over and reached for his clipboard. She set her watch. The girls were leaning in. He wanted the first lap hard.

He hit go, and Anna began to speak. Softly she said she'd been in touch with Becky's parents. That she'd updated the team because she knew he hadn't yet.

"You called a meeting?" He clicked stop on his watch before it was time. But Anna's was still going. She would get the split.

"I'm not allowed?"

Tanya was coming around first. "Relax your arms!" he shouted through cupped hands.

She'd broken eighteen minutes in Franklin Park, only once. Her performance was sporadic at best, with no prospect of placing at the championship meet in October. He still had three weeks, and Anna would start running as soon as next week.

Anna fluidly took down splits. She was good at multitasking. A quality he'd always loved about Nancy, too, the way she'd handled even the driest paperwork with passion, resolve.

Anna had spent last summer in New York City through a publishing internship with *Psychology Today*. He'd overheard her tell Becky about it in the pool one morning. How she'd done little more than fetch coffee and type meeting minutes. He'd never seen her so worked up, breathless, really. But he thought how she had her whole life ahead of her—she might get a doctorate one day, like Nancy had.

A strong crosswind troubled the backstretch. Tanya struggled. Emily used her draft.

When they were coming up, Anna cheered without looking at him. "That's it, Tanya!" she said, her hair tossed in the wind. She tucked stray strands behind her ears.

"I got everything," she said, just after practice had ended. He'd already sent the girls on their cooldown, and he was about to ask her how she was feeling, if she'd gotten his messages.

"I have to work out on the bike in the field house," she said. "I'll get stretched after."

Above, the sky was turning navy. Harder winds beat a flag above the bleachers. "Keep the resistance at 15," he said. "You should be dripping sweat ten minutes in. Every five minutes, count your RPM. Twenty strokes in ten seconds."

"I know," she said, adjusting the Velcro over her brace.

"Be careful," he said.

"It's itching, okay? I'll see you tomorrow."

"Don't forget to engage your hamstrings," he called to her back, wind shuddering through her jacket. "You have to pull back hard," he said, his clipboard cold in his hands.

~

Murray remembered the county court. He'd been there last night after practice ended, had made it just in time to dispute his traffic violation. He'd had to wait, the way those horrible courthouses made you wait ad infinitum, no clue when you'd be called to plead your case with the traffic-ticket attorney. Murray had thought about how he'd hated attorneys, waiting there, and then he'd heard a child laugh behind him. He'd turned and found her sitting between her parents, swinging her legs with little white sneakers. She had looked more like her father than her mother, and he thought they should have just gotten a babysitter. A courthouse was no place for a child. He'd wanted to cover his ears so he didn't have to hear her breathing behind him.

~

On his way out of the gym, Murray tried to think of something else, about how his car tires needed to be replaced and when he could go to fix them. How much the tires would cost. All the research he still had to do, but he could not set his mind on tires. He could only think of 2002, the year he and Nancy had had their own formal hearing, and he had signed away his assets because none of them were worth keeping. He saw Nancy in their living room, wearing the same silk bathrobe in Paris green, her hair still wet from a shower, pointing her finger at him—accusing him of an affair with Sarah, after she'd been the one—she had accused him as if to justify her sleeping with Richard, and then had demanded more from him, and he'd conceded. As if it would have made forgetting her easier, all the ways she'd wronged him; the faster he'd agreed, the sooner he'd been able to get back to his life, his work, the things that had allowed them to survive that first year.

After everything they'd been through, he thought, finalizing the settlement had only taken a few months, through a small law office downtown, one with skylights and an unused fireplace.

They'd sat at opposite ends of a long mahogany table, phone and intercom at the center, bottled waters next to them, collated copies of the agreement with little red and yellow tags that said *sign here*.

When Nancy was pregnant, she'd wanted to assess pastors and options for a baptism ceremony. She'd grown up Protestant, and he had agreed to go with her to a Lutheran service in Milford. But then his Sunday long run had gotten in the way, or had it been something else? He remembered how she'd said *they had time*. Once when she'd been in a particularly good mood, she'd wanted to talk about the kind of values and traditions they planned to instill. She'd kept stacks of books on the kitchen table, on her desk, in their bedroom—books about pregnancy and child development—titles that reached as far as adolescence, but he'd never asked her about them. He'd agreed with her about waiting to decide, because, he'd said, wouldn't experience teach everything they needed to know? Sweat hung slick on Murray's neck and under his nose, though it was not hot today. It couldn't have been much more than sixty degrees.

In his car, it was cooler, but still he was sweating: the way one felt in public restrooms, riddled by food poisoning or the flu. He turned on the car and pressed buttons and positioned the vents for a blast of cold air. He closed his eyes, and when he opened them, he turned to where Nancy might have been sitting. Then to the back of his sedan, where there used to be a car seat.

He closed his eyes again.

Nancy used to hum when there wasn't any radio music. She used to sing off-key without a thought. She would hum, and her pencil would move around little lists, the dozens of lists they kept, together and separately, to track their lives.

He started the engine, shedding the thought of Nancy in a black wool hat with matching black mittens in the winter, when they might be driving someplace with snow on the streets.

Or in the summer, if the windows were down, her hair tossing lightly, and how sometimes she'd place her hand over his on the gearshift. He turned the radio off abruptly. Why had he kept this old car?

SIXTEEN

Two hours after Nancy had left Richard for good, exactly one month before her forty-ninth birthday in March, she found herself waiting with two suitcases full of all her belongings in a hotel across from Washington Square Park. She was hungry, but more than that she needed a shower, a long, hot one that turned her skin red and offset the cold.

On her lap was Virginia Woolf's complete short fiction. She had been savoring the pages for weeks, but now her eyes couldn't focus; she felt them wandering over the red-and-gold diamond patterns of the carpet, tracing different shoes: a man's polished loafers, then the white sneakers of the woman beside him; it was unclear whether they were together or strangers. She refocused her eyes on a paragraph about burnished steel.

"Weber." When Nancy heard her name, her maiden name, she was relieved: this hope that a city's rhythms could erase, redeem, the past.

A bellboy helped her to her floor with her two large suitcases. She tipped him ten dollars and slowly oriented herself around the room, the heavy curtains she drew back for a view of the park, the television she turned on and surfed until she found a live recording of the Philharmonic performing Verdi's *Requiem*, and she unpacked her books because they would make her feel at home here, at least temporarily, and she hung up her blouses and set the baby book on her desk, also a reading light and eye mask next to the Bible in the top drawer of the nightstand. Then she turned on the shower, and while she waited for the bathroom to fog up with steam, she sorted through a little basket of soap and shampoo, two Q-tips, a miniature sewing pack, and a shower cap, which she slipped around her hair. She wished to dye it red, for the gesture to mark a new chapter in her life, but she was already splurging with the hotel, and on Monday she'd scheduled her move to a small apartment on Grove Street in New Haven, just a quarter mile from the cemetery. It would comfort her to be closer to Jean's grave, but she also feared the frequency of she and Murray crossing paths.

She considered it a miracle they'd only intersected once since she'd left him, on the sidewalk outside of the gym one Sunday. She had not told him she was on her way to the cemetery, a weekly habit she'd assumed he knew about, but he had not said anything while they waited for the light; he had merely stood still. She had been the first to speak, to wish him well before they both crossed the street and walked in different directions.

When they were dating, Murray used to remind her of characters in her favorite novels. She'd never told him this, but he often brought her back to *Giovanni's Room*. Of course this book had consumed her days in Paris, carrying with it the city's ambient gray, its smells and cadences, and so she guessed she'd been apt to make such comparisons. That moment when David and Giovanni walk along the wide sidewalk of Boulevard du Montparnasse, holding a kilo of cherries between them, laughing and spitting pits at one another like children, she always thought of Murray. How he had made her feel like a child discovering the city as if for the first time.

Nancy's parents used to scold her for comparing her life to books. Remind her that characters could never be as complicated as real people, and though this was true—a woman was as infinite as every moment passing through her, and a book was limited by language, a writer's choice over which words to leave in, which to leave out—the feelings

Baldwin described had been as true as any she'd ever felt for Murray. Not just in terms of her love but her regret, in leaving him because it was easier than accepting the truth that it was too hard to rely on your partner when certain holes had dug themselves too deep inside you: impossible to see past the desert, past the mountains, to find the ocean.

~

Not once had Murray accompanied her to Jean's grave, not once after the burial. Nancy had had the hardest time on Jean's birthday, while Murray seemed the most withdrawn on the anniversary of her death— but just one year later, the year they'd stopped sleeping in the same bed, he'd failed to mention what day it was. Nancy could still see the moment like yesterday, the way she'd been sitting at the kitchen table after a sleepless night of pacing along the strip of floor between the oven and refrigerator, when Murray had entered, not once looking up from his same bowl of bran cereal and his legal pad, not once pausing to look at her or the May sky through the window, spring, the season she'd come to loathe for its fecundity, its *new life* smells—but he had merely dropped his bowl in the sink and told her to have a good day, he had kissed her cheek while reaching for his car keys, never wasting a move.

Nancy stepped out of the shower and cleaned her ears with the Q-tips. She dressed in clothes she found at the top of the first suitcase she opened. Then she took the subway to the Flatiron District and began walking up Fifth Avenue. The streets were gray and packed with tourists in expensive coats cradling cups of coffee. She was comforted by a couple speaking French—even if she couldn't enter it directly; they made her feel part of a conversation. She found herself walking close behind them. But along Madison, when she passed Cellini and Rolex and Davidoff of Geneva, she felt foolish. She should walk farther west if she wanted to shop, but then there was the proximity to Times Square, its clogged streets and lights that flashed grotesque in her mind, especially around Christmas. It was months after that—February—but still she wound back toward Park, where the streets were wider and there were boxes of planted trees, frail from the cold city sun. Nancy remembered that one of her college roommates, Caroline, lived nearby. The last she'd heard from Caroline was years ago, when Nancy and Murray were still barely married. Caroline had sent a Christmas card, and somehow Nancy had burned the exact address into her memory, like so many details she would've liked to have forgotten. Caroline had had a child, a little boy named James, after his father—who went by Jim.

Nancy longed to call her parents, to curl up in the warm spaces of the house. She had called them with the news of the funeral. Her father had said he was there if she needed anything, but they had not made it. Her mother had not had the courage, even at a time so dire, to fly, to be there for her daughter, her grandchild.

~

It was unlikely Caroline still had the same address, but when she saw the listing for Caroline's last name, her married name, on the dial box outside her apartment building, just as another tenant was walking out, she was surprised to feel her hand catch the door so she could head into the lobby and then up the elevator. Outside Caroline's door, 12R, her hands trembled.

How stupid this was. She could still change her mind, she thought, pressing her back to the wall. Then a door across the hall opened, and another tenant walked out—no, the tenant's dog walker, with a gorgeous blue-eyed husky. The walker wore a tattered coat, hair in dreadlocks, and as he hit the elevator button, Nancy felt his half gaze, his judgment. But the elevator came and the door opened, and the walker and the dog went in, and Nancy could breathe again. Though the underpinnings of her terror had grown more acute: of what Caroline might know, what rumors might have circled despite how quiet the funeral had been, how out of touch Nancy felt with all of her friends and family in Michigan.

"Nancy!" Caroline had opened the door. "Oh my God!" Nancy returned Caroline's hug stiffly. "It's so good to see you," Caroline said, her arms gripping Nancy tighter, longer, than she could have anticipated. She was still near the door to the stairwell; not too late to tug it open and rush down the twelve flights. But as Caroline welcomed her in and told her to make herself comfortable while she went to the kitchen to make tea, she tried to focus on the moment: how Caroline's hair was dyed the same jet black from when they were roommates. By their sophomore year at Michigan, Caroline had disappointed Nancy by joining a sorority, dwindling Nancy's already slender cast of friends.

Marjorie used to remind her of Caroline in her perfect manner of dress, her positive outlook on the world. But Nancy had been wrong to assume Marjorie would be there for her after Jean, and as she scanned Caroline's stunning apartment, her eyes landing on one of the arch-shaped windows she'd seen from the street, she pictured herself looking up at the windows from the street, where she could have stayed, *should have stayed*. Why would she risk Caroline's judgment too?

She sat down on the sofa, one of distressed red leather, and admired a crystal vase full of fresh calla lilies on its adjoining end table.

"Herbal or caffeinated?" Caroline said, holding out several loose-leaf canisters. "This one is from Japan." She tipped the canister so that Nancy could smell tiny rosebuds mixed with fragrant greens. "We were just there in December," she said. "In Japan." In college, Caroline's hair had grazed her waist, dull then, but now it shimmered, this near-perfect bob.

"Herbal is fine," Nancy said. Visiting Japan had been on her bucket list since she was eighteen, a fact that made her sad and happy—sad because she could not imagine traveling there alone—and happy because she could not remember the last time she'd recalled such a list.

Caroline brought out two black pots on a tray. She sat next to Nancy on the sofa, close enough to grab Nancy's hands in hers.

"Tell me," she said. "What brings you to the city?"

"Just a weekend away," Nancy said, trying to smile, because after all, she'd initiated this visit.

"Well, I'm thrilled you decided to stop by, and I'm so lucky I'm home! Jim's away on business and James is taking tae kwon do on the Upper West Side. Usually I'm out running errands."

Nancy laughed, though she couldn't affirm that lucky feeling.

"Oh," Caroline went on, "I've been meaning to congratulate you on your work at Beinecke. I read about it in the *Times* . . . forgetting what it's on now, excuse me!" She laughed while pouring more tea, this trickle of pale amber liquid.

"Wordsworth and the Napoleonic Wars," Nancy said. She tried to take a few more sips of tea, but the chamomile was almost too sweet.

She thought of the Master's Tea she had gone to with Marjorie, how she and Marjorie had laughed over Annette's correction: *this is my home*, and as Caroline excused herself to get more honey, Nancy tasted, more acutely, the bitterness Marjorie had left her with. One morning after Nancy had continued to miss work, Marjorie had called to see how she was doing. Nancy couldn't remember exactly how it had come out, but Marjorie had made a comment that *she didn't understand how it could have happened*. Most babies were three months, not seven, when SIDS happened—Marjorie hadn't said it, but there'd been only judgment in her voice, this implication that she must have forgotten to check on Jean or had laid her down with too many blankets.

But Nancy had come to see the real truth: that Marjorie simply couldn't relate. Marjorie needed to be surrounded by "friends" who held up the mirror of her own life—and that day on the phone, she had been yet another reminder of Nancy's nightmare: that everything she'd believed to be true about friendship and unconditional love was false. Mirrors lied—and she'd had no words to fill the silence through the phone that day. She'd simply hung up, and they'd stopped speaking after that.

"I can't find the local jar from the farmers market," Caroline said. "But this will have to do." She held up a plastic bear with a yellow cap and asked Nancy if she wanted any. Nancy shook her head, but Caroline wanted to hear more about her work, as though it might be the only way for them to connect, and Nancy tried to do that, to fill the time, the silence beneath it all, with her work on Wordsworth and his Alfoxden Notebook. Caroline nodding dimly, the same way she had in college, when Nancy would go on about a particular painting or a book she'd been reading, clinging to the safety, the formality, of ideas. Caroline had always lived her ideas, Nancy thought. She didn't overthink them.

"Well, Jim and I really have been wanting to visit New Haven," she said. "We'd love to take James. But he's not so little anymore!" She pointed to a photo of her son next to the baby grand piano. On its ledge sat another vase of white calla lilies.

"Are you alright?" Caroline said, reaching for Nancy's knee. Nancy flinched, unable to remember, for a moment, what they'd been talking about.

"I'm sorry," she said, fixing her eyes more firmly on James's photograph. "He's so handsome. How old is he now?" Of course Nancy knew he was eight years old—three months and ten days older than Jean would have been—but she let Caroline tell her anyway and then add:

"He's starting boarding school next year. Can you believe it?"

Nancy couldn't, but she did not say that either: that she had no concept of time, how decades could be compressed into individual years and months and weeks so that her child might have one day grown up like James.

But now Caroline wanted to give the grand tour. Nancy didn't say anything, merely followed her past the bookcase and the piano and then the dining room table Caroline said she'd had custom built by an Italian carpenter in the neighborhood. Nancy could just picture Caroline, Jim, and James pressing cloth napkins to their lips after every sixth bite, silverware clinking against china plates, knives and forks flashing in the candlelight as they switched hands, all the while James speaking excitedly about his studies and piano lessons, his tae kwon do.

It was the life Nancy had grown up with in Michigan: the dinners and country club tennis lessons and golf matches. In Murray, she had resolved for the opposite life, for her future to follow an opposite course.

Caroline held up a lion's tooth from last year's safari in Kenya. And then a silk-and-ebony fan. "Japan was not warm," she said, tugging her sweater. "Next year we have to go somewhere warm again, to survive this winter!"

Nancy smiled, relieved to be bypassing a tour of the bedrooms, that she could safely return to the sofa. They poured the last of their tea, and Nancy took frequent sips as Caroline went on about the city, her own work, more of her travels. Nancy felt content to stay silent, half listening, half remembering; she'd been living this double existence for almost eight years—death more present than living—parroting all the things people were supposed to say in these kinds of situations, the cold winter temperatures, the latest tragedies and successes in the news, as if there was nothing between them, not the pain or the worries and disappointments that filled Nancy, unexpectedly, throughout the day—the endless triggers.

"What are your plans tonight?" Caroline asked suddenly. "We could go out for dinner? It's still early, I know, but I could fix us some appetizers here."

"Oh," said Nancy. "That sounds lovely, but—"

"Or we could order in. James will be home soon. I'd love for you to meet him. The restaurant I was thinking of is this wonderful Italian place off Lexington with homemade ravioli."

"Actually," Nancy said, "I have to be downtown for a show. I don't have tickets yet, so I should get there early to stand in line."

"Which show?" Caroline's eyes looked wide with recognition, as if she sought out theater on a regular basis or was part of some pseudo-elitist Off Broadway circle.

Yet Nancy knew Caroline deserved more credit. She had graduated summa cum laude in political science, and Nancy had been in awe of the ease at which she'd consumed Plato their freshman year, and then how she'd cranked out A papers while still enjoying a vibrant social life; upperclassmen, most of them attractive males, had knocked on their door daily and persistently with exclusive invitations to parties.

"*Incident*? Everyone's talking about it." Caroline had already gone for the *Times* and was flipping through the arts section.

"No," Nancy said. "It's a tiny production. You probably haven't heard of it. *The Wandering Jew.*"

"Oh, I haven't heard of that. Who's directing?"

"I can't remember," Nancy said, feeling her throat in her ribs. "It started at the Yale Repertory, but then Bleecker Street picked it up. It's a tiny production, written by Eugène Sue in the 1800s. I acquired one of his scripts years ago. He has a real gift for portraiture."

"But wasn't Sue a novelist?" Caroline asked, eyes gone small, pinched. "And why, if it's tiny, do you have to stand in line?"

"Oh," Nancy said, pretending to rummage through her purse.

"I can't believe I haven't heard of it." Caroline went to the dining table for *New York* magazine.

"Forget it," Nancy said. "It's silly. I don't need to go." She set her hand on top of her bag. "I came here to see you." For as much as the gesture made Nancy cringe, she felt this little pulse of curiosity for what it might be like to reexperience the company of an old friend.

~

They went to the Library Hotel on Madison, where Caroline ordered them two twenty-dollar dirty martinis. "I didn't even ask what you wanted." She laughed. Her bracelets clinked, reminding Nancy of Caroline's hippie days, when she'd worn dozens more up her arm and had dusted her eyelids in matching gold.

Caroline looked at Nancy and said, "I assume you're happy at work."

"Of course," Nancy said, unsure if she was more surprised by Caroline's continued suddenness or how unfazed she was by her own question. "I've been there ten years," she said. "Almost." She sipped her drink.

"That's wonderful," she said. "Forgive me if I've asked you this already. But you like New Haven? I keep wanting to show James the campus, to plant the idea early in his mind, you know?"

"You've said that," Nancy said, somewhat relieved to return to the surface of the Caroline she knew.

"Said what?"

"That you want to bring him to New Haven."

"I did?"

"Yes." Nancy licked her lips, wishing she hadn't already eaten both olives from her drink.

"Well—" Caroline said, her eyes evading, but also circling, closer to the thing Nancy now felt she was raring to announce any moment, that she *knew*, that she was *so sorry*, and then Nancy would have to sit with that expression again, its triteness, its vapidity.

"It's stupid," Caroline said. "I'll just say it. One of my friends, a very good friend, actually, is a department head at the Morgan Library, and the literature curator just left. He asked me if I knew anyone, and of course I thought of you, but we haven't been in touch. And then you showed up here, and I just keep thinking to myself, it's meant to be!"

"Oh," Nancy said, struggling to breathe, the tightness of her eyes too much to hold, to keep from shattering.

"It's just an offer," Caroline said. "Think about it. I'd be happy to put you in touch with him. And I think you would really love it there.

My friend—Martin, he's really open. You'd have a lot of freedom to manage exhibitions, to acquire new collections—"

Nancy should have been relieved, but she wasn't. She felt defeated, like Caroline's suggestion about changing jobs meant she appeared more generally lost and lonely than she was capable of pretending she wasn't, and wouldn't it have been better, maybe even liberating, to have just told her what had happened? But it felt too late now.

"I don't . . ." Nancy took a long sip from her martini, tears withheld, but she could taste the salt. She set the glass down. "It's tempting," she muttered.

"Really? I'll send out an intro email on Monday, and you can go from there. Exciting!"

Nancy calmly excused herself to the restroom. She wished she'd been firmer; that word, *tempting*, replayed in her head. She supposed she'd taken refuge behind it, and now she was stuck. Caroline would want to know where she'd live if she got the job, and then if she had any attachments to the city, or maybe Caroline was like Marjorie: simply too self-absorbed to express such sensitivity. Nancy supposed Caroline had asked her very little about her private life when they were roommates all those years ago.

Inside a bathroom stall, she guarded a thick wad of toilet paper in her hand, and she began to hear herself breathing. Was this what it would be like tonight, alone in her hotel bed?

Her back was hunched and aching. She stared at her shoes. Black and beaten boots she used to only wear for walking, not every day like now, because she was terrified of shoe stores, of trying different styles on.

When she returned to the table, Caroline had already paid the bill. Before Nancy had a chance to say anything, Caroline reached across the table for her hand.

"I've failed," she said. Black smeared under her eyes and her lips trembled. "I knew what happened." She wiped tears. "I failed to reach out to you, to be there for you. I'm truly sorry."

Nancy felt her own tears release in the way they'd wanted. To be seen naked for the woman who'd once taken shelter among books in their dorm room and the college library, and now to still seem to be that woman in every way, except that they both knew she wasn't. She would never be again. And maybe it was better that way, to hear the words *I've failed*, for the worst to be spoken, for what would always live in her to be named.

SEVENTEEN

Murray met Lisa outside Becky's new room on the sixteenth floor; she had moved out of the ICU. Lisa had texted that morning, just after seven. Doug would be in the office for the next two days, so he could come.

Today she wore a green sweater, sleeves cropped to reveal thin wrists, one of them bound with a small leather watch.

"She's speaking more every day," Lisa said. "Sometimes she reverses the order of words, but the ideas are there."

From inside the room, something crashed, something loud, piercing Murray's eardrums and making him close his eyes. When he opened them, he looked around, and it was quiet. He heard his heart beating in his head, but he was sure he'd heard a crash.

The door to Becky's room had been left partly open. Then he heard some moaning, followed by high-pitched laughter. Lisa rushed in first.

Brown liquid had pooled around her bed. It smelled like pureed vegetables: baby food and chicken broth. More of it splattered over her neck and forearms, which were still taped with IVs. She drew a finger to her nose.

"Stop that," Lisa said.

When the nurse arrived, Lisa had to steady Becky's jerking arms.

Becky's feeding bottle, now half-empty, ran through a clear tube. Some of her hair had grown back, but it lacked thickness. Vitality.

"I'm sorry." Lisa looked at him, crying.

Becky groaned, her words slurring. "I don wantto!"

Lisa held both of her hands over Becky's hands. She shushed her, said it would be okay. She brushed away some hair.

"Couch!" Becky said, laughing hysterically. But then her face relaxed, saddened. "I stay here," she said. "Not go to."

"That's progress?" Murray asked incredulously. And as soon as he said it, he could see on Lisa's face it had been the wrong thing.

Lisa's eyes fixed on him. Her mouth quivered. She released the grip on Becky's hands. "What?"

"I thought you said she was six," he said, part of his gaze on the nurse's station.

"What the hell are you talking about?"

"On Apgar. Whatever it was. Glasgow."

"You know," she said, "I really don't know why I even make an effort. Or take the time." She'd started crying again, her shoulders hunched. "Doug was right. You don't care about our daughter!"

He tried to speak, but thoughts blended with words. He didn't know what he'd said. *Had he said anything?*

"She's just a means for you, isn't she?" Her voice, words, they amplified. "I never felt right about it. The way you recruited her!" She was pointing her finger at the ground, not looking at him, but then she did. She met his eyes.

"My problem is I always try to see the best in people." She wept. "I was raised that way. Becky too . . . I should have taught her to be stronger." She wiped mucus from her mouth. "The first time she came home for break, she was thin as a ghost. She didn't even want to go to the movies. Her favorite." She clutched her elbows. "She always loved the movies. Since she was a little girl."

"That's enough," he said. The shadow of a cart rolling by. Supplies. "Lower your voice." He tried to keep his voice low. Diminutive.

The door to Becky's room had been left open. She moaned again, louder this time.

"Go!" Lisa shouted. "Get out!"

He saw a nurse coming this way. That way: Out of the station, out of the room?

At the elevator, he could barely breathe. He stopped and turned around to see if it was really her: Lisa, less than fifty feet away, convulsing as another nurse tried to steady her. He felt more tightening in his ribs. More shaking by his wrists, his knees. She waved her arm at him. "You stay away from *us*!"

~

He drove, not thinking about where he was going or why. His phone lay on top of loose change and odds and ends, shoe spikes and safety pins, in a small tray by the shifter. He tuned the radio to the first clear station, something acoustic, but then it went religious. He turned the knob, again and again, settling into static.

Hands restless over his steering wheel. His neck jerked. At a light, he beat his palms over leather. He hummed.

"Goddamn it!" he shouted. He pulled over and looked to the empty passenger seat. Nancy's contorted body that last drive back from the hospital. She had made him pull over. Had told him to let her out, and then she'd hobbled down Orange Street alone. He'd found her beating her fists on the sidewalk.

Outside his car, by the course, a breeze cooled his skin, but as he walked through the woods, this coolness seemed to have little effect on his lungs; he was breathing heavily. He noticed that the house before him, the one he'd been keeping his eye on all these weeks, was for sale. No cars in the driveway. Lights off. Lawn still unmowed. He read the sign again,

FORSALE, letters crammed, bleeding together, and then he thought, *There had been a man.* Murray was sure of it. But when he edged toward the back lawn, he couldn't distinguish a figure from parts of the house.

The gate to the back patio was open. He pulled out a chair and sat down. He checked his phone again. If he called Nancy . . . if she had the same number?

For a moment, he saw darkness, then a harsh slanted light. He smelled charcoal, but when he lifted the cover of the grill, there was only a rumpled magazine. Still, a fire hazard; he tore it into pieces. He watched the bits fly away.

He looked for matches. Lighter fluid. Other hazards.

"Hey there," someone said. "What are you doing?"

A man in a suit was walking toward him. Murray limped to his car as he heard heels clicking and the man shouting. "Hey!" the man said. "I'm calling the police."

But Murray was certain the man hadn't had time to read his license plate. Murray had peeled off in the opposite direction. If anyone asked, he was looking for the ball. He looked around. He was just on the edge of the golf course and wished he'd had clubs in the trunk, something to show for himself, for why he was in the neighborhood. Maybe he was lost, maybe he really hadn't been able to find the ball he was playing with and had friends out there on the sixth hole, waiting for him?

What if the house had surveillance cameras? he thought. But he wasn't in clear-enough view for anyone to detect the *Y* on his jacket, to have reason to contact the school; the main campus was over two miles away. Then, at a red light, he saw a truck parked in someone's driveway. He saw men carrying brushes and a can, and a sign that said *WET PAINT*, or had he just imagined that, because you usually didn't advertise when it was your work or your own home—you were supposed to be safe about it, wear face masks for the fumes, keep others safe.

$\sim$

He parked at a gas station, crouched over his steering wheel. His hands were blue with squeezing hard, his breath shallower. He'd started wearing a heart rate monitor again—earlier today it had been 72 beats per minute, now it was 95. He couldn't find the pulse oximeter in his glove box, his hands working furiously among maps and receipts.

He jumped when he felt on a knock on the window. It was only a service attendant. He rolled down his window.

"There's no parking here!" the man said. He had a thick accent and beard. Dark eyes.

"Oh—"

~

He turned the key to his office, thinking little of the stacks of papers he had to file, the scattering of napkins stained with coffee. He opened a window. He went to his desk. "Coach?" Rodney stood in the doorway. "We made this for Becky." She held up a greeting card. When she handed it to him, he couldn't read the words: minuscule, delicate script. "Don't you want to sign it?"

His pen was on his pad by the watch on the desk.

"Here," she said, digging around her pocket.

"No," he said. "I got it." He squeezed letters into a sliver of white space.

"When can we take it to her?" Rodney asked, holding the envelope. "She's awake, isn't she?"

"I'll take it," he said, feeling some sweat on his lips. "Haven't heard from Becky's mom."

"That's not true," Rodney said. "We've talked to her. She talks to Anna."

"What?" Murray said.

"We were just doing you a favor. We thought we could all go together, after you signed the card."

"No, I'm not taking you all," Murray said firmly, feeling his father's eyes on him, saying, *The only way you get anywhere is by working, earning your way—your privileges.*

He heard himself saying that now to Rodney. "She actually *earns* her hospital visits."

"What are you talking about?"

"Anna. Anna works harder than you do. She deserves to go with me to the hospital." He saw Nancy gripping his arms outside the hospital, Nancy's legs collapsing before they'd reached the car in the parking lot.

Rodney just stood there: eyes small, mouth slightly open. "You mean she's your *favorite*. You always have one."

"What?" He almost reached across the desk to grab her arm, to tell her to go to her room, to think about what she'd done and write that one hundred times over, like his mother had once made him do—*I will not talk back to my father. I will not talk back. I will not talk back. I will not talk back*, until his wrists had ached, the lead of his pencil dulled.

"I've seen you look at her funny," Rodney said. "You look at all of us."

She didn't speak, just stared straight at him, arms crossed.

"Get out of my office," he said. "I was going to tell you tomorrow, but you're on academic probation. That means *off* the team." He stood up from behind his desk. "I don't want you anywhere near us." He was the one raising his voice. "If I see even a trace of you, hear a mention of you, there'll be real repercussions. With the dean!"

"You can't do that," she said. "You don't have that kind of hold. You're just a deadbeat."

～

The phone rang. He picked it up and pressed the mouthpiece to his chest, his other finger on hold. "Get out!"

"Just wait!" she shouted.

"Get out!" He was louder. After three long seconds, when she was gone, he released the button: "Hello?"

"Mr. Murray?"

He listened to the silence.

"Mr. Murray?"

"Yes."

"I'm calling from Dr. Almasi's office. To remind you of your eye appointment tomorrow. At 10:30."

"No," he said, seeing little black letters, narrow, then wide. Yellow eye drops. Dilation.

"When would you like to reschedule?"

"What?"

"I asked if you'd like to reschedule."

He hung up the phone, holding it there by its neck. It took some moments to breathe again, to look around the room. He surveyed the wall with its smattering of photographs. Sarah, he had his arm around her, in front of Georgetown's track: 2001. She had just set a national record of 15:02.02 as a sophomore.

Then he started to look for a wallet-sized photo from that same year, the one Nancy had found. *Evidence,* she'd called it, in the glove box of his car.

He rifled through business cards, receipts, coupons, until he felt it, small and thin and slick. But it wasn't that. He stared at the silhouette, softly curved in the night.

"Coach." It was Victoria this time. Her eyes scorched red, as if maybe Rodney had told her something untrue. Had Rodney even been in his office?

"I'm not . . . ," Victoria said finally. "I don't think I can make practice."

"No?" he said. "Why not?"

"I can't breathe." She'd begun to cry. "Ever since Becky," she started, but had to pause. "Every time I start to run," she said, "I have to think about it." She adjusted the chain around her neck: a tiny cross. "I have to think about each breath, and then I count them. I try counting seconds instead, but I always have to stop before I reach sixty. Every workout, all I can see is the seconds." Her mouth was wet, quivering.

Murray's college coach used to ask him this every time. *Do you have what it takes? Do you?* He would lean in close to Murray's face and say that, like he was either going to be punched or he was going to go out there and obliterate himself on the track.

"You're excused," Murray said calmly, trying to focus on Victoria. It was Victoria in his office now.

"I'm not coming back." Her voice broke again.

Ten years ago, there might have been a point to patience. Understanding. But abstract philosophies meant nothing in relation to measurable, foreseeable outcomes. Murray's father said you were only ever as much as you achieved.

"I'm sorry," she wept.

He looked away, reaching for the photograph. Trapped sound-waves: the heart, this tiny throbbing star, he shoved it back into his drawer. Victoria had left without closing the door.

Nancy, she'd stormed out and gotten in the car. Said she wouldn't be back for a while. But it was just a photo. *Ask any coach,* he'd said. *They all had photos.*

It's the hiding, she'd said. *What else are you hiding?*

He should have asked her, Nancy, his wife, the same thing, but he hadn't. He'd just watched her fold the laundry that Saturday afternoon, the way she'd left his briefs and undershirts in a clump on the ottoman.

~

She used to recount the smallest details of her day, disruptions, clips of dialogue. She used to go on and on, analyzing every word, facial expression.

He thought of the logs she'd kept when they'd been expecting: the foods she ate, the frequency of kicks. Later it was the feedings, the sleep schedule.

She had borrowed his legal pads.

Once, she'd told him she thought it was a mother's job to count. *A mother never stopped counting.*

As if he didn't count every day himself, every hour, and every minute that went into a year. As if this hadn't been his whole world, as if she were the only one with charts and photographs. Milestones that gave their life meaning, an arc anyone could look at and trace and say, *Your life happened as it was supposed to; your life followed its natural course.*

~

He was counting the days. Twenty-four days since the accident. One more until another set of five, if he went by the hash marks he kept at the top of her sheet: the last day she'd run. She would again, he thought. *Patience,* he thought. Just wait a few more weeks. Maybe a few more months.

Outside his office the floor creaked. Even though plenty of people passed by at any hour on a given day, he couldn't risk another encounter, especially with Rick or another one of his girls. He stood up, the smell of broth and the brown wood of his desk. Becky's feeding tube, carts rattling down the hospital corridor, the change of light outside in the parking lot.

He had done his reading. It was all part of the process. For example, a young girl had fallen off her horse in Maine and spent six weeks unconscious before she woke. There were things she'd had to relearn, but synapses strengthened, the body provided valuable feedback. After a point, it could be like riding a bike or hitting a tennis ball. Muscle memory.

Sometimes people envisioned extremes as protection, *as preparation*, but Becky *was different*, he muttered aloud. She would surprise them.

He sought this image of her at Terre Haute, his favorite, in the late November cold, *Becky* leading the pack. But instead it was just the two of them standing in the hotel elevator.

Usually he stayed on a different floor than the girls when he took more than one with him to a competition, but Nationals was such a rare occasion, it hadn't seemed necessary to stay so far apart.

In the elevator, she hadn't locked eyes with him, not once. She'd kept them fixed above, on the ascending numbers, until the bell dinged. She looked so small when she stepped out, practically swimming in her boathouse jacket, clutching the straps of her backpack like a child.

As she flashed her key card and the door unclicked, for a moment he hadn't moved away, hadn't looked down with propriety when the door swung open. He heard Anna, then Rodney, saying that he looked at Becky, focused on her, in a way that was uncomfortable.

No, it was just Rodney causing a stir, spreading rumors. He'd better go to Rick now so there was no confusion about Lehigh next Saturday. Rodney couldn't be on that bus. But Rick's door was locked when he got there. He hurried to print out her academic record, to sign and date the official probation form. He slipped both under Rick's door.

He heard Nancy, or no, it was just the softball coach, Vivian Miller. She waved at him. He waved back, his wrist shaking. His knees again.

Nancy—evidence—words in echo: red-rimmed eyes, her arms ashen and skeletal beneath her robe as she pointed at him, like Lisa. Like he was a criminal, like he'd violated someone, when the truth, if he really boiled it down, was Sarah: the problem with Sarah was all Nancy's doing.

Before Nancy found the photo, she'd walked in on him and Sarah in his office. In the middle of a harmless meditation sequence. He never did this, meditate, but Sarah had found some New Age article and wanted to try it. She'd even suggested holding hands, but he felt afraid of that, the optics of it all. Just after he agreed, of course that was the moment Nancy walked in.

The photo had compounded Nancy's paranoia, and his explanations, his repeated assurance—they'd only made things worse.

There was no denying it: Nancy wanted, needed, a lot of things. Attention, security, his *emotional support*, as she'd put it so many times. But she was the one who'd had the affair. She had broken something in him, as if their marriage—after what they'd been through, what he'd put himself through to keep the beams up, the walls from crumbling—could be reduced to sharing an ice cream.

~

He had smelled Richard on her, under all the perfume she'd worn those first months, in the way her hands fussed when he'd asked simple questions about why she was late, again and again. His induction ceremony as head coach in September . . . He'd worn a new suit, proud to walk through Grand Central in it, into the Yale Club on Vanderbilt, greeted personally by the concierge, ushered up the elevator, to the ballroom on the twenty-second floor.

But Nancy never showed. She'd told him she needed to work a little later but that she'd be there. *She wouldn't miss it.*

He'd been mortified: alone at his table while all the other coaches sat with their wives, whispering in their ears like people did at weddings or during church. They'd asked where she was after they'd come over to congratulate him, shake his hand.

And the worst part had been knowing he wouldn't be able to tell his wife *I needed you there.* In her eyes, he'd never be able to share her pain, his would never be as crushing, because he *could manage, go on with things.* She hadn't been able to do that, and she'd never forgiven him.

He'd needed her there at the banquet—he might have said that out loud. If she'd let him, he might have proved himself capable of what she'd needed, too, those first months especially.

~

Sarah had been the only one there with him at the banquet. He had consoled himself and thought, *At least I have Sarah. Her accomplishments.* She'd been willing to put all her time and energy into training, and she hadn't suffered one injury, not until senior year when those two stress fractures had come on suddenly in her femur. She had been diagnosed with osteopenia, the precursor to osteoporosis. *Appalling*, Dr. Owens had said. *She's suffering so young from a disease most women don't get until after menopause.*

~

Nancy left before Sarah's injuries started—the year Sarah stopped running. Before that, he'd been fine. He'd had his appetite, his sleep, and his own training hadn't suffered, not as much as Nancy believed it should have. *A feeling person wouldn't know how to live with himself.* Wasn't that how she'd put it? After Sarah's injuries, he'd become increasingly restless, dependent on thoughts of when he'd see her next, how to resume their schedule. He'd needed those hours with her, that consistency.

One Saturday he'd even made arrangements, through another girl on the team, to meet her in the common area of her dorm. He'd written out notes, objective points to go over about changing her diet to optimize recovery, a projected timeline for starting PT. He'd assumed it would cheer her up, give her something positive to focus on. And she'd smiled at him when he'd walked in with a clipboard under his arm, a fresh carton of chocolate milk for her to drink. She'd had her crutches propped on the wall, these red indents under her eyes from crying or not sleeping, maybe. But he hadn't asked her about it. He hadn't been able to bring himself to, the same way he hadn't been able to ask Nancy how she was faring once she'd started work again, once she'd decided she was going to try to function.

No, he hadn't asked Sarah about her pain either. Instead he just went over his notes, highlighting the strength training she'd want to prioritize, once she could do weight-bearing activities again. In the middle, she'd started crying. *My bones are weak,* she'd sobbed, gripping the tops of her thighs. *They ache so much.*

He'd wanted to hug her. Hold her even. It had felt so long since he'd held anyone. He was disturbed by his own need, its coming on so suddenly. Of course he'd always been aware of his job: how delicate it was, the threat of a lawsuit if he crossed even the semblance of a line. Any kind of lingering embrace—even that pause behind Becky in the hallway—could have been the end of him. All he'd wanted was to show Sarah the recovery plans again, to focus on the future, any future, but that had only made things worse. She'd looked at him like he was crazy—despicable somehow—for wanting to help her. She'd refused to come back to try and finish the season. Then after graduation, they'd lost touch completely. He'd tried looking her up, to see if she was training with a professional team anywhere, but her name hadn't popped up, not even when he limited his search to major cities like New York, DC, and Chicago because she'd wanted to work in finance. For a hedge fund.

She hadn't come back for any meets either, not even Heptagonals at Van Cortlandt, like the most accomplished alumni often did. Maybe it wasn't too late to write her now, but when he checked, her email wasn't in the network. He could have tried another online search, to see if her info was attached to a link, but he didn't have the energy. He powered his computer off. Flipped his office light.

~

Later in his apartment, around 7:30, he put a slice of bread into the toaster oven and filled a pot with water to boil eggs. He pulled the carton out of the refrigerator, five left of the dozen he'd consume over a matter of weeks; he never ate the eggs in the order of their rows, but kept the patterns symmetrical along the two axes—always rotationally symmetrical—so the center of mass stayed in the middle of the carton.

When he and Nancy were first married, she used to rearrange the cartons, put the eggs back, one after the other, neat in their rows; she'd assumed he was being scattered, *rushed*—until he'd explained his reasoning, the laws of centering weight, how to keep everything balanced, but still she'd rearrange them back, as if she hadn't believed him—as if everything he did was arbitrarily compulsive, *ungrounded.*

~

The toaster oven was ticking—he listened to the timer tick, until the machine finished, dinged. He reached straight in, fingers searing, dropping the toast bare on the counter. He ate on his couch, over his coffee table without a plate, more books than he remembered stacked around him in three short towers.

Nancy had taken all the bookcases. Had them shipped to her new apartment in West Haven, and Murray would never buy a new one, not even a small one. The only thing he'd kept was their pine headboard from an antique shop on State Street. His only new purchase had been a desk, just something to fill the second bedroom's emptiness, except for scrapings of the border he'd peeled off and had tried to paint over so long ago, and a half dozen boxes overstuffed with old files, ones Nancy had wanted to convert into a digital archive for him. But he'd refused her help then—just after they'd married. She used to say, *Isn't there one thing I can help you with?* He banished that thought. *She is gone,* he told himself, nibbling his toast.

He didn't know how much time had passed before he smelled the burning. In the kitchen, he discovered the water had boiled all the way out of the pot, hot air hissing against metal, this bluish singe at its base, more gas and smoke that Murray coughed on, hands shaking as he dropped the pan in the sink, arms flailing to clear the air.

He waited for the heat to dissipate before he filled the pan with water, and he shuddered at the continued hissing, the sound of steam. On his way home, he'd picked up a bottle of scotch he'd planned to save for later, for the weekend—a long winter—but he was tugging it out of its paper bag now, crumpling the paper, the receipt. His heart rate had not gone down; it was 102 beats per minute, *tachycardia,* he thought, drinking straight from the bottle. He drank on the sofa in his living room—minutes, hours he couldn't be certain of—until eventually the books became less defined, until he couldn't hear his heart anymore, his breathing was steadier. More emptiness and quiet, surrounding his thoughts, folding him in.

He slept on the floor, crumbs at the corner of his mouth, which stayed open, breath heavy through the night.

EIGHTEEN

Somehow, in just two weeks' time, Caroline had convinced Nancy to quit her job at Beinecke for the one at the Morgan. Several bottles of wine had been involved, and Caroline had illuminated a blank canvas, and as a moth drawn to a porch lamp in the night, Nancy could not have anticipated the magnitude of that sudden light—how much this prospect trumped everything else, even her more recent successes at Beinecke. There was no denying it: work had long since ceased to offer refuge from the past. The majority of her coworkers scorned her affair, and Nancy remained silent behind the haze of this realization coming into focus, her truth like a small, luminous marble rolling down a long hill, inconsequential under the relentless force of gravity.

Of course, it had been easy for others to judge her, Nancy thought: every year since Murray's success with Sarah Lloyd, Murray had managed to bring at least one of his girls to Nationals, making him a kind of local legend. And this had made it easier, she thought, for coworkers to assume she was the broken one, the weaker one. Nancy had felt it in the lunches and happy hours she hadn't been invited to, the reluctance of her superiors to accept her ideas when they'd once extolled them. She felt in many ways that everyone had been waiting for her to leave.

～

She would leave it all behind, then.

Caroline helped Nancy land a moderately sized apartment on First Avenue in the East Village, though it was on the sixth floor of a walkup. In carrying the first of her boxes up a steep, narrow staircase, she'd barely made it to the top. She'd needed to stop and recover her breath several times. That was the day she'd taken the plunge, the fourth of March, just three days after she signed and dated her new lease. If she wanted to survive, she was going to quit smoking for good, and that was the first thing she did. In the kitchen, she used a random takeout bag on the counter to throw out her last pack of cigarettes—though it was only an hour later, when she was lying on her belly over the cold hardwood floors, encircled by all of her boxes, pen quivering as she listed essentials like trash bags, sponges, and Q-tips in a thin spiral-bound notebook, that she fantasized about the pack still within reach and the proximity of the roof, just a shoulder shove away, where she would be free to blow smoke among views of other buildings, all at various slants, the view of the Brooklyn Bridge distant and beautiful; she would be free there to dismiss and scatter her debris.

Certainly the previous tenants had left theirs in the refrigerator: tuna fish salad gray and puffy with mold, the juices of fruits and vegetables rotted and sticky between plastic crevices, soured milk and cottage cheese stinging her nose. But the worst part had been the jars of baby food, the pureed carrots and apples and peas. Many of them half-eaten, and as she added *cleaning supplies, toothbrush holder,* and *shower rack,* she felt the baby's presence even if there was no scent, no remnants of need.

The nearest corner grocery store was on Ninth Street. Under its blue awning, an elderly Chinese man cut and arranged flesh flowers. Nancy had burned her finger testing the efficacy of the oven, and when she stepped inside, the wound throbbed. She hastily picked up a few things to get by, a box of instant oatmeal, a carton of eggs. When she was in the aisle for household items, she dropped overpriced sponges and bleach in her basket, and then at checkout, she reached for a box of Neosporin, just in case. But the box seemed too light, and it was: empty. She thought, *The city, this giant rip-off with angry, entitled inhabitants stealing and leaving messes behind for others to clean up.*

There were two people before her at checkout, so she distracted herself with a tabloid. Somehow affairs among movie stars soothed her— their marriages never lasted, and the children they adopted, ones with eccentric names they'd deliberated, made her oddly hopeful.

On her way back to the apartment, bones aching up the stairwell, she reminded herself that she had moved here to embrace her singleness, but she could still fantasize, and when she did, her future was always some vague abstraction of the past. Though reality taught her it would be the opposite: starting over would require patient love and acceptance of herself, as Katherine had often reminded her. *Was she capable of that?* She'd said, *Do you think you can do that? Forgive yourself?*

Nancy didn't know. Forgiving herself meant looking in the mirror and accepting every body part that had once produced and nurtured a child; it meant choosing kind thoughts over judgmental ones when she made a mistake; it was comforting herself when she began to chase the same loops around fear and doubt; it was not this constant chastising, this berating voice that told her she wasn't good enough and wouldn't ever be. The voice of her parents, with her always, even as she tried to free herself.

Nancy had already bleached the bathroom tiles. Now she was scrubbing the hollow belly of the claw-foot tub. The stains were permanent, and she did not know if she could take a bath knowing that a child had splashed in it, rubber toys floating as he or she kicked and laughed. She could see Jean in the tub that last time, Murray there, too, as they'd rinsed under her arms, and she had splashed the water, proud of the sounds, of what she could do.

The first time someone asked them whether they had any children afterward, Murray had been there too. They'd been out to lunch and had run into the new fencing coach, who'd started after Jean had passed, and Nancy had had to tell him—*passed*, that terrible word seeming to belong only to those who had lived a full life. Murray had been silent after the fencing coach asked the question, and she'd had to answer it—to say those words alone. In time, she'd learned not to say it out of anger or tears—Katherine had taught her to say it openly, to not deny the fact that her child would always be with her, in everything, and so she sat with it, the feeling of *Jean*, even in the tightness of Nancy's breath, as she breathed and scrubbed.

When she finished, she showered in the clean tub, running soap along her body, cleaning dirt from her nails. She showered with her feet firm along the slippery porcelain she'd get a mat for tomorrow. Then she went to the bedroom and unpacked her robe, and she made her bed. She still had to order a bed frame. Tonight she'd sleep on box springs with a set of fresh sheets and the mint-green quilt she'd taken from her parents' house, the one that used to hang on a stand in her and Murray's bedroom.

~

It was 2:00 a.m., a Saturday, and she was lying on her bed, looking up at the ceiling like she and Murray had done from time to time. She breathed in dust and heat, absorbed the sputtering sound of pipes. The city noise, the diffuse bleat of taxicabs and the asthmatic wheeze of bus brakes, the rumble of delivery trucks, and the occasional prickle of sirens. She would adjust to this, she thought. She went to her box of fiction, which she'd alphabetized by author, and opened Virginia Woolf's *Mrs Dalloway*. She'd just finished reading Woolf's diaries, and she hoped they would change how she read the novel this time around. This would be her eleventh, clear by the notes flooding the margins, in different color pens, which she regretted, because now the notes distracted her, and made it impossible to see anything but the images of light and shadow she'd always been so keen to underline—markings that made her look up to see them at play in the room, and then back in the pages.

At 6:34 a.m., she awoke with the wings of her novel spread over her chest. There were the same city sounds, but she had the frightening feeling that she'd forgotten her passport or social security card. She would not be able to start work in two days without them. But there they were, in the accordion file of important papers, along with her divorce agreement, Jean's birth and death certificates. Her life, its blueprint, to be tucked away in a file cabinet.

She did not know if it was her loneliness that made her think of Murray more now so much as the fear—the fear she saw in every patched hole and the emptiness of the cabinets she had yet to fully stock, the missing bookshelves she did not know why she hadn't brought with her, this fear she'd made a terrible mistake. Had she worked hard enough to understand him? If she'd accepted his silence, his need to put everything into work, would things have turned out differently? She thought of that first walk-through of their apartment, following the broker around, sizing up the large living room, the old kitchen: this hope of leaving the person she'd been behind, even if it came with old appliances and creaking floors.

She thought of all the furniture she'd left behind with Richard, the bookcases, the kitchen table, the glassware that had been Murray's mother's, the stoneware she'd found in Aix-en-Provence when she'd taken the train there one weekend during her fellowship. She'd told herself it was too hard to manage, too expensive to move it all, when the truth was she never wanted to see Richard again, never wanted to have to call him to coordinate pickups, to have to explain her choices; she wanted to keep the past separate and removed, like a lost, forgotten limb. But she should have known you never forgot, that you always felt the ghost of that limb, of what *had been*—this ghost who told her she should have been braver with Murray, strong enough to have at least mailed him back the glassware that belonged to him, to at least have packed up the French pottery and taken it with her, the coffee cups she'd always loved so much.

She'd once taken great care to tell Murray all about how she'd met the potter at his tiny studio in the countryside—about the number of trials that went into making a single cup—and Murray had smiled and said, *I like the rims*, which were uneven, but still she'd thought he would never understand her experience inside that studio, where one man's whole livelihood depended on the ratio of clay to water, the even speed of his wheel as he spun it, pressing the pedal down, waiting for his art to reach into existence. It was this thought, like another ghost, that would remind her of her pregnancy books: one of them had warned her about stoneware, the potential risk of high-lead content—and for this, Murray had assumed she was being foolish. *These cups are fine*. She would make herself sick, drive herself crazy. But she'd blamed him for that as well, for not acknowledging her every fear, as if his denial were inextricable from the fact of the child they had lost.

~

But the truth was Nancy's own obsessions had made her blind to the details of Murray's smile as he drank his coffee, the way he'd reached for her hand in their new apartment, just three months of being married, the way he'd said, *I love that this cup makes you happy*. She felt tears gathering there, where Murray's words were, the simple affirmation of them.

Maybe people became the best and worst versions of what you projected onto them, she thought—they became the stories you told yourself, so they filled the holes of your own story, the ones you didn't want to look at. Murray would never share her own experience of joy, or love, or pain—the absence of the child she had felt form slowly week by week in her body, then leave her as slowly over the years, the burning hole of the ghost of the flesh and bones they had buried, but he had been there too; he had suffered.

When she was thirteen, Nancy's aunt Lilian on her mother's side had passed away from breast cancer. Nancy's mother had been so enraged about the late diagnosis, after Lilian had been complaining of a lump the doctor maintained was just a benign cyst, but then as other symptoms surfaced, and the second set of scans came back six months later, the doctor could see the fingernail speck of cancer had grown into something inoperable, something that had spread into her lymph nodes. The night after Lilian died, Nancy's mother had wanted her father to hold her. She had wanted him to feel the same pain, but he couldn't—it was not his sister. Nancy had wept with her mother, partly because her mother had been so hysterical and inconsolable, and partly because her father had failed to weep, failed, it seemed, to love her aunt as much as she and her mother had.

Nancy's mother never forgave her father for that, and Nancy had thought her mother was right: it was because her father, like Murray, had seemed incapable of feeling. But now she could see it was just what her mother had seen—her mother saw what she'd needed to through her grief—not that her father had been suffocated by that pressure. As much as she'd tried to be everything her parents weren't, in marrying Murray, in resolving to raise Jean differently with him, Nancy had never completely escaped the unfulfilled desires and expectations of her own childhood. The ghosts of her parents were with her always, remnants of need that seeped into her fears and desires, whether she'd wanted them to or not. It was too impossible to look at herself honestly, clearly, without needing to point her finger at Murray, for all that he should have provided and protected her from. In blaming him, she had repeated her past. And there was no telling how these same ghosts, the way she saw the world through her own parents, would have influenced her choices, in raising her child, even as she'd sought escape, an opposite future, in Murray and Jean.

Her loneliness, this singularity of experience that was *her own*, she thought, in this new expanse of space: a space only she could fill in time.

~

She already had the key to her new office. She could round out her bookcases before Monday, prepare her desk. That Saturday, later in the afternoon, she carried her most cherished classics, her whole Everyman's Library, along with reference texts, journals, and notebooks, in tote bags, just to Third Avenue, where she caught the bus heading uptown. Tomorrow would be the essentials, for which she had her own rare editions: Eliot's *Middlemarch*; Baldwin's *Go Tell It on the Mountain*; the short novels of Marguerite Duras.

She had met her colleagues already. The director, Martin Swanson, had introduced her as a "New Haven celebrity," and his assistant, Frida, had asked if she'd tried Pepe's pizza, and an office intern, Carla, had wanted to know with whom she'd collaborated at Yale. And while she was glad for a certain degree of anonymity, she was slightly annoyed at these cliché references and assumptions. But she was going to have to get over it. After all, she was the new person here and still had to prove her abilities.

~

The first week at her new job, Martin wanted her to attend a monthly review meeting to learn about extant projects, and she still had to better orient herself with several shared spreadsheets on the server with tentative exhibition names and dates, as well as the acquisition status of works the library was bidding for. How hadn't she foreseen the difficulty of this transition? The number of folders she'd have to click through one after another, only to discover that the most important files required an authorization code, and when IT turned out to comprise a third-party entity in India, Nancy was even more frustrated. Eventually she yielded remote access to a consultant—he had not given his name, and his accent was impossible to fully parse—and as she watched, her mouse moved around like a phantom. The opening and closing of more unknown folders only enhanced her sense of estrangement, led her to wonder if it was not too late to go back to Beinecke, since the familiarity of its own quirks seemed suddenly endearing, and she could reverse commute—but then Nancy shuddered at the thought of what it would mean to admit another failure to herself. She wondered how long until she'd have enough savings to start her own business, perhaps somewhere in the heart of the West Village, where there were loads of wealthy people who might like to hire her as their private archivist.

Nancy could no longer stare at the computer screen, slipping further and further from her grip. She walked across the room to her office window, fixed her attention on a small line forming across the street, outside the Polish embassy, and then on a row of brick apartments on Thirty-Seventh Street. Apparently one served as a doctor's office, and she could not imagine how the elderly managed the stairs. There was also rumor of a cat—Frida had mentioned this cat while showing Nancy her new office—how it sometimes peered through the window of the apartment above the doctor's office. She couldn't help but think of Madame Arnaud and her black stray, so many years ago in Paris: those green eyes piercing hers, and then how she'd slipped back to bed, hugging Murray tighter below the sheets.

"Nancy." Martin stood in the doorway; his fist had knocked gently at an edge. "How's it going?"

"Oh," she said. "IT is just setting me up with access. I'm admiring the view."

"I'm sure we'll have you set up in no time." Martin smiled. His eyes were a shade lighter than Murray's, his hair this silvery bristle.

"I'm sure." She smiled back.

"Well, I was just checking on you," Martin said. "If there's anything else you need, call Frida. But let's catch up later, after the meeting." He looked at his watch. "Oh shoot, I'm leaving early today. Tomorrow then?"

Nancy nodded. And then he patted her desk and walked out.

She only had twenty minutes until the meeting, so she jotted down several questions and dates to reference, and she thought about how she'd make better eye contact with Martin next time. She took a quick bathroom break and went to the kitchen for a cup of coffee. But the coffee was too hot and stung her teeth—she nearly spit it out, but she stopped herself, sacrificing a few small splashes on the green silk camisole under her blazer. She'd worn the camisole on her first date with Murray in Paris, actually, and last night when she'd tried it on, she'd been impressed it still fit, that it was in mint condition after all these years. Murray had never appreciated fine clothes, she thought, dabbing a wetted napkin over the cloth.

Then, for some odd reason—she pictured him appreciating it: his sun-weathered hands over her, brushing down a strap, caressing beneath the collapsed silk. She looked up. A miracle no one was coming, and so she walked back to her desk with her head down, in case anyone did. She couldn't help but wonder what he might be doing at this moment: preparing for his next practice, planning out the schedule for a meet—and the thought didn't upset her as she thought it might have; it comforted her that she could picture him, that she still knew his habits, his rhythms.

~

Such thoughts persisted through the long meeting, especially when she asked a question, which she'd decided on after much silent deliberation, about any plans for starting a program for digital rights. But the question must have sounded mediocre, or perhaps should never have been framed as a question in the first place, but rather asserted with conviction—she was in a director's role after all—because no one seemed to jump on it, and the topic had moved quickly to the next item on the list: the urgency of soliciting donors, and an idea for a gala next fall emerged, with Martin calling on Frida to look into venues.

At least Nancy had succeeded in looking *right* at Martin when she'd asked her question this time, but that had also been the moment when she'd thought only of Murray—and then again, hours later, after she'd been forced to socialize with other curators and administrators and archivists—after she'd locked her office and caught the bus downtown on Second Avenue, when she should have been able to hit the reset button. But at her stop, she stepped off and nearly collided with a man. He was younger than she was, with long black hair under a Sherpa hat. He smiled and asked if she lived in the neighborhood, because he thought he'd noticed her at the laundromat on Eighth Street.

This made her nervous, as did the beaten look of his hat, and the giant mole on his nose, and so she said she was late for an appointment, a doctor's appointment, and hurried ahead, her heels pinching the large tendon between her ankle and foot. Back inside her apartment, she took off her camisole and unclipped her bra. She lay back on her bed, which she'd only partially made; the sheets were tucked, but the comforter was ruffled—she lay back and imagined what it would feel like for Murray to really touch her, all the places he knew how to soften, to bring to life. Distance had done little to allay the vividness of his touch, even if it had been impossible for so long to let herself envision that, Jean palpable in her mind. She thought maybe it was the pulse of a different place that let her consider loving again.

Caroline wanted to set Nancy up with a family friend, a doctor who was in his early fifties and somewhat newly single, at least that was how Caroline had put it. Nancy had been too afraid to ask what she meant, for fear of seeming too interested, too desperate, but Nancy also supposed that just fearing this about herself implied that she was, in fact, "desperate."

Nancy could not predict, as Katherine used to remind her weekly, the reactions or judgments of others, no matter how much she tried to anticipate the future or was surprised by a person's rudeness or callousness, and rehashed the words over and over, as if she could somehow revise the past. No, how Nancy might feel in a given moment, as it was with all humans, remained an infinite mystery; the only thing she had control over was how she responded and recovered, how she conserved her energy so more of her heart could survive, could stay open to giving and receiving kindness.

Caroline continually tried to improve Nancy's life—she supposed the job at the Morgan was just the start of her friend's project—she tried to be patient, to hear Caroline out, but now, just last weekend, she'd proposed the absurd idea that Nancy join her running club through New York Road Runners, where Caroline served on the board.

~

They'd been having brunch one morning in mid-March to celebrate Nancy's forty-ninth birthday in SoHo, and Caroline had uttered the words. Nancy had had her fork poised over quarters of roasted potato, some of it submerged in the drippings of a single poached egg.

Nancy had no desire to relive her past, especially any portion that involved running, but somehow she'd found a way to answer calmly, "I don't think so."

"I really think—" Caroline tipped her coffee cup toward her lips, then set it down. "I think it would be good for you to get over these blocks."

"What blocks?" Nancy pushed her plate toward the center of the table.

"I don't know," Caroline said. "Not blocks, just barriers, I guess . . . to enjoying your life." Caroline looked down while taking a long sip of coffee.

"Blocks and barriers are the same thing," Nancy said. "And I didn't come here for a therapy session."

Caroline's lips twitched, but still she continued. "I just want you to enjoy the city," she said. "To feel like you can make new friends here."

"And running is the only way? A running team? Come on," Nancy said.

"There are so many people I could introduce you to," Caroline persisted. She speared a blackberry with her fork.

"Because you're so worried I can't make friends on my own?"

"It's not that. It's just that I've known you for a long time, and you've always just kind of had one person in your life. And I can't imagine how hard it must be for you, especially now."

"What?" Nancy said. Feeling Marjorie's judgment again, a different kind, but it was still there, this repetition of others needing to reduce her, to fail to accept her or see her as she was—a woman who'd once been married to a famous running coach. The mother of a child who could have run as well, maybe even accomplished as much.

"I'm sorry, that came out wrong," Caroline said, wiping away tears. "I really just want the best for you." Caroline's eyes were frantic. She reached for Nancy's hand across the table, but it was too late.

"The best for me is what?" Nancy stood up. "Living a copy of your life?"

"No, no. That isn't what I meant." Tears glazed Caroline's eyes.

"Maybe I'm happy alone," Nancy said, words still fuming despite nascent regret: "Maybe I'm free, and maybe I don't like exercise." She put down sixty dollars, an embarrassing amalgam of twenties and fives, to cover them both.

"Nancy, please," Caroline said, wiping a rush of tears. "Please sit back down."

Nancy wasn't going to, she couldn't, but she heard Katherine urging her to be patient, to give herself a few seconds to focus again, realize where she was, that she was more than a disembodied feeling, that she had power, control. "Okay," she said, lowering slowly. She kept her hands on the edge of her chair.

Caroline dabbed the corner of her eye, as though she was trying to find words but was too afraid of upsetting Nancy further, and Nancy sat with that, her own insecurity, more of it rising up.

"Jim says I do this thing," Caroline said. She looked up at Nancy weakly. "That I get fixated on other people's lives. Because it's easier than focusing on my own." She wiped more tears. "I don't know what there's left to fix. I've subscribed to everything already. Fitness, life coaching, marriage counseling, parent counseling." She laughed nervously like Nancy. "You must think I'm insane."

"No," Nancy said. "I don't know." She reached for her glass of water. "It's just Murray," she said. "You know it's a sore point. You know I was married to him."

"Well, yes," Caroline said. "But I guess I thought it's been years, and you never mention him."

Now Nancy was the one withholding tears. This surprised her; she supposed she hadn't realized how angry she still was, how much she still resented the sport, as if it had been the root of their problems. She supposed that running had always been there, Sarah especially—the easiest thing to feed her doubts, like blaming torn wallpaper for pulling down a collapsing house.

Caroline was looking down at her hands on the table, fidgeting with her rings. "I should have put two and two together," she said finally. "It was insensitive of me."

"No," Nancy said. "I don't know. It's just hard." She felt her tears release. "To be around new people, wondering why I'm not married. Without children. Why." She could not suppress heavier tears.

And as Caroline held her, Nancy felt as she had in college when she got overwhelmed by the pressure, so much pressure not to fail—she couldn't worry about another Marjorie, another pointing finger. Caroline was trying to be the best friend she could, given the circumstances, and it was up to Nancy to let her *continue* to be this. She would never know unless she tried, so she agreed to do that. *Try.*

~

The 5K took place just one week later, in Central Park. The temperature was low for March, in the twenties, but Nancy told herself that this cold might objectify her experience—make it unbearable enough to justify why she never wanted to run again.

Nancy showed up in sweatpants, and a thinned-out beanie, and gloves from the dollar store. She'd refused to step inside a specialty running shop—the thought of Murray's shadow as she searched for her size, hangers zinging along the sales rack—was enough to make her nauseous for days. Yet as she looked around at all the people jogging in place up the 102nd Street transverse, clapping warmth into their hands, there was no escaping him.

"Nancy!" Caroline called from a large elm tree across from a row of porta potties: what she'd said would be the easiest place marker, with hundreds of runners crowding the start. "Didn't you see us?"

"No," Nancy said. It was true she hadn't, but then she hadn't really been looking. She'd been hoping for dissolution among the crowds.

Caroline gave her one look, her hand over her mouth. "Come," she said, holding out a steaming thermos. "The perks of VIP," she laughed.

Nancy couldn't help feeling embarrassed compared with Caroline's more polished friends keeping warm in Lycra or fleece.

"This is Michael," Caroline said. "Nancy's here to give running a try."

"Very nice," Michael said. Nancy wondered if he was the doctor, the same Michael that Caroline had wanted to set her up with? But wouldn't Caroline have given advance notice? She felt a sudden desire to defend herself, to claim she'd been married to a professional runner for years, but what would she say? *I may look like an amateur, but my ex-husband is a college cross-country coach, and he swears by sweats.* Self-sabotage came in many forms.

Caroline knocked her on the shoulder. "Have you warmed up yet?"

Nancy shook her head. She'd thought of jogging from the subway, but she'd decided to save what little energy she had. She was so out of shape she doubted her ability to even walk the full loop.

"Oh," Caroline said. "This is Maureen and Katie. And Max." Everyone waved. "Max is on the board too," Caroline said.

Maureen was an investment banker, Max worked in advertising, Katie sold pharmaceuticals, and Rita—the last to join their group, then boldly stripping down to briefs and a singlet—clearly she was running this for time—was the director of a private school in New Jersey.

Around her she watched as other runners, beautiful in their name-lessness, seeped into corrals; she looked for at least one face as aged and inexperienced as her own. But no one started running this late in life, did they?

Behind her, porta potties shuddered their familiar rhythm, remind-ing her of when Murray ran the 2000 Chicago Marathon—another fact she'd scorned. He'd entered this event not even a year after Jean, and she had gone with him anyway, as "sideline support." It was something she'd always given and hadn't wanted to feel like she'd never be able to give him again. Or maybe they'd both seen it as some kind of final test, of whether they would be able to play the roles they expected of one another, whether it would be possible to forgive. Except Nancy hadn't made it to the four-mile checkpoint where she'd promised to wait for him; even before the official start, she had gotten in her car and driven back to the hotel. And Murray hadn't said anything—hadn't even looked at her when he entered four hours later to find her curled in bed, among a box of Slims and *People* magazine.

He had been hunched in his finisher's blanket, one of thin silver foil. He had turned on the hot water, and she had listened to its rain with her eyes open. That night they had slept in separate beds, and they had also woken up separately; him first, always to his hunger, and she, much later, to the sound of street construction, but she had not found him downstairs at breakfast.

"Should we move up?" Caroline asked Nancy.

"You should," Nancy said.

"We're doing this together, remember?" Caroline said. How many times did she have to remind her? But Nancy tried to counter this thought, to remember why she was here. *Try* to forgive herself for all the ways her life hadn't panned out as she'd hoped.

~

She looked up at the silver-lit sky, the sun this muted shard within it. A jagged line of trees rimmed the horizon, ethereal with mist. It comforted her against the laughter inside the corral she'd followed Caroline into—this nervous, anticipatory laughter, like the waiting room in Dr. Weiss's office: mothers comparing notes about tests and procedures, weighing written expectations against physical feelings.

But the timer above, large and black and red, reminded her of the emergency room, when she and Murray had waited for official word. They had seen Jean again, just before she went into the ER, tubes running everywhere, catheters and IVs, tiny tubes in her mouth, clips on her fingers. For a moment, they'd had hope. Maybe it wasn't too late. Yale New Haven had the best surgeons in the country; she had tried to repeat that thought, in the blur of the muted television in the waiting room. They'd held hands as nurses and orderlies rushed in and out of rooms, updating records, rolling carts of supplies, machines beeping. The sound of a man screaming about his bleeding father, others in the waiting room moaning about more benign wounds, wanting priority, wanting someone to hear them.

Somehow Nancy had wanted more time to pass, the hope of a prolonged surgery, of resuscitation, but then the spinning had stopped, all of the activity, the cries, around them. They had watched the doctor approach, his slow steps to tell them, the look in movies, but it had been their life she'd been watching—and the words as he spoke, *her* collapsing again on the floor, as she had before the ambulance, the reenactment of that repetition. Jean's death was something that *had happened*, and what she would give to go back to that moment, before the grieving curtain was closed, and they'd wept and held her, Jean in her blanket, eyes closed as soundlessly as when she'd been born, that little rush of air Nancy had felt for the first time in her arms.

~

With all her strength, Nancy wanted to turn now and run back to the subway, but a loudspeaker said the corrals were closing.

Caroline tugged at her hand, and Nancy winced. She had another nightmare last night, that Caroline was conspiring with Murray—she'd seen Caroline's face transplanted with Sarah's, and they were having an affair, and Murray had taken Caroline away on a plane to a race on the other side of the world—but then the camera lens had shifted and Nancy had found herself below the plane, submerged in the ocean, steadying a matryoshka doll in her palms, the wooden children slipping out, though somehow she had been able to save the tiniest one. The one no larger than a marble, its image still like lace over her eyes after she woke. She was surprised to picture it again.

The loudspeaker began thanking A-list sponsors—Caroline looked at Nancy while she smiled and clapped. And then a young girl—Nancy pictured her in a little wool cap with red gloves—came on to sing "The Star-Spangled Banner." Her voice was thin but powerful. The crowd roared after the last note; there were screams, finger whistles, hoots. The timer above collapsed with the last ten seconds, slow and tortuous, and Nancy closed her eyes just before it cleared to zero. She was struck by the fact of a bullhorn instead of a gun—blood surging through her, legs airy and numb, moving despite thought, any reasoning from her brain. How much watching a race, watching college girls with their lean, strong legs, differed from actually running one—this first attempt

236

of her own. She was surprised when they hit the first quarter-mile mark, her legs miraculously working in measure with Caroline's long, steady stride. Nancy heard clapping as they rounded the bend. Family members cheered for their loved ones, children held out hands to be slapped. She reached to touch a small boy's palm, then an older man's.

Cold March air filled her lungs, burned her ears and fingers. She did not think about her weak calves or knees, her nonathletic feet. *Just get to mile one,* she told herself. But the minute she saw the first mile marker, time, distance, was no longer the road ahead, but her heavy legs, and the seconds it took to breathe each breath, to place one foot in front of the other. When she rounded another bend, there was more loud cheering, more strollers and spectator signs. A man in a leprechaun costume passed, shimmering in green spandex and a matching metallic hat. Nancy lacked the strength to smile. Air flattened into the cap of her chest. She couldn't catch it, oxygen pressed in and closed.

"There is a water stand at mile two," Caroline said, stopping as Nancy had stopped.

"Go on," Nancy said. "Please, just go!"

"I'm not leaving you," Caroline said. "Five slow breaths." She placed her hand on Nancy's back. "Then we'll ease into a jog."

Nancy tried, but there was no such thing as *ease*. Didn't Caroline understand that? Her whole life, God had made uneasiness the point.

"Follow me," Caroline said, reaching for her hand. Nancy closed her eyes and opened them. She was in the ocean again, carrying a wooden marble in her hand, she swore she heard Jean crying—as if to tell her, *Mother, I was crying, I warned you, but you were unable to listen. You were my mother.*

She heard more cheering and whistling, though it felt distant, as though she were looking in at all the spectators, all of their posterboard signs: *YOU CAN DO IT, PROUD OF YOU, I LOVE YOU.* Nancy began to feel even lighter—like the fizz of a soda bottle, suddenly opened.

"You made it to two!" Caroline said at the water station. She handed Nancy a paper cup, which Nancy gulped, but most of the water spilled because Nancy kept moving. She knew if she stopped moving again, she would stop for good, and she had come much farther than she imagined she would; she only had one mile left. But these later steps did not register with her, the way her body wrenched like oranges, acidic and pulped to their skins. She did not feel minutes—each of the eleven still required to see the finish line, another black clock flashing red with milliseconds—willed forward by the waxing throb of crowds. Nancy closed her eyes tight and opened them, closed and opened them, to sustain the figment of a dream not yet broken. She thought of the sky and the road, their stillness, their indifference to time—what it would be like for Jean to run in her shoes, feel the road beneath her, that exhilaration of feeling her body overcome gravity for the first time.

"Less than half a mile!" Caroline cheered, the muted sound of gloves clapping.

Nancy pinched her lips together, salty with sweat. She tried not to think about heat on her neck, about the tiny air sacs that differentiated the lungs of a six-month from a seventh-month fetus . . . *Weak air sacs*, Katherine had maintained, were not the reason Jean had stopped breathing. Nor was it because she'd been sleeping on her stomach and not her back.

Their child hadn't died because she and Murray might have been ambivalent about having children for a time, or because they had fought the night of their anniversary, not because they'd made love in those moments, breathless, that excess of breath, while Jean took her last. There was no such thing as causality, she thought—things happened in the order that they chose to; you could try to predict the order, spend your whole life projecting into the future, but life would still arrive when it decided to; life would prove you wrong, and the only thing you could do, she thought, was try your best. *Try* and *try.*

Seeing the finish added translucence to the picture. She felt emptied of terror, of rage, of pain, the boxes she'd packed and failed to unpack for years, none growing smaller or lighter each time she'd tried. But she saw the blanket she'd knitted for Jean as light, thin and diffused through a slit of window in a room. She inhaled, exhaled. Horns and bells beat her on: beat the unidentifiable noun that lived between her throat and the base of her ribs. This invisible weight that never let her fully take a whole breath.

She heard Jean crying again, but for a moment it felt not like the one she hadn't heard, but the one she was hearing now. The one that asked her to stay here in this moment. *Here*, so there was no more holding on to what hadn't been before or could have been after. For so long she'd been carrying the marble, and she still had it, now slick with her own sweat, cold and alive in the winter air.

There were studies Nancy had found later—the ones she'd taken years to read, about how *the act* of breathing had to be learned. At some point during an infant's development, breathing moved from the lower to higher registers of the brain, from the part that was primordial and automatic to the part that was conscious and learned. Sometimes an infant got stuck, Nancy remembered; Jean had gotten caught some where in the middle, taking her breath too late.

Let it go, she wanted to say out loud, to someone, the breath Nancy had forced in and now held on to in the cold.

Letting go.

It didn't have to mean that she'd loved too little, too far between.

NINETEEN

Murray cut through Old Campus, where all of the freshman lived, past Lanman-Wright Hall with its statues of lions and its bare dogwood trees in the courtyard. *L-Dub*, it was called, reeking of beer and mildew.

Three students were throwing a Frisbee on the lawn. Exaggerated wrist flicks and lunges. Laughter.

He noticed a young girl, hair wrapped in a silk kerchief, reading on a blanket. Her tote bag bulging with books, like the one Nancy had carried around with her everywhere, in case she was ever caught waiting.

He paused before Battell Chapel: a host of flyers for theater and improv comedy and poetry readings, but he found no mention of a vigil. He turned the heavy iron handle, peering into the empty space. Inside, his eyelids twitched as he gazed up at the blue coffered ceiling, then at the sign of the Trinity on the pier walls. Apse windows by the altar. Stained glass flanking the nave.

He sat down in a pew and looked up again, tracing the sunken panels, these miniature octagon shapes. He had never painted a ceiling, only the walls of rooms: first there had been yellow, then lavender; finally white, for Nancy. It was February when Murray had painted it again. She'd said she needed to breathe.

"Do you mind if we set up?" A large bald man in a navy T-shirt gripped a white plastic bucket.

"No," he said. "I was just leaving." He felt as though two televisions played the same channel in adjoining rooms: broadcasted echo.

"Just setting up for an information session. You're welcome to stay." The man tugged at an earlobe. "If you, or anyone you know, is interested in the Peace Corps—it's never too late."

"I don't know anyone."

"Do you work here?" the man asked.

"I don't," he said. "Do you?"

"You're funny," the man said. "Coach. Now I see it." He pointed to the *XC* for *cross-country* on Murray's jacket. The stopwatch in his hands. Murray tightened his fists, eyes locking harder on the blue sandstone walls, a wood-beamed ceiling encroaching.

"I'm John," the man said, wiping a hand on his jeans.

Murray nodded.

Another man, young, walked in. He didn't shake John's hand; rather, he hugged him tightly. They talked about how long it'd been, his train ride up, what the young man was doing with his life.

Murray didn't feel himself turn the handle of the door—or drifting back—through the green, where the English major was still reading.

Becky's first semester had required reciting the first lines of *The Canterbury Tales* in Middle English. She'd volunteered a recitation for him one morning on the way to the course. She'd been giddy with the newness of college, he guessed. The first line mentioned April. He remembered nothing of the rest, the length of the journey the poem was meant to cover.

Nancy had once said that *inside they were opposite people*; she, fueled by a vivid inner life, while he understood the world as material. He had not countered her, words broken and sawed off within him, like numerated letters on a Scrabble board, this game they once played over a span of weeks.

~

He drove to the Walgreens nearest the hospital and walked up and down the aisles, searching discounted appliances, scanning flashlights and batteries and headphones. The watch was different from the kind he was used to, but it was enough, so he crushed the sides of the plastic with his hands, and when that didn't work, he tried tearing it apart with his teeth.

"I hope you plan to buy that," a voice said. A woman in a red apron: hair black with a white skunk streak.

"Yes," he said several times until the register, where he asked for a pair of scissors.

Outside the store, two seconds before the first stopwatch hit its maximum, he clutched the new one, ready to start, at the exact moment. It was a windy day, and a plastic soda cap blew near his feet, and he could hear sirens outside the hospital.

He kept the watch by the gearshift and studied, on and off, the approach of five minutes, then ten, after he'd stopped the car. When he felt he could focus on the road again, he restarted it.

At home, he boiled water and took a shower. He thought of going back to the campus at night to see if there wasn't something else going on, if maybe the men had been also helping set up for a campus vigil. He went to his door and peered out the tiny hole, expecting more sirens, a line of police cars, but of course he couldn't see that through a hole, so he stepped outside, his heart palpitating, breath short. He was wearing boxers, and he felt his bare legs, his cold ears. He went back inside and had to grip the kitchen sink. The teakettle hissed. He poured tea. He turned on the news, but after fifteen minutes, he couldn't sit there, waiting for footage. He imagined Rodney carrying a bag stuffed with little candles, rubber holders, snuffs for the vigil she might still be planning. Anna too? Didn't they know vigils were bad luck; vigils suggested defeat? You had to wait, to be patient for Becky to regain her strength.

His tracksuit had not been washed in seven days, but still he stepped back into it, in the bathroom, zipping the jacket three-quarters of the way up. He parted his thin hair as if it made a difference.

He thought of the course, of driving around at this time. His log had recorded rounds almost every hour except between 3:00 and 6:00 p.m., when he usually had to be at practice, but today was Friday and the girls had done an easy run in the morning. To save their legs.

He reached for his jacket and hopped to put on a shoe. He had to sit to tie the other one. His hands were shaking. *Murray,* he heard someone say. *We're trying to speak. Why won't you listen?*

And then there she was. Becky's mouth forming unintelligible words. *Jean hasn't crossed yet. You have to help her cross.* He saw Nancy's back over the bed, rising and falling, after waking from another nightmare. He saw himself zipping his jacket again and finding his clipboard. Saw himself turning the other way, hoping she'd fall back asleep.

He hadn't noticed the extent of the apartment's silence—hadn't heard the depth of her restless mutterings, her tossing and turning through the night, until she went missing, her side of the bed empty more nights of the week than not, her absent toothbrush.

He went to his computer and turned on the reading lamp. He waited for the machine to start, for the tiny hourglass to load applications onto his screen. He had saved three different messages from her in a folder. He had read them twenty-two different times, not to analyze them, but to affirm their existence. To consider his reply.

He opened the latest one, from last week: *Dear Murray. I am thinking of you.*

A message so simple it needed a simple reply. *Dear Nancy . . .* In typing, fingers twitching, same as this near-constant twitch he felt in his sleepless eyes, he began to inch toward other words. Longer explanations he still couldn't provide.

~

How can I know what you're thinking? she'd once asked. *How do you expect me to know anything?*

Nancy never had to know. Weren't his actions clear enough? Everything he did, *had done,* had been because he loved her. She need only to account for his actions. If she'd added them up, she would have seen.

Now he stood, looking out the window. Across the street was a white house; in the night, it glowed blue. Above it, a sliver of moon.

After some time—he didn't know how much—a car rolled by. It paused before a house, two tubes of light over the drive. The clock turned eight before a girl skipped out. She was wearing a sweater and blue jeans. Then a boy stepped out of the car. The engine still running. Murray had cracked open the window to hear its thrum. He watched as the girl hugged the boy. He was tall and lanky under a baseball cap.

When the car sped away, Murray paced back to the kitchen.

He had reheated the teakettle, and he poured more into his cup. He sat down and looked over a packet with seed times for next Saturday. He had figured Anna's performance four different ways, factoring in the time she'd taken off and the time she still had to put in. Just two days until she started running again.

Then, he thought, if she'd surprised him once before, she would again. Children surprised their parents. His girls had always done that.

He could not feel his tongue in contrast to the temperature of the tea burning it, but he hoped that if he closed his eyes and visualized Anna's strong back and thighs in uniform, her cleats digging into the dirt, no matter the time of day or temperature, his heart might steady.

～

Then Murray saw himself. *1975.* He was nineteen and standing on Scranton's crushed cinder track for the mile. There had been a dozen other runners, two rows of them, and he had stood in the second row.

It had been raining, water pulsing along his eyelids and down his mouth. He had tried to shake it off like a dog, and then leaned in as the gunman counted ten seconds before it was time.

He could not hear the sounds as they were, but the rain—it was still palpable, spitting bullets at his ankles and knees. His hair hard and cold by his eyes.

Now he had his eyes closed, and he was barefoot and crouched, knees shaking as though a line had been painted on the hardwood floor in the kitchen. If he could just hear the gun, imagine his body flying through the room—through the room—outside to the road like a catapulted car.

Maybe he could sit down and type a reply or pick up a phone to make a call. He'd write Lisa, tell her he was sorry for anything he'd said. *What had he?*

Coach!

He nearly shouted, eyes still closed, fists knotted by his side.

Becky walked toward him: hips swinging crookedly, hands closed and twisted, mouth twisted.

A spoon locked in her fist as she scooped cereal. A book with pages she couldn't turn by herself: From now on, would someone else have to turn them?

He pushed his two watches into his pocket. The library was open until midnight on a Friday, so he drove to Sterling Memorial and used a computer to write down a series of call numbers. He had checked the screen and his bit of scrap paper several times—maybe four different times—to make sure he had the numbers right, then he took the elevator up to the stacks, to the thirteenth floor, for more titles on brain injury.

He tore through case studies and dense science, a memoir by a woman who had recovered full function of her brain and body, who had returned to work and achieved impossible feats. He researched the exact nature of her injury, scrutinizing the anatomy of the brain, translating what controlled what—the process involved in this woman's surgery—where the hematomas had been removed and how regions might have been rearranged around these absences.

~

After his apartment had been emptied, Murray found a way to take up all the extra space—filled every room with his notebooks and old mail, filled each up like a sea around him. No one visited—no one would criticize him—no one to recommend the couch closer to the television, his desk closer to his bed, his manuals that belonged on shelves, not the floor.

The full rooms made it like a maze in the morning and at night on his way to bed, so he didn't have to think; he would tire himself stepping around these things, getting closer to that final point of exhaustion, always—the one that let him sleep.

Yesterday, Rick had knocked on the door to Murray's office. Printed itineraries lay over the floor, and torn sheets from his legal pad, but Rick hadn't said anything about that. He'd said, *Murray, I want to talk to you.* Murray had sat up straight in his chair, away from the new to-do list he was making.

Sure, Rick, he had said, calm as ever.

Then Rick had said, *Murray, there have been some complaints.* Then he'd paused. *I'm not talking about the accident. I'm talking about the girls. They're concerned.* He'd paused again, and Murray had asked him what he meant, and he'd said, *They're concerned that you're talking to yourself. Mumbling things they can't hear.*

Murray knew it wasn't true—he'd told Rick that the girls were young, that they misunderstood him. He was figuring splits; he always figured the math aloud. *No, Murray*, Rick had said. *I've noticed it too. You're—you look like you haven't slept.* Murray began to explain he was working overtime, but Rick had cut him off. *We're under a lot of scrutiny*

247

right now, he'd said. *We know this isn't your fault, but we have to be careful. Becky's injury is sensitive.*

Murray had felt his rage boil up. *You don't think I know that?* he'd been about to say. *You don't think I'm trying to get to the bottom of this, locate the criminal?* But he had not yielded to those words, only to the silence of Rick's stern eyes. *You have to hold yourself together now,* Rick had said, and then, *It couldn't hurt to see someone, before the season gets more chaotic. Or maybe take some time off.*

Time off. Murray had felt the words boil over, this singeing heat—he'd wanted to lean in and grab Rick by the collar, remind him there wasn't anyone to fill his shoes, that he was saving the season, the program for that matter—if they wanted to seal recruits, if they wanted to continue his legacy. But Murray had bit his lip hard, had gripped his pen firmer, and watched Rick just pat him on the shoulder. *Think about it,* Rick had said, before closing Murray's door.

∼

"Coach?" A finger brushed his back. Liu was gripping a heavy tote bag. A large white sweater slipped from her shoulder.

"I come here to do the same thing." She smiled dimly.

Murray had to work saliva into his mouth. And when he spoke, when he said, "Oh?" his voice wasn't familiar. But he focused on her pale cheeks, and he thought of the ceramic Nancy had put into storage because of the lead content when she was pregnant. *You're crazy,* he'd said.

"I have to study chemistry for school anyway. So I come up here to read."

"Be careful," he said.

She was silent, her face scrunched.

"You might break it. It's expensive."

"These books?" she said, laughing quietly. "I usually use them when I'm here. I am about to put them back."

"Good," he said. "That's very good."

"It's not true, is it?" she said, her voice tinny and hollow like a can Murray and Patrick had once used to talk between rooms.

"What?" he said.

"That you want to get rid of Rodney?"

He was silent again. The pages of the book he was reading were sticky. "No," he said finally, counting to ten, imagining his arms square below him, and then his chest falling to the floor as his abdomen squeezed him up.

"I didn't think so," she said, eyes hazy like formula. "I don't believe what the others say anyway," she said. Her hand reached for his, wrist thin as a candy cane.

"Is that right?" he asked.

"Yes," she said. "I think you are doing the best you can."

Her forgiveness?

He scooted his chair closer to the small desk he was using, pressed to the wall before a window that overlooked the street. He was high up, and he could see streetlamps—and students gathered along the quad and by the women's fountain.

"I think the architect was like you," he said. "She achieved this—built that fountain."

Liu just looked at him.

"Maya Lin, just like you," he went on. "But she was a mediocre student." Murray had heard the tour guide say this about Maya Lin, when he and Nancy had taken their first walk around the campus, and they had paused at the fountain, the water steadily flowing over the edges of the rounded gray stone.

Rodney, he thought. *Her poor grades*—and then he wondered if it *was* Rodney there, Rodney in the stacks looking at him now?

Liu looked away, down toward her feet. She wore silken flats. They weren't supportive; she needed to wear better shoes. He closed his book and asked her to leave.

"You aren't right," Liu said, but now she was crying. He wouldn't stand one more girl crying. Didn't they all see—everyone—that he had his job to execute, all the hours he put in? *Who* would do it, if he didn't?

Liu had left him, and so he put the books back, and he folded the notes he'd taken—all on scratch paper—into his pocket.

He paused to take a sip of water at the fountain. It was 11:43, according to the clock above the checkout desk. But his second stopwatch read 5:39.785. Zeros, digits between numbers flooding his brain.

TWENTY

Nancy began running with Caroline in the mornings. They met at 6:30 a.m. for two loops around the bridle path in the park, where the ground was soft and smelled sweetly of manure that forced owners to yank the leashes of their dogs harder, collars jangling in the mottled darkness. It was when they neared the reservoir—or the slivers of path that offered a clear view of the water, when the sun began to rise three miles in, that Nancy could ease into a pace. It was here, even at the age of forty-nine, that she was surprised she could focus on something else besides the stiffness in her muscles and joints, the endless cold in her lungs. She could focus on the morning light, how it flickered over the silver slant of high-rises, casting their impressions, silent and still, over the water's glass. Or the snow, when it snowed, like ribs, along the path. Or bare trees crisscrossed black like uneven spokes.

In time, over the course of seven months, she learned to abandon the pain of every step, to at least accept it as part of the process, as a discomfort that came and went. If she was patient, the pain always passed. And it was one of the few times in her life when there was no room for thought—the sensations of her body superseded it, and if focusing on those sensations was the only thing she could do, when she finished each run, her mind felt that much freer to think new thoughts, to feel hopeful, she supposed, about what the day might bring.

She grew strong enough to hold a conversation with Caroline, grew open to talking across subjects that had not come easily before. Yes, there was always the weather and upcoming weekend plans, but there were also the movies she'd seen at the Angelika, the plays at Barrow Street Theatre, the two-hour lunch break she'd taken one Wednesday to try Korean barbecue with Martin and Frida, the Sunday evenings she spent perusing contemporary books at the Strand. They could talk about running practice on Tuesday evenings at the East River Track. Nancy didn't mind running in the slowest group, and she took frequent breaks between sets. And when it came time to race, she wore the singlet and shorts she got as a member. In these uniforms, she felt Murray's presence deeply. His sweat, the faded blue each item took on from repeated washing, and sometimes, no, often, really, she felt him adjusting her form. She knew from the diagrams he drew, her shoulders needed to be square, though they'd never be square, and her knees at ninety degrees, though her hip flexors were too tight to fulfill such a range. But she also felt him when she wanted to quit but didn't—when it was raining or snowing or below ten degrees the following year, when she had to double up on spandex and gloves to get out the door— she felt him every time she braved uncertainty or forced order onto the disorder of a given day. And she was thankful for that, to picture him zipping up his coat and tying his shoes under the worst possible conditions.

Nancy thought of him, too, as she began to discover new routes by running down the East Side, past South Street Seaport, to Battery Park. She ran through the gardens that hooked through the West Side and continued down a path along the Hudson, scintillating in the sun, all the way up past Chelsea Piers and the *Frying Pan*, and the Sea, Air & Space Museum, past the Fifty-Ninth Street bridge, up Riverside Park and Washington Heights—once all the way to the Cloisters in Fort Tryon Park, where her knees ached over cobblestones and the tamed grounds of its gardens, and she walked its magnificent halls, its chapels with illuminated manuscripts. Before her body chilled with sweat, she ventured to part of a great stone ledge and leaned over it, looking down at the water, this revised view of the small and distant river, still quiet and shimmering.

One Saturday the following October, she ran through Chinatown, where the smell of fish was strong, the piles of fruit wobbly and over-flowing from barrels, the street signs foreign, the voices frenzied, but she ran through the maze, and she focused on remaining calm, being a force of calm, which carried her up the Manhattan Bridge, this eggshell-colored steel that took her to Brooklyn, to Jay Street, which was wide and flat, and she ran to the farmers market in Grand Army Plaza—gourds and pumpkins and apples robust with autumn, pies glinting under plastic wrap that she had to stop to appreciate, to admire the delicacy with which berries had been tucked below folds of sugared crust. She curved around past the Brooklyn Public Library and entered Prospect Park there, where there were fewer people than at the main entrances. Over many Saturdays of running the loop, she would learn its specific sequence of hills, which were at least shorter than the hill in Harlem, but they happened in close succession. She learned to distract herself with the fragrance of the surrounding woodlands, to imagine the proximity of the Botanical Garden, efforts of conservancy not unlike her own at the library.

Sometimes she stopped at a stand and bought yellow Gatorade, the electrolytes Murray insisted on, enough energy to exit the park and jog through Prospect Heights, then Brooklyn Heights, where she admired the brownstones, the shaded, tree-lined streets that connected to a promenade for a view of the river. If she was patient and fol-lowed the signs through the construction, the scaffolding, she found the staircase to the Brooklyn Bridge. She squeezed between tourists taking photographs of the stone towers and steel-wire suspension cables. At one point there was a girl, no older than twenty-five, balancing over a truss; Nancy felt rifts building between breaths, blood flooding her face, her quickening pulse—the desire to say *life was precious*—but this was someone else's life and she had to let that be, to step outside the image, to let it recede. There was just the snake of the river again, Manhattan a stagger of rushed script across the way. It glimmered over the water, clouds sifting between the sharp, narrow bodies of the buildings, the sky soft and cyan blue against anthracite, at turns silver—she could see again the largeness and the smallness of the world, time endlessly stretching and contracting the spinning orb of its arms.

Some evenings, especially in the winter months, when daytime was short and she left her office for the darkness, she ran through the bar-lit Lower East Side to the Williamsburg Bridge, guided by her footsteps as they shuddered over cast-iron steps. Never so dark that she couldn't detect a clamor of neon graffiti—or notice the shadow of a bicycle on the adjacent path. She could catch a twinge of conversation here or there, too, sometimes—she liked best to hear a listener's pause after something was said. And she didn't know how to express in words the simultaneity of traffic rumbling below and above her—the sudden, illumined windows of a subway car—the J/M/Z train she'd rode home once after a run through some Hasidic quarters. It was a symphony that elevated and exalted her, and if she wrote Murray a letter now, she would tell him all this—how the distance between them was ever shifting, modulated by a single step, a single breath—and in this movement, this sound, she also found silence, a reigning silence that obliterated barriers between one thing and the other. In silence, weren't they two of the same? Weren't they part of some continuance that found its origin in Jean?

The silence in her chiseled cheekbones, the sharpness of her eyes, the crow's-feet that had formed from miles of squinting in the sun— they reminded her of him. She wished to tell Murray she felt him there, in her body—different from desire. It was the way of repeated distance, of starting in one place and arriving at another, and the time it took to get there, printed by the map of sinew and tendon, veins rivering with blood, muscle fibers that frayed and rebuilt themselves into fortresses overnight.

Nights, as she lay in bed, legs heavy with exhaustion, she pictured Murray's view of the body as a clock. Minutes and seconds never pointed to a continuum; rather, they were fixed and measured. They were results. Running, for him, represented a mountain whose peak never ended at the top. She wondered as she ran if maybe each peak represented a new summit he hadn't been able to help but climb. So Nancy ran on, crossing bridges that connected her to Queens and Roosevelt Island and Randall's Island.

She took the train to Long Island and ran through Roslyn Heights and Sea Cliff—took it to Westchester and ran along the Old Aqueduct Trail—through Dobbs Ferry, Irvington, Tarrytown, and Sleepy Hollow. Several times she connected from the trail to the Rockefeller Preserve, where she crossed farm meadows and ran loops around the lake. She licked sweat from her lips, listened to the crunch of dirt, the throb of roots under her shoes . . . and living, she thought, was the way light, temperature, breeze changed, in seconds. It was the sound of her feet falling in echo, distant from any pack, three falls for every one breath. It was bound by the borders of a moment one had to learn to hold for hours: daylight relaxing into dusk, dusk into evening, black. An accumulation of moments in which she grew ever smaller, her body no more than time's vessel, this tremor of universe, tiny and self-contained and spinning on.

Caroline was surprised by the depth, the constancy of Nancy's new habit. But she congratulated Nancy and cheered for her at road races, made signs that she held up from the sidelines as Nancy ran by.

Caroline didn't scold Nancy either, the first time Nancy had pushed herself to the point of injury. By fifty-two, Nancy's injuries had become more frequent and took longer to heal—yet she ran through them. She ran through tendonitis and hip bursitis, through turned ankles and gluteal strains and tarsal tunnel. Ran through piriformis syndrome and IT band syndrome and compartment syndrome. Several of these conditions were self-diagnosed; in fact, most were, but the point was over time she had come to laugh at her neuroses.

Only once did hypochondria surface in its harshest reality, after nine years of steady running; it happened the February before Nancy turned fifty-eight, as she was exiting the park at East Sixtieth Street. It had been below freezing that night, and she'd felt a sharp stab in her groin. She'd had to stop, had waited for the pain to dull before she began again, in a hurry to the subway—the train would be warm—but the pain only pierced more sharply. She'd had to limp down the stairs, peg-legged as Murray after a marathon. She was sure she'd broken a bone, and two days later, when she went to Columbia Medical Center for the X-ray, she was right. Her skin felt cold and clammy in the dark room, sequestered by the machine's secret intelligence; she closed her eyes as it thrummed photographs. Afterward, the technician asked if she'd fallen on ice, and she'd said no, she hadn't, but she had to wait for an orthopedist, one Caroline insisted she see on the Upper West Side, to point to a hairline crack, its halo ghosting through the screen.

"Your pubic ramus," the doctor said. Dr. Patterson. He was a slightly bulkier version of her old obstetrician, Dr. Weiss—and she was surprised the resemblance didn't bother her, that his voice, his presence, felt oddly comforting, familiar.

"It must be painful," Dr. Patterson said. "It's rare." *Rare*. She closed her eyes at the word. As rare as Murray in Paris, as getting pregnant unexpectedly at forty, as losing Jean at seven months instead of the average three months for SIDS—the narrowness of each percentage, like a hangnail she wanted to tear off with her teeth. As Dr. Patterson had Nancy lay on her belly, he traced his hand up her spine and noted the curve. "Very interesting," he said before advising she choose a different activity, to consider swimming or cycling—or even better, yoga.

"I'm not stopping," she said, picking at the hangnail. Wondering if it would bleed.

Dr. Patterson shook his head and scribbled a prescription for physical therapy. He tore the blue slip from his pad and recommended someone experienced in the Schroth Method.

The next day, Nancy ordered an instructional video, which she followed morning, noon, and night. Some evenings she did the stretches in combination with the stationary bike at the gym, or on weekends she began aqua jogging at the 14th Street Y. She remembered how religious Murray had been about the pool, after he'd had surgery to remove arthritis in his hips the year she left him. And then later, at night, before she fell asleep, skin saturated in chlorine, she thought of how if they'd stayed together, they would never have grown so similar as they were now, apart.

~

But Nancy made sure they were still different. She let herself rest. She treated herself to chiropractic adjustments, massage, and acupuncture. There was a "miracle worker"—Dr. V—whom Caroline had recommended. Dr. V treated multiple patients at one time, his electro-stim machines chiming every ten minutes, the sound of him greeting patients, or commending them for *doing something* about their conditions: *You're going to feel grrreat,* he'd say before he was finished. The walls were covered in Broadway posters, signed by all the dancers he'd cured. Dr. V played Enya while he poked needles at various angles along her rear, two along her earlobes, which made her sleepy and flushed her face with color, grateful for the gifts of Eastern medicine. Dr. V gave her a yellow exercise band and told her to tie one end to her ankle, the other to her bedpost, and he showed her how to keep her leg straight while she did ten repetitions. He lay on the floor and demonstrated. "Light, light," he said. "Your hamstrings are short. You don't want to pull anything."

And she did that at home, this light stretching and strengthening. Which, at her age, was an accomplishment; Dr. V said it during her tenth session, when he moved to lavender oil and massage.

It took four months' time, but Nancy ran again. She ran through the scar tissue, the fear of breaking other bones. She ran through the discomfort of unfit lungs. She ran the loops she knew best, the shortest loops she'd first run with Caroline, though they felt longer than her longest runs through the city. She ran past what had been before. No matter how slow her pace, she was passing the past the way a train passes a row of houses shouldered by hills, a church, or industrial complex, a cemetery half-covered in snow.

In fact, the next January, when she was running the hills in Harlem, she sensed the old constriction in her lungs, the way it could come on suddenly without warning. She had thought she'd have to stop, just a minute, maybe five, to breathe. But then she'd closed her eyes, and thought of Murray in East Rock, all those mornings he'd climbed to the top of its summit, in snow, in freezing rain. She'd pictured him, and then she'd felt it, her lungs expanding in the cold, oxygen filling her legs, soothing their burn, arms pushing harder, past numbness.

She thought, *Is this what Murray was seeking after Jean died?* She nearly stopped again, her eyes burning, her heartbeat stronger at her wrists, under her watch, numbers moving up, approaching the next minute, and the next one after that. *These minutes, they had been Murray's survival,* she thought. He had lived these minutes the only way he'd known how to.

The next time she traversed the Manhattan Bridge, she sought to feel what Murray might have, to encompass the entirety of that view: the whole island, all the places that become one—she saw out of herself, as though she were part of the buildings, smaller and smaller the higher up she went.

She could look down at that world and say that living on was a choice she and Murray had made—that their life together, in their child, could not have been anything other than what it had been. It was how Nancy came to one day run past playgrounds and carousels, ice rinks dotted with children—to imagine a school or theater or newly erected apartment building filled with happy children. Could stop to finger violets or forsythia in spring, to really laugh at a movie or buy a lottery ticket. Cut her hair without regret. Hang photographs or brush the covers of her favorite children's books with her palms.

She was thinking like this seven months later, one early morning in August. She was fifty-nine and curating an exhibit on *Alice's Adventures in Wonderland*. The original manuscript had just arrived in her office from the British Library in London, and Nancy had already begun sifting through pages and illustrations, imagining Charles Lutwidge Dodgson's pen over paper, how he'd written it for the Liddell sisters one evening when he'd been rowing them up the Thames for a picnic in Godstow, and the little girls had asked for a story.

∼

The phone rang. It was Caroline.

"James," she said. "He's being a typical senior, but he doesn't tell us where he's spending the night and he's been lying about his summer work, a few essays he's supposed to turn in before his first day back. How is he going to be prepared for college in a year?"

"Caroline," Nancy said. "Relax. Take a deep breath." And then she waited until she heard it. *Breathe.*

"I'm sorry," Caroline said. "You're at work."

Nancy had her finger over an illustration of Alice shielding her face amid a spiraling vortex of cards. The six of spades was most pronounced, distended.

"It's alright," Nancy said.

"I suppose I panicked," Caroline continued. "But I had a thought. That James loves to draw." She breathed through the phone. "He has private lessons and supplies, his own charge account at Blick, but I realized he's never really developed an *appreciation*, and I thought—"

Nancy closed her eyes, waiting for Caroline to finish.

"Well, I wondered if you could take him to the Met. Maybe as soon as next weekend before he goes back to school?"

"I don't know if one trip to the museum . . ." Nancy focused on the two of hearts, three behind the six of spades. Its proportions more balanced, its coloring soft.

"Jim and I aren't expecting change overnight. But it would just make us feel so much better to try now. Because then he's gone until Christmas. I know he looks up to you. He keeps a print of the Rembrandt you gave him in his room. Nancy, you know the self-portrait, *Etching at the Window*, or—"

"*At a Window*," Nancy said.

"What?"

"It's called *Etching at a Window*."

"Oh," Caroline said. "Right. That one."

"I gave you that print."

"You did? You did! I remember. Well, I gave it to James." Caroline's breath was heavy again. "He loves Rembrandt, and he was really moved by the picture—the image, I mean—and so I framed it for him and hung it above his desk. I told him what you do, and how hard it is to make a career in the arts, and how you are an example of perseverance, brilliance, really, and he listened . . . no, *hung on* is better, to every word."

"Caroline," Nancy said. She had slipped the illustration into a clear sheath, which she pressed her finger over. "Save it, will you?"

"What?" Caroline said, her voice soft.

"The lip service. I get it. I'll do it," she said. Now she had her pen poised over a Post-it note, on which she'd recorded the correct catalog number and the date.

It took them over six minutes to pin down a time in the morning next Saturday—the day before James would leave for Choate. Caroline explained how he'd need time to eat breakfast and shower after tae kwon do, then they had to factor in travel time, because *he liked to walk places*. When it was done, Nancy drew a circle around the date on her wall calendar: August 26.

Inside she printed *James. 11:30.*

TWENTY-ONE

Monday
6:02:45 a.m.

On Anna's first practice back, Murray had her warm up for twenty minutes on the bike and complete eight by 400 meters on the treadmill. The idea was to work out in a controlled environment so they could pinpoint a target speed slightly slower than preinjury training. They had easy access to the training room if anything went awry. Anna was working out twice a day with resistance bands to strengthen her hips and glutes and getting regular chiropractic, massage, and electro-stim therapy. She looked like she may have gained a few pounds since the sprain.

He told her to increase the treadmill's incline to 2.0, speed to 9.5: effectively a 6:13 pace. Once she could maintain this for two minutes, he set his timer for 1:20 and had her increase the speed to 10.5.

"Shoulders relaxed. Head up," he said, thirty seconds into the first interval. "See your competition. Imagine passing her on a hill."

Anna's right foot still looked a little weak, the way she was collapsing on her instep. Once Becky was well enough, she'd have to do at least three one-hour sessions of physical therapy a day.

Last night he'd stayed up reading about brain injury—not in the stacks, at home. He had not fallen asleep until 3:22 a.m., but right now his head felt surprisingly clear.

Becky would need to start with a roller walker. Patients, like athletes, needed experts to set milestones, ones that at first seemed out of reach but that were, ultimately, attainable.

"Rest," he said. Anna had forty-five seconds of rest before the next quarter. Thirty seconds in, she should start ramping up the speed.

Becky was getting regular massages: experts managing her limbs, and he had to assume it wasn't all passive. That they had a plan to engage her core muscles, her pelvic stability.

"Go!" he said. His left eye twitched as he thought about bed rests and how they made for weak lower backs. For a moment, he saw Nancy's body-racking contractions, and then the sound of her heaving—the searing red of her face. *A one two three four five six seven eight nine and ten!*

He imagined doctors marking Becky's progress through tiny hash marks on a whiteboard or along the wall.

"Thirty more seconds!" Then he told her to notch up her base speed. "Hold it . . . hold it." Twitching seized the right side of his mouth. "Five . . ." He began counting down. Last night he'd dreamed of Nancy reading in the bathroom. Shrouded in steam. He had wanted to join her there, but couldn't move through the opacity of heat.

"Three down, three to go." He and Anna were on better terms now, but she still felt far away. When was the last time she'd smiled or told him to have a good night after evening practice?

"Twenty more seconds!" he said. "After this, you're halfway through!" Anna's breath labored, not wheezing, but searching. She breathed through her mouth. "Rest!"

Rick had shown him one of Becky's medical reports Lisa had sent over before the university settlement. Hyperbaric oxygen therapy. Long-term neuropsychological assessment.

"Go!" Anna was starting interval number five. He thought of the piston of Becky's ventilator, moving up and down. *Less than 50 percent chance patient will regain normal cognitive function. Level 3 on the Rancho Los Amigos scale of cognitive function.*

"Rest!"

He thought about the other possible obstacles to Becky's progress that he'd read about: involuntary eyebrow movement, blurred vision, the struggle for balance, to relearn language; but he had not been convinced. Not by any of it.

"Go!" he said. "This is it!" He had her amp the incline to 3.0 and her speed to 12, the highest the machine would go, for five minutes. Halfway in she was grunting. Moaning. But Lisa had not given ample warning about Becky—the outbursts.

"Keep it going! Keep it going!" He said it repeatedly over the next fifteen seconds. Anna's head and arms struggled to remain square. Knees perpendicular. Hair along her neck was soaked. Sweat blackened her blue T-shirt.

"Done," he said. Treadmill twenty minutes exactly, including rest. He told her to jog for another twenty minutes, to grip the handlebars for twenty seconds, so they could measure heart rate.

"One-eighty-two," he said, after numbers stabilized. "How is your foot?"

"Pretty good," she said, breathless. "I feel it, but not bad pain."

"It stayed the same?"

"Yes." The machine said she slowed to 7:30 pace. When he asked her how this felt as a cooldown, she said fine. Said she'd averaged about that on her first run back.

It was Monday. They had five days until Saturday, the invitational at Lehigh. She should run four miles on Saturday, and a pace run under 6:00 to start. If she felt good, she could work toward 5:30 or faster. Then for Sunday's long run, she'd do nine miles, instead of the twelve she had managed preinjury.

He'd read that some patients benefited from listening to Mozart's Sonata 448 every morning. A form of *expressive therapy* that expedited healing.

He'd read about all the other forms: *cognitive* for everyday functioning, *recreational* for engaging in social leisure activities, *occupational* for daily demands—showering, dressing, personal hygiene.

He wished he'd pressed Lisa about the physical exercise Becky needed. Becky's muscles had to learn how to relax and relearn certain sensations. *Reflexology* and *water therapy*: other options he could have stressed.

Anna had finished the first five minutes of her cooldown. He had to remind her to relax and square. To still her pelvis and imagine her navel. Told her to see her hips as two headlights, staring into the dark.

"I'm trying," she said.

He merely wanted Becky to be able to transition from walker to cane sooner. To practice taking real steps. Independent ambulation first and foremost.

He told Anna to grip the handlebars again. They waited six seconds for the heart rate sensor to activate, numbers adjusting around her pulse. "One sixty. Keep that." More sweat had splashed over the treadmill's belt. Her feet had no other choice but to fall over it. How fast would she go on the road at this stage? Or in a race, along less predictable trails?

When she finished, he sent her to the trainer for rehab. They went over the exact sequence of strengthening exercises, and then how long she'd need the stim machine. He wanted to confirm they were putting electrodes along her calves, feet, and glutes. That she left with ice plastic-wrapped to her ankles and shins.

"I'll tell them." She walked away: no sign of her limping.

~

Later, at the diner, he asked for two cups of coffee. He had not slept in two days and needed the caffeine.

Becky's face had looked sallow, as if improved diet and mobility made no difference. And her left arm had been in a brace, because the left hemisphere controlled the opposite side of the body.

Coffee was better with sugar and cream. Real sugar, not the pink stuff so many of the girls consumed. At away meets, when they stayed over at hotels and gathered early in the morning for complimentary breakfast, he'd watch them tip packet after packet into their cups.

Today they were working out on the IM fields. Since Anna was through with her workout, she'd help him take splits, at least for the first half. For the last, they'd agreed on some added supplementary training so she would reach over sixty minutes of cardio today. The plan was for a thirty-minute tempo, hitting her max speed and resistance twenty minutes in. Exertion was exertion. It didn't matter if she did it all in one go or sporadically throughout the day, though mentally it was always better to push through pain for a longer period of time.

Sarah Lloyd had won the Eastern College Athletic Conference in 2002, six months postinjury her sophomore year; she'd had acute Achilles tendonitis, nothing like the stress fractures she would endure as a senior, but still the tendonitis had required a long, arduous recovery. Murray had customized a plan for her: three and a half hours of intensive cross-training daily, coupled with physical therapy, intensive calf stretching, and strengthening at least four times a week.

~

Sarah came in just as Murray was ordering his eggs over easy. She wore a long black skirt with a purple blazer. Usually this place was full of locals and college kids. Hands worked frantically around her purse after she took her booth.

She was searching for medication; he saw the white top of the bottle and then its dark, shadowy orange. She took a capsule with water, still unaware, it seemed, of him.

"Home fries?" the waitress asked. He'd seen her before—she had large eyes, but had they always been this vibrant, glistening green?

"No," he said, "just toast. Whole wheat."

"You got it." She smiled.

Murray waited for Sarah to turn a bit more in his direction so he could be certain before he said anything. But she didn't—she just looked out the window, hands resting on the purse in her lap.

He was sure Sarah saw him here, even if she never turned to confirm it, *him*, in her periphery. He'd thought of waiting, something to prompt her, but then—he wasn't certain how much time had passed—his eggs came. He studied their soft, wobbling centers.

She's done. Sarah's parents had called him, after that last moment with Sarah in the common room when he'd brought the chocolate milk, when he'd wanted to hold her but hadn't. The phone had quivered in his hand as Sarah's father said, *She is done*, and that he didn't want Murray contacting her with any more of his "plans and timelines."

She's going home after graduation, her mother had interjected, voice as shaky as Lisa's. They didn't want her staying on with him to train for the Olympics, like he'd hoped from the beginning. More like they'd forgotten what they'd signed up for. A Division I program in the Ivy League. That was the best there was.

~

He closed his eyes, felt himself sink into the padded seat at his booth, where he had his eggs and toast. He raised his fork to pierce the yolk, but he couldn't push down, couldn't break it, feeling the yolk overtake the size of the white. Usually he liked to dip the bread, but the thought of that taste—he pushed the plate away.

You don't look good, Rick had said. *You should see someone.* Murray's hands shook as he raised his pen to his pad and noticed the dry patches around his knuckles. Eight hours before practice, he told himself. *You just have eight hours,* and he wrote down every hour as a list, with the things that had to be accomplished. He had the itinerary and final roster to print for Lehigh. Stats and seed times to review. Several recruiting emails to send. He had to stay within those boundaries—there was no going past the minutes he allotted.

When the waitress asked if he wanted his food to go, he said no, and as he waited for cash, he looked once more in Sarah's direction, his eyes twitching, his mouth dry. He reached for his water glass, sipping slowly.

The whole while, she remained there, turned away from him, silent, by the window.

When the waitress came back with his receipt, he asked if the woman was a regular.

"What woman?"

He explained, without pointing, but the waitress didn't understand.

"There aren't any women here. Just me." She laughed.

Was she joking with him? Was this a joke? He thought so, then didn't, as he looked down at his watch, its face glazed with sweat. The running time: but he could hardly differentiate *six* from *nine*, seconds from minutes. Hours, arbitrary numbers. Letters. Words.

"Sir, can I get you anything else?" The waitress stood before him, holding water. "Are you going to be alright to leave?"

It wasn't a joke, Murray thought. No woman had been there by the window. The booth was empty.

You're muttering to yourself, Rick had said, *the girls are concerned.* Murray shook his head, then looked up and took the water the waitress was still holding. He sipped it, trying not to cough as he breathed. "I'm fine," he told her when she asked again, and from the black plastic tray she'd brought, he scraped what change from his breakfast was left, and he stood up and made his way out.

TWENTY-TWO

James had not arrived yet. Nancy waited in front of the Met, on the steps, precisely according to plan. It was a hot day, even for August. She wore golfing shorts and a polo with her running shoes, the most comfortable outfit she'd been able to conjure for this weather. Still, she felt stupid. She had not held a club since she was a small child, no older than eight, when her parents had insisted on lessons. Funny, she thought, when she'd first come to the city, James had been eight. Had it already been ten years? Yet, still she hardly knew him. She supposed for most of those years, she had not wanted to get to know him.

She looked for his face among the herds of people toppling in, many of them speaking languages she couldn't decipher—the air thick with human sweat and musk. Nancy looked for James's blond hair, his tall, lanky build, a near copy of Jim, at least when he was young, as Caroline had once pointed out in photographs, after she'd dug out an old album to peruse on her sofa. Jim had been away on business then, and Nancy recalled several of the photos: Jim carefree on a tire swing. Jim fishing with his brother. Jim poised for a baseball pitch. Now, Jim, hunched and bald, spent most of his time running his own consulting firm—a sight that had led Nancy to wonder whether stress or loneliness had been as unkind to Murray over the years. She had seen a few photos of him as a child, photos before church or at family gatherings, never ones of leisure. Murray had been afforded meager comforts his whole life, but his hair, it had been as full and blond as Jim's as a child. What did he look like now in the eighteen years since Jean, in the fifteen since she had left him completely?

There he was. James coming up the steps with his satchel. He wore cropped pants in this heat. Flip-flops for all this walking. She reminded herself that her job was to act as friend, mentor. Her job was not to scold him, the admonishing finger, the packed lunches, the sunscreen—things that had never been required of her.

"Hi!" she said, surprised by her nervous lilt.

"Hi," James said. His voice was deeper than expected, his eyes a soft green she'd never noticed before. He carried a pocket-sized paper journal, its cover fire red.

"What's first?" she asked. "What would you like to see?" She began to unravel her map, tracing her finger along the numbers, the many rooms she'd never been to. "Egyptian art? European painting?"

"Whatever," he said, refusing to look at her.

She scrunched her eyes, unsure of whether to take the lead or let James decide.

"Move!" A woman pushed past. "You're blocking the door." The woman was carrying shopping bags and a backpack, which security stopped her to inspect.

Nancy shrugged; she knew it was important to set a precedent of calm, so she led the way through security. James wandered in after her, looking up at the banners, the high ceiling. Nancy donated twenty dollars for their tickets. Then she thought maybe she should donate more—she worked in art, at a museum, for God's sake, she should give more—so she pulled out another twenty.

James looked annoyed. He did not seem pleased, in general, about the way she did things. The trick was confidence. She told him there was a painting he might like in Modern and Contemporary Art. She showed him on the map, drawing down the Great Hall and left after the two-dimensional staircase, which they could see from where they stood. He walked ahead of her, toward Medieval Art, but it was easy to get lost in here.

"James," she said. "It's this way. We have to turn now." She had her hand on the map, but that was ridiculous. Of course it would be too hard for him to see. She hurried to catch up. "This way," she said.

Reluctantly he turned to follow her, and they crossed through European Sculpture, where she was tempted to point out French medals from the 1600s and artifacts from the Renaissance. Or to take a slight detour to stand before Canova's stunning *Perseus with the Head of Medusa*, acquired, she believed, through the Fletcher Fund. But James was moving too fast. He reminded her so much of Murray, the way he skimmed through rooms, never pausing to read a caption. She'd made him stop, listen to what she'd had to say about a particular artist or moment in time.

"Lucky you have a sketch pad," she said. But he pretended not to hear her—or maybe he really didn't hear her through all of the clicking heels, the incessant chatter—the vastness of the space. So she waited until they were in Modern and Contemporary Art, where it was slightly quieter, to tell him about Agnes Martin—the artist whose painting they were about to see.

"She was born in Canada," Nancy said. "Have you been there?"

But James wanted nothing to do with a history lesson. He was edging his way into the main exhibition gallery, when she wanted to bypass that. "James," she said. "This way." Her voice had begun to aggravate her, its sheer repetitiousness. "Gallery 908," she said. She wouldn't bore him with the accession number she'd memorized, or the details of the loan through SFMOMA, gift of Mr. and Mrs. Moses Lasky—she had copied the details in her own journal last night, after several hours of extensive research—in case James did look up to her or was considering a similar path—but she could see Caroline's skewed expectations. Her projection onto him.

James had followed her. She felt him behind her when she paused. Here was the one.

"There you are," she said, smiling. "I wanted to show you this one." But still he didn't seem to hear her, so she spoke louder. "James," she said.

He turned and looked at her as he might have his mother. Irritated. She focused on the dimensions of the painting, six feet long by six feet wide, and the material, oil on linen.

"Look closely," she said. "At those lines." And then after a few moments: "See how close together they are."

Still he said nothing.

"She did each one of these tiny horizontal lines with her steady hand, one after the other—see how the vertical lines form a grid?"

"I get it," he said. "I see it." James pushed his bangs back again, but this time he held his hand there, over his forehead.

Nancy moved away from the canvas, because if she walked farther away from the gridlines, the painting was like a wave, these undulating saturations of blue, but if she moved close again, all she saw was the detail, the patience, the precision.

"What does it make you think of?" she asked him.

"I don't know," he said. "The sky." He rolled his eyes at her.

"Okay," she said. "I think that's fair. But what else in the lines, the color?"

"Fabric," he said. "It looks like a clean piece of fabric." He sighed.

"And—"

"That's it," he said, turning to walk toward the elevator. Light poured through a slant of windows along the curved ceiling.

"James," she said, reaching for his arm.

He jerked away.

"I'm just—I—" Nancy's pulse was dizzying, like a sprint to a bus she couldn't miss, not without great expense. "I just want to hear your thoughts. I'm really interested to hear what you think."

"Aren't they the same thing?" he said. "Thinking and thought?"

"James," she said. Just saying it, the single syllable sound, the *J*, she didn't know how many times she'd have to repeat it.

"What?" he said.

She shifted her attention. She thought of something else. "That very shade of blue," she said. "It was a color the artist chose . . . and don't you think? Have you ever thought that painting, or drawing, or any kind of art, is about a series of choices?"

"No," James said. "I don't. Because isn't that obvious?" He sighed. He opened his notebook and wrote something down.

"I don't know," Nancy went on, her head light, heart accelerating further—for reasons she could and couldn't place. "I think about this a lot. That every single moment an artist has is a choice about how she wants to look at her subject, and in an instant that decision can change, that choice can change, so in some ways we could consider the final piece an accident."

"What?" he said. He had started walking again, and she alongside him, forgetting all of the paintings they were missing, but he was talking. "You really believe painting hundreds of lines together was an accident?"

"It might have been planned, you're right—at least to a degree, but I don't think her painting is about perfection. I think it's about patience."

"Maybe," he said.

"We don't know what she was feeling when she chose this blue oil or this quality of linen."

James stopped. "I still think it's pretty simple," he said. "She likes solid colors."

"I think you're onto something," Nancy said. "Solid colors. Why does she like them? Maybe she's searching for something."

"Patience," James said, his tone mocking. But then, after a few seconds of silence, he said, "Didn't you say it was about that?"

"I did!" Nancy laughed. "You're right. But that's just my interpretation. And when I look at it, I feel something more too." The light from the windows had formed shafts over the floor, dust spectral in the light. "I think it's about healing."

"*Falling Blue,*" James said. "That's the title." Which he wrote down, his eyes hiding like she didn't see him do it. "What is she falling from?" he asked. "Grace?" He laughed, as though it could be a joke.

"I don't know, maybe it's simpler, like you said before. Because it's just the light falling, different patterns of light depending on the angle—or maybe it's like rain."

"Over the ocean," James said. "That's what I think it is." He did not look at her when he spoke, as though he were thinking out loud, and this gave Nancy a certain unprecedented joy, for James to see only as he could.

~

Afterward, they went for soft pretzels from a stand just outside. James squeezed mustard over his, while Nancy picked off a few kernels of salt. He had not shown her his notebook when she asked to see his sketches, nor had he answered her questions about the classes he was taking, his roommate at Choate. He merely let her walk with him down the East Side. She took the subway at Grand Central, cutting through the main concourse, where the clock glowed the time. 4:32. She gazed up at the ceiling, admiring its constellated stars, and she thought of how easy it was to dream a dream for a child that did not have a chance to be broken, how much harder to watch a child slowly break it. She wished to tell Caroline there was a kind of beauty in this destruction—through it, James would create himself over time.

It was the same with Murray: shards she'd had to learn to leave as shards, some which pearled in the sand, others jagged and sharp under her feet. Eventually they led her back to the ocean, the dream of it always as vast, as silent.

TWENTY-THREE

Saturday
7:06:38 a.m.

The Lehigh Invitational was in Bethlehem, not too far from where Murray had grown up. Every year he took his top three girls. Ross did the same for the men's team, and the whole ride up in Ross's Jeep, he attempted small talk with Murray, imagining what the predicted cold would do to his number one, also nursing an injury, a minor hamstring strain. But Murray, too concerned about the competition, only half paid attention. He'd read up on Penn State's number one and two girls, and a few other top names at Gettysburg and Villanova, since both were having remarkable seasons. If all went well, Anna would be up there with the best of them, running sub-5:20 miles. On Wednesday, her second workout back, she'd clocked in three repeats at close to five flat. Granted, the intramural fields lacked ample hills to simulate a real race, but it showed she had the foot speed and might have a real breakthrough this morning.

Lehigh's course wove through dry cornfields, the kind he'd grown up running around too—stretches of countryside always in his periphery. Racing spikes, he imagined them snapping husks and crunching earth.

"Let's go," Anna told the team a few minutes after Murray and Ross finished setting up the tent. After Thursday's practice on the track (200-meter striders), he'd tried to tell her about his second visit with Becky, but she'd insisted on catching the shuttle for the team dinner.

He was looking around for Kate Reinhart from Gettysburg, the girl Anna needed to follow if she had any chance at setting a new record. But Murray only had a vague idea of what she looked like from another meet last year.

Now he was too afraid to search Becky's name, for the sheer number of articles destined to populate. More every week. Rumors that he worked his girls like horses, that he starved them, but they had him confused with Jana, the Princeton coach. The calls and messages from journalists that kept piling up. No one could see all the calls that had accumulated through his lifetime, every moment he'd endured between his father's death, and his mother's too—his wife leaving him after he'd done everything that had needed to be done so they could get on with their lives—Murray had kept himself and Nancy afloat those two years before they'd separated, and still people would call him and leave him messages wanting answers to their questions, as though he were a machine, a robot operating on command.

If Nancy were there, she'd say, *How is it you can't think to say one thing in the paper about what's happened to your team? You really think you can just pretend?*

It had been March, around her forty-second birthday, when he'd tried to surprise her with flowers. *You think this will take my mind off things?* She had stuffed the flowers in the trash. He had thought her cruel—how blind she'd been to his every gesture, his every attempt to save their marriage—how could he have said it out loud, like she wanted, to everyone? Let the words in every day, while still giving his girls the focus they needed, the resolve to compete like it was the last time they would.

The first time he'd raced the mile, when his father was still alive, he'd run hard enough for the world to turn hazy—all oxygen had gone to supplying muscles, not enough to the brain, causing him to finish in a delirium, dizzy and heaving by his knees. He had heard his coach's cheering as an echo, the whistles of the crowd, reverberations that had led him into the pain, to choose it, and surpass it, eventually; if he pushed hard enough, the pain would always leave him.

~

"Stay loose," he told Anna. He reminded her of where he would be, pushing pen hard into pad. Numbers. But she wasn't looking at him. And then she walked away to join Tanya and Ginny by the tent. He watched their three foreheads press together, arms looped, hugging.

"Let's get to mile one early this time." Ross, the men's coach, had tapped his shoulder, and then as they headed to his Jeep, he spun on about how his number one, Ryan Thompson, wasn't running well, and no one could figure it out. Ross thought something was off at home, or even more likely—girl troubles, because Ryan was a junior and had been singularly focused on school and running until last summer, when he was studying abroad in Spain and probably met someone.

"Murray?"

"What?"

"I called you a bunch of times by the tent."

"I didn't hear you."

"I know it's been a lot," he said, his face scrunched. "The stress."

"I'm fine," he said, but he was looking at his forearm, thinking about the time Nancy had gotten some soap under her wedding ring. The skin became irritated, and at night she used to scratch—until she got eczema and had to apply dime-sized amounts of cortisone daily. She'd taken a break from wearing it for months, or maybe that had always been an excuse?

Ross had said something else in the car, about "being there" if Murray needed anything, and Murray had said something else, but he couldn't remember what.

"Ahead of the curve." Ross smiled. They were standing at mile one with the other coaches. One had four different stopwatches looped around his clipboard.

"Three minutes." Ross looked at Murray. Ross had started coaching men's after Murray had already been coaching his girls for ten years; he'd once asked Murray if he had any children, and when Murray had told him, Ross had asked more questions. *What do you mean?* he'd said—not understanding the conditions of Murray's loss, the vague description he'd provided. *Minimum facts,* he thought—*it had never been anyone's business*—as Ross's number one runner approached, part of a tight pack.

Murray watched Ross click his watch after his first runner, Wes Michaels, clocked his first mile at 4:25—there were at least nine men in the pack, and Ross told Wes to hold on. Murray had recorded the split, but the next twenty seconds felt much longer; he watched fractions dissolve.

One minute and seven seconds later, Murray spotted the lead woman, on pace for 5:05. He waited another fifteen seconds, but still no sign of Anna. Had she fallen again? Was it her ankle? Ross didn't have time to stay with him, so Murray gripped his watch alone.

At 5:25.49, his heart rate was elevated, and at 5:32.17, it beat at triple speed. His lips cold with sweat. At 5:48.53, he wasn't sure of the order of numbers, of what came first, a five or a three? There would be no heeding his clock's cross into six minutes—or seven—or eight—or nine—until ten: the rolling green of that misted hill on the golf course that morning, the quiet, the sight of Becky lying there, at *10:23.57.* He felt his pulse like a frog's tongue inside his neck, flicking dim, but fast. Two fingers by her pulse. He closed his eyes, shaking off more cold sweat. He felt a hand on his shoulder. He flinched. And then he heard: *"Coach."*

"You have to go back. Right away!" The voice was loud, nearly shouting, as someone, a woman, got him in her car. If she was another coach, where was the logo on her jacket? She spoke rapidly, and he wanted to ask her to slow down, but his lips wouldn't move. They were gelled and cold. Something serious had happened—he knew this much, and she drove them a half a mile and then parked in the grass, in the open space between the tents and the course.

Then he saw them all there. Rodney in front, in a hooded sweatshirt and jeans, Anna right next to her, after that was Liu, Tanya, Victoria, and Emily. *How had they traveled here?*

All their hands were locked together, in a barricade. Their mouths hung open, and they were chanting, but he couldn't hear what they were saying. Something about *Becky*, but as he hobbled closer, he still couldn't hear *words*—like those dolls his mother had kept along the windowsill during Christmas: a silent chorus of dolls.

He felt the other teams, other coaches watching. Felt the land, smell of the earth, at his feet. The air was growing colder, mountains turning redder, when he was a child and would look up and think: *No other place but here*, hills and mines. All of it, *closing him in.*

Silence roared through his ears like an ocean as he approached. He was close enough to see Anna's eyes, rage, *greener*. Nancy's shards *piercing*, suddenly he felt his head light, hovering above him; a planet against its universe, black centrifugal forces. He did not feel himself fall, only the unbearable weight of his limbs, like watching oneself bleed.

Nancy had cut her nipple in the shower once. She'd fainted over a bath mat before he found her. A small pool of blood.

He had not heard her cry, just as he did not hear them now, people around him: someone calling for help.

His whole life, Murray had known how to suppress pain, but it always came back.

TWENTY-FOUR

Nancy arrived on a day when the light was clear and warm, the way it sometimes was in September. She had a particular way of entering the lot, which was not by going through the main gate, wrought ironed and chained, but through the east side, on Canal Street, where there was a sliver of grass, a narrow opening. Nancy carried a paper bag with hydrangea clippings, no longer from a garden bush, but from the Ninth Street corner bodega. She'd held the bag on her lap on the train, looking out the window, light casting shadows over the bag. The man at the bodega knew her by now—knew she'd come in the morning every other Sunday after her run. He knew to add fresh greens in with the blue, these tiny clumps of petals whose shade depended on the variety he had available. Today the blue was pale and partly cream, like the sky, though less muted and more brilliant, as she walked to the place where Jean lay.

The grass was wet by the stone; it had rained the night before, though shouldn't it have dried? But then Nancy thought this was lucky: that the grass hadn't dried. She studied the clean carving of the stone, the absence of a nickname she'd always regret, the last name that would never be the same as her own. The bold-faced letters: Murray had chosen the engraving. And there were the dates, this sliver of time that united them.

Jaclyn Gilbert

Nancy always tied the flowers with yellow yarn from a spool she kept in her dresser drawer.

Nancy's mouth felt dry, her eyes twitched, yet there was some joy in remembering Murray's reaction anytime Jean had smiled at him and grasped toward his face, smooth from shaving, in the mornings. A memory Nancy didn't know she'd forgotten.

Over the years Nancy had left Jean short letters, poems, words of wisdom, tucked in with the flowers. She used to clip them onto a stalk, but later she'd let them blow away, and now she didn't bring them at all, because Jean was her wisdom, not the other way around.

Nancy used to think about the car they'd taken, alone, to and from this cemetery, the way the driver had spoken of the weather, as though it were any other day. She used to think about Jean's tiny satin-lined casket lowered into the earth: how Murray had held back that one webbing strap—she hadn't considered how it must have felt for Murray, in helping the pastor backfill Jean's grave, in tamping down on the dirt alone.

She used to think of the box light as air, the temperature of the earth, the question of whether the blanket she'd knitted and the little terry cloth bear they'd tucked in with her would be enough in the cold.

There was a sanctuary for meeting her child. Nancy had never spoken or written of it, and it had taken her many years to find it. Katherine had once mentioned the possibility of a place where she might like to meet her child. She had asked Nancy to close her eyes, and Nancy had done that, but when she told her to see a place, to imagine its contours of light and sound, she had seen only gray, and when Katherine had continued to prompt her, the image had only turned grayer, a deeper shade of gray. She had reached for her coat. She had walked out that day, shoulders crouched, hand waving goodbye to Katherine behind her head, the way Nancy's own mother had one day in August when she'd left for college. And that was the last time Nancy saw Katherine.

The idea of a meeting place had felt impossible—until recently, when she'd been in the middle of an eighteen-mile run in Rockefeller

Preserve, a Saturday morning in September when mist shrouded the green meadows, the sky gray and diffuse like fog. She had suddenly pictured hills, golden brown, grass angled in the wind, which she could see up close, though the hills were far away—and there had been Jean, standing in the grass, her legs long, her hair haloed copper—though Nancy could not perceive her face, like in dreams, when there was only shadow, yet which felt as real as any living body she'd felt or seen.

You can go here anytime, Katherine had said before she'd first tried to find the place, and Nancy had looked up from her chair to the only window of the room, dim with natural light. She may have walked away then, but she'd learned not to punish herself for walking away, because only *now* mattered, and she was not afraid to walk away.

She'd found this place unexpectedly, when her mouth had been dry, lungs exhausted from fueling oxygen through her heart. And she could find it again and again, only without expectation, such as now, when she closed her eyes, remembering the scene: the grass golden brown, the sun pouring down, she waited for Jean to appear. She did not know how long it took, but eventually she detected long legs and arms cutting the air, the way they would have been if she were here. Light twitching through the shadow of Nancy's mind as if through the tinted windows of a moving train—Jean, there, the age she was today: eighteen. Her child was happy, free, unweighted by circumstances, the brevity of her life.

The day they'd buried her, the pastor had said that she'd lived a full life, that she'd known joy and love and pain, and though Nancy had listened to the words, it had taken all these years to hear them.

When Nancy opened her eyes, she had to place herself amid angled stone, some flat and pressed like plaques, or propped and square, rounded at the edges. There was another person, two people, holding one another, necks locked, one of them a man, holding his coat between his hands. Nancy watched the image from the corner of her gaze as she left. The ground was soft, air rich with leaves and bark, the roundness of time.

She walked down Prospect Street until it became College Street, and eventually reached Chapel, where she entered Claire's and found a table by the window. She ordered a slice of carrot cake with the restaurant's famous icing, thick with sparkling granules of sugar. She savored each bite between sips of tea, edging the side of her fork into the layered brown.

Next to her, two students leaned in toward each other as they spoke about classes and fall break. One had long tendrils of hair running down her back, and the other wore a nose ring. It became clear they were sophomores. The student with curls said she'd written a book of poetry around the objects she'd helped archive at a museum over the summer, and the other said she'd helped paint houses in New Orleans. They gossiped about other girls in their dorm and groaned over the subject of math and the difficulty of making office hours around their volunteering and intramural schedules, their terror over a recently assigned series of problem sets. Nancy had wanted to tune it out, to let the clatter of plates behind the kitchen, the smell of the cinnamon in the cake, the sweetness of raisins, subsume her, but the energy of the girls made her curious. They made her wonder.

She could not picture Murray, in all their years apart, surrounded by such conversation. She could not imagine him in this world, unaffected by its energies, steadfast in his dogma, his structure. She thought about how his girls always did long runs on Sunday, on trails around the golf course. Murray sometimes took these days off, and she hoped he'd gotten better about that, about taking at least one day off for himself.

~

She would think this thought again, almost exactly a year later, when she would read about the accident, in her office. One Monday morning in early September, when she would spread out the *Times*, systematically folding it around salient articles like she did, so she could focus on one story at a time, and then she'd see it, what happened to his runner Becky Sanders. She would see the photograph of him from his first year of coaching—his light hair, his narrow, focused eyes—and she'd wonder what time might have done to him. Then she'd be struck by the white noise of a fan in the room, the ticking of a small clock by her computer. She'd be swept in a rush of panic, and she'd reach for her phone to call him, but she would stop before pressing the tenth digit, the 5, at the end of his number. She'd wait several days to email him, to express her concern, to offer her help, and then she'd wait for weeks, in radio silence.

TWENTY-FIVE

Murray awoke alone, confined to a room. There were tubes running fluids to his arms. A heart rate monitor's green, jagged rhythms. He closed his eyes and opened them again. He would see the girls standing there, refusing to run—the order of events was unclear, the cause of them vague. Only the sound of voices—Lisa's in the hospital, Nancy hysterical over the folded laundry, Becky, her smile, her laugh—before silence had overtaken him, filling his car rides, all the time he spent alone.

His eyes fluttered open and closed. Now he heard only machines, the rasp and ripple of shadows, this gray, windowless space that made it impossible to know how long he'd been here, how to call for help, unless he shouted or rang a bell, but he lacked the energy to be seen or heard.

～

Sometime later, after his machines were unhooked, he was led into another dimly lit room. He was wearing sweatpants and slippers. Taped gauze ran along his inner arms. His knuckles were bruised.

"My name is Dr. Andrews."

Murray scanned the woman's white pin, her photo ID: *Dr. Susan Andrews.* He waited for her to position two beige chairs. Then he took a seat, pressing his back in firmly.

"I was hoping we could talk for a bit," she said. "Does that sound alright with you?"

Murray just looked at her, the quiet blur in her eyes.

"Do you remember a meet at Lehigh yesterday?" She had a pen pressed to her clipboard.

When he didn't answer, she said, "Do you remember falling? Feeling panicked?"

Then Murray saw cornfields, the ones he'd run through as a child, and also other fields, the ones his girls had run through. He pushed the chair's hard edge with his thumb, against the silence.

"Maybe we should start with your medical history?" she said. "Can we talk about that?"

Murray studied the glassy film over her eyes. He willed his pupils to tighten. He thought of the detectives in their apartment, Nancy in the other room weeping, the questions he'd tried to answer alone.

"Are you on any medications?"

"No," he said.

"Any medical conditions I should know about?"

"No." He blinked, steadied his eyes' tremor.

"How about in your family? Any history of illness or hospitalization?"

"No."

"I'd like to test more of your memory," she said. "How does that sound?"

He waited. Nodded.

"What day is it?" she asked.

"The thirteenth," he said.

"It's the fourteenth, actually," she said. "But how about the month?"

"October," he said.

"Good," she said. "Where are we?"

"New Haven." He reached for his pockets.

"No," she said. "You're in St. Luke's Hospital. In Pennsylvania. Near where you're from?"

"Yes," he said.

"Where are you from?"

"Luzerne County," he said.

"And when were you born?"

"January thirteenth," he said. "1956."

Then she wanted to know where he'd gone to college, and how long ago he'd graduated. She asked him to name three major rivers and what happened to John F. Kennedy. She asked him to count a series of numbers forward, then backward. She told him a random address and asked him to repeat it back.

"Good," she said. "Very good."

Murray breathed. Then the doctor moved some papers around. She made her pen ready.

"Can we talk about why you're here today?" she said.

Murray searched for a clock in the room, but there was only the black screen of a mounted television.

"Let's start with the bruise on your head." She pointed her pen to her forehead. "Do you know how you got it?"

He reached up, feeling for a tender spot.

"Do you remember hitting your head?" she asked.

"No," he said. Then he thought he'd seen the doctor before, or was it the woman that had driven him in her car? Had he slipped?

"Do you have thoughts about hurting yourself?"

His chest felt crushed. He swallowed.

"How about any unusual voices?" the doctor said. "Have you heard any lately?"

Murray stared at her, the sound of the girls again, in unison. And then there was silence, growing full beyond measure.

"Or any thoughts?" the doctor said. "Thoughts that come into your mind but are difficult to remove?"

Becky, he saw the curl of her again in the grass. Nurses plugging their arms under hers, lifting her from bed to wheelchair.

"Is there anyone you've thought of harming?"

He shook his head.

"Are you under any stress at work?"

He saw a tube jammed into Becky's throat, a tangle of tubes and wires. He saw the surgeon's scalpel, and then blood drained from her skull. He saw her trying to form words again.

"Do you remember pushing on the ground, doing CPR? The emergency report said you seemed concerned about someone's survival. Is that true?"

He waited and watched, as if that would save him: silence growing full.

"Anyone you're worried about?"

Then she asked if he'd had any unusual experiences that bothered him. Like the feeling that people were talking about him?

Murray heard sirens. The vigorous pace of a pen.

She asked again if thoughts ever entered his mind, thoughts he couldn't stop. Lists? Numbers he counted? He tapped his thumb at his wrist. If he avoided elevators or tall buildings or certain animals. She asked him if his job had become stressful lately.

~

"Did you hear me, Samuel? Have you been under stress at work?"

He saw his child there, before she was gone. Jean on the changing table, kicking her legs while he fumbled over a diaper. Jean on Nancy's lap, tugging a clump of red hair. Jean forgetting to breathe.

~

"Who is she?" the doctor asked.

He looked at the doctor through the dim light, heard a clock on the mantel ticking, but there was no mantel. Where was his watch?

He pressed two fingers into his temples and held them there. He closed his eyes.

"Who is Jean?"

"I said so before," he said.

"What did you say before?"

"—Nothing." He kept his eyes pinched tight.

Dr. Andrews went on. "Are you married?"

"No," he said. "Not anymore."

"You said Jean. Is she your wife?"

"No," he said.

"Someone you miss?"

"Yes," he said.

"Where is she?"

"She's gone," he said.

"Your child?"

"Yes," he said, wrists shaking, soft static filling his ears: what he should have heard.

TWENTY-SIX

Nancy was on the train. The *Autumn Express*, a line that had been dormant since the eighties but that had reopened fairly recently—though with spotty service—but she found a line connecting New York to Bethlehem. And she watched the valley come into view, purling through ghost towns; she saw Murray running past these fields again, and then taking his team here every year.

She still could not believe it had happened, could not imagine how it must have been for his girls, seeing him break. The weight of holding his grief in, never talking about what they'd been through, to anyone—she assumed—for all these years. His girls, she guessed they saw him the way she always had, as someone applying this constant pressure—not the one feeling it himself.

~

She had been stretching on the floor of her living room when the doctor had called her. *Hello, Mrs. Murray?* She'd corrected it with *Weber, Nancy Weber*, but when the doctor had clarified, *You're not the wife of Samuel Murray?* she said, *No, not anymore*, and then the doctor had said he'd listed her in his emergency contacts, that they needed to collect some information about his medical history. She had answered their questions over the phone, but they'd refused to provide the details of his diagnosis. She just knew that he'd suffered a *brief reactive psychosis, most likely due to stress or trauma.*

It was five days later, and he was about to be discharged. She had offered to pick him up. She did not know why, but she had, and he'd consented, and here she was, already thirteen miles from Bethlehem.

The doctor had asked her about Murray's parents, and she had confirmed how they both had died. Nancy thought of the coal mining accident: the image of the collapsed shaft, the cold dirt, Murray's father's face black with carbon.

Murray once told her, after they'd visited his mother together, and he'd taken her to see his high school, that he'd started running at thirteen—two years before his father's accident. He'd told her that the rhythms of his feet, against his breath, three steps for every one breath, had always soothed him. She'd been stunned that he'd found speed through all the overgrown fields, the lack of cleanly paved roads, so unlike in the neighborhoods where she'd grown up riding her bike. He'd broken records on a grass track, too, not the red Tartan she'd assumed all tracks required.

The fields Murray had taken her through eventually met the woods, and a series of trails of which they'd walked a portion together. When they'd emerged and wound back through town, past the abandoned tattoo of railroads, the smell of soft earth lingering, she had felt hopeful. That despite their divided upbringings, their disparate paths, they had something to offer one another.

Nancy only had this moment, she thought, to be there for Murray if he'd let her. She'd packed a duffel bag with the things she thought he needed. A bar of soap and a fresh change of clothes from Kmart.

Were there other things he might want? Books? Records to play? But where to play them? Did he wish to see her face?

In the waiting area, she took frequent sips of water. There was a television playing the travel channel. The show featured a resort in Alaska that caught and prepared fresh fish. Zoomed-in images of a salmon's belly severed in half. Egg whites whisked with saffron and poured over salted halibut. A panoramic shot showed the flicker of a campfire, then the Aleutian Range distant and gleaming.

She entered when he was awake. Numb with medicine, but he was awake and could recognize how she'd once been before her hair turned gray, shoulders and cheekbones—he didn't remember them so sharp. She didn't seem to mind his gaze. His weak body trying to stand up in the room.

~

Nancy knew he wouldn't look the same, but time—these years had printed the lines of his face, the hunch of his shoulders, the thin, weathered look of his hair, all these years between them, the years she used to believe they'd never survive. She had pushed down toward the bottom of the ocean, she thought, but she could help her husband through those depths. Here they were, still surviving.

"Murray," she said, setting the bag she'd brought on the floor. She kept enough distance as they stood there, in silence, for several long moments. He tried to focus on her eyes, the way time was supposed to soften things. Quiet in the way *it had been*, just after Jean was born, when he'd sat a few feet from Nancy's bed in the delivery room, Jean asleep by her chest—he'd watched them so peaceful, two breaths rising and falling. Why had it been so hard for him to tell her? That he saw her strength, in all she'd given of herself, to create and sustain their child's life.

Now Jean was filling the space between them in the room. Wobbling toward his outstretched arms. Smiling at him with gaps in her teeth. She waved at him through the window in a house they all might have lived in together on Orange Street, the house Nancy had picked out one winter. In the daytime, the house had been a simple clapboard, but in the evening, it had scintillated: eaves and windows and tree branches dripping with light.

He saw her older still: passing her driver's license test, passing other exams. Saw her throwing her hat on graduation day. Saw her stripping tape from boxes on the floor of her college dorm. Time contracting into the moment his arm crooked hers: the slow, long walk down an aisle somewhere. Somewhere where he might have had the chance to let her go.

Last, he was lying on the floor, balancing Jean on his knees: propped by elbows before the television. Jean, no more than one month old, a fuzzy sheen along her forehead and nose, the soft lines of her eyebrows. His baby had been so warm and still on his knees, sleeping there. It had been the Fourth of July, but they'd put the fireworks on mute, so he'd had to imagine the sound of the lights, the smell of gunpowder.

He'd thought, *One day I'll take her to the top of East Rock to watch the lights and name the shapes. One day she might run to the top, too, for a view of East Haven, remembering that sound, her heart like ticker tape at the end of a race he'd be waiting at the end of.*

Nancy held him.

He said something she could barely hear, words broken, his body shuddering. She asked him. She said, "Tell me," as though nineteen years no longer divided them, and she was the one in his place, steadying him the way he had her, in the grieving room.

"I was supposed to go first," he wept.

He felt the weightlessness of Jean in his arms, in the hospital, holding her that one last time. The doctor had sealed her eyelids: peaceful and sleeping, as if untouched by suffering, the way life started and stopped on its own.

"I know," Nancy said, tears filling her eyes.

"She could have been anything," he said. "I would have been proud of her."

Nancy pulled him closer. "I know," she wept. "I would have too."

~

Minutes passed, then hours, darkness filling the room—just a glimmer of light under the door—unperceivable to anyone.

~

They left in the car Nancy had rented, back to New Haven. Murray slept most of the drive, only fluttering his eyes a few times.

When they reached Bridgeport, he opened them. She thought about a restaurant in New Haven, but then she drove past New Haven. She pulled into the parking lot outside of a sandwich shop in Mystic.

Inside there were a bunch of high school students buying potato chips. Nancy ordered a grilled vegetable panini and swiss cheese and pastrami on rye. She got the order to go, had it placed in a brown bag with sodas. She carried it for them to a bench on the boardwalk in Ocean Beach Park.

Above, gulls circled. One swooped down, skimming the water. Another approached Nancy's sandwich. She shooed it away with her napkin. She looked around at the scarcity of passersby, just the occasional jogger or walker. The pastel awnings of abandoned food stands and shops absorbed stillness.

They took a walk and watched gray specks flood the sky. One gull never strayed too far from its flock.

The day they'd met, Nancy had thought it odd Murray was running through Paris alone, how odd for their lives to have felt parallel, him racing a marathon, while she'd spent days holed up in the archives of the National Library, taking breaks only for coffee.

Lucky she'd decided for a longer break that day. That Murray had interrupted her, forcing anew the rhythms of the metro, his map sticky with sweat, his eyes searching, always for a better view.

Jaclyn Gilbert

He had reached for her hand then, but now she reached for his as they neared the end of the pier.

When they were first dating, Nancy remembered how they used to guess what the other was thinking; one person asked a question, while the other imagined often ridiculous possibilities. The game had grown more silent and less ridiculous as the years went on, more like perpetual hide-and-seek, never claiming the thing between them, love and its failure, need and its denial—then the dream and its breaking.

But Jean was here with them, she thought, in the salt of the cool breeze, in Murray, too, when she looked in his eyes; here, their child was more alive than she'd ever been, in all this time.

Nancy paused to lean over the guardrail. She watched the soft, silvery ripples of ocean. After several minutes of waiting, Murray turned to her, her eyes and gray hair, which used to remind him of burnished copper, pennies he'd waited for trains to flatten as a child with his brother, for speed to imprint a given year. He held her hand tighter as the gulls squawked above, and the sun grew dimmer over the water.

He had never told her she made time like that for him, specific and infinite at once: each moment greater than the second it carried, this one breath that had taken him his lifetime to find.

ACKNOWLEDGMENTS

This book would not be possible without the people who first believed in its potential as a short story at Sarah Lawrence College. Thank you to all of my loyal readers: Aliza Bartfield, Jessica Denzer, Olivia Worden, Alicia Schaeffer, Krystal Padley, Yaron Kaver, Carolyn Silveira. I am also grateful for the incredible mentorship I received from David Ryan, Nelly Reifler, Mary La Chappelle, David Hollander, Kathleen Hill, Melissa Febos, and Brian Morton—without your guidance, "Murray" would never have attained the expanse of a novel.

I remain indebted to the support of Alex Levenberg and Stephanie Koven through every stage of my journey as a writer of this story. Alex, you have been the most devoted and enthusiastic of readers, certain *Late Air* would one day reach bookshelves; you've taught me the meaning and beauty of friendship, seeing me through each up and down that *is* life and always finding room to laugh. Stephanie, thank you for urging me on while I was just starting out at Sarah Lawrence, and for holding me accountable for every draft. Your mentorship affirms how inextricably linked writing is with living—the importance of waking up each day and setting pen to paper because we have to. I am grateful for the brilliance of my agent, Marya Spence, whose vision for this novel allowed it to reach its fullest potential as a human story about love. Your contagious energy propelled me forward through the hardest stages of the process, challenging me to arrive at difficult articulations about marriage and loss, and what it means to translate both experiences most concretely on the page. I am also grateful to Clare Mao for her perceptiveness through each revision, and everyone else at Janklow & Nesbit Associates who helped realize *Late Air*.

I remain in awe of my editor, Hafizah Geter, whose luminous intuition at the sentence level guided me through the final rounds, probing the text into its deepest emotional truths. Thank you to all those at Little A who have championed the book: Carmen Johnson, Vivian Lee, and the whole international rights, sales, and publicity teams working restlessly to bring it to market.

I am equally indebted to the community I found at the Bread Loaf Writers' Conference. Sanjay Agnihotri, Megan Weiler, Jenessa Abrams, and Stephen Fishbach: your revelatory insights helped me to deepen my process, to interrogate each graph most honestly as I worked to finish this book. Thank you to all of the other friends and colleagues who have believed in my work: Johanna Van Straaten, Adam Golub, Tim DiGiulio, Jessica Henderson, Ashley Campbell, Betsy Adams, Julie Mackay, Cecile Barendsma, Katy Reedy, Kristina Bicher, Jennifer Convissor, Julie Surbaugh, Spencer Guo, Amy Kvilhaug, and Andrea Burdett—and all of my students who have inspired me to understand writing as a constant state of becoming. Thank you to the generous support of the New York Public Library's research fellowship program for their overflowing shelves and the quiet space to convene with other writers.

I offer a special thanks to my first writing professor at Yale, Marian Thurm, for planting the seed that I *could* write a novel that summer of 2005, and to my cross-country coach at Yale, Mark Young, and all my teammates who have been my family away from home. Thank you to my parents, my mother for her steadfast love and encouragement since I was a child writing stories; my stepfather, Dave, who has been my biggest champion through every obstacle course; my sister, Samantha, whose spirit has always inspired me to savor each moment; and my brother-in-law, Michael, for supplying me with journals and pens. Thank you to my grandparents for fostering my passion for books since I could walk, my aunt Marci and Reggie, whose generosity in all things cannot be matched, and my uncle Steve, for sending me my first books on writing and taking me to Barbara's Bookstore in Chicago. Thank you to Kim and Brian for becoming another set of parents, and I cannot forget to send my thanks to my Weimaraner puppy, Phin; thank you for sleeping faithfully by my side while I drafted hundreds of pages that never made it in.

My deepest gratitude I owe to my husband, Jared Gilbert, whose love and faith has changed me in more ways than I can say in words. You have shown me that marriage is a daily gift of understanding, in giving all of ourselves to the greater whole of our being. This is for you.

ABOUT THE AUTHOR

Photo © 2017 Jared Gilbert

After completing her BA at Yale University, Jaclyn Gilbert went on to receive an MFA from Sarah Lawrence College. Since then, she has received a research fellowship from the New York Public Library and contributed to the Bread Loaf, Colgate, and Tin House writers' conferences. Jaclyn has also led writing workshops at the Valhalla Correctional Facility, the Writing Institute at Sarah Lawrence College, and Curious-on-Hudson in Dobbs Ferry, New York.

Jaclyn lives in Brooklyn with her husband and her dog, Phin. *Late Air* is her first novel. For more information about Jaclyn, visit her website at www.JaclynGilbert.com.